The ferocity of the snow-tiger was unlike anything Paul had ever witnessed. The scent of its prey was alive in its nostrils and it thrashed at the logs, leaping and turning in its efforts to get beneath. The animal's body was massive and stretched from one end of the log covering to the other. Its eyes burned like red-hot coals.

For several minutes the great beast tore at the roof. Then, its fury momentarily spent, it paced the logs. From its throat came a deep, raspy growl. Saliva dripped from six-inch teeth. Suddenly the beast whirled and tore at the log directly above Paul. Bark flew and fell between the gaps. Paul's heart was in his throat. It was like a creature from the worst of nightmares! Its head was so large that its eyes stared down at him from either side of the log above him. He pulled down on his rope with all his strength....

——————

Other  Books

THE CLOUD PEOPLE

Robert B. Kelly

THE CLOUD PEOPLE

First printing: October 1991
Printed in the United States of America
Library of Congress Catalog Card Number: 90-71515

9 8 7 6 5 4 3 2 1

ISBN: 1-56076-077-X

TSR, Inc.
P.O. Box 756
Lake Geneva, WI 53147
U.S.A.

TSR Ltd.
120 Church End, Cherry Hinton
Cambridge CB1 3LB
United Kingdom

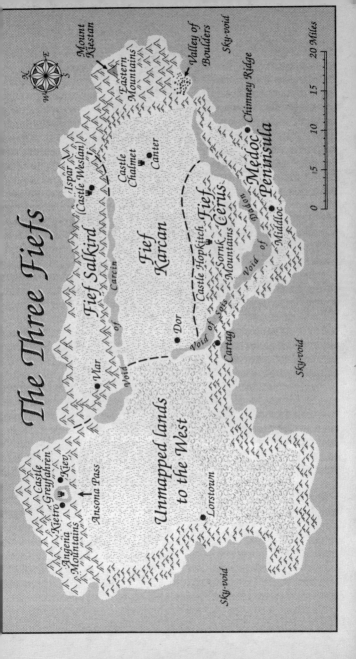

PROLOGUE

 The noise rumbled like thunder across the wooded hillsides. Duke Whitin Benjarth jerked his head skyward. A seamless canopy of cobalt blue stretched from the curved horizon of the planet Calferon to the distant cliff tops.

It was a perfect autumn sky, one that allowed the warmth of the sun to shine down on the slopes of the northern ridges. Duke Whitin toiled in his short sleeves, clearing a path to drag the logs uphill in the coming weeks when they would work the lower slopes bordering the Void of Dadon. The felled trees had to be winched uphill because the only road servicing the sawmills ran in the valley between the two ridges. Through a break in the cliff face that fronted the Void of Dadon Duke Whitin could see the thin line of clouds that marked the approach of a storm. But the clouds were distant. *Too distant.*

It was then he realized his mistake.

A man born on the thin finger of the Medoc Peninsula and reared in the logging camps would have reacted differently to the sound. He would have looked uphill immediately. But Duke Whitin had lived among the loggers for only the past three years.

He had lived most of his life on the flat, fertile plains of Fief Karcan, the largest of the three fiefs settled by the Jarred. It bordered the Medoc Peninsula to the north. The sounds of his childhood had been the ring of the smith's hammer rather than the woodsman's axe. He'd sat atop corral fences and listened to the whinnying of the horses as their hooves pounded the ground in their stampede to get out to pasture. Now the only animal sound he heard was the occasional bleating of a mountain goat. He remembered how the rain had fallen with a crisp, drumlike cadence on the tiled roofs and flagstone courtyards of Castle Chalmet. On the ridge tops it would fall with a soggy thud into the soft earth. Footsteps had always echoed slightly in the long corridors of the castle, warning someone of another's approach. Here all sound dispersed without reverberation. On the plains of Fief Karcan the distant rumble of thunder was the only warning one had of the rapid approach of the violent rainstorms that swept down from the Eastern Mountains. But on the Medoc Peninsula a thunderlike rumbling was the sound of a runaway log pounding the ground as it rolled down the slope.

Duke Whitin whirled around. The log hurtling toward him was massive, for the trunks of the asharen trees grew five to six feet in diameter. He knew its length immediately. All the trees were cut into lengths of fifty feet. The winch cable must have snapped and the log had turned because its length was now perpendicular to the grade. He couldn't get out of its path. He'd lost time, precious time, looking up at the sky. Quickly he scanned the terrain between himself and the moving log. He saw stumps cut smooth to the ground, knew they had been cut that way to allow the logs to be winched uphill without obstacle. He realized then that a logger who found himself similarly trapped would have already dived to the ground, flattening himself and wriggling into the soft earth as much as possible. But Duke Whitin realized this too late. He dove, but the log hit his left side while he was still in the air. Its spin drove him into the ground. He heard the crunch of bones breaking. Then he felt himself being lifted again, the rough bark gripping his clothes and skin, and he was flipped to his back.

Duke Whitin lay there, strangely calm, amazed that he was still alive. He did not feel pain, but the realization of what that meant did not come to him at that moment. Slowly he became aware of the things he could do. He could breathe, though only in shallow gasps, as if biting at the air. He could move his eyes and roll them forward. He saw that his body faced downhill. Somehow he had spun around as he'd flipped over. Far downhill, the leafy boughs of the unharvested asharen trees formed a smooth, unbroken flow of emerald green that reminded him of the gently sloped grazing land near Fief Karcan's northern border with Fief Salkird. For a moment he imagined himself a young boy again. He imagined lying atop a small knoll watching the stallions and mares grazing. But then the wind rose up, gusting and swirling, and it broke the smooth expanse of the treetops into a choppy sea of green. The memory faded and Duke Whitin was left with only another reminder of how much he had missed his homeland these past three years.

He lifted his gaze farther north. The southern cliffs of Fief Karcan bordered the Void of Dadon. He could see the smooth stone of the cliff face and the knobby, porous stone of the fief's crohephite rock base. The stone's porosity was a factor of the number and size of the core-vines running through it. It was these vines that produced the selevium gas that filled the jooarie sacs and held the aerial world aloft. The outer membrane of each jooarie sac was sensitive to atmospheric pressure and the core-vines would adjust their production of selevium gas in order to maintain an average altitude of twelve thousand feet. The core-vines were continuously adjusting gas production due to surface weight changes. Stone quarried from one area to build a castle in another was a change in surface weight distribution. The jooarie sacs located beneath where the stone was quarried would release gas, while the sacs located where the castle was being built would expand with the production of additional selevium gas.

Duke Whitin rolled his eyes to the right. He could see the flow of sky that marked the northeastern turn in the Void of Dadon. Its grayish tint lingered like a fine mist and was the result of billions of microscopic particles of screula being drawn to the exposed edges of the core-vines on either side of the sky-void. The duke had always thought fascinating the geophotosynthetic process that turned screula into crohephite rock. The hair-thin spinolla fibers that grew on the stems of the core-vines wove it to the existing rock. Farther to the east, beyond his line of sight, existed the eastern land bridge joining Fief Karcan to the Medoc Peninsula. It was there he had crossed to the Medoc Peninsula in self-exile three years ago.

Duke Whitin heard voices. Then, as he tried to tilt his head to see from which direction they came, he realized he could not move his neck. Panic seized him. He tried to move his arms and legs, to thrash about on the ground like a beetle flipped on its back. He had to be able to move his limbs. A paralyzed man could contribute nothing to the survival of the loggers. They might as well cast his useless body into the Void of Dadon! But he experienced no sensation in his legs or the left side of his body. All he could move was his right arm and the fingers of his right hand. He coughed and tasted blood. He realized then he was bleeding internally and dying. It wouldn't be long, maybe only a matter of minutes, before his lungs or throat would fill with blood and he would suffocate.

For a moment his vision blurred. Then the distant cliffs of Fief Karcan came into focus again. He thought it would have been nice to see his son again, but he knew he wouldn't make it back now. He'd left them all rather mysteriously: a cryptic note, a single rider heading south through the darkness of the night, a stable hand sworn to secrecy. He'd had to leave them. It had been the only way to save them. Now a sense of urgency pressed upon him. He had to tell someone what he knew.

A rush of motion swept past him. Someone had tried to stop beside him, but the soft earth had given way and he had slid past. A moment later the figure of a strong young lad loomed over him.

Duke Whitin knew the boy, Mark Elbtas. He was a slender lad with tousled black hair and light gray-brown eyes. He was tall like his own son, like most Jarred were, at least those of pure blood. It was rare on the Medoc Peninsula, which had been a mixing ground of the Jarred, Sinese, and Phlogin races, to find someone so pure in Jarred features. Duke Whitin considered it a good omen.

Another figure appeared. It was the daughter of one of the loggers. She was younger than the boy, perhaps only fifteen. She was slender like he was, but her flat cheekbones, the broad bridge of her nose, and her wide-set eyes were evidence of a mixed genealogy. The girl helped her mother, who cooked for the loggers, to gather mushrooms, roots, and the wild clandi-cabbage that grew well in the acidic soil of these slopes. All would be mixed in a stew pot: the mushrooms and cabbage as stock; the roots, depending on the plant they were from, as seasoning.

Duke Whitin's eyes darted back and forth between them. So there would be two *bashans*. That was good. It was the number of observers he desired. If there was only one and his or her life should be taken unexpectedly, then the knowledge would be lost forever. Too many bashans, and the knowledge might leak out prematurely. The fact that one was a female posed a problem: the boy and the girl mustn't be lovers. Not now, not ever! It was important they go separate ways. Otherwise they might perish together in a house fire or similar tragedy.

"I'm going for help," the boy said.

Duke Whitin wanted to shake his head. There was nothing they could do for him. They had to stay here and hear what he had to say. He formed the word "no" with his lips and tried to expel it in an exhalation of breath. He felt droplets of blood hit his face and neck.

"I must get help," the boy said again when he saw the blood.

Duke Whitin formed the word again with his lips and then spat it out in another small shower of blood. "No."

"He'll be dead before we can even get a stretcher down here," said the girl. She bent forward on one knee and turned the duke's head very slowly. Blood flowed from the side of his mouth.

"His neck is broken," she said, whispering to Mark.

Duke Whitin motioned with his finger for the girl to lean closer. "Are you lovers?" he asked her.

She drew back from the duke, perplexed by his question. "He asks if we are lovers," she told Mark.

"Perhaps he is delirious."

No, you fool, the duke thought! It's important. He called upon a last reserve of strength, grabbed the girl's wrist and pulled her close again. "Are you lovers?" he asked again. His voice felt stronger and he found he could talk easier now that the girl had tilted his head to the side.

"No," she answered, frightened by the intensity with which he had asked the question.

"You must never become such. Promise me that."

They nodded their heads, though he suspected they might be humoring him. He couldn't control where their future paths would take them. It was better he got to the point. They would understand if he told them of the medallion.

"You know I am not one of you."

A waste of breath! Of course they knew. They'd seen the softness of his flesh and pockets of body fat when he'd first arrived. His hands had been uncallused as well, unusual for a logger.

"We know you are from the land of the three fiefs," Mark said.

"Until three years ago I was *ruler* of Fief Karcan. My son rules there now. Safe in the castle's vault is a medallion. The medallion is hollow. Within it lies the power that created our world and can in turn destroy it."

A wave of painful dizziness swept over Duke Whitin, and he found his eyes shutting involuntarily. A memory flickered into consciousness. He saw himself trudging across the wind-swept surface of Calferon, the medallion he had found there secured about his neck.

The medallion was the size of his fist and was joined by an eyelet to a thin chain. It was constructed of an indestructible substance known as *metal*. That had been the translation from the old tongue. It was the only piece of metal that existed anywhere in their aerial world. The medallion's two silver-gray convex halves fit together so perfectly that the seam was visible only with the aid of a magnifier. A representation of a winged creature had been etched into the metal on what the duke considered to be its front half. Its backside had a small, rounded indentation into which a cylindrical key fit.

The memory continued. He saw himself surrounded by a wall of swirling sand rising twelve thousand feet from the planet's surface. It concealed a set of stairs that wound around the center of a spiraling core-vine. The climb back up the stairs to Fief Karcan had taken days. A painful wound inflicted just below his abdomen had forced him to rest often. At night he had chipped a hole in the stone railing and tied his belt through it so he wouldn't fall while he slept.

"My son does not know of the medallion's power," he said when his dizziness had passed. "Nor do the dukes of Fief Salkird and Fief Cerus. It is better they don't. The dukes are jealous of each others' power. The medallion could give my son and his lieutenants the power of life and death over the other fiefs. The other dukes would not tolerate such an imbalance of power. War would break out and many lives would be lost. That is one reason I had to leave Fief Karcan. The medallion can only be opened with a special key. That key is secured around my neck by a fiber chain. The two of you must find a safe hiding place for it."

The duke spat some more blood. "You may wonder why I chose to live in self-exile rather than simply toss the medallion into the sky-void. I did so because the medallion may one day prove useful to us. The unmapped territories west of our borders are lawless. Perhaps we are to blame for this, since we banished many of our criminals there. Unfortunately, I fear that one day a tyrant will rise to power and organize them into a formidable army. He will talk of the conquest of both lands, for such is the talk of madmen. When that day arrives, the medallion and the key must be brought together so that its power can be unleashed to defeat these forces of evil. Only then will our people put aside their jealousies and unite behind its power."

A wave of pain shot through Duke Whitin's head and he struggled to remain conscious. "Please understand the responsibility I have given you. The lives of our peoples may one day rest in your hands. Now take the key from around my neck."

Mark bent down on one knee and pulled open the duke's shirt. Duke Whitin couldn't see the boy's hands. He couldn't feel them either. But he watched the boy's face, followed his eyes as they followed his hands. He thought: *He takes too long to remove the key!*

Mark held up a broken piece of fiber chain.

Duke Whitin knew immediately what had happened. The fiber chain had broken when the log had crushed him and the key had come loose. Now it could be anywhere downhill. Perhaps Mark had already buried it when he had slid in the soft ground. Then again the log might have pressed it into the sod. The duke felt himself beginning to lose consciousness. It was so hard to concentrate now, but he had to. Just a little longer.

"Search for the key! But, if you can't find it, . . . it *must* be able to be duplicated. The Jarred religion preaches that an enlightened one, the Malhah, will aid his people in their time of greatest need. Perhaps it is his destiny to make a new key. He must if this one is lost!"

The duke sensed he only had a breath or two of life left. "It is prophesied the Malhah will appear to us through the Saulcar Mass. Observe the sky during the times of its passage. Watch for his arrival."

Duke Whitin tried to suck in another breath of air, but it was only a bubble of fluid being drawn back into his throat and down his windpipe.

An image of pure blue sky filled his mind. Thin, feathery clouds were driven across it by a high wind. The clouds took the shapes of horses. A herd of powder-white stallions and mares galloped from one horizon to the other. Then the scene faded into darkness as all thought ceased and death took Duke Whitin Benjarth.

CHAPTER 1

"Did you watch the storm last night, Benerit-woman?"

The old woman remained standing by the window, her back to the boy. The window looked out upon the stables, but the boy doubted his Benerit-woman was looking at anything in particular. His mother had once explained to him that older people suffered periods of "mental distraction." His Benerit-woman had taught three generations of Benjarth and so had to be in her seventies.

He repeated his question in a louder voice.

The old woman turned from the window. She seemed irritated by the question and her voice lashed out at the boy like a whip. "Why should *I* watch these storms? The lightning, well, perhaps it holds the interest of a child such as you, but . . ." She hesitated as if she'd lost her train of thought. "Ah, well, it's . . . it's all such a foolish waste of time."

Paul Benjarth stared wide-eyed at his Benerit-woman. To speak as she had was a blasphemy! She knew full well the reason they watched the quarterly passages of the Saulcar Mass. It was a star-gate. Through it, so the Book of Prophecy stated, the Malhah would appear.

"What causes these storms? he asked. "I mean, what are the physics involved?"

She shot him a cross glance. "You know that answer already."

"I know they are caused by the movement of the Saulcar Mass across the top of our atmosphere," he snapped, irritated by his Benerit-woman's sour mood. "But I want to know more!"

The old woman sighed wearily as she made her way to the bookcase. Age had bent her body forward and shortened her gait to a plodding shuffle. She pulled a manuscript from a shelf and cradled the heavy volume against her chest. Then she lifted her eyes to the pale expanse of wall above the bookcase, where portraits of the six generations of Benjarth dukes hung.

Such remarkable similarities of features, she'd always thought. It was as if the Jarred genotype that was uniquely the Benjarth's was impervious to any other gene mix. All six dukes had large, gray-brown eyes. All had thick, straight eyebrows, a straight nose, and a bow-shaped mouth with the characteristic thin upper lip and fuller lower one. However, it was the portrait of Paul's great-great-grandfather, Duke Whitin Benjarth, that reminded her most of Paul. It was the rigid set of his jaw and face, as well as the squint of his eyes, that gave the duke a stubborn, intense look. She saw this same expression on Paul when he became intense about a subject, as he was now.

She placed the book on the table where Paul sat and thumbed through the manuscript until she found the drawing she was looking for.

Paul studied the drawing. Depicted was the sun and the orbital path of their own planet, Calferon. Also shown encircling the sun was the Saulcar Mass. Its orbit had been drawn as a flattened ellipse, its ends open. It intersected the orbit of Calferon at four points.

"Does the Saulcar Mass cross the orbital path of the planet Palastrides, Benerit-woman?"

The woman eyed her young charge curiously. "It does."

For a moment Paul remembered the atmospheric disturbance he had watched last night. He had stood in Tower Satchkind with his parents and his younger sister. When the storm had been directly overhead, his sister had run to their father and grabbed his leg.

"Don't let him eat me, Daddy! Don't let him eat me," she had cried.

"Don't be afraid, Christina," her father had said, "Saulcar's belly is full tonight. See how it scrapes across the sky."

That was the fable. Saulcar was a mythical winged dragon who slept in a cave on the planet's surface. Awakening after months of sleep, he encircled Calferon in search of food, gorging himself in order to satisfy his ravenous appetite. It was a child's fairy tale, but one the scizans had borrowed from to name the gaseous mass.

"What are the chances of life on Palastrides?" Paul asked.

"Do you mean intelligent life?"

Paul began to stroke his Adam's apple with the thumb and forefinger of his left hand. "Yes, intelligent life."

"Quite unlikely. Palastrides is farther from the sun than Calferon. It's hypothesized that the temperatures on Palastrides range from minus two hundred to minus one hundred degrees Fahrenheit."

"But it's not impossible, is it? Especially if there were a more advanced civilization on Palastrides, one that had learned to cope with such temperatures. Perhaps one that lived in subterranean caverns?"

The Benerit-woman slouched wearily in her chair. "What is it you are really trying to figure out, Paul?"

"What I am trying to figure out is if the Malhah could be a man of flesh and blood, no different than ourselves! An inhabitant of the planet Palastrides."

"And you see the Saulcar Mass as his means of passage between Palastrides and Calferon?"

"Is there not some logic to this, Benerit-woman?"

She straightened in her chair. "Very little. How, for instance, would your Malhah survive the bitter cold of space within the Saulcar Mass?"

Paul had been waiting for that question. "Why must he be exposed to the void of space at all? Why can't he be encapsulated within, say, a life-sustaining shell?"

"A flying machine?"

Paul caught the mocking lilt of her voice. It annoyed him. "Yes! A flying machine! Do you think ours the most advanced civilization in the universe?"

"It is the only one in this solar system, Paul."

That episode of his youth had happened twelve years ago, but Paul still took a certain pleasurable satisfaction in remembering it, because his Benerit-woman had been wrong. Unfortunately, she had not lived to see the first of the flying machines come through the Saulcar Mass. It had happened seven years ago, two years after her death. Since then, three other flying machines had come.

Paul returned his gaze to the east. A thin, pulsing edge of light was just now visible above the peaks of the Eastern Mountains. It marked the approach of the Saulcar Mass.

Paul directed his eyes downward to one of the castle's four corner towers. It was crowded with members of the castle's court who, like himself, had gathered to watch the passage of the Saulcar Mass. The crenelated stone of the tower's roof formed a chest-high wall that was punctuated by breaks in the stone only half as high. The design had been for the defense of the castle, allowing archers to kneel in the openings, fire their arrows, then duck back behind the wall. Sometime in the two centuries of peace following the Jarred invasion of Fief Karcan, the stone had been notched and a wooden railing installed across the more open areas. Now children gathered by these railings, the smallest among them peering through gaps between the boards. The adults stood a few paces back, huddling in groups to talk and watch.

Paul stood in Tower Satchkind, the castle's central tower. It rose a full seventy feet above the corner towers. It was traditional for members of the ruling duke's family and their invited guests to watch the passage of the Saulcar Mass from this highest tower. Paul was not alone in his vigil tonight. Illad Rahman, his father's security captain, and Jessie Wanthrop, a friend, were with him.

Paul heard footsteps on the stairs leading to Tower Satchkind. He turned to see his sister's head poke through the narrow opening in the floor. "How is mother?" he asked.

"Asleep. The surgeon gave her a sedative."

Christina climbed the few remaining steps into the tower and stood beside her brother. There were lightning bolts in the sky to the east. They watched them a moment in silence.

"The surgeon feels her illness is psychosomatic."

"Why is she giving up so easily?" cried Paul. He recognized the tension in his own voice. Weren't they both forcing themselves to be optimistic now?

"She's not giving up," protested Christina.

"She is! She believes father's . . . dead."

A silence fell over them. It was the first time either of them had admitted that possibility to the other.

Paul turned his gaze back to the mountains. The storm was almost over them and the uppermost peaks were illuminated by flashes of lightning that flickered continuously. He could see their jagged edges and he knew of the deep, rocky chasms between peaks. All four flying machines had crashed in those mountains.

"Why did he have to go, Paul? He had more than enough volunteers among his own lieutenants."

"You know why he went."

"Yes, I suppose I do. Still, it was . . . foolish."

Paul could see that his sister was near tears. These past few months had taken a toll on her physically. She'd been thin to start with, but she'd lost even more weight worrying about her mother's health and her father's safety. Her face had sunk inward around her mouth, her pale skin drawn tightly down across her cheekbones and jaw. The fact that she had pulled back and tied her dark hair in a ponytail only accentuated the thinness of her face.

"Shhh, don't talk like that," said Paul softly. He put his arm around his sister. She started to cry.

Christina was right. It had been a foolish thing to do. It would have made more sense for their father to remain at the castle and direct operations from within the safety of its walls. He was too important to be a pawn in these scouting expeditions. Yet it had always been his father's philosophy to be in the thick of things with his men. His father's reconnaissance party had headed west to the unmapped territories controlled by Lord Thyden three months ago. They were the second such group to venture west to gauge the strength of Thyden's forces and probe for weaknesses. The first had not returned either.

"They should have killed him," his sister said.

"Killed whom?"

"Belshane." She gazed up at her brother. "Banishment! What kind of punishment was that? Didn't grandfather realize what he was doing?"

"Belshane was a sick man."

"Does a surgeon show mercy to a cancer cell?"

"They gave him two injections of tronocyanimide before escorting him to the border of Fief Karcan. It guaranteed sterility. How were they to know he would find an antidote and father Thyden? None was thought to exist."

"None was thought to exist," repeated his sister. "Thought to! Don't you see? It was a gamble."

"It was all so many years ago, Christina. What is the point in debating it now?"

His sister averted her eyes like a child who had just been scolded. "None, I guess."

Paul returned his gaze to the mountains. The storm was directly over them now. Screula boiled in a rolling motion, simultaneously being sucked in and pushed out. Light pulsed from within. Jagged bolts of lightning ripped across the storm's perimeter, but no thunder followed these flashes. The Saulcar Mass made no sound as it rolled, oblong, across the top of the atmosphere. Paul always thought it eerie how such a violent aberration of nature could be so completely soundless. Suddenly a towering flare of screula arced across the night sky. Too far from the storm's center of gravity to be sucked back in, it dissipated harmlessly over the mountains.

Paul shifted his gaze from the storm to the mountains. The stone washed into soft focus as his thoughts and fears colored his sense of sight. A memory of a face appeared to him. It was the old, wrinkled face of his Benerit-woman.

What concerns you tonight, Paul?

Paul had spent so much of his youth in the company of his Benerit-woman that even after her death she remained in his mind as a confidant.

What if father doesn't return?

What if he doesn't?

Well, what'll I do? Send out another spy party to probe Thyden's kingdom?

The first has not returned, and the second appears to have fared no better. Do you propose to waste even more men?

Attack in full force then?

Against a kingdom whose strength you do not even know?

Sit and wait for Thyden to attack us?

And give him the chance to surround you? To dictate the plan of battle?

Well then what? What do you propose I do?

"Paul!"

His sister's voice shattered the image of the old Beneritwoman like breaking glass. Something had flickered in the sky above the mountains. Something had reflected the light from the storm.

"It was a flying machine, wasn't it?"

Christina nodded.

Paul felt a shiver of excitement ripple his body. "The Malhah comes, Christina. Illad! Jessie! Did you see? The Malhah comes!"

"Do not let your hopes get the best of you, my brother. It was over the mountains." Christina remembered that search parties had found mangled bodies and charred skeletons in the wreckage of the other flying machines. Her voice dropped a shade in volume. "None of the others survived."

Paul's heart pounded beneath his breastbone. "But they weren't the Malhah. Don't you understand? The Malhah will survive!"

Christina spoke in a calm, nonchallenging manner. She did not wish to get into an argument with her brother. "So the Book of Prophecy states. But it may not happen in our lifetime. Or even in our children's lifetimes."

Paul looked at his sister, puzzled. "Why do you think that? There have already been four flying machines in the past seven years."

She knew of his theory: a Palastrides' man conveyed to Calferon by way of the Saulcar Mass. She wasn't sure she believed it, but she did see a certain logic to it. And the Book of Prophecy was certainly open to interpretation.

"But look how flimsy they've been," she reminded him. "It may be a hundred years before the technology on Palastrides evolves to where a flying machine could survive a landing in our mountains."

Paul felt betrayed by his sister's comment and lashed out at her. "So we should give up hoping? Is that what you are saying? That we shouldn't investigate these crashes for the next one hundred years?"

"Of course not, Paul. That's the last thing I'm saying. It's just that I . . . well, I don't want to see you disappointed tomorrow."

For a moment, all Paul could do was stare at his sister. It seemed like only yesterday they had squabbled the way siblings do over every little thing. Now they were so close. When had the change come? Had it come with age, with maturation? Or had it come because of the difficult times they now faced?

"I won't, Christina."

A knowing smile curled up the ends of her mouth. "You will."

Paul managed a smile, too. "Well, maybe."

A bolt of lightning flashed directly above them. Christina's mind leaped back to her childhood. She remembered how she used to run to her father and hug his legs as the Saulcar Mass passed overhead. Tears came to her eyes. She turned and ran down the stairs.

For a moment, Paul stared at the empty space where his sister had just stood, wondering about her abrupt change of mood. But then the thought of the flying machine he had just seen turned his attention back to the mountains and his thoughts to the Malhah.

What if this time it was?

What leaps their technology could take under the guidance of an enlightened one! What advances could be made in physics, math, astronomy, chemistry . . . and weaponry. That science interested Paul most of all. A man from Palastrides could teach the Jarred to construct weapons powerful enough to crush Lord Thyden once and for all, no matter how large his army.

"Illad," he called out.

Illad Rahman's hard-soled shoes click-thudded, click-thudded across the stone of the open tower roof. His right leg had been crushed below the knee in a rock slide. Surgeon Farant had managed to save his leg, but the accident had left him with a pronounced limp.

It still pained Paul to watch Illad walk. He had been a much different man before the accident. He had been lean, muscular and tremendously fit. No one could beat him in a sprint or distance race. He had been the one to teach Paul how to ride and how to fight with knife and sword. But the accident had limited his mobility. Consequently, he had gained weight in the years since. Now his shoulders sloped forward and he walked with his head bent. But his mind was keen, and his attention to detail still made him a respected security captain.

"I want to leave for the mountains first thing in the morning."

Illad dipped his head and shoulders. "I'll see to the arrangements immediately."

Paul watched Illad descend the narrow staircase to the lower tower chambers. He'd been about to thank him for seeing to his wishes. But Illad's bow had taken him by surprise and the words had never left his lips.

Now you, Illad! You're a friend, not castle staff!

Paul was ill at ease with the formalities now being used in his presence, formalities previously reserved for his father, Duke Jaiman Benjarth. Those who had been his friends and peers now acted awkwardly, distantly, and at times subserviently. He did not like what their change in manner foretold. It was an unspoken acceptance of the reality that his father might never return.

A moistness formed about his eyes. He glanced at Jessie, then turned his head away. He stepped over to the railing and placed his hands atop it. *Why did you have to go, father? Why?* He bowed his head and let his tears flow freely.

CHAPTER 2

Metal debris lay scattered across the rocky floor of the bowllike depression, but the body of the flying machine was still intact. It gave Paul hope. Had the Malhah survived? Was he only unconscious within the wreckage? He motioned the search party to descend from the lip of the bowl.

"We'll be blind down there," said Cristo. "It would be wise to leave a guard up here."

Paul glanced at Cristo. He was one of two lieutenants in charge of his father's soldiers. He was a tall man and this, as well as his thin neck, were the only true Jarred features he possessed. His wide forehead, flattened cheekbones, and wide mouth were Sinese characteristics. His nose was large and hooked, a trait believed to be Phlogin in origin. He was beginning to bald and this was rarely seen. Baldness was thought to be linked genetically to the Ornan race and only one-half to one percent of the population at large was believed to be of Ornan extraction.

His caution seemed unnecessary to Paul. "We are only two miles from our own fields, Cristo."

"And only four miles from the Medoc Peninsula."

"We're that close?" Paul had lost track of the fact that they had moved steadily southward through the mountains. When he had first seen the light from within the Saulcar Mass reflect off the flying machine, it had appeared to be more to the north and they had started their search there. That had been two days ago. He found Cristo's remark revealing for another reason as well. "You think Lord Marthan has made an alliance with Thyden?"

"It was your father's belief as well as mine, Paul. No people are neutral."

Paul had doubts about Cristo's observation. "I can't see the loggers taking up arms against us."

"I suspect they won't, Paul. They have no interest in the business of war. Lord Thyden knows that, too. I doubt he was looking to recruit new soldiers other than those already in the employ of Lord Marthan. The ability to amass troops on the Medoc Peninsula is what is important to him. Strategically it gives him two more crossing points into the three fiefs."

"But there are three sentry posts guarding the land bridge between the Medoc Peninsula and Fief Karcan. Certainly Duke Leipedes has posted ample guard at the crossing point into Fief Cerus. That's thirty men! Thirty men to guard a strip of land no more than a quarter mile wide. No one could get past. Not spies, anyway. And the topography of the land bridges would help the sentry posts stall an attack until reinforcements arrived."

"Do not underestimate the craftiness of Lord Thyden."

Cristo's warning made Paul uneasy. There had been fear in his voice.

"Steven," Cristo commanded a tall youth, one of Duke Jaiman's ablest fighters. "Stand watch up here."

Although it was only thirty feet to the floor of the depression, the grade was steep and the men had to pick their way down carefully. In the final ten feet the slope curled back underneath itself, creating a cutaway in the rocky bank. To jump from that height was to risk turning an ankle, so the men lowered Solman, the biggest among them, to the floor of the bowl. In turn they lowered themselves onto his broad shoulders and then to the ground. The five of them approached the craft and halted ten yards before it.

"It is wise you remain here, Paul," said Cristo. "One never knows." He gave orders for Stilgart and Hannah to search the craft.

Again that caution! Paul figured he would have to get used to it. He was, after all, the only male heir to the throne of Fief Karcan.

Cristo pointed to the south end of the bowl. "The craft entered the bowl from that direction. See how the debris from its tail section traces a path to its final resting place."

Paul glanced at the trail of debris with only casual interest. He took a step forward, felt Cristo grab his arm. "Well?" he called out to the men searching the craft.

Stilgart's head poked up from within the remains of the craft. "There's no one here."

It took Paul a moment for the facts of the situation to register through his disappointment. He had prepared himself for two possibilities. Either they would find a corpse or a living man.

"Maybe it was unmanned," suggested Cristo.

Hannah shrugged. "Maybe, but the other four weren't."

"Nor was this one," said Paul. He turned to Cristo. "He's alive. Don't you see? He's walked away from this wreck."

"The inside of this craft is all twisted members," said Stilgart. "No one could have walked away from this."

Stilgart's simple logic angered Paul. Stilgart was too much a pragmatist and too little a believer. "The Malhah could walk away from this wreckage," he said. "That he will survive is prophesied. It is the cornerstone of our faith!"

Stilgart turned his back on Paul and took a few steps away. He would not argue with the son of his beloved duke.

"Do not question Stilgart's faith," Cristo said to Paul in a low voice. "It is as strong as my own. But he has seen the other wrecks, as I have. He has seen the decapitated bodies and the charred skeletons." Cristo returned his gaze to the debris. "This wreck is as bad as any of them. All I can think of is that the pilot was thrown from the craft before it hit the ground."

"That means we have more territory to cover," said Paul, still as convinced as ever that the Malhah lived. "We'll need more men. The sentry posts! Can we enlist the aid of the men there?"

"Aahh!"

All heads turned to the west end of the bowl to see Steven

rolling down the rocky embankment, the shaft of an arrow protruding from his chest.

"This way," cried Cristo, motioning to an upthrust rock thirty feet away.

Paul and Cristo made the shelter of the rocks just as four archers appeared atop the bowl's west rim. A moment later, Solman hobbled in after them, an arrow stuck in his right calf. He collapsed an instant later.

Cristo put his hand to Solman's neck and felt for a pulse. "He's dead," he mumbled. He removed the arrow from Solman's leg and examined the tip. It had been coated with a dull orange substance. "Poison," he said to Paul. "Fast acting, too. We'd better warn Stilgart and Hannah."

Cristo yelled across the way to Stilgart and Hannah, who had taken refuge within the wreckage of the flying machine, then he and Paul assessed their situation. Through an opening in the rocks they could see only the archers' heads. They lay prone atop the ridge, their faces little stabs of pink flesh, featureless at this distance. They wore gray hoods, and Paul suspected they wore gray tunics and trousers as well. Such was perfect camouflage for this area of the Eastern Mountains.

What Paul couldn't figure out was how the archers had crossed to the three fiefs. The land bridges were natural formations of rock half a mile long. They not only joined Fief Karcan and Fief Cerus to the Medoc Peninsula, but they also defined the eastern and western boundaries of the Void of Dadon. The only passage across them was a thirty-foot-wide trail that had been cut into the rock centuries earlier. This path was just wide enough to allow horse-drawn carts loaded with timber, meat, textiles, and other goods to enter and leave the fiefs. The rest of each land bridge was a weathered expanse of fragmented rock surfaces pitched at different angles to each other. This ground was crisscrossed by deep crevices and punctuated by mounds of broken rock. There were three checkpoints along the length of the trail. Also, lookouts were posted up on the rocks. They would spot anyone who attempted to make the dangerous traverse away from the trail.

Paul's eyes swept the expanse of sloping gray rock to the south end of the bowl. The crater measured three hundred feet north to south and one hundred eighty feet east to west. It was a uniform depth and the crater floor lay thirty feet below its rim. Paul thought it a strange and unique formation for this mountainous area. Perhaps the partial collapse of a huge jooarie sac had created it. Or perhaps it was formed by the collapse of several smaller jooarie sacs along a core-vine running north-south.

There were three other upthrusted pieces of rock in the bowl. One was in front of and to the south of the two men. Part of the tail section of the flying machine lay against it. Two were located behind and to the north of them.

Paul's gaze returned to the archers. The advantage was all theirs. It was next to impossible for he or Cristo to shoot them from the floor of the bowl.

We're as good as dead if we move from behind this rock, he thought, his lower lip trembling.

He drew his head back from the opening in the rock. "We're safe here, aren't we?" he asked, desperate to get a fix on Cristo's thinking.

Cristo did not turn his head from the opening.

Paul grew impatient with Cristo's silence. *What was he thinking? Did he have a plan?*

"Could they loft their arrows over these rocks?" he asked. "I mean, aim them up in the air so they fall behind here? Those tips would only have to scratch us."

"Paul, please be still," said Cristo. "I've got to think!" He turned his head from the opening. "How long do you think the archers will be content to wait for us to make a mistake?"

"What do you mean?"

"They're here to kill us, not lay siege to us! The longer they're stalled, the more chance there is for something to go wrong." Cristo pointed to the north rim of the bowl. "Look how exposed we are from that flank. It's the same to the south and east. It won't be long before they fan out." He looked again at the archers atop the ridge. "Damn it! They move already."

Paul peered through the hole in the rocks at the archers' position. He saw only two archers. "Which way did they go, Cristo?" He began to move toward the left edge of the rock. "Do they move toward the north or south rim?"

Cristo reached out and grabbed hold of Paul. "Stay behind

these rocks!"

Paul fought back the urge to panic. Cristo was one of his father's cleverest strategists and would surely come up with a plan of action. He wouldn't let them die! Yet Paul also realized that Cristo was only a man, not the Malhah. He could accomplish no more than the situation would allow. Paul was reminded of a saying his Benerit-woman had told him: "A man can accomplish no more than the tools he possesses will allow. He can't build a castle without stone, nor scale a mountain without rope."

"We've got to get beneath the overhang along the west wall," Cristo told Paul.

The cool, matter-of-fact tone of Cristo's voice gave Paul hope. "But how?" he asked.

Cristo looked once again at the two archers atop the rim. They were prone. That would slow their reaction time. They were also close together. He had an idea. "Whose pack has the storm lanterns in it?"

"Mine."

"Get them out."

Paul knelt and removed the lanterns, then he glanced up at Cristo with a puzzled look.

"Do you know what will happen if you light one of these and then smash it open on the rocks?" he asked Paul.

Swiftly they set to work enlarging the narrow slotlike openings where the wicks soaked up the fuel. This would let the fuel spill out freely. Next Cristo removed a match stick from his pack, adjusted the wicks and lit them. He picked up one and gave Paul the other.

"Should we alert Stilgart and Hannah?" asked Paul.

Cristo bit down on his lower lip in thought. "No. They have farther to run to reach the overhang and I'm not sure we'll make it. Hopefully they can find shelter enough within the wreckage to protect their flanks."

Paul gripped the handle of his lantern tightly as he judged the distance to the archers on the rim. "I'm ready," he advised Cristo.

"Now!" cried Cristo, throwing his lantern in the direction of the two archers.

Paul's lantern, the first to strike the west wall, burst aflame a good twelve feet below where the archers lay. Cristo's throw was more accurate. His lantern exploded into flame atop the rim between the two archers. Paul and Cristo sprinted to the overhang and reached the shallow alcove beneath it safely.

Paul saw an opening in the rock above them. "Give me a boost up, Cristo."

Cristo formed a saddle with his hands and Paul stepped into it.

"Well?"

"It's a tunnel through the wall," said Paul.

"Can you fit through it?"

"It's narrow, but yes, I think I can crawl through. But you'll never make it, Cristo. You're bigger than I am."

"Let me have a look."

They switched positions. Cristo cursed softly to himself and then stepped down. "It's up to you, Paul."

Paul went numb when he heard those words. He thought they were just trying to escape, to find a better hiding place, a safer one. A stalemate would force the archers to enter the bowl and then they would be an easy target for a marksman like Cristo. But he was forgetting about Stilgart and Hannah. The wreckage of the flying machine provided only minimal protection to the north, east and south. The archers would be shooting down into the bowl and that vantage point might give them a clear shot at either of them.

"I'll give you a hand up," said Cristo, again forming a saddle with his hands. He shot a nervous glance at the north rim of the bowl. "Let's go!"

Paul moved less of his own free will and more in response to the authoritative tone of Cristo's voice.

Cristo handed him his bow and a quiver of arrows. "Drag these behind you."

Paul began to panic. "I'm not that good a shot, Cristo."

Cristo reached up and clasped Paul's hand. "You're an excellent shot, Paul. I know. Illad and I trained you. Now relax. Take a few deep breaths."

Paul did as he was told.

"That's it. Focus on the mission." Cristo waited a few seconds. "Feel calmer?"

"A little."

"Good. Now listen to me. Don't concern yourself with the archers on the west rim of the bowl first. Stilgart and Hannah are well protected on that flank. If they weren't, the archers would have cut them down by now. This tunnel is north of the archers and below them. You should be able to exit it unseen. Use caution, Paul. And steady yourself before you shoot. Aim for the chest or back. An arrow there should make a kill."

"What will you do?"

"Try to find another way out." He reached up and clasped Paul's hand again. His eyes spoke of the concern he felt for Paul's safety. "You can do it, Paul. Trust in yourself."

The tunnel was wide enough the first fifteen feet for Paul to crawl through on his hands and knees. But then the way became narrow, so narrow in fact, that Paul had to turn on his side, find fingerholds and pull himself forward. When he peered out the end of the tunnel he saw he was midway up the thirty-foot mound that sloped down from the rim of the bowl. Much of the mound was overgrown with a hearty scrub grass and would muffle the sound of any loose bits of rocks he might set free. He gave a glance toward the two archers, who were above him and to the left about seventy-five feet away. Their attention was elsewhere. Paul pulled himself from the mouth of the tunnel and, crouching as low as he could, ran swiftly toward a low shelf of rock and ducked behind it. There he knelt for nearly half a minute, peering back over the wall of rock, waiting. No one pursued him.

The mound that encircled the bowl was punctuated by narrow ridges. These tapered as they rose toward the rim of the bowl. Paul moved stealthily from one ridge to the next, using each as a barrier to hide behind. There he would pause, check the way ahead, then, crouching low to the ground, sprint to the next ridge.

He caught sight of the first of the archers halfway around the circumference of the bowl. The archer was bent over and using all fours to climb the rocky slope, which was steeper at this end of the bowl and without scrub grass. Paul sprinted to the next ridge. His heart hammered beneath his breastbone. His hands were sweaty. Too sweaty! He wiped them on his pants so his fingers wouldn't slide from the bowstring. He removed an arrow from his quiver and strung his bow. His heart pounded even faster. Now all he had to do was step from behind the ridge and take aim. He sucked down a deep breath.

He froze with fear. This wasn't a game or contest set up by Cristo or Illad to hone his skills as a marksman. It was the real thing. He froze because . . . he had never killed before. It didn't matter that the archer would kill *him* without a moment's hesitation. Or would kill Cristo or Stilgart or any of the Benjarth! It didn't matter. *He* had never killed before.

The archer's foot slipped and he slid back several feet. He shook his head as if disgusted with his own carelessness. Then he continued his climb up the embankment.

Paul watched the archer's progress in helpless frustration. His fingers felt numb. His legs felt rooted to the ground.

The archer neared the top of the grade.

Paul could no longer think clearly or logically. Blood pounded at his temples. Images came to him. He saw Steven tumbling down the grade, the bloodied shaft of an arrow protruding from his chest. He saw Solman's eyes roll up into his skull as he died.

The archer paused at the top of the slope and peered over its edge.

The images came faster now. He saw Stilgart and Hannah with arrows in their backs. He saw Cristo's face twist in anguish as an arrow cut him down.

The archer removed an arrow from his quiver and strung it to his bow.

The worst of the images came next. He saw his father. His father's face was scarred in pain—constant, unmitigated pain!

Father!

Every muscle and tendon in Paul's body came to life at once. He leaped up from behind the ridge and let his arrow fly.

His shot was low, the arrow piercing the archer's left thigh. The archer yelped in pain, and his bow fell from his hand and slid down the embankment. He whirled to view his assailant. A knife flashed against the gray of his tunic.

Paul's reflexes, fine tuned from his years of training with sword and rapier, saved his life. He twisted his upper body to the left and the archer's knife flashed past him. Unfortunately he had been standing on loose stone and his sudden movement caused him to lose his footing and tumble to the ground. The archer crouched, ready to leap. Paul turned on his side, yanked an arrow from its quiver and planted it on the ground beside him. The arrow split in two under the archer's weight, the splintered end of the upper left tearing across the backside of his hand. The point of the arrow did its job, though, puncturing the archer's heart.

Paul rolled the lifeless body from on top of him and got to his feet. He felt a surge of emotion so primitive, so base, that he felt like an animal as he let it consume him. He had killed! He had been the hunter and he had killed his prey. The man's blood was smeared on his tunic, but Paul was not disgusted by it. It was his badge of victory. He felt strong, powerful. He felt something else, too. A barrier had been crossed. He could kill again.

Just then he heard the soft crush of stone behind him. He whirled around and saw the other archer standing, his bowstring taut, thirty paces away.

"What a mess you've made of poor Armen." The archer feigned a look of sadness. "A pity. We were drinking buddies, you know."

Paul found himself capable of surprisingly clear thought. He remembered a fact his father had once taught him. Men about to make a kill, he had said, were of two personalities. There were those who were machinelike and quick about what they had to do, and there were those who liked to toy with their victim before dispatching him. Against the former, one hadn't a prayer. Against the latter, a slight one.

This one's a talker! Stall him!

"What is it you want?"

The archer looked genuinely surprised. "Isn't it obvious?"

Paul glanced to the left. His bow lay on the ground ten feet away. "Not the reasons."

The archer pulled at his bowstring. "You are in no position to ask questions."

Paul glanced to the right. The dead archer's knife lay on the ground behind a stone. He doubted the archer could see it from where he stood. "It's a condemned man's right, isn't it?" He took a half-step back. "To get a few answers?"

The archer cast a thoughtful glance toward the top of the

bowl. "Why not? Your friends aren't going anywhere. We fight, Paul Benjarth, to take back lands rightfully ours. Lands Matthew Sinoms and the Jarred took from us."

So that was the stratagem Thyden had used to motivate the Sinese and Phlogin to follow him! Paul knew his history. In the year one hundred eighty-four, Matthew Sinoms did lead the Jarred in an invasion of Fiefs Cerus and Karcan. But what the archer was omitting was that it was the Sinese and Phlogin who had driven the Jarred from those lands in the first place.

"Why must you go to war with us? he asked. "The Benjarth share the bounty of Fief Karcan with all those who live within its borders."

The archer looked puzzled. "What exactly are you saying?"

Paul delayed his response to buy himself a little more time. He rocked back and forth on his feet, took a slight step back and to the right. "The rewards of the good life are available to all living in Fief Karcan. Set up residency here."

The archer looked dubiously at Paul. "You think me a fool? The Jarred share only with their own kind."

Paul took a half-step to the right. "There are Sinese and Phlogin living among us now."

The archer's face hardened. "As what? Your servants? Your maids? Your stable hands? That's not for me."

Illad had taught Paul to relax when throwing a knife. The knife must slide from the hand, he had said. A tense person will hold onto a knife a fraction of a second too long. The knife will miss to the left, or wound or graze when it should have killed. Paul took a calming breath, exhaling through the nose. He now stood directly beside the knife. All he had to do was stoop, grab it and throw.

"Do you think you will fare better with Lord Thyden?" he asked. "His lieutenants and field captains alone will share in the riches of the three fiefs! There will be nothing left for a soldier like you."

Paul worked his feet apart to better his balance. He flexed his knees ever so slightly, once, twice. His move for the knife would have to be instantaneous, flawless. And his throw, perfect.

"He who kills Master Paul Benjarth will be well rewarded by his superiors," remarked the archer with a self-assured air.

Paul took another calming breath. It was now or never.

The archer raised his bow. "Make a move for that knife and you'll only prolong your agony. A clean kill is immediate."

Paul stiffened, and as he did he realized he had no chance now to make a clean move for the knife.

It was then the archer did an odd thing. As if an unseen hand had slapped him across the back, his upper body pitched forward, then recoiled back. His arms fell limply to his sides. He swayed forward, caught himself. Then he crumpled to the ground. The handle of a knife protruded from between his shoulder blades.

A man stood forty feet away. He was of average height and thin. His hands and forearms were disproportionately large. His eyes were deeply set and his face worn, aged. His long hair was brushed back. A crimson-colored cloak covered his sinewy frame from shoulder to knee. Stitched just above the cloak's bottom edge was a blue-and-white patch. Centered on the patch were three thin vertical lines surrounded by a broken circle.

"Who are you?" asked Paul.

"A friend." The stranger turned. "Charnen," he called out to the rocks behind him. "Charnen!"

From behind those rocks appeared the largest man Paul had ever seen. He had to be seven feet tall and weighed in excess of three hundred pounds.

"Take care of the two archers on the other side of the bowl," the stranger commanded.

With two strides the man called Charnen was beside the dead archer. He reached down and pulled out the knife. In the man's massive hand the knife looked but a toy, its thin stone blade no longer than one of his fingers. He brushed past Paul and was on his way.

"Charnen will not fail," the stranger said.

"How do you know of the other archers?"

"We saw the attack from up there." He pointed to a ridge that overlooked the east end of the bowl. "There is a concealed path behind the rocks. I figured some of the archers would circle to the east side of the bowl. You were exposed from that flank so we climbed down."

"Have you a name?" Paul asked.

"My name is Arnun Weldlin. I am a bashan."

"Bashan?"

"The word is of the old tongue. It means 'watcher.' One of my tasks was to watch over the Benjarth medallion."

The Benjarth medallion! Paul was confused. *Of what concern of yours is the Benjarth medallion?*

"It was an easy enough task with your grandfather," continued Arnun. "He kept it safely under lock and key. But your father took to wearing it like a piece of costume jewelry about his neck. He felt it a good-luck charm." Arnun paused. "I wish it had been. Now Lord Thyden has it."

"You've news of my father?"

Arnun nodded solemnly. "He was captured, blinded, and put to work in the chemical gardens beneath Lord Thyden's castle," he said.

Paul felt a stabbing pain in his chest. *Blinded!*

"It is an unusual fate for one of his position. Commoners are usually blinded and enslaved. Those of nobler bearing are put to death in the maze-box."

"Maze-box?"

"It is said to be a drug-induced state of mind and place. That's all I know." Arnun paused a moment in thought. "Drug experimentation? Wasn't that why Belshane was banished from the three fiefs? For experimenting on human subjects?"

"It was," acknowledged Paul.

His voice had been little more than a whisper. His thoughts were elsewhere. They were on his father, on the pain he must have felt, the knife ripping through the soft tissue behind the eyeball . . . Tears formed and slowly rolled down his cheeks.

"Hold your tears, lad. What I have to say demands your full attention. There exists, somewhere beyond the mountains to the east, a way down to the planet's surface. Why? Who built it? Both are unknowns. Your great-great-grandfather led an expedition of nine men to Calferon."

Paul snapped at Arnun, bitter he had not shown more compassion concerning the news of his father. "I know that history! He returned alone with the medallion. The others were killed in a rock slide."

Arnun gave Paul a hard stare. "Everything is at stake, Paul.

The lives of thousands! That medallion Duke Whitin Benjarth brought back was hardly just a piece of jewelry. It was hollow. Within it lies the power that created our world and can in turn destroy it."

Paul found Arnun's statement incredible. "A power that created this world? And can destroy it? I don't understand."

"I'm afraid I don't either, Paul. Duke Whitin alone glimpsed its contents. Yet it must be a force of terrible power! Remember that he exiled himself to the Medoc Peninsula to live as secluded a life as possible. Perhaps he feared being interrogated by those who knew of his journey to Calferon. He would be defenseless to guard what he knew after an injection of a truth serum like styranotide."

Paul reflected upon what Arnun had just told him. "Now if what you say is true," he said finally, "why then does Thyden not possess this power?"

"Did you ever note the medallion's construction?" Paul's silence was answer enough for Arnun. "No, perhaps not. Your father was quite possessive of it. It cannot be opened by Lord Thyden. Or by any of us! The hottest of fires cannot melt it. The most acidic of solutions will not etch it. A key once existed that could open it, but it was lost. Now only one can open it. The Malhah."

Paul noted the nervous way Arnun kept squeezing his heavily veined hands—the hands of a woodsman, he realized—together. "What do you know of the Malhah?" he asked eagerly.

"He was captured by Lord Marthan."

Paul was stunned by that news. "Here? In these mountains?"

"No. On the Medoc Peninsula."

"But how is that possible? The wreckage of the flying machine is right here!"

"I don't know," replied Arnun.

Paul collected himself. "We are all in terrible danger then, aren't we? When Lord Marthan turns the Malhah over to Thyden, he will be able to open the medallion."

"Lord Marthan does not have the Malhah anymore. My men sprang him from his cell in Middloc, but it was a costly action. We lost many and we've revealed ourselves. Now Lord

Thyden's and Lord Marthan's soldiers search for us. That is why we need your help."

"How can the Benjarth help?"

"We need men who know the geography of the frontier. We plan to take the Malhah around the Void of Sois. We can't bring him into Fief Karcan any other way. The land bridges are too heavily guarded."

Paul remembered that Kalin Merteuse, an adviser to his father, had been a trader and had traveled the frontier before Lord Thyden had seized control of it. He would know its geography and could draw a map of it.

"We will help you," said Paul.

Arnun nodded his thanks. Then he added a caution. "Be wary of who you tell the medallion's secret to. The thought of possessing such power can turn a good man bad. You are only the fourth now living to know of the medallion's power."

"Who is the other? Lord Marthan?"

Arnun shook his head. "Lord Thyden would have been foolish to tell him. Such knowledge might have made Lord Marthan reluctant to turn the Malhah over without first striking some sort of deal that gave him a share of the medallion's powers."

"Then who is it?"

"I don't know. There have always been two bashans. Your great-great-grandfather set it up that way. I am the third bashan in an order that goes back to a boy named Mark Elbtas. We were to reveal the potential of the medallion when our peoples were threatened by an oppressor's armies." Arnun paused. "Duke Whitin seems to have been gifted with foresight. He predicted the rise of a tyrant such as Lord Thyden in the western territories. Yet I'm sure he did not foresee *these* circumstances."

"These circumstances?"

"That the medallion would leave Fief Karcan." Arnun paused. "Perhaps it is my fault that it has. But then again, my task was to observe. I could not take it from your father.

"Somehow," he continued, "Lord Thyden must have learned the identity of the other bashan. Most likely it was by coincidence. He took Jarred prisoners when he raided the border settlement of Dor, needing slaves to work in the chemical gardens. Perhaps one of those taken was the other bashan. Had this individual been randomly interrogated with styranotide, Lord Thyden would have learned of the bashans and their mission.

"The greatest dangers now lie before us. If Lord Thyden recaptures the Malhah and the Malhah opens the medallion for him, then he will be all powerful. We must prevent that at any cost."

Paul heard the crush of stone behind him. He whirled around. Charnen trotted past him.

"It is done," Charnen told Arnun.

"Your contact is Varth Medo," Arnun told Paul. "He lives in Cartag. Send one down from the edge of the forest to locate him. He will organize your men."

Arnun turned and the two men disappeared behind the rocks.

CHAPTER 3

Lord Thyden stared down at the messenger from the elevated vantage point of his throne. "Speak, lad."

"Lieutenant Fargo is in your quarters."

"Is he tied securely?"

"Quite."

Lord Thyden studied this messenger carefully. He had not seen him before. The captain of the guard took care of security and that included the hiring and firing of castle staff. The guard captain had a number of drugs at his disposal. A truth serum such as styranotide helped weed out those who possessed too much ambition and might eventually challenge him for his throne. It also helped to weed out those of weak character, as such individuals were prone to take bribes. Men of strong character believed in causes and would lay down their lives for them. So he'd let his people believe they were going to war to reclaim the kingdom of the three fiefs. He alone knew they were only pawns in his personal vendetta against the Benjarth.

"What's your name, lad?" he asked.

"Keith Harkins, my lord. I'm from Lorstown."

"Spare me your personal history! All I asked for was your name." He watched with delight as the boy's Adam's apple leaped to the top of his throat and plunged back down again.

"Sorry, my . . . my lord."

Lord Thyden dismissed the boy with a wave of his hand, then studied him as he walked from the room. He noted the ripple of the boy's leg muscles, their outline clearly visible beneath the folds of his pea-green slacks. His shoulders were broad and his back tapered in a perfect vee to slender buttocks. His calves were as rounded as fully-flexed biceps.

"Your age, boy?"

The words left Lord Thyden's mouth unexpectedly. He had not consciously thought of the question. The desire to know the boy's age was a link to a memory from the past, a memory so painful that it surfaced only when there was a lapse in the conscious brain's suppression of it.

The messenger spun around on his heels. "Fifteen, my lord!"

Fifteen!

So engrossed in his own thoughts did Lord Thyden then become that he was not aware of having waved the boy away again. It was only after he looked up, hoping for another glimpse of him, that he saw he was gone. So handsome the boy had been! And tall, too. Almost like a Jarred. Lord Thyden knew his own son would have grown up no less tall or handsome. *Fifteen!* It was the same age *his* son would have been. Lord Thyden's face twisted into an ugly mask of hatred. *The Benjarth be cursed! They shall pay dearly for what they've done to me!* He rose from his throne.

When Lord Thyden entered his living quarters, he saw with satisfaction that all was in readiness. Lieutenant Fargo was tied to a chair and the chair bolted to the floor. A jar of cymethadrenatyne was on a small table that had been placed next to the lieutenant. A syringe lay beside it. He struck a match and touched it to the wick of a candle. He placed the candle in a holder, which he then placed on the table beside the drug. Then he turned and gazed down at the bound lieutenant who, in addition to Duke Jaiman, had been the only one to survive his ambush. His men had knocked the lieutenant's sword from his hand early in the fight and the lieutenant had had no choice but to surrender.

"You need a shave, lieutenant." He sneered.

From above a thick stubble of gray-black whiskers two icy

blue eyes stared back at Lord Thyden. "You'll get nothing out of me," the lieutenant snarled.

"It's not my intention to try to make you talk, lieutenant. You know nothing I don't already know." He unstopped the jar of cymethadrenatyne and slowly filled the syringe with the purplish liquid. "I intend to kill you."

"By injection," scowled Lieutenant Fargo. "You're just like they say. A coward to the very core."

"I think you'll find me quite the contrary," remarked Lord Thyden. He held the syringe up to his eyes and counted off the gradients to himself. "I'm really quite a sportsman."

The lieutenant spat on the floor in reply.

Lord Thyden glanced in disgust at the glob of spit. "You really should appreciate what I'm about to offer you."

"And what's that?"

"As equal a chance to kill me as I'll have to kill you."

There was both interest and skepticism evident on Lieutenant Fargo's face. "Tied to this chair? And drugged?"

"It's not your physical prowess that will aid you," explained Lord Thyden, "rather the ability of your mind to think. Being tied to that chair will not handicap you."

In one swift motion of hand and arm, Lord Thyden jabbed the syringe into the lieutenant's upper arm and depressed the plunger halfway down. The lieutenant winced in pain.

"Now as for the drug," said Lord Thyden, passing the syringe needle back and forth over the flame of the candle, "you shall see that it's no more of a handicap for you than it is for me."

As the lieutenant looked on in amazement, Lord Thyden pushed the needle into a vein in the palm of his hand and depressed the plunger the rest of the way down.

"Now that that is done," he said, placing the syringe back on the table, "I hope you'll permit me the opportunity to boast a bit. I'm really quite proud of my drenatyne series." He placed a chair in front of the lieutenant and sat down in it. "Cymethadrenatyne is, for lack of a better word in describing it to your simple mind, a powerful hallucinogen. Yet the hallucination we are both about to experience is not shaped by our individual minds, but rather by the molecular structure of the drug itself. The hallucination is preprogrammed for us down to the last detail. Everything that happens to you will happen to me. That is until we descend into the maze-box. Then we take control of our own destinies. One of us will kill the other."

"Great Malhah," screamed the lieutenant. "What's happening to me?"

Lord Thyden pushed his own chair aside and stretched out on the floor. His thick robe and a pillow placed beneath his head cushioned his body against the hardness. He had learned through trial and error that lying supine prevented the muscular stiffness that could result from collapsing into an awkward position when the drug took effect. He folded his hands on top of his stomach and gazed dreamily at the ceiling. And, as he lay there, he felt his body grow rigid. It was a most unique feeling! It was as if his skin layers had fossilized and he was but a gelatinous substance floating within. Then the pressure came, the substance of his self expanding against the shell of his body. The sensation evoked the fear of being crushed against something hard, like a wall or rock. And then the shell of his body gave way to the pressure, exploding into a million luminous orange-yellow fragments. Lord Thyden's mind was free of his body. For an instant there was darkness everywhere, then he was floating above the maze-box.

CHAPTER 4

———

Paul walked with the relzan. Both men listened to the sound of the rain falling on the flattened stones of the courtyard below. Paul hoped it would clear soon. He was scheduled to leave for Fief Cerus in the morning.

"But why would Duke Whitin put such knowledge in the hands of the bashans?" he asked. "Would it not have been more useful to the Benjarth?"

Paul had remembered Arnun's warning that if he should choose to tell another of the medallion's power, he must be very selective in that choice. Illad Rahman was like a second father to him. He would lay down his life for his beloved duke or any of his family. He could be trusted. Paul needed to confide in him because he needed Illad's help in selecting the best individuals to accompany him on this mission, as well as his help in organizing the materials necessary to equip them. The relzan could be trusted as well. Those saddled with a personal problem or with guilt over some wrongdoing often consulted him. The relzan was familiar with the Book of Prophecy and could interpret passages concerning the Malhah. He was also knowledgeable in historical matters. It was Paul's hope that the relzan could help him better understand the medallion's powers, his great-great-grandfather's exile, and the Malhah. There was still another reason he'd needed to confide in someone. He was only twenty-one and inexperienced in matters of state and warfare. Naturally he was insecure about the responsibilities he was assuming since his father's capture. If nothing else, it was important to have someone whose advice he respected confirm that he was making the right decisions.

"Perhaps you've answered your own question," the relzan said. "*Useful.* There were strong rivalries between fiefs in the time of your great-great-grandfather. He may have feared that high-ranking officials of his own court, even his own son, might have used the medallion's power to invade the other fiefs. His actions give one reason to believe this was the case."

"How do you mean?"

"It is said that for days he stood alone atop Tower Satchkind. Always his gaze was fixed to the east. Soon thereafter he packed provisions and hiked into the Eastern Mountains."

"What happened to him?"

"He crossed to the Medoc Peninsula and labored three years on the ridges as a logger. It was only at the time of his death that he revealed his true identity to those people. They brought his body back for cremation."

They had come to the end of the walkway and now had to turn to the left or right. To the right was an archway secured by a heavy wooden door that swung inward. Through it lay the busy corridors of the castle proper. A fire had certainly been lit in the great hearth of the dining hall as well as in the smaller fireplaces of the bedrooms. It would be warm inside the castle. To the left was another walkway. It joined the north and south wings of the castle's living quarters. It was open on one side and let in the chilling dampness of the night air. It was deserted. Paul turned to the left and the relzan followed.

The stones of the walkway were triangular and had been laid so that every two stones formed a square. A grayish green mortar had been used to fill the joints between the stones. The walkway was lit by ascama fiber lanterns hung every twenty feet. When exposed to light, trace amounts of morcain gas in the semitransparent filaments of the ascama plant's stems would glow brilliantly for up to sixteen hours. This meant the plants had to be grown in the complete darkness of a basement room. Should a single ray of light, be it from sunlight or another ascama fiber, permeate the room's darkness, then the chemical change within the ascama stems would begin and the entire crop would be ruined. The castle's ascama fiber growing room was accessed by either of two winding staircases. The geometry of the turns prevented light from reaching the bottom landings. There was a door at each end of the room. Each closed against the stone of a slightly smaller opening.

"What do you think lies within the medallion?" Paul asked the relzan finally. "What force can both create and destroy our world?"

"I do not know, Paul. There is no mention of it in the Book of Prophecy."

Paul stopped. "Do you think it all a hoax?"

The relzan put his arm around Paul's shoulder and they began to walk again. Paul could feel the soft fleshiness of the relzan's body press against him. "Perhaps it is not religion you should look to for proof. Instead consider the dilemma of the geoscizan. Core-vine dating reveals the Eastern Mountains to be the oldest of all rock formations. So who planted the first core-vine there? And how was it accomplished?" He raised his eyebrows. "Remember, we are twelve thousand feet above the planet's surface."

"The histoscizan faces a similar puzzle. Why does the formation of the Eastern Mountains predate history? And is it not the same with Castle Chalmet? Open the history books to page one and already Castle Chalmet is fully constructed."

The relzan removed his arm from Paul's shoulder and placed it on the inner railing of the walkway. Rain fell on his hands, but he seemed not to notice it. "The early years are hidden from us. Purposely, I believe." He looked at Paul. "The medallion may well be a link to those early years."

Paul acknowledged the relzan's remarks with a nod of his head as he stood absorbed in his own thoughts. He was overwhelmed by how much had happened in so short a time. He reviewed the preparations he and Illad had made for tomorrow's journey, wondering if they had forgotten anything. Everything had been put together so hurriedly since his meeting with Arnun.

Arnun!

"I've something to show you," cried Paul, suddenly remembering the sketch he had hastily drawn and stuffed in his shirt pocket. They stepped into the light of an ascama fiber lantern. "The patch was blue and white and sewn on Arnun's cloak. There was some intricate line work along its borders, but I was not close enough to see the detail closely. This was its central design."

The relzan studied Paul's sketch. "It would appear Arnun and I have something in common," he said at last. "We are both relzans."

"He's a relzan?"

"He is one of a few who travel among the logging camps on the Medoc Peninsula." The relzan pursed his lips in thought. "It is a hard life."

Paul remembered how lean and sinewy Arnun's build had been. "It's reassuring, though," he said.

"What is?"

"That he is a relzan."

"Oh?"

"Well, I've always believed that those who devote their life to interpreting the Book of Prophecy and preaching right from wrong, as you have, are honest men and less likely to mastermind a hoax."

The relzan smiled. "Your comment is most complimentary, but you should be wary of judging another man's character by his profession alone, or by comparing him to others who practice the same trade. You are still young, and to generalize is one of youth's naivetes. You have a far better reason to trust Arnun."

"And that is?"

"He saved your life."

CHAPTER 5

———

Thirty riders left the stable compound on the north side of Castle Chalmet two hours before sunrise. They rode east through fields of peas, corn, and squash, reaching the slopes of the Eastern Mountains by daybreak. The sun would not clear the high peaks for another hour. The riders turned to the south and rode in the blue-gray shadows of the mountains.

Illad Rahman had selected this route. Certainly it was a roundabout way of getting to Fief Cerus. It would have been shorter to ride southwest across Fief Karcan rather than ride east first, circle to the south and then head west. But the plain southwest of Castle Chalmet was grazing land, and shepherds and ranchers tended their flocks and herds night and day there. Certainly their attention would be drawn to a band of thirty armed riders. The Benjarth could not be sure who was in the employ of lords Marthan and Thyden and paid to spy on them.

It was midmorning when they reached the easternmost tip of the Void of Dadon. They rode west along the southern slope of a ridge that concealed them from the shepherds tending their flocks southwest of the castle. It was afternoon when they crossed the border into Fief Cerus. It was nightfall when they set up camp at the foot of the Sornk Mountains.

The next day the Benjarth procession began the slow, winding trek south through the mountains. Paul was immediately aware of how different these mountains were from the Eastern Mountains. For one thing, they were not as steep and, secondly, they were not devoid of vegetation. A yellowish brown scrub grass thrived on the rocky slopes while clumps of kejote bushes clung stubbornly to the ledges beside cliffs. Boulders were covered on their top sides with a dark green mosslike fungus. Here and there an asharen tree towered beside the trail.

What magnificent trees they were, thought Paul, his gaze turned skyward.

For one hundred and fifty feet their thick trunks rose without branch or leaf. Then, in an explosion of boughs and branches, the trees spread their leafy canopies in circular domes one hundred feet in diameter.

"How I wish the Eastern Mountains had trees like these," he said to Kalin Merteuse, who rode beside him.

Kalin looked at Paul, his thin smile only another line on his wrinkled, leathery face. Kalin had been a trader for twenty-five years and had lived outdoors for most of his life.

As a boy Paul had enjoyed listening to the stories of the traders when they had stayed at Castle Chalmet. He had felt so grown up in the presence of these rugged men who plied the trade routes between the three fiefs, the Medoc Peninsula, and the border territories now controlled by Lord Thyden. He liked the smell of the smoke from their pipes as it curled lazily toward the ceiling. He liked their gruff appearance: their unshaven faces, their unkempt hair, the heavy clothing they wore, the worn shoes. He liked the sound of their voices, most of them deep, some gravelly, one or two slurred slightly because they drank too much Reiswaner.

"They are magnificent, aren't they?" said Kalin. "And so easy to log. One cut and the tree is completely clean of branches."

"Is there any logging done here?"

"On Fief Cerus? No. Duke Leipedes never tried to establish a logging industry. He didn't have to! Wood was plentiful from the mill at Middloc. But now, with the closing of the land bridges, it might not be a bad idea if he did."

It had been his father's and Duke Leipedes' d

years ago to close the land bridges joining their fiefs with the Medoc Peninsula. It was believed spies for Lord Thyden and Lord Marthan were posing as traders in order to enter the fiefs and gain information about the strength and size of the Benjarth forces, as well as those of Fief Cerus and Fief Salkird. Now the land bridges were like fortresses, each side posting a small army to prevent the spies of the other side from crossing.

"Tell me of the Medoc Peninsula, Kalin."

"Ninety percent of it is covered with forest. Those who live there make their living as loggers or as soldiers in Lord Marthan's army. A narrow valley winds like a ribbon down the peninsula's entire length. The only known east-west road follows the course of that valley."

"How far is Cartag from where we cross to the peninsula?"

"A day's journey on foot."

They rode on together, each busy with his own thoughts.

It was Kalin who finally spoke. "Cartag was, at the time I was traveling the trade routes, quite a boisterous town." He smiled at Paul. "Loggers have always been free-spirited individuals. You know—drinking, carousing, women-chasing. I guess there is a lot to get out of one's system after being up on the ridges for months at a time. The traders always got along well with the loggers. I guess we both were from the same mold." Kalin's face seemed distant now. Paul knew he was reliving some pleasant memory from that time of his life. "There was no hatred then, Paul. The Sinese, Phlogin, Ornan, Jarred—we all drank together. Time had healed the wounds since Matthew Sinoms's invasion of fiefs Cerus and Karcan." Kalin's face clouded over. "It was Belshane who rekindled that hatred. I know Cartag is not what it once was. It may well be a garrison town now."

The procession came to a halt.

"Form a line," cried Dimistre, another of Paul's father's lieutenants. "There's a bridge ahead."

The bridge was hewn from the trunk of a single asharen tree. It had been split lengthwise and the two halves bound with cord. It spanned a gully fifty feet wide and thirty feet deep. Fully exposed to view in the gully were core-vines three, four, and five feet in diameter.

"That crevice is artificial, isn't it?" asked Paul. "Why else would the core-vines be unearthed?"

"It is," explained Kalin. "It is a fire ditch. In the old tongue the word is *orquil.*"

Paul understood. "So a fire can't leap across it."

Kalin smiled as one bursting with a secret to tell. "That's part of it, Paul. There are no ursulas this high up on the ridges. Yet even if there were, the terrain would make it difficult to bring buckets of water to where a fire was."

Paul saw nothing unique in Kalin's explanation. *So what was he grinning about?* "So it contains the fire to a specific wooded area. That means the whole of the Medoc Peninsula must be so divided."

"Right again, Paul. But you are forgetting something. Think about it. You've studied geology. The heat from a fire?" He raised his eyebrows. "Eh? Eh? Eh?"

Of course, realized Paul. The jooarie sacs would rupture. They could hold only a finite volume of selevium gas. The heat would expand the gas within them and they would burst. The surface rock would be unsupported in those sections and its weight would tear the core-vines like dead tree limbs being snapped off. The burning brush and trees would fall from the sky with the rock.

Kalin nodded his agreement when Paul told him his thoughts. "That is why the gullies have been dug," he said. "The land will break cleanly at those joints where there is no crohephite rock holding it together. Therefore no additional land will be lost. Eventually new rock will form as screula is drawn to the spinolla of the exposed core-vines."

Paul found it difficult to imagine the disintegration of so vast a piece of terrain. "Has there ever been such a fire?"

"Only once. And that was by lightning. Care with fire is religion to a logger."

The procession halted again. This time Dimistre had them dismount. Quickly four stable hands gathered the horses' reins, for it was their task to return them to Fief Karcan. The others followed Dimistre up a narrow trail cut into the very ledge of the mountain. Three hundred feet they climbed to the top of the perimeter cliffs. There they were fronted by a rock wall eight feet high. To their right it tapered down to where it became broken and open in places.

"We will cross after dark by that broken rock over there," said Dimistre.

The men did their best to find comfortable resting places among the rocks. Paul undid the straps that held his blanket, unrolled it, then folded it until he'd fashioned a pillow. The rock still held some of the heat from the noonday sun. Paul curled up against it and fell asleep.

It was night when Dimistre woke him. "Food's over there," he said, indicating a shelf of rock where capoi bread, dried meat, and dried fruit had been laid out.

Paul saw the others had already eaten and were busy preparing themselves for the crossing. "Why did you let me sleep so long?"

"You were tired," answered Dimistre matter-of-factly.

As Paul's eyes grew accustomed to the dark, he saw that the shelf of rock held what he was sure were more generous helpings of food than the rest of them had eaten. "You'll not treat me any differently than the rest of these men," he told Dimistre sternly.

Dimistre gazed at him with an uncertain face.

"It's not right," Paul whispered, his tone of voice less harsh.

"It is right. You are the duke's son."

"But the others, Dimistre. What will they think? That I'm soft and need pampering?"

"That you are here tells them otherwise."

Paul drew his head back and gazed into Dimistre's gray-brown eyes. Such unusual eyes. They always seemed in motion, their glance darting this way and that. One who had never met and talked with Dimistre at length would have trouble getting used to those eyes. Yet what appeared to be a nervous manner was in fact just energy, an energy that told you Dimistre was always alert, aware. His face was long and narrow, and his nose thin. His hair was brushed back like Arnun's had been, but it was not as long. He was not big-boned, yet there was a certain presence about him, an intensity that might make a physically stronger opponent still fear him in a fight.

Paul saw no point in arguing with him further.

As he ate, Paul watched his friend, Jessie Wanthrop, one of four archers selected for this mission, work a polishing stone up and down the barbed tip of an arrow. When he was satisfied with his workmanship, Jessie attached a length of rope to the special connector fitted to the arrow. Then he took a kneeling position at the cliff's edge beside the other archers. The wind gusted and the four men waited patiently for it to subside. When it did, the rip of bowstrings cut the air. Hardly an instant later four dull thuds, sounding much like axe blows, echoed back. The arrows had lodged in the trunks of the asharen trees across the way. Jessie climbed the rock formation behind them and secured the four ropes. They now pitched across the Void of Dadon at an angle of twelve degrees.

Paul stepped to the edge of the sky-void. He'd rarely been to the fiefs' perimeters and the majesty of what he saw filled him with awe. Twelve thousand feet below lay Calferon. Consumed by sand storms, it appeared a peppery swirl of grays and blacks. Paul wished he'd seen the sunset. The windblown sand, tinted innumerable shades of red and orange, would look like a boundless fire engulfing the planet. Paul lifted his gaze to the Medoc Peninsula. The interlocking boughs of the asharen trees formed a vast canopy, allowing neither starlight nor moonlight to penetrate. The peninsula's crohephite rock base, a broad band of dark gray punctuated by areas of black, was sixty feet thick at the perimeter. To the left, like an airy, transparent river, the Void of Dadon flowed away to the east until, curling back toward Fief Cerus, it disappeared from view.

The soft whistle-screech of a slide-harness ripped Paul's attention back to the immediacy of the mission. For a moment, a figure was suspended over the void. Then it disappeared into the forest.

Paul located his own slide-harness and attached the safety line to his belt. He was to cross last with Kalin and Dimistre, so he waited his turn at the foot of the rock. The crossing itself seemed to take but an instant. There was an incredible rush of air across his face and then a pair of hands reached for him and slowed his momentum.

The smell assaulted them. It was a heavy, greasy scent.

"Kalin," Paul whispered. "What is it?"

Paul attempted to take a step forward but found his way blocked by a tangle of branches. He stepped to the side and stumbled. His hand plunged into a pile of branches. He felt grease.

"Kalin!"

A wall of fire erupted in front of them. Fueled by the grease-soaked branches, it raced along the ground.

"Back across the ropes," cried Dimistre.

The men zigzagged their way through pockets of flaming brush. Some were on fire. Two soldiers, consumed in flames and blind with panic, ran off the edge of the peninsula into the void. Those who reached the ropes shoved and pushed each other in their haste to cross. Paul already stood by one of the ropes, having been one of the last to cross. But he'd been numbed by the sheer horror of what he saw happening around him and his body did not respond to his mind's command to flee. He was knocked to the ground by his own men.

The first of the Benjarth soldiers to reach the halfway point in his crossing dropped from the rope. An arrow had severed his spinal cord. Those soldiers crossing on the same rope immediately turned around. Those on the other ropes hesitated, confused by the retreat of their fellow soldiers. They'd seen the soldier fall, but not the arrow that had struck him. Suddenly the air over the void was thick with arrows. Seven, eight, nine men fell, screaming, into the void.

"They've archers at the peninsula's edge," shouted Dimistre.

One soldier, an arrow in his leg, leaped for the cliff's edge but missed. Another, too far from the peninsula to make it back without getting shot, cut the rope with his knife. He swung across the void, struck the crohephite rock base of Fief Cerus and fell, unconscious, into the void.

A wall of flame raced up the trunk of an asharen tree. Its light silhouetted the motion of two figures to Paul's left. One of them raised a knife high above his head and let it fall on another of the ropes. Grabbing the end of it, the two men leaped from the peninsula, swinging out beneath the base of Fief Cerus. After waiting out the swing of the rope, they began their climb.

Paul grew hopeful. It looked as if they were going to make it. He unsheathed his own knife and prepared to cross similarly. But moments later their screams told him the archers had cut them down, too.

"Help me!" cried a voice.

"A soldier, his shirt aflame, fell to the ground beside Paul. Paul wrapped his blanket around the soldier, smothering the fire. An arrow struck the ground near them. Paul pulled the soldier behind a tree.

"What'll we do?" cried the soldier, his eyes glazed with shock.

A tremor shook the ground.

The jooarie sacs!

There followed a loud pop as a jooarie sac burst. An area of burning trees and brush to Paul's left collapsed. There followed the sound of rock smashing and grinding against rock. Another tremor shook the ground. And then that section of land fell from the sky.

"What'll we do?" cried the soldier, who Paul now recognized as Janon Alpur, Jessie's half-brother.

"I don't know!" Paul screamed back.

Another jooarie sac ruptured. The scent of selevium gas lingered momentarily in the air.

"The rock breaks apart," Janon cried hysterically.

The ground suddenly pitched, and Paul was thrown from his feet. A tree fell ten feet from where he lay, splitting in two as it struck the ground. Paul rolled away from it until a rock prevented him from rolling any farther. He lay on his stomach, facing the void. His view was of the crohephite rock base of Fief Cerus. The elevation of Fief Cerus, at the point where they had crossed, was higher than that of the Medoc Peninsula. It was then his mind made the connection. Crohephite rock was porous! Those areas of deepest black were tunnels into the rock!

Paul saw it as their only chance. He cut one of the ropes still spanning the void and secured it about his waist. "Dimistre! Kalin! Listen to me! The crohephite rock is porous. It's riddled with tunnels and holes!"

He lowered himself over the edge, slipped down the face of the rock, and pulled himself into the first large hole he came to. From his pocket he removed a box containing an ascama fiber-stub. Its light revealed depth to the hole.

A tremor shook the ground. Paul dropped the fiber-stub

and it spilled into the void. Something exploded through the rock by his shoulder. It was bulbous and felt leathery.

A jooarie sac!

A figure filled the opening.

"Give me your hand!" cried Paul. He grabbed Dimistre's hand and pulled him in. "Have you a fiber-stub?"

A lit stub appeared in Dimistre's hand. It was brighter than Paul's had been. "The tunnel appears to curve around to the right."

Paul glanced back at the opening. "Did you tell the others to hurry? Where are they?"

As if in answer, a figure appeared. Paul grabbed his hand and pulled him in. After Kalin came Jessie, then Janon, and then Merlin Kantor. Only the six of them had survived the massacre.

Dimistre led them forward.

Suddenly there was an explosion behind them. The jooarie sac by the opening had burst. The rock gave way there and brush and timber were swept into the void. There was another tremor and the floor of the tunnel cracked open. Through the gap Paul could see the debris falling like a fiery meteor to the planet's surface.

"This way! Hurry!" cried Dimistre.

For a distance of roughly two hundred feet the men were able to run upright through the tunnel. But then the way narrowed and they had to turn their bodies and walk sideways. Protruding knobs of rock bruised their legs and backs.

"Can't you go any faster, Dimistre?" asked Jessie, who was third in line.

Dimistre lowered his right arm, which he'd been holding up alongside his head so the rock wouldn't bruise his face, and peered ahead. "The tunnel widens ahead. Maybe twenty feet. We might be able to go faster—"

The rest of Dimistre's words were drowned out by the sound of rock grinding against rock. The left wall of the tunnel dropped two feet.

"Against the right wall!" screamed Kalin. "She's going to fall!"

In rapid succession three jooarie sacs exploded. The left wall of the tunnel fell. There was a scream as a figure hurtled into the falling rock. Merlin, who only an instant ago had been standing beside Paul, had been sucked into the void.

Paul pressed himself against the rock. What had once been the floor of the tunnel was now only a ledge twelve inches wide. That time a huge wedge of forest had fallen. Paul knew it was now only a matter of minutes before the rest would fall.

The men inched their way forward, backs against the rock. For thirty feet they made their way, each of them so very conscious of their slow progress. Finally they reached the point where the rock had sheared. A few feet farther the tunnel widened. They ran until they came to a fork in the path.

"We must continue to go west," Kalin said. "We've got to be close to the orquil there."

"We go straight then," said Jessie.

"No! We've been curling around to the north." Dimistre swept his hand in an arc, indicating how they had traveled. "Straight would be toward the Void of Dadon!"

The wall beside Paul exploded and the swollen membrane of a jooarie sac hit him broadside. He would have been crushed against the other wall of the tunnel had the rock there not already given way to a jooarie sac. The expanding membranes began to envelop him.

"He'll smother!" yelled Jessie.

Paul tried to climb out from between the two jooarie sacs, but the plant membranes pinned him about the waist. Already the jooarie sac behind him pushed against the back of his head.

"Help me!" he cried.

His friends attacked the jooarie sacs with their knives, but the tough leathery membranes resisted their blows.

Paul brought his arms up in front of his face and formed an air pocket as the plants enveloped him. He could no longer hear the cries of the others and had no way of knowing their progress in freeing him. He could only hear his breathing and a hollow echo that he knew was his heart pounding. The expanding gas pushed back on his arms, taxing his strength. The exertion caused him to breathe rapidly and he feared he was too quickly using up what little air he had been able to trap. He sucked in what he sensed was his last breath of oxygen and held his breath.

He thought: *Push to the side! Push where the jooarie sacs overlap!*

A hand grabbed his wrist and pulled his left arm straight out. His other arm alone did not have the strength to hold back the jooarie sac, so it collapsed around him, sucking onto his face. An instant later the jooarie sac ruptured and Paul was swept forward into the hole where the jooarie sac had once been. But the arm held him tightly and pulled him back into the tunnel.

Dimistre would explain later the turn of events that had saved his life. Some burning brush had fallen through directly atop the jooarie sac. The entrapped gas had then expanded so rapidly at that point that a bubble had formed. It was Kalin's arm that had grabbed him as Dimistre's knife punctured the weakened membrane at the point of the bubble.

Suddenly the ground shook and the five of them were knocked from their feet. The tunnel's ceiling split open and the selevium gas pocketed there rushed out with a loud slurping sound. The howling roar of the flames swept into the tunnel like a blast of foul air. They could all see that the forest above them was an inferno. The tunnel ended around the next bend. The men leaped into the orquil and scrambled into the shelter of a hole on its far side.

Seconds later everything collapsed. The separate fires flared up into a single blinding lick of flame. Paul turned his face from its brightness. When he looked back, only the emptiness of the void was before him.

He closed his eyes and slumped down into the curve of the rock. Visions came to him. Horrible visions! He saw Merlin fall, shrieking, into the collapsed rock. He saw the two burning soldiers running toward the sky-void, the wind from their own flight fanning the flames higher. He saw his soldiers drop from the crossing ropes. A part of him felt responsible for their deaths. Hadn't he been the one to organize this mission? Hadn't he been the one to lead them to the slaughter?

Somehow lords Marthan and Thyden had learned of this mission and where they would cross. Someone had tipped them off. Paul considered the possibility that there might be two spies. The first would act as Lord Marthan's and Lord Thyden's ear. He would gather information but never leave the castle's grounds so as not to cast suspicion on himself. A second spy, perhaps a stable hand or even a rancher, would ride south with the information to either Fief Karcan's or Fief Cerus's border. A note might be attached to an arrow and shot across the Void of Dadon to a waiting contact. Or the message might be spelled out in coded light flashes from a mirror fragment. But it was the identity of that first spy that concerned Paul. He had discussed the details of this mission with only trusted confidants. Arnun Weldlin had told him of the medallion and had requested his help. But Arnun did not know the day they would leave or the mission's crossing point. The relzan knew the day but not the crossing point.

Illad!

Paul forced that thought from his mind. Illad would never betray those he loved so well. That left Dimistre and Kalin. They were the only other ones who knew the details of the mission. Yet to suspect them was absurd.

They waited one hour. It seemed a reasonable enough time to ensure that Lord Marthan's and Lord Thyden's men had left the area. Then Dimistre climbed the peninsula's edge. He secured a length of rope to an asharen tree and lowered it for the others to climb up.

"What do we do now?" asked Jessie, once they were all again standing on the forest floor.

"I suggest we continue with the mission," Dimistre said, after giving the matter some thought.

"But we've lost our provisions and most of our weapons," cried Janon.

Jessie was in agreement with his half-brother. "We're not an army anymore, Dimistre."

"That doesn't matter," replied Dimistre. "We are five ablebodied men. That's five more men than Arnun's people have now." He looked to Paul, who nodded his support. "We go to Cartag."

They climbed the wooded slope and descended its backside to the valley floor. Keeping the road to their left, they paralleled its course westward. They stayed far enough from the road so as not to be seen by any who journeyed it with lanterns, yet not so far as to lose sight of it. Slivers of palest pink and turquoise streaked the early morning sky as the Benjarth climbed a narrow ridge. From its crest they gazed in awe at the scene before them.

Cartag lay nestled below in a narrow valley no wider than two throws of a stone. It was a most remarkable compression of terrain when one considered that where Paul and the others lay atop the ridge—half a mile east of the town—the peninsula was two miles across. Cliffs of dark stone towered above the town on its north and south flanks. These looked more like dams built to hold back the sky-void than wind-swirled aberrations of the core-vine growth process. Dwellings had been built into the sides of the cliffs, homes atop homes. In some instances these were six stories high.

"Wait until the morning sun hits here," said Kalin. "She's painted up like a carnival." He noticed the others looking at him with amused smiles. Grinning sheepishly, he said, "Aw, give an old trader a moment to reminisce. She is a colorful town. Really!" An uncertain look crossed his face. "Or was."

"She looks like she'll be a busy place come midmorning," Paul remarked to Dimistre, noting the vending stalls that split the main way into two thoroughfares. "Perhaps we can blend into the crowd in our search for Varth Medo."

"In years past it would have been possible. But I've no doubt Cartag's activities are carefully monitored by Thyden's soldiers now."

Janon overheard their conversation. "Who is Varth Medo?"

To Dimistre alone Paul had confided the name of their contact in Cartag. This he'd done for security reasons. The less the others knew, the less they could reveal if interrogated with a truth serum such as styranotide. Now Paul felt obligated to tell the others. "He is our contact in Cartag. It is who will bring us to the Malhah."

As the sun rose higher, the shadows blanketing the town receded. The wind picked up and the mankekin that covered the hillsides to the east and west of the town began to undulate in the breeze.

"See how the terrain here forms a natural ursula," pointed out Kalin.

"And how convenient it must be for collection," remarked Janon, whose duties, among others at Castle Chalmet, was to collect water from the ursula southeast of the castle and transport it back in barrels.

"This one ursula here," continued Kalin, "provides the water needs for the entire peninsula. I'll bet in a heavy rainfall they'll collect in the neighborhood of one hundred thousand gallons."

Paul could see the massive wooden collection troughs located at the east and west ends of the town. The mankekin was tapered and its short side overlapped one edge of the collection troughs. The fabric itself was closely woven and then shrunk by flame to flow the threads together. This process made it watertight. The troughs were nearly as high as a man. Several pipes equipped with spigots allowed the collected rainwater to be directed into wooden barrels and casks. Excess water was allowed to drain through another set of pipes into the ground.

There was activity in the town now. Striped awnings of bright green, red, yellow, and white were unfurled as wooden posts were driven into the ground to support them. Shutters were thrown open to let in the sunlight. A single horse-drawn wagon, led by one man, emerged from the wood and headed down the road into Cartag. It was soon lost behind the mankekin.

"All of you remain here," advised Kalin, who, crouching low, scurried downhill and out of sight. He returned fifteen minutes later. "It is as I suspected. Soldiers watch the road. We can't see them from this angle because of the mankekin. They searched that wagon before letting it pass."

Paul could see the wagon just now entering the outskirts of Cartag. "What will we do? If they question but one of us with styranotide . . ."

"I've an idea," said Kalin. "It's a risky one, though, especially for Janon."

The others turned to Janon.

"The blood of the Sinese and Phlogin is strongest in you," explained Kalin. "You have the best chance to pass for a logger."

From the vantage point of the ridge Paul and the others watched Janon stumble down the road to Cartag. They were now no more than fifteen yards north of the road and from there the checkpoint was clearly visible. The pungent smell of symorine, a coagulant, lingered in the air around them. The scent was close to that of alcohol and as much as could be spared had been dabbed on Janon's lips.

"Great Malhah," remarked Jessie. "He couldn't walk more drunkenly even if he were drunk!" His subsequent laughter was forced, his way of relieving the tension. They all awaited Janon's confrontation with the soldiers anxiously.

Kalin's years as a trader had afforded him many glimpses into the hard life of a logger. Many lived for months at a time away from their families in logging camps. Many drank heavily, for it helped pass the long nights on the ridges. So Kalin had reasoned that a drunk logger wandering the road into town, one who'd had some words with his boss, grabbed a flask and skipped camp, should not draw undue suspicion.

"You must be wary of what you say to the soldiers," Kalin had cautioned Janon. "Do not try to befriend them. Hatreds exist between logger and soldier and it would be out of character to act as if they didn't. Just don't say anything so strong to give them cause to draw their swords."

"And if they do make a run at Janon?" Paul had asked Kalin, as Janon had stepped out onto the road.

"There is nothing we can do from here, Paul. We cannot reveal ourselves and so jeopardize this mission. I do not think they will, though. There is no honor or satisfaction for any soldier, even one who follows Lord Marthan, in killing an unarmed drunk."

Paul watched Janon weave his way downhill. Once he sat down as if weary or unsure of his balance. Then he was up again, stumbling. As he drew near the checkpoint, one of the soldiers took a few steps laterally until he stood in the center of the road. He was a monster of a man. He had a beard and mustache that so enveloped his face that he appeared more animal than human. A sword sheathed in a scabbard hung from his side. He removed a flask from his pocket, spun off the cap and gulped some of the contents down.

Paul nudged Kalin in alarm.

"I see it," acknowledged Kalin. "A worse twist of fate could not have happened. But there is nothing we can do about it now."

The minutes crept by. Janon never sped up nor slowed his

pace. For his part the soldier never budged from the center of the road. Gradually the other soldiers filled in positions beside him.

The distance was too great for Paul and the others to make out much of what was said. Janon gestured in a drunken manner with his hands. The soldier did likewise with his big, brawny arms. Then in words they could hear, the big soldier bellowed out, "Spineless scum!" Having said that, he stepped forward and shoved Janon to the ground. He then spat on him. The laughter that followed rolled up the valley.

Paul saw Jessie's hand slide across his back toward the quiver of arrows there. Jessie was an ace marksman and could probably hit the big soldier, even at this distance. Paul grabbed Jessie's arm.

The soldier drank from his flask and then held it out for Janon. Janon got to his feet and grabbed for it, but the soldier pulled it up out of reach. He laughed again. Then he clubbed Janon across the side of his head with his forearm. Janon fell to the ground, rolling to absorb the blow. When he got to his feet again he was right beside the soldier. Words were exchanged. The soldier took a step back and drew his sword.

In a single motion consummate with his skill as an archer, Jessie removed a bolt from his quiver and strung it in his crossbow. In an instant Dimistre was atop him, wrestling the crossbow from him. The bolt flew free and struck a nearby tree.

The big soldier took a swipe at Janon with his sword. However, the soldier's height worked to his disadvantage. His swing was high and Janon was able to duck under it. The quickness of his own move, though, caused Janon to lose his footing. He rolled as he hit the ground, his momentum carrying him downhill twenty feet. The soldier turned to pursue him, but another stepped in his path. They exchanged heated words, the voice of the other soldier surprisingly loud. Paul and the others could catch traces of his words: "Trouble . . . don't need!" The big soldier raised his sword as if to strike the other down. He then appeared to think better of it, turned, took a few giant strides to the roadside and slammed his sword into the bench there. He then sat down beside it.

CHAPTER 6

——

 Paul lay supine on a bit of ground beneath a kejote bush. Although the bush was in full bloom, there were gaps between the boughs. Through them he could see the forest's darker green canopy.

Something had awakened him.

He closed his eyes again. His dream lingered on the edges of consciousness and he wanted to commit to memory all he could still recall of it. It had been a most fascinating dream. He'd been in a mammoth cavern, one far more vast than any he could imagine might be hollowed out of crohephite rock. Within the center of the cavern a small fire burned in a containment vessel. All else had been in darkness. Paul had approached the fire until he'd stood beside it. It was then he had done a crazy thing. He'd reached for the fire. Not the vessel it was in, but the fire itself! There had been no heat, no searing pain, no burning flesh. He'd held the flame aloft in his hand and felt a power of incredible scope possess him. Then the cavern had spoken his name. Like a swirling wind the sound had enveloped him and its turbulence had extinguished the flame.

"Paul," the voice repeated. "Wake up."

Paul turned his head to the side. "Kalin?"

"It is your watch."

"How long have I been asleep?"

"Six hours."

Paul propped himself up on one elbow. "Any sign of Janon or Varth?"

"None. I'm not discouraged by it, though. They may not be able to make contact with us until nightfall."

"Has there been any other activity?"

"Two more wagons have gone down the road to Cartag and are now returning. That wagon we saw enter this morning returned to the wood during Dimistre's watch."

"Any soldiers?"

"Not a one."

Lying prone atop the ridge, Paul watched the second of the two wagons disappear into the wood. It was midafternoon and warm. The soldiers at the checkpoint had taken refuge from the sun beneath the mankekin. In and around the vending stalls there was only token activity. At the far end of town, a timber wagon sat with its load of logs. Kalin had told him that the wood was most likely bound for the mill at Kietro, and Lord Thyden's use. Beyond the town the hillside rose sharply. The mankekin that clung to its slope framed all in a brilliant white.

To the northwest was a passageway through the rock bordering the town. It opened up into a field. Beyond, a forest bordered the Void of Sois for miles. Farther still was a tremendous plain, its green expanse broken only by an occasional patch of gray. The farthest reaches of this plain disappeared into the shadows of the Angena Mountains.

Angena. Paul felt it a logical name for these mountains. The word was from the old tongue and meant shadowy or dark. It had, in fact, been their black stone that had been quarried to build Castle Greyfahren, Lord Thyden's residence. Yet there was another translation of the word *angena*. It also meant death. Paul wondered if that wasn't the more accurate of the two translations, for it was believed that those who had died building Castle Greyfahren had been buried in the mountains.

Paul felt something sharp pinch at the small of his back. He turned. Lord Marthan moved the blade of his sword until its point lay against the bridge of Paul's nose.

"How nice it is to finally meet you, Paul Benjarth."

CHAPTER 7

 The door to Paul's cell opened. Four guards stood outside. Two of them entered and took up positions on either side of the door. They were big men for Sinese. Their arm muscles bulged as they folded them across their chests. Paul saw he had no hope of overpowering them.

"Come, Master Paul," said one of the guards. "Will you walk freely as executioner? Or do we drag you to your task?"

Paul would have thought the guard's choice of words—*as* executioner—strange had he not watched them build the gallows from his cell window. For three days he'd watched Lord Marthan's men fit the trapdoors, position the overhanging beams, and knot and cut the thick ropes to size. Because they'd knotted only four nooses, Paul had at first figured Janon killed. But then work had begun beneath the platform. From a pile of stones a hearth had been built, its firebox just beyond the far corner of the platform. Chopped wood had been piled neatly beside it. Next, a hole had been made in the firebox and one end of a fifteen-foot rod mounted and hinged within. Rope had been tied to the other end of the rod. A cylinder of rock had then been provided as a counterweight. It was interconnected through a pulley system.

Yesterday morning Paul had watched the two guards act out

a trial sequence. One had fired up the hearth while the other had held down the far end of the rod. Slowly the bar had heated up.

"She gettin' warm yet?" the guard tending the hearth had asked.

"What do you think, genius?" the other guard had replied.

He had then let go of the rod. It had shot upward as the counterweight fell. The trap doors had sprung open.

Paul stepped through the door of his cell. The two guards who had remained outside fell in place in front of him. The other guards fell in place on either side of him. Each grabbed hold of an arm. The stones underfoot clicked as they walked down a long corridor.

Kalin's plan had failed because Lord Marthan's spies had ferreted out Varth Medo's link with Arnun. Varth was secretly being watched. When Janon had made contact with him, the soldiers had closed in and captured Janon. They had given Janon an injection of the truth serum styranotide and then questioned him. The two wagons returning to the forest during Paul's watch had concealed soldiers, not food and supplies. Once in the forest, the soldiers had slipped from the wagon and surrounded Paul's group. Lord Marthan himself had participated in the operation.

They descended a winding staircase. Small, barred windows let in light. The men passed through a wooden door and were outside. The two guards in front worked feverishly to clear a path through the crowd that had gathered. Paul, being a Jarred and taller than many of those around him, could see the platform ahead. He could see his friends atop it, their hands tied behind their backs, a guard standing beside each one. The crowd's cries became deafening as he approached the platform.

All at once, people were being pushed and shoved. The hand that gripped Paul's left arm suddenly went limp. A knife was thrown. The guard to his right doubled over and fell back into the crowd. The two guards ahead of Paul turned and charged toward him. Suddenly a body flew out from the crowd, striking them both about the knees and toppling them.

"This way, Benjarth," a voice said by his ear.

He was shoved through the crowd. He knocked over a woman; an old man toppled in his path. He risked a glance toward the platform and saw the soldiers of Lord Marthan engaged in hand-to-hand combat. An arrow flew and a man fell from the staging. All at once, Paul found himself past the fringes of the crowd and into the gap between the cliffs.

"Run for the wood," a voice cried from behind him.

Paul sprinted through the gap and into the field. He ran as hard as he could and only after he had covered a hundred yards of ground did he dare a glance back. Others now sprinted into the field. Dimistre was through the gap. And Janon! About two dozen men in all.

An arrow struck the ground not more than twenty feet ahead of him. Paul began to weave his sprint. Another arrow lodged into the ground to his left. He looked back and saw that archers had taken up positions atop the cliffs bordering the field. The elevated vantage point would allow them to shoot their arrows farther and more accurately, since they would not have to loft them so much to get distance. Paul feared the archers might be able to reach the forest itself.

Paul had run two hundred yards now and had that distance again to go to the forest. His sides ached and the blood pounded at his temples. He wasn't going to make it to the wood, not at a full sprint, anyway. He paced himself at a three-quarter sprint. He took encouragement from the fact that no arrows had fallen near him. Maybe he had been wrong. Maybe he was out of range already. Maybe he was just too distant a target for any archer to realistically hope to hit.

He plunged into the safety of the forest, sprawling forward on the soft earth as his foot caught an uplifted root. He was too exhausted to get up and so lay on the ground. Soon others entered the forest. Thirteen men in all. Paul raised himself on his elbows. Across the field, a dozen men lay sprawled about the ground, arrows sticking up from their backs. Most lay near the far end.

"Young master!" cried Dimistre, catching sight of Paul.

Janon and Jessie hurried Paul's way and helped him to his feet.

"Where's Kalin?" Paul asked.

"Over here!" Through the forest to their left Kalin's burly

form came crashing through a tangle of brush and low branches.

"This way," a voice commanded. "Quickly!"

They ran along a path that paralleled the field until they came to a small clearing. Brush had been piled at its near end, and they threw the brush aside. Concealed beneath were several weeks' worth of food, medical supplies, several coils of rope, weapons, backpacks, and digging implements.

"Grab a backpack," a bearded man instructed them. "Stuff it with whatever you can. Make sure each of you carries a shovel or an axe."

All fell to the task. Only Janon lagged. He stood facing the field, which was visible in spots between the overhanging boughs of the trees.

"Lord Marthan's men do not pursue us into the wood," he said, loud enough for all to hear. "Instead they spread out in a line across the field."

"They will not enter the forest this late in the afternoon," came a reply. "Neither should we, but we have no choice. Now we must hurry."

"What is the danger we face here in the forest?" asked Paul.

"Snow-tigers. Please! We must hurry."

Paul had never seen a snow-tiger. Their habitat was the forest west of the Void of Sois. What little he knew of them he'd learned from traders such as Kalin, who had traveled the roads between Castle Chalmet, Cartag, and Kietro. The snow-tigers were monstrous animals, carnivores that would kill a man as readily as another animal for food. They would even kill their own kind in times of shortage! Their fur was a dark gray-black, the color of a thundercloud about to burst. But they were named for their paws and a patch of fur on their bellies, as white as the virgin snow that occasionally fell in the mountains. Paul knew why the soldiers had not entered the wood. The snow-tigers hunted only at night.

"Down this path and hurry," came a command.

They moved at as brisk a pace as possible, the weight of their gear making it impossible to run. They'd gone about a mile when the wood opened up into a large clearing. Two men separated themselves from the group and paced the confines of the clearing, their heads bent as they studied the ground. After a short discussion, they returned to the others.

"Those with shovels come with me," said one of the men.

Paul, Dimistre, and six others put down their gear and stepped forward. The man led them to the clearing's north-west end.

"The roots are few here and the ground soft," the man explained. "The digging should be easy." He marked off the corners of a rectangle sixteen feet by nine feet with four stakes.

It took them two hours to dig a pit four feet deep. In the meantime, the others felled and trimmed several trees to lengths of twenty feet. These logs were then tied together, two individual strands of rope used at each tying junction. The forest was in semidarkness when, one by one, the men squeezed through a narrow opening one log wide. Ropes had been tied to that last log at both its ends and middle and it was pulled into place and secured from within the pit. Fifteen individual ropes hung down from the log roof. To each was tied a stake. Each man drove his stake into the ground beside him. Each had the responsibility to secure the roof should his rope break or the stake to which it was secured work free from the ground.

Within minutes night came to the forest.

"Master Paul Benjarth," a voice called out.

"Yes?"

"We've had little time for introductions. I am Etan Kamir. Those around you, besides your own men, are members of a group dedicated to the overthrow of lords Marthan and Thyden."

"How did this escape come to be planned?" asked Paul.

"There are two among us who served Lord Marthan as guards. Jair was present at Janon's interrogation, so we learned of your presence on the ridge overlooking Cartag. However, we were unable to do anything to warn you, so quickly were soldiers dispatched to bring you in. We hoped to be able to spring you from your cells, but the guard was increased and we had to abandon that plan. We made our move at the only time we could."

"We are most grateful," said Paul.

"Listen," cautioned a voice. "One has our scent now."

All talk ceased as each man strained to hear above the rustle of the wind through the tree boughs.

"Perhaps you were mistaken, Svent," said a voice. "I hear nothing."

"Me neither," said another.

"One is nearby," warned Svent. "Be ready on your ropes."

There came, an instant later, a deep, throaty snarl that prickled the skin the length of Paul's spine.

"She is right beside the pit!"

The ferocity of the snow-tiger was unlike anything Paul had ever witnessed. The scent of its prey was alive in its nostrils and it thrashed at the logs, leaping and turning in its efforts to get beneath. The animal's body was massive and stretched from one end of the log covering to the other. Its eyes burned like red-hot coals. For several minutes the great beast tore at the roof. Then, its fury momentarily spent, it paced the logs. From its throat came a deep, raspy growl. Saliva dripped from teeth six inches long. Suddenly the beast whirled and tore at the log directly above Paul. Bark flew and fell between the gaps. Paul's heart was in his throat. It was like a creature from the worst of nightmares! Its head was so large that its eyes stared down at him from either side of the log above him. He pulled down on his rope with all his strength.

The logs held.

The snow-tiger leaped from the structure and paced the pit's perimeter. Soon Paul and the others heard a scraping sound.

"She tries to tunnel her way beneath the logs at that end!" cried Etan. "Pull hard on your ropes!"

Paul felt an upward pull on his rope and, although it was too dark to see it happen, he thought the roof had been raised a bit. The thought of that monstrous beast being able to tunnel into the pit enabled him to find a new source of strength. He pulled down on his rope with even more vigor, every muscle of his body drawn into the effort.

"She's gone," a voice said at last.

Slowly Paul relaxed his grip, his fingers unfolding like stiff cardboard. His hands burned from the impression of the rope.

"Was this end raised slightly?" asked Janon.

Janon's voice had come from Paul's right. There were five rows of men in the pit, three across. He was in the second row at the left outside position. Dimistre was beside him at center position and Janon was to Dimistre's right. Jessie was behind him. Kalin was to Jessie's right.

"It was indeed," Svent answered. "Their strength is incredible."

"Has this one given up?" asked Paul.

"For the moment, it would seem so," replied Etan. "But her attack will bring others. We have a long night ahead of us."

"But surely there is easier prey to stalk than us?" Dimistre asked.

"There are great herds of scherlings to the southwest," replied Etan. "They are the tigers' main staple. Yet many things affect the mating habits of the scherlings. It is said now that herd size is small. In such times the snow-tigers will roam farther north and east in search of food."

"Can they see us here in the darkness?" asked Paul.

"As if the pit were lit up by a dozen ascama fibers. That unusual ability forces them to be nocturnal animals. The light of the day blinds them."

For a time the forest was still. Some of the men talked among themselves; others fidgeted with their gear. A canteen was passed and water shared. As the night dragged on, Paul found it increasingly difficult to stay awake. He'd not slept well a single night in his cell, and he doubted Dimistre, Janon, Jessie, or Kalin had, either. He felt his eyes closing, popped them open, felt them closing again.

He awoke with a start. Two red eyes, which glowed as if lit from behind, stared down at him from either side of the log above his head. A strong animal scent filled the pit. A second snow-tiger clawed the log roof at the other end. Suddenly it leaped up and threw its great weight down on the logs as if to smash them apart. Again and again the beast did it.

"Hold those ropes down!" cried Etan.

The other cat did not thrash about so. Methodically it scraped at the log directly above Paul. The sound of Etan's voice made it look up momentarily and snarl, but it quickly returned to its scraping. All at once the great beast swung its body about sideways and began pawing at the log frantically. A rope broke. The log above Paul moved and in a flash the cat was around upon it and had thrust its paw through the narrow gap there. Paul felt motion in the air above him, and he slithered to the ground.

"She's got her paw through the logs!" he cried.

The gap was narrow and the beast could only get a little of its paw through. The cat pulled its paw out and again clawed at the log. Another rope snapped and the log moved still more. Again the great cat thrust its paw through the gap.

Paul tried to shrink into the ground. He could not see the cat's paw, but he could hear the swishing sound it made as it circled inches above him. "She's going to claw me!"

"Everyone at this end lie flat," Dimistre ordered.

The other cat, as if further enraged by Paul's and Dimistre's voices, leaped up and crashed down upon the very center of the log roof. All within the pit heard the crack of wood.

"Great Malhah! The cats are going to bust through!" cried Svent.

"Stay down," ordered Dimistre.

Paul heard Dimistre's knife slide from its holder.

The gap between the logs opened more.

"Dimistre!"

A swoosh of air swept over Paul's head and then around behind him. The cat shrieked as it leaped from the log roof. Its dismembered claw fell on Paul and he swept it off his body in a single motion of his arm. The other cat leaped from the logs. From the forest came the most hideous of cries and growls.

"Great Malhah!" cried Jessie. "What is going on out there?"

"The best thing we could have hoped for," cried Etan. "The cats fight among themselves. Most likely the wounded cat will be killed. The other cat and any others in the area drawn by the noise and the scent of blood will feast upon her and not us."

The sounds of their fight trailed away into the night and once again the calm of the forest descended upon them. Many hours later, the first light of dawn slipped between the gaps in the logs and woke the men. Etan organized them quickly. They cut the ropes and pushed the logs aside. Then they gathered their gear.

"Our breakfast must wait," said Etan. "We're still too near

the edge of the forest to be safe. With dawn the danger of the snow-tigers is passed. Lord Marthan's men will enter the forest in search of us." He approached Dimistre. "I commend you on your actions last night." A smile crept across Etan's face. "That must be some knife that can slice off the paw of a snow-tiger with a single pass."

Dimistre removed his twelve-inch blade from its holder. It glinted silver in the morning light on one edge; the other was dull-stained with the snow-tiger's dried blood. "She's served me well."

"Do you wish the snow-tiger's claw?" asked Etan. "It is said to be good luck."

"I wish no particular remembrance of last night," replied Dimistre. "We are fortunate to be alive."

For the better part of an hour they followed the course of a trail west through the forest. Throughout, Etan seemed edgy and Paul thought he knew why. The path, while not wide enough for a rider and horse to overtake them, looked to be well traveled. Certainly it was known by Lord Marthan's men. They veered off the trail at a point where the forest was especially dense. Here their pace slowed considerably. Vines twisted in their path and they had to hack at them with their knives. When they'd traveled several hundred feet in this manner, they stopped and ate a quick breakfast of dried fruits, dried vegetables, and capoi paste. Water was provided from canteens and Etan instructed each man to drink only what he must. When they continued their journey, Paul walked up front with Etan.

"Does Thyden know of our escape?"

"Not yet," replied Etan. "A rider needs two days to make the journey between Cartag and Castle Greyfahren."

Paul reflected on that bit of information, then asked, "Where do you lead us now?"

"To the Malhah."

Malhah! The word lingered in the air like the crisply struck note of a chime bell. *Malhah!* Paul inhaled deeply, feeling as if he were standing in a vast field of wild flowers and each bud, each stamen, was fragrant with the scent of the word. He looked up and saw each of the six letters carved into the azure slate of the midmorning sky. For a moment, it was enough to experience the word in this pseudosensory manner. And then the questions came. "What does he look like? Has he spoken to you? Has he revealed any powers? Is he as the prophecies say?"

Etan grinned broadly. Paul's curiosity was understandable. "I can tell you he is not one of us. His hair is the color of the wheat at harvest time." He arched his eyebrows. "You know that a genetic impossibility among our races."

Etan suddenly halted the group. "Listen," he cautioned.

Paul heard nothing at first. Wait! Now he could hear something. Louder it grew. And then he recognized it.

Horses!

"Everyone down on the ground," said Etan. "We are nearer the road than I thought."

The pounding of hooves grew louder and louder. Suddenly orange flashed against the vegetation ahead of them as riders swept by.

Etan motioned them to their feet when the thundering of hooves had faded. He commanded Jair and another to head in opposite directions along the road. "Check for sentries and other riders," he advised them. "Signal us if the way is clear."

When the signal came, they crossed. Again Paul walked up front with Etan.

"I've something to ask you," Etan whispered. He glanced quickly over his shoulder, then back at Paul. "Do you know of the medallion and its powers?"

"Yes," Paul blurted. "Arnun told me."

Paul remembered Arnun's warning an instant too late. He'd been careless.

"I thought as much. Arnun and I are a team. He is my eyes on the eastern half of the peninsula and I am his on the western half. Some time ago he told me he harbored a secret he could never share. It was his appointed destiny, he had said, that he could not." Etan smiled, though his smile was not one of smugness. "Little did he know."

"But how is it that *you* know?"

"The other bashan is a woman." The tone of Etan's voice softened and his eyes grew misty. "A woman who just happens to be . . . my wife." His mood swing was abrupt. "The bastard," he hissed. "He kidnapped her! She and the entire town of Dor.'' There were tears in Etan's eyes now, and rage beneath. "He blinded her! Blinded and made slaves of them all, so he could send his castle staff to the fields to be trained as soldiers. He blinded her, Paul. Do you hear me? He blinded her . . . like he did your father."

There was something calculated in the way Etan had spoken those final words. What Etan had really said to him was: "Lord Thyden has captured and blinded your father. Now what are you going to do about it?"

"What do you know of Castle Greyfahren and the Angena Mountains?"

Only the faintest trace of a smile betrayed Etan's pleasure at Paul's question. "There is only one route through the mountains. That is Ansona Pass. The trail forks at the bottom of the pass. One road leads east to Kiev, a small settlement, most likely a garrison town now. The other road leads west to Kietro. Kietro is the principal settlement within the circle of the Angena Mountains."

"And the lay of the land? What are its features?"

"From the sheer sides of the mountains to the beginning of the sky-void ring is perhaps a mile and a half. Some of it consists of hills. Most of it is flat."

To the beginning of the sky-void ring!

Paul remembered Castan's theorem from his school years. It stated that crohephite rock structures would remain at a fixed altitude and position above a rotating planetary body if that planetary body had a gravitational constant of 2.37 or larger. For centuries Castan's mathematics went unproven. The swirling sand storms that raged across Calferon's surface made it impossible to sight a landmark on the planet and note their motion with regard to it over a period of time. Belshane had been the one to prove the soundness of Castan's equations. It had been his genius that had devised a way to build Castle Greyfahren and then separate it from all adjoining land masses.

"How could we cross?"

"There is a drawbridge. It is joined to the rock at the base of Castle Greyfahren. It is lowered and raised as needed to bring in supplies."

"But surely that bridge is well guarded?" Paul paused in

thought. "How wide is the sky-void ring?"

"I've been told it is two hundred feet at its closest point and four hundred at its widest."

You've been told! "You've never seen it?"

"No," admitted Etan, who added, perhaps too quickly, "but Jair has. Jair will lead us."

Paul felt Etan had let his emotions cloud his good sense. What could they, a hastily assembled handful, possibly accomplish within the very lair of Lord Thyden's stronghold? They had task enough ahead of them ushering the Malhah to Fief Karcan. He expressed these concerns to Etan.

"It is not only that I wish to see my wife again," Etan replied when Paul had finished.

"Revenge? I, too, would like to see Thyden killed."

"It is not that, either. If this world is to have any chance of escaping Lord Thyden's domination, then we must retrieve your father's medallion."

Etan's remark puzzled Paul. "Is it not enough to keep Thyden and the Malhah apart?"

"Do you really think Fief Karcan safe ground for him? Lord Thyden's troops outnumber those of the Benjarth three to one."

Paul was indignant. "Do you feel sheer numbers alone will dictate the course of the battle? We've built fortifications across the entire breadth of the frontier. Thyden will be hard pressed to dislodge us, whatever his numbers."

A look of incredible sadness crossed Etan's face. "Lord Thyden will throw but a token force against your fortifications. The majority of his troops, approximately eleven thousand men, are in barracks at the eastern end of the Medoc Peninsula."

"But that is sheer madness," cried Paul. He had spoken too loudly, for some of the others now looked his way curiously. He lowered his voice. "The land bridges are impenetrable. The rock alone will only allow a few men to pass at a time."

"I wish it were madness, Paul. Lords Marthan and Thyden have built a bridge beneath the eastern land bridge. Do you understand? Its support stakes are driven up into the crohephite rock."

Paul's mind reeled from the horror of Etan's news. Eleven

thousand men would overrun Castle Chalmet in a matter of minutes! "But why didn't Arnun tell me of that bridge?" he angrily demanded of Etan. "He must have known!"

"He didn't. Arnun never had time to question the Malhah and learn how he crossed to the peninsula. He had time only to spring him from his jail cell in Middloc."

Paul lashed out at Etan in an accusatory tone. "But you knew! Why didn't you tell us of this last night?"

"Weren't the snow-tigers enough distraction?" Etan grabbed Paul by the shoulders and looked him straight in the eye. "We need a plan, Paul, a carefully thought out plan. And we need a place to launch this plan, a place where Lord Thyden's men won't accidentally stumble upon us."

They reached a glade by late afternoon. It was bordered on its far side by a concentric row of trees. So thickly tangled were the boughs and limbs of those trees that, viewed collectively, they seemed the wall of an impenetrable fortress. Etan led them in a northeasterly direction across the clearing.

"Be careful here," he cautioned as he pulled back on a tree limb. "The way drops."

They descended into an oblong bowl whose floor, on average, was five feet lower than the surrounding forest floor. Trees grew thickly along its entire perimeter, their roots visible in the earthen banks that were the sides of the depression. Most of the bowl was littered with rocks. A towerlike structure forty feet tall shot up from the center of the hollow. It was conical, and its smooth sides told Paul it was a natural formation, not a manmade pile of rock. An opening in that rock hinted that it might be hollow.

A stranger stood leaning against the tower's west wall. His face was raised toward the sun and his longish hair fell about his shoulders. The stranger's hair was yellow.

CHAPTER 8

 Since childhood Paul had tried to imagine what the Malhah would look like. The prophecies had mentioned no specific physical characteristics. When Paul had been nine, he had hypothesized that the Malhah would be a being from the neighboring planet of Palastrides. He'd clung stubbornly to that theory, but as he had grown older and learned more about probability and genetics, he began to accept the likelihood that the genetic development of beings from different planets, despite being in the same solar system, would be different. There had been times when his imagination had formed a picture of the Malhah with the face of an animal, or with green antennae protruding from his skull, or with one eye, four arms, or taloned feet. But to see him for the first time and see the similarities to his own people—he appeared virtually identical to them, except for his hair—filled him with a powerful sense of awe. Established scientific fact, as well as the mathematics of probability, argued in favor of the uninhabitability of most of the universe, Palastrides included. Paul realized then that the exceptions to these laws of probability, such as the Malhah, were the foundation upon which organized religion was founded. They were the miracles that were not supposed to be!

The stranger turned his head their way and returned their

stares. Paul averted his eyes, embarrassed by how openly he had been gaping at the man. He thought for a moment to drop to one knee and bow his head in reverence, but the stranger turned his head away then, seemingly uninterested in them.

Paul spoke to Etan in a whisper, "How do you communicate with him?"

Etan looked at Paul with a puzzled expression.

"How do you communicate with him?" Paul repeated. "He's from Palastrides, isn't he?"

Etan's look of befuddlement turned to one of disbelief. "Are you making a joke?"

Etan's remark caught Paul by surprise. It took a moment for him to remember that *his* belief that the Malhah was a man from Palastrides was not shared by all who believed in the revelations foretold in the Book of Prophecy. The book gave neither birthplace nor birth date for the Malhah. That opened the way for interpretation.

Paul forced a smile. "Yes, I'm making a joke," he said finally. It was easier to lie to Etan than debate the Malhah's origins. He knew of the flying machines' wreckage and suspected Etan didn't. "How do you speak with him?"

"He speaks our tongue." Etan gazed at Paul curiously. "Why would you think he wouldn't?"

Paul found Etan's remark too incredible for a reply. *He speaks our tongue! That's impossible!* Paul quickly became suspicious that this whole thing was a masquerade. Hair could be dyed yellow. No matter the coincidence that beings from separate worlds could develop similar genetic characteristics, it was inconceivable that their language would evolve similarly. That would be too much of a miracle to expect! He boldly walked over to where the stranger stood.

"My name is Paul Benjarth," he said. "My father is Duke of Fief Karcan. We discovered your flying machine—"

The stranger lurched toward Paul. "My airplane," he cried. "Where? How badly damaged is it?"

Paul had stepped back when the stranger had come at him. His left forearm had gone up defensively to shield his face and his right arm to shield his body. The stranger had moved so quickly, so fluidly. It impressed Paul. He'd been trained for something. Paul sensed also both the spontaneity and genuineness of the stranger's outburst. The flying machine did belong to him. He wasn't an actor. He was the Malhah.

They talked with the stranger for hours. He confirmed the existence of a suspension bridge beneath what Paul knew by the stranger's description was the land bridge joining Fief Karcan with the Medoc Peninsula. The man had parachuted from his plane and landed in a valley strewn with boulders. He'd found the entrance to the bridge purely by chance while looking for a way across that valley. This news was followed by a great deal of debate that ended in a course of action.

They would divide into two parties of five men and one party of six. Dimistre would head one group, Kalin another, and Paul and Etan the third. Dimistre's and Kalin's groups would follow the forest's border with the great plain to the north. With separate paths to be chosen later, each group would try to cross into Fief Karcan along its western border. Benjarth sentries were positioned just inside the border. If they could reach them, troops could be dispatched to the eastern land bridge. The danger lay in the suspected buildup of Lord Thyden's forces along that border. Etan and Paul would lead their group northwest across the plain to Castle Greyfahren.

The day grew late and Etan suggested they eat a hasty dinner in the hollow, then retreat for the night into the shelter of the fortress. Rocks were piled into the opening from within until it was sealed. The men stowed their gear along the walls and lay their bedding out in the tower's center.

Paul lay awake after the others had fallen asleep. The Malhah preoccupied his thoughts. He'd said his name was Brian. He was slender, even compared with Paul's own people, and the Jarred were the slimmest of the four races. Paul had expected him to be otherwise. He had expected him to be a great warrior, big and strong. Didn't the Book of Prophecy state that the Malhah would lead his chosen people against their enemies, and all who opposed him would perish? Most disconcerting of all, Brian knew nothing of the part he was to play in their history. He knew nothing at all of the medallion he was supposed to open!

Paul tried not to think of Brian anymore. He rolled onto his back and fixed his gaze on the fortress's ceiling. The sides of the rock tapered to a hole twenty-four inches in diameter. That opening, Etan had assured them, was too small for a snow-tiger to wriggle through. Through it Paul could see the night sky and a single distant star.

A shadow passed across the opening.

Paul's heart leaped into his throat. Etan be damned! He'd seen what those monstrous beasts had done to the log roof of the pit. Would it be any less difficult for them to claw away the rock around this opening until it *was* big enough for them to fit through?

Again a shadow passed across the opening. This time Paul felt a drop of something strike his hand.

Rain!

He took a deep breath and almost laughed as he exhaled. Those shadows had only been wind-driven rain clouds.

Paul moved his bedding a little farther from the opening. He closed his eyes and tried to relax, but couldn't. The shadow remained focused in his memory. The perception of depth, shadow to sky, had not been as it should, not for a rain cloud. The shadow had been too close, too solid. He opened his eyes. The shadow lingered by the edge of the opening. He raised the back of his hand to his nose. Saliva would have an animal scent. He sniffed.

Chemical!

He jerked his head up. Voices? He had heard voices!

Marthan's men!

Paul did not possess Jessie's skill with bow and arrow, but the shadow was an easy target perched as it was over the opening. The air whistled sharply as an arrow flew from his bow. There was a shriek and the shadow fell away from the opening.

Paul woke the others.

Etan sniffed the residue of the droplet on Paul's hand and recognized it immediately. "Nicomene." He glanced up at the hole. "If they get a chance to pour that through the opening, we'll all be asleep in seconds."

Etan's men knew what to do without being told. There were six vertical slots cut into the walls of the fortress and they took up positions beside each.

"They're on this side," Jair cried.

Arrows flew from his bow as well as the bow of another on

the other side of the rock-filled entrance. Within half a minute they had shot seven arrows between them.

"They've taken cover behind the rocks," Jair said, lowering his bow.

"How many were you able to kill?" asked Etan.

"Can't be sure," Jair replied, speaking for them both. "It was difficult to see them."

Etan glanced again at the opening above them with grave concern. "Shoot at anything that moves." He turned to Paul. "How are your men with bow and arrow?"

"I'll put Jessie up against anyone."

Etan nodded. "We must keep a careful vigil throughout the night. We'll rotate people every four hours. In the morning Lord Marthan's men will be easier to spot."

Daybreak saw one of Lord Marthan's men, arms raised above his head to show he was unarmed, approach the fortress. "Who will speak for you?" he called out.

"I will," Etan shouted back. "What is it you want?"

"We ask you to surrender. If you do, no harm will come to you. We can wait indefinitely out here. Supplies can be brought daily to us from Cartag." The man waited half a minute. "Well? Your answer?"

"Give us a few days to think about it," Etan replied.

The man shook his head angrily before turning and exiting the bowl.

"How many of them do you count?" Etan asked Jair, who stood before the slot on the other side of the entrance.

"Eight."

"There will be more tonight," he said.

There was a message implicit in Etan's remark. The longer they waited to put a plan of escape in motion, the less likely its chances for success were.

"Two of us could pin them down," Jair suggested.

"We haven't enough arrows."

Etan paced now, visibly upset. It had been his idea to make camp in the hollow for the night. Now he felt responsible for getting them out of their predicament.

"Why didn't the snow-tigers devour the soldiers last night?" Jessie asked.

Etan never paused in his pacing. "The snow-tigers kill only

for food. More than likely Lord Marthan's men killed two of their own horses some distance away from here. A snow-tiger can pick up the scent of blood a long way off."

"Why not tunnel our way out?" Janon suggested.

Etan glanced at the lone shovel propped against the wall. They had left the other shovels in the pit, figuring they wouldn't need them again. "Where would we come up?"

"I've seen no activity on this side of the bowl," Dimistre advised him. His slot faced northwest.

Etan kicked in frustration at the hard rock floor of the fortress. "It would take forever with one shovel!"

That one shovel, though, gave Paul an idea. Its thin stone blade would become red-hot in a fire. If they were to unstring two or three of their bows and tie them together, and in turn tie them to the shaft of the shovel's handle, the assembly just might be long enough.

It was near dusk when Paul removed the shovel from the fire and handed it to Etan. Ever so carefully Etan lowered the shovel through a narrow slot in the rock floor beside the west wall. Then he paused in his task to give Dimistre and Kalin a final piece of advice.

"The moon's arc will be across the southern sky," he said. "Keep it to your right in the early part of the evening. As the night progresses it should be at your back."

"How do we defend ourselves against the snow-tigers?" asked Kalin. "We won't have time to dig a pit."

"I've no doubt Lord Marthan's soldiers have already butchered a few head of cattle and left them in the forest. Such a feast will satisfy the snow-tigers' hunger."

Just then a soft glow of greenish yellow light entered the fortress through the slots in the east wall. The soldiers' lanterns had been lit and the shutters adjusted to direct their light at the rock.

Etan lowered the shovel into the earth. "I'm there," he said.

The others moved to the far side of the fortress.

There was no sound when the jooarie sac ruptured. The shovel blade had formed a bubble on the membrane of the sac and the gas had expanded only within that bubble before the heat had opened up a hole. What Etan had done was akin to rupturing a partially inflated balloon, since the jooarie sac was not full to capacity. The strong odor of selevium gas that momentarily filled the fortress told Paul and the others something had happened. Simultaneously a crack ripped up the west wall. The sound of the rock separating gave Etan a few precious seconds of warning. He leaped back just as the ground opened up and the wall caved in.

Ironically it was the light from the soldiers' ascama fiber lanterns that helped them pick their way along the edges of the hole. Quickly they crossed the floor of the depression to the western embankment. As they climbed it, the soldiers' shouts alerted them that their escape had been discovered.

Paul emerged from the trees into a glade. Fifty yards away lay forest. "Dimistre! Kalin! Organize your men quickly!"

The men had entered the glade from different points across the length of the western embankment. Now it was imperative that they regroup with their assigned leader because they had different directions to travel.

A horse and rider came charging up the embankment behind them. Sword raised above his head, the soldier spurred his horse into their midst. There was a shriek. The soldier raised his sword above his head again but was yanked from his steed before he could deliver another deathblow.

"Let's go!" cried Dimistre, motioning them across the clearing.

They sprinted for the wood.

Two more riders appeared. Jessie whirled, knelt, strung his bow and cut down one of the riders. The other was felled by an arrow from one in Dimistre's group.

Suddenly Paul was aware that Brian was with *them*. "No," he cried, pointing to the running shapes of Dimistre's and Kalin's groups. "Go with them!"

Brian took off in their direction.

The boughs of the trees ringing the hollow parted and three more riders appeared. Two held lanterns.

Jessie, still kneeling in the clearing, nocked another arrow.

"No, Jessie! There'll be more," shouted Paul. "Go for the wood!"

Jessie let his arrow fly, then raced after them.

"That's him!" cried one of the riders.

The three soldiers spurred their horses in Brian's direction. Two of the riders cut him off and the third fell in place behind him. One rider raised his sword to strike him down.

"No," another commanded. "Lord Marthan wants this one alive."

An arrow flew from Etan's bow. It missed the rider but struck his horse's neck. The horse toppled onto its side, crushing its rider's leg beneath.

Brian leaped over the fallen horse and ran for the wood.

"Over here!" yelled Etan.

The riders followed. A branch knocked one from his horse as he tried to enter the wood. Etan's knife felled the other.

"He can't come with us," Paul told Etan. "The castle . . . Thyden . . . it'd be crazy!"

The trees that sheltered the hollow's west side seemed to come to life. Men poured into the clearing.

"He's got no choice," said Etan.

It was fortunate Jair knew the paths of the western wood and Lord Marthan's men did not. It was fortunate also that the trees were too thickly clustered for riders on horseback to pursue them. They put half a mile between themselves and the soldiers after fifteen minutes of running. Only an occasional yell, shout, or barked command told them they were still being pursued.

Brian dropped to one knee in exhaustion. His chest rose and fell in an exaggerated, almost convulsive manner as he gasped for air. "It's the altitude," he said between breaths. "Not used to it. Hard to breathe."

Etan caught Jair's gaze and jerked his head to the east. Jair backtracked twenty yards and listened for approaching soldiers.

"We can't afford to rest too long," said Etan.

Brian nodded that he understood.

Jair returned a minute and a half later. "Let's go," he said.

The trees pressed close on both sides of the path, so they ran in single file. This species of tree had few lower boughs, but the leafy branches of the upper boughs formed an interlocking canopy that prevented any celestial light from reaching the floor of the wood. Even the trunks bordering the path were indistinguishable from the forest at large.

Paul ran close on Jair's heels. He couldn't lose sight of him, not for an instant. Should he veer but a yard from the center of the path he would strike a tree and be knocked unconscious. That was the risk they took running at this pace along so narrow a path. Yet it was the only way to put distance between themselves and the soldiers. Soon a band of light stretched across the vastness of the forest ahead of them. The trees became silhouetted and therefore much easier seen. Paul relaxed his gaze on Jair's back. A minute later they emerged from the forest into a windswept field of waist-high grass.

"We must cross the field tonight," said Etan. "We'll be spotted if we wait until morning."

The moon now cleared enough of the forest to coat the tips of the grass blades the same silver-gray as moonlit water. The wind blew steadily out of the west, rippling the grass in a wavelike motion. Twenty miles distant, the Angena Mountains towered above the horizon, mountains that somehow, eerily, failed to reflect any of the moonlight that struck their slopes.

Etan, ever mindful of the soldiers, kept one eye on the wood while they crossed the field. They had traveled nearly a mile and a half when he ordered them to the ground.

Soldiers emerged from the forest. Each carried a lantern. They came a short way into the field and then, in an orderly fashion, spread themselves along its width. Those on horseback rode to the farthest corners of the field, then turned inward. From the northwest came more soldiers on horseback. So distant were they that, at first, their bobbing lanterns were only specks against the horizon, fireflies skimming the tops of the grasses. Five miles distant, they also began to spread out. They moved quickly to surround the field.

Etan watched the proceedings solemnly. "They will wait until morning to close ranks. There will be less chance of us slipping through by daylight."

"Then we will have to slip past tonight," Jessie said spiritedly.

"They are too close together," replied Etan.

"Then let's go right at one of them," suggested Jair. "He wouldn't stand a chance against the six of us!"

"And then what?" demanded Etan.

"We break for the wood."

"The soldiers are a quarter mile into the field. They'd converge on us like a swarm of hungry flies."

"So what do you suggest?" Jair snapped.

Etan gave his friend a long, hard stare before allowing a sly smile to crease his lips. "We commandeer a timber wagon."

Paul had first seen the timber wagon from atop the ridge overlooking Cartag. That day the first of many logs was being loaded. The day before the hanging, the wagon had left on its four-day journey to the mill at Kietro. Three of those four days were spent crossing the woods. The reason that part of the journey took so long was because of the snow-tigers. The forest was too vast for a team of horses to pull the heavy timber wagon through it in one day. By midafternoon the horses had to be unhitched from the wagon and galloped back to Cartag. The next morning the horses were ridden back into the forest and rehitched to the wagon.

"The wagon is about three miles from the wood," Etan pointed out. "It's a good bet the loggers feel it is far enough from the forest domain of the snow-tigers to simply tie the horses to the wagon for the night."

"Where do the loggers sleep?" asked Paul.

"There is a narrow cage running the length of the timber wagon. It is dome-shaped and thirty inches at its crown." Etan traced the shape with his hands. "The logs are piled around and atop it, so in effect the cage is a tunnel beneath the logs but above the bed of the wagon. It is entered from beneath. The shelter can protect a man from the snow-tigers if he is injured and unable to ride."

It took them two hours to crawl on their hands and knees to the timber wagon. Their wrists ached and their knees were sore. They halted thirty yards from the timber wagon to finalize their strategy. Etan talked mostly with Ewechuk, who, like Jair, had aided the Benjarth in their escape from Cartag.

Etan had suggested that Paul consider assigning Ewechuk to their group rather than Dimistre's or Kalin's, advice that had at first puzzled Paul. Ewechuk was small-boned, frail, and wore glasses. He looked anything but a fighter.

Etan had explained. "His expertise is in pharmaceuticals. He can mix a potion to put a man to sleep or a nerve poison to paralyze him instantly. Lord Thyden will be beaten by cunning and trickery, not force, Paul. Another marksman like your friend Jessie gains us little."

Etan and Ewechuk slipped beneath the wagon. Each held a syringe and a vial of chemical. One of the chemicals in the syringe was nicomene, the very same sleep agent the soldiers had tried to pour through the opening in the ceiling of the fortress. The other was locusan, an astringent. The vial contained riacin. Locusan and riacin were chemically such that, when combined in the presence of oxygen, they formed a clear, odorless gas, which was to be the carrying agent for the nicomene. Yet so rapidly did these two chemicals gasify that the riacin would not be added to the syringe until both men were in position beneath the wagon.

Etan nodded to Ewechuk that he was ready. The vials were uncapped and the chemicals mixed. The syringe needles were inserted into cracks in the worn bed of the timber wagon and the sleep-inducing gas released into the narrow chamber. A minute later they unfastened the latches of the trapdoor and pulled four sleeping bodies from the chamber.

"How long will they be out?" Etan asked.

"Twenty-four hours," replied Ewechuk.

Etan had never considered killing the four men. They were not soldiers of Lord Marthan or Lord Thyden but were instead villagers from Cartag. Unfortunately that made it more difficult to deal with the unconscious bodies. Were they to kill them, they could simply bury them and there would be no trace of them for Lord Thyden's soldiers to find.

Jair looked up from the bodies at Ewechuk. "Can another injection wake them?"

"Not from the effects of nicomene."

It was Jair's turn to smile slyly at Etan. "Why don't we give the soldiers what they want?"

CHAPTER 9

 Slowly the timber wagon creaked and pitched its way along the worn, rutted trail. Etan and Jair sat on top. Etan held the reins. Paul and Jessie walked alongside.

At the approach of the wagon a few of Lord Thyden's soldiers began to move toward the road.

"Now," Etan told Jair.

Jair jumped from the wagon and ran toward the soldiers, waving his arms above his head. "The yellow-haired stranger," he cried. "We've captured him! Come see!"

The division commander spurred his horse forward. Two other riders followed.

Jair ran alongside the horses, babbling all the while like an excited school child. "Yes! He attacked us, he did! Tried to get our food! Yes, yes! This way!"

Etan reined the horses to a halt as the riders drew near. Paul and Jessie ran forward to meet Jair and the soldiers.

"We tied them across the horses," cried Paul. "See! Right there!" He pointed at the horses. "See! It was I who saw the stranger first. He came upon us from the southeast."

"How could you see anything?" snapped Jessie. "You were nodding off. I saw him first!"

"Who cares?" cried Jair. "I was the one who wrestled him

to the ground."

"Silence!" bellowed the commander.

The soldiers dismounted and approached the bodies draped over the rear two horses. One man held a lantern aloft.

"Look at his hair!" cried one of the soldiers.

"He is as the legends say."

There was both fear and awe in the two soldiers' voices.

The commander was all business. "Who is this other?"

"He was with him," said Jair, again feigning an excited, rapid manner of speaking. "He grabbed me from behind when I grabbed—"

"Just shut up, will you!" shouted the commander.

The soldiers huddled together. Paul, standing closest to them, could hear every word of their conversation.

"Maybe this other one is the Benjarth prince. They were said to be together."

"What a find this is! Lord Thyden will be most pleased."

"There'll be promotions for all of us."

"You! On the wagon!" The commander cast a quick glance at Paul and the others. At the same time his hand moved to his sword. It was a warning. "How did you come to capture these two?"

"It is pretty much as my friends have told you," said Etan. "We were sitting beside the wagon, smoking, talking. It'd been a hard journey up to this point and we needed—"

"Hurry up your story," snapped the commander.

"They approached us from out of the field. The yellow-haired one wore a cap, so we did not know who he was at the time. They asked for food and water. Said they were lost, separated from their group. We were suspicious of their story and questioned them. A fight broke out, but we were able to subdue them. No doubt they were weak from hunger."

The commander laughed. "Hunger is the least of their concerns now."

"Broder," said one of the soldiers, addressing his commander by name. "Something's wrong! These men are out cold."

"What trickery is this?" the commander demanded of Etan.

"We subdued them with nicomene. Why not? We are not soldiers. We've not the weapons nor the time to hold them prisoners. What's important to us is getting this load of timber to Kietro."

For some time the commander stood buried in thought. "Your name?" he asked at last.

"Jashua Corbs," Etan lied.

"Listen well, Jashua. You never saw these two men. Your crossing was without event. My soldiers captured them. If rumor comes out to the contrary, be assured I will hunt you down and kill you." He rattled the scabbard holding his sword. "I'll kill the whole worthless lot of you!"

They left. Minutes later the northern line of soldiers withdrew. One galloped to the south to inform the commander of Lord Marthan's division that the Malhah and the Benjarth prince had been captured.

Paul could only be pleased with how well their plan had worked. Ewechuk had managed to concoct a coloring agent to dye one of the logger's hair a mustard yellow. Then his body, along with that of another logger, had been tied across the horses. The other two loggers had been left to sleep off the effects of the nicomene in the field. Brian and Ewechuk had stowed away in the cage of the wagon. Unfortunately, neither looked like a logger—Brian being so slender and Ewechuk so short and frail. In case the soldiers had insisted on inspecting the cage, Brian's hair had been shorn to the skull and a pasty mixture of earth and water had been rubbed into the stubble to give it, temporarily, a brownish color. Bundled thickly in blankets to mask their body sizes, they would appear as resting loggers. However, to discourage the soldiers from a search of the wagon, Paul, Jair, and Jessie had tried to appear as petty-minded chatterboxes, hopefully giving the impression they were too simple-minded to mastermind a deception of any sort.

Somehow, though, in spite of the successes they'd had so far, Paul found it difficult to relax. The Angena Mountains' imposing slopes towered before him, their peaks jagged and sharp. It made Paul think of teeth, and the ring of mountains, the lower jaw of a monstrous beast. Somewhere in the sky, masked by the darkness of the night, hovered the other half of that huge jaw. The beast waited, because it knew it would feast tomorrow. It waited because it knew its great jaw would come crashing down and taste Benjarth meat and bone.

CHAPTER 10

———

The courtyard was small. It measured eighteen feet on a side and had been carved from the rock on the south side of Castle Greyfahren. A sundial, mounted on a pedestal and base, stood waist high in the center of the courtyard. The hour numerals and the quarter-hour gradients had been carved into the dial's stone face and the shadow line flowed into these niches, filling them as water would a pool. The gnomon consisted of a naked male babe-child. The die from which it had been cast had been meticulously crafted, and each crease of baby fat, each wrinkle of skin, spoke well of its craftsman's understanding of anatomy and skill as a sculptor. The babe-child clutched a narrow staff, which formed the sharp edge across which the sun cast its shadow onto the sundial. Child and staff together stood twenty-two inches high.

Lord Thyden reached out and touched the babe-child. The fingers of his right hand gently stroked its hard thighs. His left hand squeezed its buttocks. He'd been bitter, terribly bitter, when he'd come of age enough to understand his father's reason for having the figure cast. His father's desire for a son, a son unblemished by the tronocyanimide injections of the Benjarth surgeons, was for a time an all-encompassing obsession. Two sons and four daughters had been born to Belshane by three wives. All were deformed. All were cast into the sky-void ring. He was the seventh child. No less deformed than his brothers and sisters had been, he'd been spared their fate because his father needed him. His father was old now and needed a son, blemished or otherwise, to orchestrate his revenge against the Benjarth, an act that he would be unable to realize in his own lifetime. So here in the courtyard, preserved for eternity, was that child Belshane had longed for but could not produce. Here was the perfect babe.

Suddenly, as if the statue had turned red-hot, Lord Thyden jerked his hands away. The son he had conceived so many years ago had been as unblemished as the babe-child before him. For that reason he'd paced the hallways of the castle for days and tossed sleeplessly at night. He feared his son's rejection because of the gross deformities of his own body. By the fourth day he'd no longer been of stable mind. He was exhausted, paranoid, depressed. He'd suffered hallucinations, always of the same subject. His son stood pointing at him (his forefinger greatly exaggerated) while his head rolled back in derisive laughter or bent forward in scornful inspection. Lord Thyden then had ordered his son cast into the sky-void ring.

A waist-high wall of interlocking stone enclosed the courtyard. Lord Thyden stepped away from the sundial and let his hands come to rest on the adjoining walls at the southeast corner. To the south, two miles distant, were the Angena Mountains. Lord Thyden scanned their jagged peaks until he located Ansona Pass. A speck of brown stood out against the worn gray of the trail. The timber wagon, realized Lord Thyden. The timber wagon commandeered by Paul Benjarth!

You've proved most elusive so far, my young friend. Four times you've slipped through Marthan's and my grasp. But you were foolish to believe that I did not have an antidote to the nicomene you subdued the loggers with. Now you've trapped yourself within the mountains' ring!

Lord Thyden had given his soldiers orders to capture Paul Benjarth at the base of the pass. The rest of his lot they could kill. The duke's son had some questions to answer. Surely he knew where the Malhah was being held.

Lord Thyden removed the Benjarth medallion from his pocket. He'd had it polished to a brilliant radiance, and the sun's light glinted across its surface as he slowly turned it in his hand. The workmanship amazed him. It was truly flawless. The two halves of metal fit together so carefully that even under a magnifier a gap could not be seen in the seam. He'd had the medallion heated in the hottest of fires, yet the seam had remained tight. His guard captain had smashed it with a hammer while it was still hot, but it had not opened. He'd even poured undiluted acid along the seamed edge in the hope it would eat away enough of the metal to allow them to insert a blade and pry it open. That had not worked, either.

"Within it lies the power that created our world and can in turn destroy it."

The words alone set Lord Thyden's imagination soaring. Imagine! A power that could destroy all. Or what he chose to destroy. Yes, *chose* to destroy. For wasn't power meant to be manipulated and controlled?

It had been fortunate the guard captain had questioned, one by one, the captives from the village of Dor. This had been done as a standard security precaution. Those captives whose personalities were defiant and wills resilient—those capable of sacrificing their own lives for a chance to take his— were blinded and put to work in the chemical gardens beneath the castle. Guards would watch them day and night from the balconies that ringed the gardens. Those who were more servile were blinded but allowed to work in the castle proper. Each had a simple task assigned to them, one that could be mastered through repetition despite their handicap.

A woman named Moria had told the guard captain an incredible tale while in a styranotide-induced stupor. She had spoken of being a bashan, the third in a line dating back to a logger's daughter named Tella. She had spoken of a hollow medallion with strange powers possessed by the Benjarth. Lord Thyden had thought little of her story at first. But then, by chance, that fool Duke Jaiman had brought the medallion to him and he'd seen for himself its construction. He realized it was not of their world. That was reason enough to believe it might possess unique powers.

Lord Thyden descended the stairs from the balcony to his quarters. A few minutes later there was a knock on his door.

"Enter, young master Harkins," Lord Thyden said.

The door opened and Keith Harkins's head popped out from behind it. "We have Duke Jaiman, my lord."

"Well, don't let our guest stand out there. Show the good duke in, my boy. And make sure you secure him well." He indicated the chair he wished the duke tied to.

Lord Thyden observed carefully as the duke was led in and tied to the chair. How thin he's become since his capture, Thyden thought. He noted the hardened scar tissue within the hollows of Jaiman's empty eye sockets. How drawn and pale his face now was. Surely, chuckled Lord Thyden, this couldn't be the once proud ruler of Fief Karcan.

"You'll find them quite secure," remarked Lord Thyden as he watched the duke twist at the ropes that now held him.

"You fear a blind man?" Duke Jaiman laughed. "What a cowardly specimen of a man you must be."

Lord Thyden's cheeks burned red from the insult, but he managed to keep his temper in check. The duke would not get the better of him. "Perhaps you have learned of *my* physical limitations from those you toil with in the chemical garden?"

"Are mine any less? Surely it would be a fair challenge."

Lord Thyden watched the duke again strain at the ropes. How spirited he still is, he thought. He waved Keith Harkins and the two guards from the room.

"Your boy, Duke Jaiman," he began when they were alone. "He's really quite a resourceful lad. My compliments to his Benerit-woman."

"Spare me, Thyden. Is there something you wish to say?"

"My, my, we are testy, aren't we? I suppose it is to be expected when talking about one's son. The helpless father's concern . . . no, fear. Yes, I'd be safe to say that, wouldn't I? The helpless father's fear for his son's well-being. How very touching, Duke Jaiman."

"What could you possibly understand about paternity when all you've been able to engender from your shriveled organ is fear and hatred?"

"How foolishly you talk to your executioner," cried Lord Thyden. "Let me remind you, Duke Jaiman. Your death can take many forms. I can be merciful and make yours quick and simple, or I can drag out the pain for days."

"Having to sit here and listen to you is more painful than

any death sentence you could pronounce upon me."

"Then I shall make it even more painful for you! Fate's dagger lies but an eyelash away from your boy's throat. I could have him killed now! Or I could put him to work beside his father in the chemical gardens."

Lord Thyden relished the silence that followed his threat. How very weak is a man burdened with a son, he thought. How simple it is to cripple his spirit. Truly the stronger of rulers is he who fathers none. Such a man gives his enemy no leverage to use against him.

"Why so quiet?" he asked at last. "Actually, you needn't worry about your son. I'll not order him executed. Not yet, anyway. You see, I want to question him about this." He held up the medallion. "Oh, forgive me. I forgot you can't see. Ah, but what is the difference? You were just as blind when you had your eyesight. It is your medallion. Or rather what you thought was just your medallion." He went on to tell Duke Jaiman what he knew of the lore surrounding the medal.

When he had finished, Duke Jaiman laughed. "And do you have the winged dragon Saulcar tied up behind your castle?"

"You force your laughter, Duke Jaiman. Still, I commend you on your spontaneity. You joust well, even though it is in a losing cause. There are facts about this medallion that you have overlooked. Yes, in your pompous vanity to wear this thing around your neck as a woman does her best jewelry, you failed to see it for what it really is."

Duke Jaiman scoffed.

"And you deny it? And so quickly? How unfortunate. Your son, in contrast, believes as I do, that there is some truth to it. He heads a party of four whose impossible mission it is to wrest it from me right here in Castle Greyfahren."

Lord Thyden paused but a moment before continuing. "You remember earlier in our conversation how I complimented your son. You never did let me explain why. Your boy, clever lad, has managed to escape death four times. Not that the incompetence of Lord Marthan's men, as well as a few of my own commanders, who have been disciplined on account of their failure, didn't have something to do with his good fortune. Still, your son has proved most elusive. And resourceful! He has commandeered a timber wagon bound for the mill at Kietro. Could any plan be simpler than to cross the Angena Mountains via Ansona Pass in the guise of loggers? At this very moment he stands near the top of the pass. The view from there is quite fantastic and I daresay he is overwhelmed by what he sees. A sight you unfortunately missed, my dear duke, as we dragged you through the southern tunnel at night. But his capture is imminent and this time there is no escape." He clucked his tongue triumphantly. "I've given orders to take him at the base of the pass."

Duke Jaiman said nothing.

"Again so little to say?" Lord Thyden watched the duke twist at the ropes that bound him to the chair. His hands were clenched, knuckles showing white. Lord Thyden could sense the rage boiling within the duke. "Isn't there one thing you're curious to know? One thing above all else?"

Again Duke Jaiman said nothing.

"Too proud to ask, huh? Well, keep your stupid pride intact! I shall ask and answer the question for you. How do you know, Lord Thyden, about all these things? Let us consider your son first. He made an unwise assumption. He assumed I had no antidote for the nicomene he subdued the loggers with. A chemist of my genius not possessing an antidote to a simple barbituric acid derivative! I should feel insulted! Well, so much for your son's error, Duke Jaiman. You will find your own downfall far more intriguing. How did I know where to position my men to ambush your reconnaissance party? Why, I've had a spy in your castle all these years!"

Lord Thyden watched Duke Jaiman's reaction carefully. The stiffening of the facial muscles, especially around the empty eye sockets, told him that Duke Jaiman's eyes, had they been there, would be bulging now.

"I'll wager you are curious about something else, too. Who is it? But you won't ask me, will you? Too proud, you are. Well, it wouldn't do you any good, because I won't tell you. No, it will give your feeble mind something to occupy itself with while you're toiling in the chemical gardens. Then, just before I'm ready to kill you, I'll reveal his identity."

Lord Thyden laughed to himself. If he were to tell Duke

Jaiman that the spy was his wife's first lover, he doubted that even then the duke would know the man. Arrogant fool! The duke probably believed he'd been Lady Benjarth's only suitor. No doubt, like a dutiful wife, she had never spoken of a past involvement in order to keep her husband's stupid ego unbruised. What husband didn't want to believe he was his wife's first lover!

Lord Thyden eyed the duke curiously. "You smile, Duke Jaiman. Such a strange change of mood. May I ask why? Or do you force it to mislead me?"

"I smile," said Duke Jaiman, "because all your talk, spy or not, is hollow. You've yet to wage battle against the armies of the three fiefs. I smile because I already know what you're about to learn. Your sick dreams of conquest will be quite impossible to realize."

"On the contrary, my dear Duke Jaiman, I think I'll find them boringly easy to realize. Over the past couple of years, Lord Marthan and I have engaged in quite a feat of engineering. We've built a bridge. Mind you, not an ordinary bridge. Our bridge is quite unique, for two reasons. One, it passes beneath the land. Do you understand? Its supports are driven up into the crohephite rock itself! Two, it is built beneath a most strategic piece of rock, beneath the land bridge joining Fief Karcan to the Medoc Peninsula!"

Lord Thyden watched with immeasurable delight as the duke's mouth fell agape. "Hear me well, Duke Jaiman." The excitement of what he was about to say gave him cause to stand. "It is my troops who will surround yours! It is my troops who will surprise yours! It is my troops who will know victory!"

CHAPTER 11

 The trail fell into shadow as a cloud passed in front of the afternoon sun. The wind that blew was cooler, much cooler, and Paul glanced skyward. A storm front stretched across the northern sky. Its clouds were tall, jagged, dark, a mirror image of the land they now crossed. Paul sensed the beast's jaw beginning to close.

"It's all gone too smoothly," he said to Jessie. "The stable hands must have broken records hitching up that second team of horses at the entry checkpoint. And did you notice some of them? Out of the corner of your eyes you could just catch a trace of a smile. Not all can hide so well what they know."

Jessie shared Paul's suspicions. "Look at the number of guards milling about at the bottom of the pass. Too many for an interior checkpoint."

They were halfway down the backside of Ansona Pass, on the east side of the trail. Paul and Jessie walked up front. Etan and Jair, who led their team of horses down the steep incline, followed. To their left, the timber wagon creaked as it rolled forward. Two thick ropes, which were slowly being let out from atop the pass, guided it down the incline. A single horse steered it.

"I will do as you instruct, Paul," continued Jessie. "You are the leader of our group, but I fear our mission is in jeopardy."

Paul glanced at the ropes that held the wagon, then back at the horses Etan and Jair were leading. He and Jessie slowed their steps, allowing Etan and Jair to catch up with them. Paul discussed his and Jessie's observations with them. Etan and Jair shared their concerns and were in agreement that they risked capture if they didn't put some plan in motion.

It was Etan who organized them. "One of us must slip beneath the wagon and unhitch the horse that steers it. Also, Brian and Ewechuk must be cued when to jump. Jair?"

"I can handle it."

"Good. I'll take care of the horses. Paul? You and Jessie take care of the ropes."

Jessie unsheathed his knife and Etan handed his to Paul. "We must work in perfect unison," explained Etan. "Understand that the slightest delay in any of us accomplishing his task will allow Thyden's archers time to set themselves for a clean shot. Jair? Go!"

Jair slipped beneath the wagon. He alerted Ewechuk and Brian to their plans, then made his way to the front of the wagon. When Etan saw that Jair was ready, he advised Paul and Jessie to get into position. Both already walked at the back of the wagon, so it was simply a matter of slowly drifting over to the left . . .

"Now!" cried Etan.

The blades of the knives glinted in the afternoon sun as they were momentarily raised overhead. Then they fell in unison, their keenly sharpened edges slicing through the taut ropes. Simultaneously Jair dropped the hitch that joined horse to wagon and whacked the animal about its hindquarters to shoo it. It bolted down the incline. Brian and Ewechuk had dropped from the wagon at Etan's cry. Within seconds the wagon rolled beyond them and they were able to mount. Brian rode with Paul, and Ewechuk with Etan. Paul urged his horse to a gallop and the others followed his lead.

The wagon hurtled down the incline, caught a wheel, flipped, and spilled its contents. Logs four and five feet in diameter smashed through the two wooden guardhouses at the checkpoint. Men cried out as they tried to leap out of the way. Some were crushed beneath.

Paul was the first to reach the bottom of the pass. At a full gallop he spurred his horse over the first log that blocked his way. Suddenly a man appeared in his path, a sword raised above his head. Paul's horse reared up on its hind legs. Paul grabbed its mane as Brian's weight pulled him back. There was an embankment to the right and, as the horse's front feet struck the ground, Paul twisted its head to the right and drove his knees into its flanks. With but two powerful strides the horse was up and over the embankment.

For a moment, Paul halted the horse atop the embankment. Ahead of him the colorful blossoms of half a dozen species of wild flowers peppered the foothills of the Angena Mountains. Wild grasses grew knee-high. Here, too, twisting spires of rock, many several times the height of a man, rose from the earth like fingers thrust up through the knitted weave of a quilt. In the distance there was a wood. To the north the foothills fell away to flatter terrain. A road wound eastward across it to Kiev. Farther to the north was the sky-void ring and Castle Greyfahren.

Suddenly there were shouts from behind them. A horse whinnied. Paul urged his horse to a gallop. Within moments they were racing across the foothills.

"Riders come!" yelled Brian, glancing back.

They charged down the slope of a hill and the riders were lost from sight.

Paul's first thoughts were to ride for the woods. Once there, he and Brian could climb a tree and conceal themselves among its branches or find a hiding place within the crisscrossing branches of some tangled underbrush. Unfortunately, the woods was also where Lord Thyden's soldiers would concentrate their search.

They rose out of the depression and onto the high ground again.

"The riders gain!" cried Brian.

"Yeeahhh!" Paul whacked his heels against the horse's flanks.

The ground sloped away again and the riders were lost from sight. The woods loomed before them. To their right rose a final spire of rock.

"Jump off!" Paul commanded as he brought the horse to an abrupt halt and literally threw himself and Brian to the ground. Paul grabbed both packs. "Aiiyahh!" he shouted, striking the animal sharply about its rear quarters. The horse bolted for the wood. "Behind this rock!"

They reached the rock just as their horse plunged into the shadows of the wood. A moment later six riders descended from the crest of the high ground.

"Stay low," whispered Paul.

The riders streaked by the north side of the rock and fanned out as they approached the wood. They entered it and again became unseen.

Paul scanned the rock face of the Angena Mountains for any niches that might conceal them. They'd moved north of the mountains as they'd galloped across the foothills and now the Angena Mountains were a good quarter mile distant.

"The footing here is unsteady," commented Brian.

The ground moved beneath him as if he stood upon something springy. Then, abruptly, it gave way. Brian fell three feet through the earth before he rooted onto something more solid. "What's happening here?" he asked as he pulled himself back up.

"Stay down," directed Paul. He'd heard hooves. They'd been distant but they were drawing closer rapidly. "More riders."

Sure enough, within seconds another six riders plunged down the incline from the crest of the high ground. They, too, passed the rock spire on its north side. However, this time only four riders entered the forest. The other two dismounted at its fringe and, on foot, began to work their way along its edge.

There was no way to make it to the mountains now, Paul realized. He kicked the earth around where Brian had fallen through and dislodged a big piece of sod. "Do you think we can conceal ourselves beneath this loose layer of earth?"

"You mean make a hole, drop ourselves inside and cover the opening?"

"Precisely."

They set to work on the task and in a short time had fashioned a hole that dropped onto a more solid ledge of crohephite rock. They capped the narrow opening with a flat rock, atop which they piled sod. Brian slid it into position from within the hole. However, the rock did not quite cover the entire opening.

That it did not worried Brian. "We're sure to be seen if Thyden's men come near here."

"I don't think so. It is already well into the afternoon and the Angena Mountains tower beside us. Soon the sun will dip behind them and we'll be in shadow. It will be difficult to see us then, and I doubt Thyden's men will abandon their search of the woods for some time."

At this Paul guessed right. It was several hours later when they heard the soft plodding of a single horse circling the spire of rock. For a moment, horse and rider halted. But then they moved on, the sounds of their passage fading as they climbed the slope to higher ground. As night approached, a comforting silence descended upon the valley.

It was dark when Paul and Brian climbed from their hiding place.

"Be careful with my pack," Paul told Brian as the latter lifted it from the hole.

"Oh?"

Paul smiled as one with a secret he was bursting to tell. He opened his pack and ever so carefully cradled a small, frightened, birdlike creature in his hands. He'd trussed its wings to its body with some makraw-leaf thread. Brian was still standing in the hole, so Paul lowered his hands, enabling him to see the creature for himself.

"Where did you . . . ? What is it?"

"A Seguna bat."

Paul had found the Seguna bat on the floor of the timber wagon. The creature had been nesting in the logs and the nicomene had put it, as well as the loggers, to sleep.

"I never shared Etan's confidence that our group would be able to sneak into Castle Greyfahren across the drawbridge," he said. "I wonder if Etan really thought his plan a good one. No matter. Now that Thyden knows we are here, an obvious crossing point like the drawbridge is out of the question. But this little fellow here," he said, stroking the terrified creature, "will allow us to cross the sky-void ring in a not-so-obvious manner."

Brian looked dubiously at Paul. "That?"

"He's all wing, Brian. Got a span of four, maybe four and a

half feet. He's strong, too. Can fly with twenty pounds strapped to him." He carefully returned the trussed creature to his pack. "The moon will rise above the peaks of the mountains soon enough. We must make our journey now."

"Do you think they still search for us? I mean now, at night?"

"Thyden may figure us trapped within this ring of mountains and so figure it unnecessary to continue the search into the night. Still, we can't be sure."

They ate first, for they had not taken nourishment since breakfast. As they did so they gazed with keen interest at Castle Greyfahren. Its enormity overwhelmed them. Its base was three times that of Castle Chalmet and comprised five tiers of living and working quarters. Exploding from its center was the tower, a black monolith shooting upward into the very soul of the sky. The tower's base was two hundred feet in diameter. It was one thousand feet high. One-fifth of the way up, four massive quarter-circles of stone, spaced at ninety-degree intervals, joined the tower to the castle's flat roof.

"Like staring into a void," mumbled Paul. The awe he was experiencing was uncomfortably mixed with an evil foreboding. *A void that sucks us toward it!* He turned to Brian. "Is there a structure like it in your world?"

"There are many tall structures where I come from. We call them skyscrapers."

Skyscrapers! Paul liked the word. It was poetic. *To scrape the sky.*

"Two of the tallest stand side by side in New York." Brian cocked his head as if to obtain a slightly different view of Castle Greyfahren. "It is hard to judge. This structure seems nearly as tall. Yet this is built completely of stone! Perhaps only the great pyramids rival it in grandeur."

"Are they also skyscrapers?"

"They are ancient monuments made from stone blocks. Their fascination lies in their age. They were built many thousands of years ago and were truly incredible structures for their time. There are theories that visitors from a far more advanced civilization—space travelers is what we call them—masterminded their construction."

Paul glanced at Brian but found the latter's attention once

more riveted on Castle Greyfahren. *Space travelers!* Was that what Brian was? Had that been what Belshane had been? A being from Brian's world? Had there been the crash of a flying machine in his grandfather's time that none had recorded? Paul pondered the implications of such a line of thought. If Belshane was from an advanced civilization, and Thyden partial to his father's knowledge, then they were truly up against a powerful foe. Perhaps only the medallion could ensure victory over Thyden and his armies.

"We must go," he told Brian.

They crawled on their hands and knees through the high grass. The wind, which had picked up considerably since sunset, swirled the grass, its motion masking Paul's and Brian's movement through it. The going was slow but at last they came to the end of the foothills. Here they encountered the road that ran east to Kiev. Paul put his ear to the ground and listened for the sound of hooves. He heard none and they crossed. The grass of the flatter terrain was also knee-deep, so they continued as before. An hour later, they halted at the edge of the sky-void ring.

The moon had just risen above the peaks of the Angena Mountains and much of the detail of Castle Greyfahren's southern face could be seen in its light. A sweeping staircase descended from the third tier to a miniature courtyard carved from the rock at the edge of the sky-void ring. Jutting half-circles of stone formed balconies along the fifth tier. Rectangular pillars ran the full height of the castle proper. Spaced at relatively close intervals, these pillars, which adjoined the wall on their back face, gave the castle a ribbed appearance. Located between these pillars and rising the full height of the first two tiers (approximately forty feet) were shadowless voids, where the moon's light was not reflected. The design of Castle Greyfahren's southern wall appeared to carry over to its eastern wall as well. Here, too, the upper three tiers were dotted with small rectangles of light while the lower two-fifths remained steeped in absolute darkness.

Paul's gaze shifted downward to the crohephite rock base that supported Castle Greyfahren. What an incredible formation it was! The base plunged to depths of—Paul peered over the edge of the rim to take it all in—six, perhaps seven hundred feet! When he'd formulated his plan to enter Castle Greyfahren, he'd never imagined that the crohephite rock might fall to such incredible depths. Yet he could see an aberration within the rock that would work to their advantage. There was a small protruding area of rock along the northeastern perimeter, where the crohephite rock had formed to a depth of only thirty feet. Paul knew he could accurately shoot a bolt under that piece of rock.

Paul returned to where they'd left their packs and to where Brian lay on his back gazing up at the tower structure. "Tired?" he asked.

"A bit."

"Rest yourself while you can."

Paul removed the Seguna bat from his pack and gently placed the creature on the ground before him. Next came his crossbow. Paul swung it open. He started to string it but paused in the task to speak to Brian.

"When we journeyed across the plain, you told me of a bomb that could destroy an entire city. Do you remember?"

"I remember. I was referring to a nuclear warhead."

"Can it also create?"

Brian's response was not immediate. "I do not understand your question," he said at last. "What do you mean, 'create?'"

Paul finished stringing the crossbow as he thought how best to explain his thoughts. "We've journeyed this far to locate a medallion that once belonged to my father but is now possessed by Thyden. It is said that within it lies the power that created our world and can in turn destroy it. I could not imagine such a power until you told me of these nuclear warheads. Now do you understand my question?"

"I do," said Brian, "however, a warhead is an instrument of destruction only." Brian pondered Paul's question a bit more. "Yet the same forces unleashed within a nuclear explosion have been harnessed for use in other ways. Like in the generation of electricity."

"Electricity?"

"It's a form of energy, like lightning, only it is harnessed and used to run thing such as appliances and lights."

Paul thought about Brian's remarks as he removed a bolt, a

grappling hook, and two coils of makraw-leaf rope from his pack. The leaves of the makraw plant were most unique in that they were transparent. Thus, rope woven from the broad, flat leaves of this plant, besides having extraordinary tensile strength, were nearly invisible.

"Brian! Give me a hand a moment."

Paul had Brian hold the creature's wings tight to its body while he retied them. This time he used a bow knot, one end of which was the coil of rope itself.

Noting Brian's curiosity, he explained, "When this rope pulls taught, this knot will undo and the bat will be free to fly. We have only to be careful that this rope is shorter than the rope I've tied to the grappling hook."

The grappling hook was twenty inches long, had four prongs, and weighed three pounds. Paul secured the other coil of rope to it. He cut a short length of line and tied the bat's claws to the coil of rope a foot back from the grappling hook.

"Our little friend will find it uncomfortable flying with this added weight. She'll roost in the rock beneath the castle and work at the rope about her claws. Eventually she'll pick clean through. In the meantime, we've got to hope the grappling hook lodges within the rock."

Brian looked at Paul warily. "And then what?"

"We cross, hand over hand."

Brian had only to glance into the sky-void once. "Are you crazy?"

Paul was taken aback by the vehement tone of Brian's remark. He felt himself begin to anger. "Have you a better plan?"

"A better plan? Why should I have a plan at all? Why should I be a part of your plan?"

Paul struggled to keep his own voice in check. A shouting match would only alert Thyden's sentries to their presence. "Will you not accept your destiny? Your importance to my people?"

Brian sensed the need to lower his voice also. "I have tried to be patient, to keep an open mind about what's been going on. I probably owe you my life, but this talk of a medallion and . . . and . . . some sort of mumbo-jumbo powers?" Brian became frustrated with his inability to convey to Paul what he was really trying to say. "Perhaps I just bumped my head when I bailed out of my plane and now lie comatose in a hospital somewhere. Maybe I'll wake up soon."

"This is no dream, Brian."

"Then what the hell is it? Where I come from these floating islands would be clouds. Thin, vaporous clouds!"

"All this was once cloud-mass, but it is the core-vines, or more precisely the receptor sites of the spinolla of the core-vines, that chemically alter cloud-mass, which we call screula, to crohephite rock. The flowers of the core-vines are the jooarie sacs, which fill with selevium gas and keep the land afloat. You've seen for yourself what happens when a sac is ruptured."

Brian started to say something, then, thinking better of it, turned his back and walked a few steps away.

Paul returned to the task at hand, but his concentration was not what it had been earlier. Now he couldn't help but wonder if Brian were truly the Malhah. Granted, he had survived a crash in the Eastern Mountains, but perhaps other flying machines would come and other strangers survive. Perhaps one of *them* was the Malhah. Yet the Book of Prophecy spoke of the Malhah's coming at a time of great need, and that time was certainly now! When else had they faced an army of such superior numbers? If Thyden were to prove victorious, the Jarred might well be wiped out as a race. And it was the Jarred who were the Malhah's chosen people!

Paul looked back over his shoulder at Brian, who sat on the ground with his back to him. He found his friend's sulking scornfully juvenile. How like a child to try to deny reality by shutting it out of his mind. He felt like shouting at him, waking him up, screaming some sense into him. This was reality! Castle Greyfahren was reality! Their mission to retrieve the medallion was reality!

It was then he remembered something the relzan had told him concerning the Malhah. "He will be a stranger to our lands, our ways, ourselves." Perhaps he should be more sympathetic, he thought. Certainly Brian was disoriented. Perhaps he was lonely and homesick as well. His plane had been destroyed. Paul remembered well the grave expression that had crossed Brian's face when he had explained to him how damaged it was. Maybe he expected too much of Brian too quickly. The prophecies had been general and no powers mentioned specifically. Perhaps his vision of the Malhah had been shaped too much by his imagination and too little by good, sound logic. Perhaps he had been foolish to fantasize that with a wave of his arm the Malhah could vanquish Thyden's armies, or with a few thoughts from his mind their technology would take quantum leaps into the future. Yet was he wrong to believe that the Malhah might possess some power?

Paul shook his head in denial of everything. His old Benerit-woman had told him that one's loss of faith was a gradual process. Yet Paul suspected it was more a series of distinct moments of disillusionment and that it only seemed gradual because the tenets of religion one was reared on were too firmly entrenched to be dissolved by a single point of crisis. If Brian would not help him retrieve the medallion, then he would do it himself.

He used another bow knot to join the grappling hook to the bolt. Twice he wrapped the rope around each, then he carefully uncoiled and recoiled each length of rope. It was important there be no snags or knots that might release either the bat's wings or the grappling hook prematurely. Nearby was a tapered finger of rock seven feet high. Paul gauged the length of rope needed to cross the sky-void ring and secured the rest about the base of that rock, then he knelt by the edge of the void and studied the crohephite rock beneath Castle Greyfahren. Gravity would aid the weighted bolt, since it would be shot downward. He tugged again on the ropes to ensure that they were secure.

He felt himself growing anxious again. His muscles began to tense. He had doubts. Maybe he was insane to attempt to cross the sky-void ring in this manner. Maybe he was insane to expect to be able to wrest the medallion from Lord Thyden in his own castle.

Don't think about it! Just do it!

He fitted the bolt into the crossbow and raised it to his chin.

Do it!

He sucked in a deep breath, held it, and squeezed the crossbow's trigger.

Almost instantly both ropes went taut, then fell slack again.

The grappling hook had separated from the bolt, and the bat's wings had been freed. Now the Seguna bat would seek the underside of the crohephite rock. It was instinct to do so because these creatures were cave dwellers and nested in ceilings. Paul counted off the sixty seconds to himself, then took in the slack of the rope still secured to the bat's claws and the grappling hook. It went taut. Paul yanked on the rope with all his strength, let it go, then pulled it taut again. The grappling hook had snagged itself! He looped the slack once around the rock and knotted it.

"Are you with me?" he asked Brian. "Or do I do this alone?"

Brian slowly got to his feet. "Yeah, I'm with you."

Paul unsheathed Etan's knife and cut two seven-foot lengths of rope. "Make yourself a safety line," he instructed Brian, handing him one of the lengths.

They made a loop and knotted it. After helping each other secure their packs across their shoulders, each looped the other end of his safety line through his crotch and around his waist.

"Wait until I'm beneath the rock," Paul told Brian.

The rope bowed slightly under Paul's weight. He moved with deliberate care because the rope was transparent and nearly impossible to see. He had to gauge where the rope should be as he swung forward, his fingers closing around the rope only when he felt it strike the palm of his hand. He felt strong enough to make the crossing, that is if he rested every so often, which he could do simply by letting go of the rope and allowing the safety line to hold him.

Yet, in spite of the fact that he knew he should pace himself, he found himself rushing. Too many fears pushed him. He was not afraid of heights, and yet he would not look down. He knew he would see images if he did. He would see fiery bits of forest and rock falling. He would see Merlin tumbling through space. He kept his eyes focused ahead, but even then his mind began to play tricks on him. Shadowy figures dropped from the ropes ahead of him. The whisper of the wind sounded like the crisp whistle of an arrow shot from a bow. Did archers wait concealed in those shadowless voids of the castle's lowest two tiers? Had the guard heard him and Brian arguing earlier? Damn it! Brian's outburst had been unnecessarily loud.

Paul swung forward, grabbed for the rope, and felt it slip through his hand. He still held the rope with his other hand and so remained upright. He had to relax. His hands were wet with sweat. He wiped them on his trousers before continuing his crossing.

Eventually he reached the underside of the rock. He felt a tug on the rope and realized Brian was beginning his cross. Paul took momentary comfort in the fact that Brian had not deserted him. His friend had courage. He rested a moment.

The moonlight reflected up by the dust storms on Calferon enabled him to see the definition of the rock around him. To his left the main body of crohephite rock supporting the castle fell away hundreds of feet. That rock was riddled with holes, and the rock above him was equally porous. Paul pulled himself forward. Unfortunately his weight bowed the rope so much that he could not reach up, grab a fingerhold, and pull himself into an opening. He realized he would have to follow the rope to its end and shinny up it. That they might only be able to explore that one opening the Seguna bat had flown into certainly narrowed their odds of finding a tunnel up into the castle. Paul could only hope they'd be lucky.

Suddenly there was a great fluttering in front of him. Wings brushed against his face and a claw ripped into his arm. Paul's arms flew to his face to shield it, and as they did he fell.

An unexpected fall, even one of short distance, often produces disorientation. So as the safety line attached to Paul's belt snapped taut, he reached in a blind panic for the rope only to miss it. He twisted and found himself staring into the void. Down, he told himself. He forced himself to relax. He was all right. The safety line had caught him. He twisted around and, grabbing hold of the safety line, pulled himself up enough to grab hold of the makraw-leaf rope.

He licked the area where he'd been clawed and tasted blood. He knew that the Seguna bat carried no venom and decided to tend to his wound later. Right now it was more important to climb up through the opening. He'd seen the bat fly off, its wings spread, the reflected moonlight making it momentarily visible as it had flown around the edge of the rock. It would not return once he established his own scent within its roost.

Fifteen feet up into the hole, Paul could feel stone above his head. Realizing it was the underside of a ledge—he was able to reach up and around it—he kicked off from the near wall, shinnied a few feet farther, then sat down atop it. He reached around into his pack and removed a tiny wooden box containing an ascama fiber-stub that had been exposed to sunlight atop Ansona Pass. The fiber-stub would glow brightly, but for no more than sixteen hours. He slid back the cover to the box and held the light aloft.

What he saw next any geosciczan would have given his diploma to witness! In front, behind, and above him were jooarie sacs. They were yellowish-green, though Paul realized the light from the ascama fiber-stub probably gave them more of a greenish tint than they would have if viewed in sunlight. He ran his hand across the smooth surface of the jooarie sac behind him. It was paper thin. Above him he could see the core-vine from which the jooarie sacs had formed. It was encrusted with crohephite rock, which made it difficult to gauge its size. Paul judged it to be about eighteen inches in diameter. Yet here the rock was only thirty to forty feet thick! Paul could imagine that some of the core-vines had to be as large as twelve feet in diameter in order to support as massive a structure as Castle Greyfahren.

When he finally began to view his surroundings less as a scizan and more in response to the needs of their mission, he saw that there was only one tunnel they could follow with the hope of finding their way up and through the rock. It was to the left, and they could follow the ledge into its mouth.

There was a noise below him. Paul looked down and saw that Brian was about to enter the hole.

"You've got the hole lit up? How?"

"An ascama fiber-stub." He slid over. "There's a ledge up here. You've fifteen feet to climb. Can you make it?"

"Yes."

As Brian climbed the rope, Paul tended his wound.

"What happened?" asked Brian as he sat beside Paul.

"The bat. It's nothing serious." Paul repacked the medical supplies in his backpack, then he held the light aloft. "Look around you, Brian. Can you see how swollen the jooarie sacs

are with selevium gas? It is the core-vines themselves that produce the gas. I'll bet as much as seventy-five percent of the
crohephite rock base of Castle Greyfahren is actually selevium
gas." He continued to hold the light aloft while Brian looked
around.

"Yet Castle Greyfahren must have taken years to build," he
said.

"Without doubt," said Paul. "The core-vines produce the
selevium gas only as it is needed. Yet the sacs can only fill up so
far. After that they will burst." He ran his hand across the surface of the jooarie sac behind him. "These must be at capacity."

Perhaps therein lay a part of Belshane's genius, realized
Paul suddenly. To understand the physics of the core-vines and
the jooarie sacs well enough to build a structure such as Castle
Greyfahren atop it.

"Ready?" asked Paul.

"Ready."

Paul led the way into the tunnel. After a few yards, it bent
around to the right. Paul peered around the corner and saw
with disappointment that the tunnel narrowed and became
impassable.

"There may be a way through here," said Brian hopefully.
"Hand me the light."

The tunnel was too narrow for Paul to turn around in, so he
passed the box between his legs and waited for Brian to tell
him what he'd found.

"The way through here is narrow and it curves," Brian reported. "It's like a chimney with a bend in it. Still, I think I
can make it through."

When Brian's feet had left the floor of the tunnel, Paul
wormed his way back and beneath the opening. "What do
you see?"

"I'm in a cavern. It's maybe ten, twelve feet high."

"Does it go on?"

"Yes. There seems to be another tunnel of some sort near
the top."

Paul stuck his head up into the mouth of the opening. That
faint lingering odor that permeated everything, but which
Paul had been unable to identify until now, hit him with a

potency that was like a blast of cold air.

Capoi!

"Put out that light," he instructed Brian.

"What?"

"Keep your voice down and slide the cover over the box. Do it now!" Paul watched all plunge into darkness. "Now open it slowly. No more than a crack. That's it. Now hand me the light." Paul reached up through the opening and took the fiber-stub from Brian's outstretched hand. He placed it in a hole in the tunnel wall. "Now remember to keep your voice down when you answer me. Is there any light from the ascama fiber-stub in the cavern now?"

"It's very faint."

"Good. I'm coming up." Paul snaked his way up through the tunnel and emerged into the cavern. "Where's that opening?"

"It's in the wall to our left."

Paul looked up and saw that the bottom of the opening was nine feet above the cavern floor. He would need Brian's help to reach it. "Crouch down and let me stand on your shoulders. Can you lift me?"

"Yeah. What's the alarm?"

"I'll let you know in a minute." He steadied himself against the wall as he climbed atop Brian's shoulders. "Okay. Lift me."

A portion of Paul's view was blocked by the underside of what appeared to be a table or a bench extending several feet out from a wall. However, his peripheral vision was not impeded by any structures and he noted immediately the vastness of the chemical gardens. It was a room the size of which he had never seen before. Surely it ran the full width of the lower two tiers of the castle. Paul could see the outlines of the waist-high troughs where the capoi was grown. He could see men and women sleeping on the damp stone floor. They had no blankets and had huddled together in groups to keep warm.

"Bring me down."

In a moment he was standing on the cavern floor beside Brian.

"Well?"

"Let's climb down. I'm concerned our voices may carry."

Once within the tunnel that led out to the ledge, Paul told Brian of the vast chemical gardens he'd seen. "Like the ascama fibers, capoi is grown in troughs filled with an aqueous solution of nutrients. It grows rapidly. The seed, which is the edible portion of the plant, can be harvested in seven to nine days. The roots and stems are discarded. It must be the main staple of those enslaved by Thyden."

Paul wedged his pack across the mouth of the tunnel in case the Seguna bat returned. "We'll sleep here tonight," he told Brian.

CHAPTER 12

—

Paul awoke shivering. It was damp within the rock and the night air had been cold. He awoke Brian and they shared a meal of dried meat and spiced capoi bread. When they had finished, they stowed their packs beyond the bend in the tunnel, then pulled themselves up through the rock and into the cavern. Paul again stood on Brian's shoulders and peered through the opening.

Light entered the chemical gardens from the east and, in the moisture-laden air, the beams were well defined. In a sweeping glance Paul saw more than one hundred people working alongside the many troughs that ran north to south the length of the room.

They're all blind!

Paul could imagine all too vividly Lord Thyden's butcher-surgeons methodically carving the eyes out of these people. It was a barbaric act made even more heinous by the scale on which it had been carried out. Paul wanted to scream. He wanted to scream profanities, to scream curses, to scream of reprisal, and to scream of the immeasurably painful variations on torture and death Thyden would suffer at his hand. Most of these people were Jarred villagers who had had no quarrel with Lord Thyden. Paul's anger so consumed him that his body trembled and he felt Brian's grip tighten around his calves.

Suddenly it all peaked—a thunderclap within his head—and then his anger began to fade as his heart went out to all those who'd felt the unanesthetized pain of the knife and now saw nothing. His eyes darted from one figure to the next, studying each for a brief instant, until finally . . .

Father!

Duke Jaiman stood beside a trough. He was a tall man, and with the way he held his carriage erect, he seemed a giant compared to the stooped figures working around him. His hair had been shorn and he'd lost a great deal of weight. The clothes he wore were tattered and ripped. Still, he carried himself with the pride and dignity befitting the leader of the largest and most powerful of the three fiefs. This in spite of the fact that all around him were blind and couldn't see him! Tears welled in Paul's eyes. Never would his father bend or bow to Lord Thyden. Never would he give Thyden the satisfaction of seeing him defeated.

"I'm crawling through," he whispered to Brian. "Wait for me here."

Paul pulled himself into the opening, turning sideways to slip through. He saw he was beneath a table. There were other tables around him, and some chairs, too. A balcony ran along the inner perimeter of the castle at a height just above the top edge of the openings in the wall. Two guards chatted on the west balcony. The south and east balconies were empty. The north one he could not see.

Paul pondered his next move. Did the guards know by sight the one hundred or so individuals who worked below them in these gardens? Could he slip among the workers, his head down (so the guards could not see his eyes), and do so without being detected? He decided he would have to chance it. He didn't know where to start looking for the medallion on his own. He would need his father's help. He ripped the sleeves of his shirt because the clothes of those who toiled in the chemical gardens were similarly tattered. When the two guards turned for a moment to greet a third, he slipped from beneath the table and made his way to his father.

His father was bent over a trough, swirling the water with his hands. He straightened slowly and looked in Paul's direction.

Paul averted his gaze. Only slowly did he allow it to drift back to his father's face. At first he focused on the man's mouth, but he felt ashamed doing this. Couldn't he look his own father squarely in the face? Slowly he raised his glance and looked up into his father's hollow eye sockets.

The pain you must have felt! I'll make Thyden pay for it, father! Pay for what he has done to all in here!

"Yes? Is someone there?" queried his father.

Paul breathed the word more than said it. "Father."

"Paul," his father replied in a choked whisper. He stepped toward his son with his arms outstretched.

Paul stepped back. "No, Father. The guards. They'll see."

"What does it matter now, Son?"

"I have eyes, Father. I can see."

"What? How can that be? Thyden had his men poised to capture you at the bottom of Ansona Pass. He boasted of it to me."

So he did know!

"Jessie and I suspected as much. We sent the timber wagon smashing into the guard shack and then rode past them."

"Is Jessie with you now? How did you get in here?"

"I'm with another. We crossed the sky-void ring at night using makraw-leaf rope. We came up through the crohephite rock base beneath the castle. Thyden does not know I'm here."

A smile passed quickly across his father's lips. "You must not linger here, Paul. You will draw suspicion. Against the east wall are stored trays to gather the capoi. My trough is ready to be harvested. Go! And mind you that you do not sidestep anyone. Better you should collide."

Paul found the trays stacked in several piles. The bottom of the trays were perforated. He took one and returned.

"Tilt the tray forward and drag it across the surface of the water," his father instructed. "The water will pass through the tray, but the seed and plant will collect in it. I have already separated the plants from their roots."

Paul placed his tray so its bottom edge was just a few inches below the surface of the water. Slowly, he dragged it forward.

"Thyden has built a bridge beneath the eastern land bridge," Duke Jaiman said.

"We learned of such ourselves a few days ago. Kalin and Dimistre each led a group of men on separate paths across the frontier. I can only hope they alert Illad in time."

"Thyden has a spy in our castle, Paul. He boasted of it to me."

"His eyes and ears seem everywhere! Who is it?"

"He wouldn't say."

"But *you* must know who it is? A guess at least?"

His father shook his head. "No one I brought into my confidence would betray the Benjarth, Paul. I'm afraid I don't know."

Paul sensed his father's embarrassment with that admission. He looked down at the soggy plant matter he'd collected in the tray. "My tray is full, Father," he said finally. "What do I do with it?"

"There are processing tables against the south wall. Dump your load there. There are others whose job it is to separate the capoi seed from the leaf."

Paul found the tray quite heavy. He let it rest against the wooden side of the trough. "Do you know why I'm here?"

Duke Jaiman nodded. "I've always known the medallion was from Calferon. Still, I never thought it more than a trinket. If only Thyden hadn't been the one to tell me of its value. Go, now! Before you draw the guards' attention."

Most of the area along the south wall was given over to several large tables. These tables had three-inch lips to contain the seed and plant, as well as drains to carry off the water. Eight people worked at each table (three on either side and two at the end). The large, oblong seeds were separated out by the workers along the sides of the processing table and the soggy mass of leafy vegetation continually pushed back. The workers at the end of the table threw the waste into bins.

"There is enough capoi for you to make one more pass with the tray," his father said, when Paul returned. "So listen carefully to what I have to say." Paul placed his tray in the trough and slowly dragged it forward as his father spoke. "Against the north wall there is an area where we take our meals. There are some tables and chairs, you will see. There is a girl, Elsa is her name, who brings capoi bread down a back stairway from the kitchen. She alone has this task, so you cannot confuse her with another. She will guide you out of the chemical gardens and into the castle proper. Give me fifteen minutes to pass the word along."

Paul glanced down at the leafy clump of vegetation that had built up in the front of his tray. He had harvested his father's trough. "Father . . ." His voice faltered as tears came to his eyes.

"My heart is with you, too, my son, as are the hearts of all who toil in these gardens." Here, too, his father's voice faltered, and for a moment neither said a word to the other.

"I love you, Father."

Paul waited in the cavern. As he did, a group of laborers gathered in the eating area. Paul knew his father had had something to do with arranging this crowd and knew it was his cue. He advised Brian to move slowly through the group, to feel his way along as if sightless himself.

They saw Elsa sliding a tray of freshly baked capoi bread onto a cart. She was a slim-hipped woman of average height. Her head was turned, as she was not yet aware of their presence, and Paul noticed that she had used a bit of the stem from the capoi plant to tie her hair back in a ponytail.

"Elsa?"

"Yes?"

Paul averted his eyes when Elsa turned her head. It was the shock of that first glimpse, the eyes missing and the hollow, scarred sockets staring back at him; it would take some getting used to. Slowly he returned his gaze to Elsa's face. Her skin was smooth and unwrinkled. She was young, perhaps no older than he was.

"I am Paul Benjarth. Duke Jaiman's son."

His voice was their signal. The laborers converged on the bread cart.

"This way," Elsa instructed Paul and Brian.

The workers raised their arms to reach the loaves on the upper shelves, effectively shielding Paul, Brian, and Elsa from the eyes of the guards on the balconies. They moved to the back of the cart, then through a doorway and up an unlit flight of stairs. Three times the stairway wound around itself. There was an archway at the top of the stairs, and they paused there. The smell of capoi was particularly strong. It was warm, too.

"Peer into the kitchen, Paul Benjarth," said Elsa. "How many women do you see?"

Six open-hearth stone ovens lined one wall of the kitchen. Two women labored in front of each. Some pulled sweet-scented loaves of capoi bread from the ovens while others fueled the fires with wood and kindling scraps. Against the opposite wall were tables. Bread pans were neatly stacked atop them. A variety of baking utensils protruded from canisters arranged on a shelf that ran across the wall at eye level. Chopped wood was neatly stacked against the same wall. A door exited the room at the far end. Beside it stood a tall, bone-thin woman holding a tray of bread.

"Thirteen," said Paul.

"Does one stand by herself against the far wall?"

"Yes. She holds a tray of bread."

"That is Shyla. Now go! She will take you to the fourth tier. And remember well the route she takes. You will have to backtrack without her assistance."

Quickly Paul and Brian crossed the kitchen. Paul reached for Shyla's wrist. The woman tensed at his touch.

"I am Paul Benjarth," he said. "Elsa says you can take us to the fourth tier."

"You must be my eyes. My hearing is far better than yours and the stone echoes. I will be able to hear if someone comes. But if they are already there, standing still, I will not know. Some of the guards make a game of this—standing there and letting us walk into them. Open the door before you and tell me if the way is clear."

Paul opened the door. A corridor ran to the right and left. "The way is clear."

They stepped into the hallway and turned left. Ahead the corridor bent to the left. Shyla motioned them to a stop just before the bend.

"Is the way clear?"

Paul peered around the corner. "It is."

"Good. There is a door directly in front of us. Follow me."

Shyla opened the door and led them into a corridor so narrow that they had to proceed single file. There were no ascama fiber lanterns. The only light seemed to come from ahead and up.

"There are steps here," said Shyla, after they'd gone a short distance.

Paul was amazed at how well Shyla knew the corridors in this part of the castle. Her gait had been brisk and yet she had stopped precisely at the base of these stairs. She was barefoot, as were most of the captives, and Paul realized that this was probably by choice. It would allow them to feel the imperfections in the floor, or a change in surface texture from one stone to another—little things that would serve as markers to tell them exactly where they were.

The light came through a bend at the top of the staircase. Here they entered a wide corridor. Windows opened to the north and ran its full length. Sunlight streamed in.

"I like this corridor," said Shyla. "I can feel the wind as I walk past these windows."

Paul saw that Shyla was smiling. He marveled at the strength of her spirit. She was blind, malnourished, and a prisoner in this castle; yet, in spite of these adversities, she had found something to take pleasure in. She'd discovered a sanctuary among the castle's many hallways of despair.

A steep, narrow set of stairs cut into the middle of the corridor. It dropped perpendicular to it. The stairs led to a small room cluttered with brooms, mops, pans, and carts. Shyla closed the door.

"I have only a few minutes to talk. This bread is for the noonday meal of Thyden's guard captain. If it is cold, he will question me, for it is normally a short walk to his quarters. There is one whose task it is to clean Thyden's chambers. Her name is Adrian. She will retrieve the medallion for you. I will leave you shortly in a room where you can wait for her."

"We are grateful for your help," said Paul.

"All of us who slave here are committed to the overthrow of Lord Thyden."

"I am confused by one thing, Shyla," said Brian. "Why did we need to come this far? Would it not have been safer for us if the medallion had been brought to the cavern beside the chemical gardens?"

"Adrian must bide her time and make the theft when the opportunity presents itself. The minute the medallion is taken it must leave this castle. Once Lord Thyden discovers the larceny, he will seal off all the exits."

"Could not Adrian have brought it to the chemical gardens herself?"

"You forget she is blind, as we all are. She knows no more of the castle than the fourth tier. I know no more of the castle than the kitchen and these back corridors. Together we know the castle better than Lord Thyden or any of his guards, but separately we are limited." She touched one of the loaves of bread. "We must go now."

They exited the room and reentered the window-filled passageway.

"This corridor ends at the base of a stairway. The stairs lead to another corridor. You'll see an archway directly across from where you enter it. Through it is a repair shop. You are to remain there. Adrian will come when she can."

"A repair shop?" Paul was concerned. "Are we safe there?"

"Those whose job it was to fix the odds and ends about the castle have been made into soldiers and sent to the fields. Only security personnel remain. You'll be safe there. Now, please! I must go."

The repair shop consisted of four rooms. The first was the largest and contained mostly furniture in need of repair. There was a table with a broken leg, a chair whose fabric was torn, and a ladder whose wood was split by a crack running half the length of it. Tools were scattered about the floor or hung from wall-mounted pegboards. The inner rooms were much smaller and identical in size to one another. They were cluttered with a vast assortment of junk.

"He's a pack rat," said Brian.

"A what?"

"Thyden's a pack rat. It's an expression. It means he can't throw anything out."

For the first time in quite a while, Paul allowed himself the luxury of a smile. "It would seem so," he said.

All of a sudden Brian cried out. "My parachute! I don't believe it! How did it get here?"

"Keep your voice down," warned Paul.

"My parachute is here! How?"

Paul saw that Brian was indicating a pile of white-and-blue fabric. A cord or two of rope seemed intertwined within it.

"You said you left it in the Valley of Boulders, didn't you?"

"On a ridge overlooking it."

"That needle you were given when you were captured by Lord Marthan's men was styranotide. I'll bet on it! Your hiding place must have come out in the questioning and Lord Marthan later sent men to retrieve it."

Paul thought he heard someone step into the repair shop. He raised his finger to his lips and glared at Brian. When he saw Brian nod that he understood, he slowly peered around the edge of the doorway. A small, wiry woman with short, cropped hair stood just inside the archway. Her head turned this way and that, as if she could see and was searching for something. She drummed the fingers of her left hand against the wall.

"Adrian?"

"Y-Yes?" The woman seemed to be laboring with her breathing, and her voice came in spurts. "I am she."

"You have the medallion?"

"No. I only . . . I only came to see . . . to see if you are here. To be sure before I . . . I must go."

She was gone in an instant.

How different she was from Shyla and Elsa, thought Paul. Both had seemed so composed. But this woman seemed a nervous wreck. It worried him. Could she handle the theft of the medallion?

She returned a half hour later. "You must leave this room," she said.

"I don't understand," said Paul.

"It is not safe . . . here. There is another room. We must . . . go there. Please, follow me."

"Have you the medallion?"

"No, but . . . but I will. Please! We must go."

They moved swiftly down the corridor, made one turn, and headed straight down another. Paul continued to marvel at how well these blind women could negotiate the castle's corridors.

"The medallion is in a box Thyden keeps locked in the third drawer of his dresser," said Adrian. "It is a small box. The key is taped beneath the dresser."

They turned into another corridor. Suddenly armed guards

stepped into the path ahead of them. From behind came the footsteps of more guards. Adrian ran forward and the guards parted to let her pass.

She's betrayed us!

"Why such a puzzled look, Paul Benjarth?" asked the guard captain. "Did you really believe the medallion that easy to steal?"

Gloating bastard!

Guards stepped up from behind and bound Paul's and Brian's hands. They were searched and Paul's knife taken.

"Do not fault Adrian for what she has done," the guard captain said. "The rule here is quite simple for her kind. For each transgression a child will die. Adrian has four of her own here."

A guard ran up from behind the guard captain. "Olef! She is dead!" He held up a bloody knife. "She has taken her life with this."

For a moment, Olef stared at the knife. "A pity, really," he said, as he turned again to Paul and Brian. "She was a good worker."

They climbed a flight of stairs and entered the base of the tower.

Paul's eyes followed the curve of the wall around him. Jair had told him the tower was six hundred feet around. It was not lit by lantern light. Instead, thin radial planes of sunlight entered the tower through staggered slits that appeared to run the full height of the tower. These slits were cut horizontally into the stone and were about six inches high. Each traced an arc one-fourth the circumference of the tower's wall.

"It is one thousand feet to the top, Benjarth," said Olef, grinning satanically. "A long way to fall, don't you think?"

Paul continued to look up. The tower's size was truly spectacular, but what Paul found more intriguing was what it lacked. There was nothing in it.

Had Belshane sacrificed function in order to build a monument to height? The jooarie sacs can only handle so much weight, and he's chosen to pile these stones skyward rather than build floors and walls for rooms and chambers. Is this all an architectural frivolity?

A stairway wound around the tower. It was narrow and was

separated by a wall from the hollow shaft of the tower. An occasional opening afforded them a glimpse of their progress upward. When at last they came to the top of the tower, they found themselves on a rounded ledge protruding ten feet from the tower wall. At one end of it was a small room with a stone door. A guard made his way toward it. He held a fiber loop with a single key fastened to it. Centered in the tower and suspended by a column of stone was a disk twelve feet in diameter. The top of the column was joined to a massive beam of wood. This beam swung out from a pivot point centered midway over the small room, the walls of which fell short of the tower ceiling by several feet in order to allow the beam the freedom to pivot fully around to the platform.

"A simple cell would have been sufficient," remarked Paul.

"Running you through with a sword would have sufficed, Benjarth," countered Olef. "Fortunately for you, I have orders otherwise."

He turned toward the disk and spoke above the noise of the machinery. Paul knew that the guard who'd entered the small room was turning a wheel or other mechanism to move the disk. "As for this, well, it is Lord Thyden's toy. He himself designed and oversaw its construction."

Within another minute the disk bordered the ledge. Paul and Brian were prodded onto it by sword point. Once again the machinery was set in motion. The disk moved away from the platform. When it stopped, the guard emerged from the room and relocked the door.

"I bid you a most pleasant evening, Benjarth," called Olef.

The guards' laughter echoed in the tower as they descended the stairs.

Paul and Brian found that their hands had not been bound tightly, and they were able to work the ropes free within minutes. Paul then studied their situation. The distance from the disk to the ledge looked to be thirty-five to forty feet—too far to jump. The center post that held the disk was four feet in diameter. Paul felt the smooth, polished texture of its stone and realized he could not shinny up it. He gauged the distance to the wooden beam above them to be twenty feet. He could not reach it even if he were to stand on Brian's shoulders. He sat down and buried his head in his knees.

It was several hours later when Paul heard a voice calling his name.

"Paul? Paul Benjarth?"

He scrambled to his feet. A blind serving girl stood on the ledge. "Yes? Who are you?"

"My name is Lysa. I bring you food. Am I near the edge?"

"Yes. The ledge is narrow. You are three feet from the edge."

"I will stand here then. Speak! I will throw this packet of food in the direction of your voice."

"How did you get up here?"

"It is my task to bring food to the guards here in the tower. I asked if I could bring you food. They laughed and wished me luck. They are fools! My throw will be accurate. Now guide me with your voice."

"We stand forty feet apart. You face us now."

"Are you any bit above or below where I stand?"

"No. We are at the same level."

Her throw was accurate and Paul caught the food. "Thank you, Lysa."

The serving girl seemed to hesitate briefly, then said, "Did Adrian tell you where the medallion is hidden?"

"Can you get it?"

"I . . . I think so."

"It is kept in a small, locked box in the third drawer of Thyden's dresser. The key is taped beneath the dresser."

"Can you get us some rope, Lysa?" asked Brian. "Say sixty feet?"

"I don't know where they keep rope."

"Can you get the key to the door here?"

"Door?"

"To your left is a door," said Brian. "Behind it is housed the mechanisms that slide this disk back and forth."

"The key? No, I don't think . . . no. It would be impossible. The guards must have it."

"Maybe they hang it on a peg somewhere?"

"I . . . I don't know. I'm sorry."

For several minutes none of them spoke.

"Your parachute, Brian! Could we not use it to jump down from here? You used it to jump out of your flying machine!"

Brian stepped to the edge and eyed the distance down. "It is risky, Paul. We would hit the ground hard. And the tower is narrow. No, it is too dangerous."

"Dangerous?"

"Keep your voices down," warned Lysa.

"Dangerous?" repeated Paul. "Do you realize the dangers we face if we remain here? We'll be injected with styranotide and after we've told all we know, we'll either be executed or blinded and put to work in the chemical gardens. I'll not give Thyden the pleasure to decide my fate!"

"And how does Lysa slip it by the guards? It is not so small that it can be concealed on her person like the medallion."

To that Paul had no answer.

"Wait a minute," said Brian, having given the matter some thought. "Perhaps . . . yes, it might work. As a wraparound. Or a cloak. Yes! She could wear it as a cloak! It must get cold here in the tower in the evenings. Hasn't it become cooler already?" Brian thought more about his idea. "Yes, if she were to wear it inside out, so that the cords fell inside the cloth and the guards wouldn't see them . . ."

"It's worth a try," agreed Paul.

"I've heard what you said," said Lysa. "I'll do what I can. Where is this parachute?"

They told her of its location. She left.

Brian peered over the edge again. "I don't like it. Even if we survive the fall, one of us will more than likely twist an ankle. Maybe even break a leg. How will we run then?"

"We'll get out of this castle," vowed Paul, "even if we have to crawl out on our hands and knees."

Gradually the light that shone through the slots ringing the wall of the tower faded. It was several hours later, after sunset, when Lysa returned. They could not see her in the darkness.

"Have you the medallion and the parachute?" asked Paul.

"Yes, I've both. You must hurry, though. I'm not sure I can get back to Thyden's room in time to cover the theft."

"What do you mean?"

"I am one of several he beds if he so chooses. He lines us up like livestock and takes who he wants for the evening. I made sure he chose me tonight. He is asleep now, but for how long I don't know."

Lysa set about the task of folding the parachute into its pouch. "I have put the medallion in the bottom of the pouch, but I can't get all of this material in." There was frustration evident in her voice. "What'll I do?"

"Have you anything to wrap around the pouch? To tie it with?" asked Paul.

"No, nothing," she replied at first. "Wait. Perhaps . . ." Less than a minute later they heard her voice again. "It's secure."

"Your throw must be accurate this time," said Paul. "It is dark and it will be difficult for us to see it. Your throw last time was good."

Her throw this time was no less accurate. At the very last second, Paul picked out the pack from the surrounding darkness and was able to block it with his body and fall upon it before it could slide from the disk.

"Have you got it?" asked Lysa.

"Yes."

"Good. I must go now."

The parachute had been tied together with her straplet. Paul undid the simple knot, rolled the straplet up, and stuffed it into the left front pocket of his trousers. They had to be sure to leave no trace that Lysa had helped them. Paul next removed the medallion from the pack. For a moment he held it in his hand, his fingers wrapped tightly around the smooth metal. Both a feeling of power and triumph roared through his veins. *He* now possessed the medallion! He secured the medallion's chain around his belt and placed the medallion in his right front pocket.

All of a sudden the bottom of the tower flickered with lanterns. Brian, who had been peering over the edge, watched them disappear through the opening to the stairs. "We must warn Lysa," he said, turning to Paul.

"What do you mean? What goes on?"

More lanterns appeared in the base of the tower.

"See for yourself," said Brian.

Paul watched the lanterns of the second group of guards disappear through the opening to the stairs. "There is nothing we can do for her," he said.

"My God! We have to do *something!*"

"There is nothing we can do! Do you understand? Our concern now is the medallion. We must get it out of Castle Greyfahren. In twelve minutes the fittest of Thyden's guards will be up here. We must jump soon. Your parachute is here. Do what you must with it!"

How Paul wished there *was* something they could do for Lysa. Surely she would be discovered and made to account for what she had done. And Adrian already dead! Paul vowed then and there that no more Jarred would forfeit their lives on his account. And Thyden's men would pay in kind.

"Hurry," he urged Brian.

It took Brian several minutes to repack the chute and secure it via the harness strap to his back.

"Okay," said Paul. "Now how do we do this?"

"Give me your belt," said Brian.

He looped Paul's belt beneath the two harness straps that fell down across his chest, centered the buckle between them, and pulled the belt taut. With the other end he formed a loop by securely tying the belt back onto itself. "Your hands go here," he told Paul. "Grip this with all your strength. It is your only link to me."

Paul sat by the edge of the platform. Brian straddled him.

"One, two, three, now!" cried Brian.

They jumped in unison.

For the first few seconds Paul was totally disoriented, aware only of an incredible rush of air. Which way was up, down, right or left—it was impossible to tell. The darkness masked reference points. And then the rush of air stopped. Completely stopped! Paul felt as if he and Brian were suspended like puppets on strings to the underside of the platform far above them. It was Brian's voice that told him otherwise.

"We're about to hit, Paul! Let your legs go limp and roll to the side!"

Paul's legs kicked out from under him when he hit and he fell back. He twisted his body as he tried to roll and his right shoulder crunched to the stone as Brian fell on him and rolled off.

"Are you all right?" Brian asked, unbuckling the parachute's harness.

There was a throbbing pain in Paul's shoulder. He rolled his arm in a circle, then thrust it forward and back. Nothing was broken. "I'm okay," he said.

The stairway exiting the tower was deserted. So, too, was the hallway beyond. But before they reached the bend at the far end of that corridor, they heard a shout from behind them. A guard gave chase. They made the door at the end of the next corridor just as the guard set himself to throw. *Whoosh-thud.* His knife bit into the wood of the door as they slammed it shut behind them.

There was little moonlight in the northern sky, so the windows that lined the corridor ahead of them let in insufficient light to break the black expanse before them. The corridor was wide and without obstacle except for the opening in the floor to their right, which led to the storage rooms. They ran single file along the left wall, then descended the narrow flight of stairs to the third tier. It was then they heard the echo of many pairs of footsteps in the windowed corridor and realized just how close at hand was their pursuit.

Paul opened the door that exited the back corridors. The hall before them was well lit by ascama fibers. There was a guard at its far end, but his back was to them. They ran for the kitchen.

"Halt!" cried the guard, turning and seeing them.

They crashed through the darkness of the kitchen, disrupting pots, pans, and cooking utensils, but somehow managing to keep their footing.

"Which way?" cried Paul when they were through the kitchen.

"To the left!"

They descended the winding staircase and entered the soft, moonlit darkness of the chemical gardens. They crawled through the opening and dropped to the floor of the cavern. The hole in the floor was narrow and they snaked their way through on their backs. They grabbed their backpacks, crawled out onto the ledge, and helped each other put them on.

All at once they heard voices at the entrance to the cavern.

"How did they find us?" cried Brian.

"The guards atop the balconies must have seen us. Be careful! We are on the ledge."

They heard a thud as a man jumped to the floor of the cavern.

They are too near!

Paul realized that he and Brian would not get far along the rope—thirty, perhaps forty feet—before the guards would discover their means of escape. Then it would be an all-too-simple matter for them to alert archers to position themselves in the windows of the east wall and wait for he and Brian to begin their crossing of the sky void ring. The two of them would be an easy target in the moonlight. Or would they even bother to do all that, wondered Paul? Perhaps they would just cut the rope, thinking they were sending him and Brian to their deaths thousands of feet below.

That's it!

He'd been disarmed by Olef's men and so he was without any means to cut the makraw-leaf rope, but if he were to dislodge the grappling hook, it would, in effect, be the same thing.

Another guard jumped to the floor of the cavern.

"Squat down and let me stand on your shoulders," Paul said.

"What?"

"Trust me! It's our only chance."

A muted grating sound came from behind the jooarie sac to their left. One of Lord Thyden's guards had started to climb through the hole in the floor of the cavern.

Once atop Brian's shoulders, Paul leaned forward. He'd remembered the height and contour of the ledge above him when he'd studied it last night by the light of the ascama fiber-stub. He grabbed onto the ledge across the way and, bracing himself with one arm, located the grappling hook with the other. He twisted and turned it until it came free. He looked down at Brian and saw the glow from an ascama fiber lantern issuing from the mouth of the tunnel.

"Listen to me, Brian. I'm too far over to get back without your help. On the count of three I'm going to push off from this ledge. Grab me about the waist as I fall and pull me toward you."

The light within the tunnel grew brighter.

"One, two, three!"

Paul pushed off from the ledge with his free hand. Brian dropped his shoulders and grabbed Paul about the waist. Throwing his weight back, he managed to pull Paul onto the ledge.

"Surrender, Benjarth!" cried a voice from within the tunnel. "You haven't a prayer."

There were two loose rocks on the ledge. Brian picked up one and hurled it into the tunnel. The guard blocked it with his arm. Brian threw the other one. This time the guard cried out as it bruised the same arm. The guard drew his knife.

"May this blade be your death, Benjarth!" he shouted as he moved forward through the tunnel.

The grappling hook had four prongs. Paul grabbed onto two of them. Brian did likewise.

"Hold it upright like this," Paul said. "This way the hook won't twist when the rope goes taut."

The guard emerged from the tunnel and raised his knife above his head. Paul and Brian jumped. There was an incredible rush of air as they fell. Then their bodies kicked out to the side as the rope pulled taut and they began the arc of their swing.

CHAPTER 13

———

 "Can you pull yourself up?"

"I think so," said Brian, "but I wish I could see the damn rope better."

They hung from the prongs of the grappling hook. They were close enough in weight that the grappling hook did not pitch toward either of them. They had waited out the swing of the rope, which had carried them several times across the sky-void ring and then back again beneath Castle Greyfahren. Now only the wind rocked them.

Brian let go of one prong and reached for the rope. The grappling hook pitched and he grabbed the prong again. "It's too unsteady," he said. "We've got to distribute our weight differently."

"Lock your legs around my midsection," Paul suggested. "Then pull yourself up."

Paul's plan worked and within moments Brian stood atop the grappling hook, his feet secure in the curves of adjoining prongs.

"Now give me a hand up," said Paul.

Brian grabbed Paul's wrist and pulled him up. They stood facing each other atop the grappling hook.

"How high a climb do you figure it is?" Brian asked.

Paul glanced upward. The coil of rope had been two hundred and fifty feet long. Of that, thirteen feet had been wrapped around the rock spire, fourteen feet had been cut from it for both their safety straps, and roughly twenty-five feet lay on the ground between the rock and the edge of the sky-void ring. "Two hundred feet," he said.

Brian grunted an acknowledgment as he began to climb.

The crohephite rock base supporting the flat lands encircling the sky-void ring dropped to a depth of forty feet. Paul and Brian found a narrow opening in the rock and pulled themselves in. Their arms ached from the climb and they needed to rest before continuing. The opening itself had depth to it, as a cave or tunnel would, and they wandered back from its edge and sat down. They hadn't rested a minute when they noticed the night sky grow lighter. Paul, curious as to the source of the strange light, rose and approached the mouth of the cave.

"Stay back," warned Brian. "They're flares!"

Suddenly the cave was flooded with light. Paul had to shield his eyes from the flares' brightness.

"Get back from the opening," cried Brian.

It took only a few seconds for the flare to pass by the mouth of the cave. On all sides of the rock supporting Castle Greyfahren they could see flares descending. There were six of them in all.

"I've never seen anything like those," said Paul in amazement.

Brian had other concerns. "Could they see you?"

"No. A ledge overhangs the mouth of the cave." He paused a moment in thought. "The rope is transparent. They won't see that."

"They'll see the grappling hook, though," said Brian.

Paul stepped back beside Brian as the night sky began to lighten again. This time a single flare briefly illuminated the walls of the cave.

Paul ran forward to the mouth of the cave. From his pocket he produced a second box containing a single ascama fiberstub. Quickly he slid back the cover and, holding the base of the plant stem to the inside of the box with his thumb, he turned it toward the dwindling light of the flare.

Be enough light!

There was. The fiber-stub began to glow. Paul slid the cover of the box back in place.

"Why did you do that?" Brian asked.

"Because we need light to explore this cave. We can't continue our climb. No doubt Thyden's men have seen the grappling hook and archers will be positioned among the rocks on the east side of the castle. Our only chance is to explore this cave further in the hope of locating a fissure through which we can crawl back up to the surface."

Paul held the ascama fiber-stub aloft as they explored the depths of the cave. Swollen jooarie sacs bulged in their path and at times they had to turn sideways to slip by them. But always they were able to continue forward, ever deeper into the rock. At last they came to a wood-and-rope suspension bridge.

"It's similar to the bridge I crossed beneath Fief Karcan," remarked Brian. "Not as long, though. I can see the outline of the rock on the other side."

"No doubt Thyden plans to slip into Fief Salkird the same way he does Fief Karcan." Paul sat down and placed the ascama fiber-stub on the ground beside him. "It's odd, though. I didn't notice any other tunnels entering this one."

Brian spoke with disinterest. "So? What of it?"

"Well, I should think there would be! How else would Thyden's soldiers enter *this* tunnel? Remember that a ledge overhangs the mouth of the cave. It would be a risky climb down from the rim of the sky-void ring. How much easier to dig another tunnel from the surface to join this one." Paul saw that Brian was confused. "The point I'm trying to make is maybe Thyden didn't build this bridge."

Brian stepped to the edge of the bridge and pushed down on the first plank of wood with his foot. "Do we go on?" he asked wearily.

"What choice do we have?" Paul snapped, annoyed that Brian had not shown more interest in what to him seemed a most curious observation.

Brian's eyes flashed and held Paul's gaze for several seconds, then his eyes shrunk back into his skull and he yawned. "We'll have to cross in darkness then," he said. "We'll need a hand on each of these ropes to manage this bridge."

Paul held back as Brian crossed. Damn it! He was tired, too, but they had to push on. Didn't Brian understand that? They had the medallion now and were sure to be pursued. They couldn't rest. Not yet.

The tunnel widened on the far side of the bridge.

"Let me get the fiber-stub out again," Paul said.

But before he could slide back the cover of the box the shutters of four ascama fiber lanterns opened. Paul and Brian instinctively took a step back as they shielded their eyes from the blinding glare of the lights.

A voice spoke from the direction of the light. "Do not be foolish enough to go for your weapons. We've archers poised to shoot and they won't miss from this range. Slowly now. Throw your weapons down on the ground in front of you."

"We carry no weapons," said Paul.

"You take us for fools?"

"Search us if you like."

"Be assured we will! Now take your backpacks off. Slowly." Paul and Brian did as they were instructed. "Now kick them forward toward us."

Two of the lanterns were turned and focused on the backpacks. This, plus the fact that Paul's eyes had become accustomed to the glare, enabled him to make out the shadow-figures of the men. There were eight of them: four with lanterns, two with bows, two now inspecting the contents of their packs.

They're all so tall! Are they Jarred?

"Kellan! They speak the truth. There is nothing in their packs but food and a coil of rope."

"Search their persons."

The other two lanterns were refocused on them.

"This one is clean," announced one of the men after he'd searched Brian.

"What's this in your pocket?" demanded the fellow searching Paul. He removed the medallion from Paul's pocket.

"Jewelry," replied Paul.

The man studied the medallion by the light from one of the lanterns. "So it is," he said, returning it to Paul. "This one is clean, too."

"It indeed appears you speak the truth," said Kellan. "A

coil of rope, food, but no weapons? Who are you? What is your mission here?"

Paul decided to speak truthfully. A suspicious tale would only invite an injection of styranotide. "I am Paul Benjarth, Duke of Fief Karcan."

None of the eight spoke immediately.

"You are young to hold such a title," said Kellan, his tone suspicious.

"My father, Duke Jaiman Benjarth, is a prisoner in Castle Greyfahren. Until his return is secured, I am the acting duke."

There again followed a silence.

"We saw your light from afar," began Kellan. "That is how we came to intercept you. But how did you and your friend learn of and enter the western passage? And why?"

"We are two of six whose mission it was to learn what we could of Thyden's troop strength and to learn of means to free my father and others held with him."

Paul went on to reveal how they had crossed the Angena Mountains and made their way into Castle Greyfahren. He summarized their escape. He was, however, careful to omit any reference to the medallion. While he sensed Kellan was a friend, he felt it wiser not to speak of the medallion's powers.

Another voice spoke when Paul had finished. "Those bright lights that fell from the sky. The second time there was only one and it was directed to the east." He had spoken this to Paul as if to confirm its accuracy. "Kellan! Hadn't we better cut the bridge?"

"Yes! See to it immediately. Hermph and Jace will stay with you. You must do more than cut it, though. It must be removed. Not a single rope or plank is to be left as evidence of our people."

Three men broke ranks and brushed past Paul and Brian.

"You will come with us," said Kellan.

They had not traveled far to the east when the rock south of them opened up to the sky. Moonlight angled in and washed the cliffs bordering the hole in a silver glow.

"The Void of Carcin," Kellan said for the benefit of Paul and Brian.

The trail dropped sharply and the way became narrow and winding. Paul could see how closely spaced the jooarie sacs were. There were mountains above them and Paul knew them to be the western end of the mountains encircling Fief Salkird. Abruptly the path turned steeply upward and they had to use the rock on either side of them to help pull themselves forward. Where the path leveled off Kellan halted.

"Behold, Paul Benjarth and friend! Behold what none from your world has ever witnessed!"

Paul was speechless. All he could do was stare in wonder at what lay before him. It was a city—suspended beneath the crohephite rock base of Fief Salkird!

The rock into which the city had been incorporated was uniquely shaped. It was as if, thought Paul, a giant hand had used a knife and with surgical precision carved out a semicircle half a mile in diameter from the underside of Fief Salkird. The city was likewise semicircular, its flat side facing the sky-void. It was inset from the curve of the rock around it by thirty yards. Five suspension bridges, the westernmost of which lay just before them, joined it to the rock.

The city consisted of dozens of tiered structures suspended from tapering projections of crohephite rock that hung down from the ceiling like stalactites. Remarkably the buildings of the city seemed of rock also, as if somehow the core-vines had been made to grow straight down, then branch off to form walls, floors, roofs. Hundreds of these core-vine aberrations supported these buildings and the many bridges that joined them.

The lights from dozens of lanterns glowed throughout the city. Where a lantern happened to illuminate an outside wall Paul could see dull traces of color: reds, oranges, and yellows. Come morning, sunlight would be reflected upward from Calferon and the vivid hues of the painted stone would brighten. Paul realized the city might be every bit as colorful as Cartag was when the striped awnings of its vending stalls were unfurled for morning traffic.

The curve of the rock encircling the southern half of the city had been hollowed out and subdivided into rooms. Some were growing rooms. Paul could see the nutrient troughs and the rows of ascama filaments mounted above them. He suspected capoi was one of the crops harvested because of its fast growing time as well as its ability to grow under artificial light. Some of the other rooms were workshops. Paul could make out tools and benches in these. A few pipes with flared ends dropped from the rock and angled into an unlit room. Paul guessed that these pipes directed rainwater, which trickled down through fissures in the rock, into barrels.

"Your silence is most complimentary, Paul Benjarth," said Kellan. "We often wondered about the reaction of an outsider to our city."

"It's amazing! It truly is! But how did it come to be? Who designed and built it?"

"It was conceived by my great-grandfather, Jamis Caalton. It was his obsession and his alone. This ledge blocks our view, but above and behind us is the mouth to a small tunnel. It was there my great-grandfather, as a young man, knelt and envisioned his city, his creation, in this space beneath the crohephite rock. That tunnel was a natural fissure through the rock and his little secret. He'd drawn up plans for much of what you see here, though I daresay we've expanded it beyond what even he'd imagined, but he hadn't the manpower nor the resources to pursue it. He thought the project too much a frivolity to approach Duke Orsinc the second, ruler of Fief Salkird, for support. Yet, if you know your history, Paul, you know the years 256 to 261 to be dark ones for the Jarred."

Paul remembered. *The plague!*

"Jamis saw in his plans an escape from the baccillium virus and the death it brought. His family and relatives fled through the tunnel. Fortunately, it was the time of the harvest and there were ample foodstuffs to store in the many passageways they found. Here they hollowed out a home, rupturing a few of the jooarie sacs and cutting and stripping the crohephite rock from a few of the smaller core-vines. A simple beginning to the complexity before you."

"But the ravages of the plague lasted only five years," remarked Paul. "Why did your great-grandfather and his people not return to the world they knew?"

"It was said that my great-grandfather had a captivating manner. I daresay that all became as caught up in the idea of starting their own civilization as he was. To govern themselves by their own rules! To police themselves by their own laws! And to create this!" Again he motioned to the city with his arm. "Who would want to leave?"

"Have any returned to the fiefs?"

"Not a one, Paul."

"Not even out of curiosity?"

"Curiosity? Yes, I daresay it has crossed all of our minds on occasion. But it is curiosity we have learned to control. It is a trust we are all bound to. Can you not see the danger in satisfying such a curiosity? We risk discovery! Then what would our city become? A stop for the curious? A town taxed and governed by the duke of Fief Salkird? The home of a people whose values would gradually become polluted by the evils of the surface world?"

The city was crisscrossed with walkways. Stairs zigzagged downward, level after level. Some stairs were nothing more than thin, flat pieces of stone protruding outward from a wall. Others were elaborate suspension bridges that sloped gently downward and had double rope railings on both sides. These swayed as the men crossed in single file. Eventually they reached the city's lowermost tier. There Paul and Brian were shown into a small room furnished only with a table and three chairs. Two guards were posted by its only door. Kellan returned with bedding. Food was brought by others.

"These will be your quarters for the evening," said Kellan. "The council will meet in the morning and you will be granted an audience before it."

"And then what?" asked Paul.

Kellan averted his eyes. "It depends on what the council decides."

Before Paul could question him any further, Kellan departed with the others. Seconds later they felt motion.

"The room is being lowered," cried Paul.

Both he and Brian rushed to a window. Sure enough, the floor of the city seemed to rise away from them. When the motion finally stopped they had dropped twenty feet.

Paul slumped down into a chair in the corner of the room. Brian pulled one up to the table and began to eat.

"Tell me of this plague," said Brian between mouthfuls. "I heard you talk of it with Kellan."

Paul pulled a chair up to the table. "The first infection of the baccillium virus was reported in the year 256 in Fief Cerus, somewhere in the mountains."

"I do not know your calendar, Paul. What year is it now?"

"Three hundred fifty-eight."

"Continue."

"The tragedy lay in the diagnosis, or misdiagnosis, of the virus. It was first thought to be another outbreak of the reno-cocci bacterium. The early symptoms were similar and the virus tested the same. So the same vaccine was again prepared and the populace injected. What was unfortunate was the fact that the mountainous area of Fief Cerus bordering the Medoc Peninsula was predominantly Phlogin and Sinese then, and they were to prove naturally immune to the deadly effects of the baccillium virus. Those who died were Jarred, but because their numbers were small, the death count was low relative to the overall size of the population. There are always a few deaths associated with any mass vaccination program, because not everyone takes to the vaccine. There are many histoscizans who believe the Sinese and Phlogin surgeons administering care in that region of Fief Cerus covered up the fact that only Jarred were dying."

"Why?"

"The Jarred are not liked by the Sinese and Phlogin. It's been that way always. So it wasn't until the outbreak moved farther north and entered Fief Karcan, which was and still is predominantly Jarred, that *our* surgeons realized something was wrong. The viral strain was new, unique; it took five years to develop an effective vaccine. By that time the Jarred population had been cut in half."

"But why have the Jarred never settled outside the borders of the three fiefs?"

"The bond is strong between those of the same race. Histos-cizans have remarked that even as early as the year one there was a marked preference for racial segregation. Of the three earliest known settlements, Castle Chalmet was seventy-five percent Sinese, Castle Hopkitch was eighty-one percent Phlo-gin, and Artan was ninety-five percent Jarred."

"Yet Castle Chalmet is now your home, isn't it? Is it not now Jarred?"

"Castle Chalmet and Castle Hopkitch are now Jarred settle-ments. Artan no longer exists. Where its walls once stood are grazing fields. Between the years 57 and 184, Fief Salkird was the principal settlement of the Jarred. This was because they had been driven from Artan in the year 57 by the combined armies of the Sinese, Phlogin, and Ornan."

"Ornan? I have not heard that race mentioned before."

"They are a minor race as far as their numbers are concerned. Quite truthfully, they are a genetic puzzle. I'll give you an idea of what I mean. Up to the year 256 the populations of the principal three races were nearly identical. Let's say thirty-three percent were Jarred, thirty-three percent were Phlogin and thirty-three percent were Sinese. That would leave one percent Ornan. Their numbers are hardly significant, so in general discussions they are often omitted."

"It's interesting."

"Isn't it?" Paul paused, then asked, "Where was I?"

"The year 57. The Jarred had just been driven . . ."

"Yes, yes, of course. So, for many years, let's see, to the year 176, the Jarred developed the resources of Fief Salkird, the Sinese of Fief Karcan, and the Phlogin of Fief Cerus. In 176 the twins Michael and Matthew Sinoms contested for the throne of Fief Karcan in the week of games set up by their father. Michael was declared the winner and heir to the throne. Less than a year later, Matthew married Cythin Benjarth, niece of the duke of Fief Salkird."

"An intermarriage between the races?"

"Granted, a rare occurrence. But in this case the marriage had political overtones. Many viewed the marriage as a bridge of peace between the Jarred and the Sinese peoples. But Matthew was hardly so idealistic. In fact, his thoughts were quite to the contrary. He used the marriage to gain access and acceptability into the ruling nobility of Fief Salkird. In time he was able to rekindle the hatred that had always existed between the Jarred and the Sinese and Phlogin, reminding them constantly that it had been the Sinese and Phlogin who had driven *them* from the rich farmlands of Fief Karcan. The year 184 saw the Jarred launch a successful military campaign against the Phlogin and Sinese, driving them from their homes to that narrow strip of land that is now the Medoc Peninsula. The Jarred have been the dominant party of the three fiefs ever since."

"So those who now hold us are Jarred?" Brian indicated their confinement with a glance toward the window and the underside of the city. "Some way to treat those of your own kind. Especially after what we've been through!"

Paul nodded his head in agreement. *Some way, indeed!*

They were brought before the council the next morning. Seven men sat behind a curved table. Kellan was seated to the far right. Guards were posted at either end.

"I am Simon Seagarth," said the man seated centrally at the table. "I am the council head."

Simon did not stand to greet them. Instead he leaned back in his chair and peered at them over the tip of his nose. He was an old man, the eldest of the seven. His hair was white and had receded almost to the midpoint of his skull. He had large, probing gray-brown eyes and thick, bushy eyebrows. His forehead was deeply wrinkled. He wore a gray tunic with two green stripes that ran downward right to left across his chest. There was a small patch sewn to the fabric over his heart, but Paul could not make out its design at this distance. Each of the other council members wore identical uniforms.

"Kellan has told us of your journey to Castle Greyfahren and of your escape from it," he continued. "A most incredible tale. We admire your courage."

The eyes of the council members fell upon Paul, and he felt obliged to respond. "There are those enslaved within Castle Greyfahren who are more deserving of such praise. Robbed of their sight, they have managed nonetheless to form an alliance to aid all who work for Thyden's defeat. Faced with the penalty of death and the death of their children for the slightest transgression, they aided us in our escape. Most are Jarred or of Jarred blood. May they stand as truer examples of courage."

"A noble sentiment, Paul Benjarth," replied Simon. "Tell the council, if you will, of Lord Thyden's ambitions."

"Thyden's goal is nothing less than conquest and domination of the three fiefs."

"Why?"

"He is a madman obsessed with conquest! He fires up his soldiers with talk of taking back the land 'rightfully' theirs, land the Jarred took back from the Sinese and Phlogin with the invasion of Matthew Sinoms. He's raised an army no less than three times the size of ours."

The councilmen talked among themselves in whispered tones. Simon Seagarth spoke at last. "What chance do the armies of the three fiefs have of defeating Lord Thyden's forces?"

"We have the advantage of fighting on our own turf. We've had the advantage of setting up our defenses because we knew of Thyden's invasion ahead of time. He has the advantage of numbers. It is a difficult question. However, I will tell you this," Paul said, his fists clenched, his voice spirited with passion. "The Benjarth will not surrender to Thyden! They will die in combat first, slaying many before falling themselves! Such is their courage."

"Their courage aside, Paul, they may still lose the battle. Am I right?"

Paul's face dropped. "It has to be considered a possibility, yes."

Again the council huddled.

"Simon Seagarth," Paul cried out, taking a step forward. His voice rolled like a thunderbolt through the whispering councilmen. All heads jerked upright and their talk ceased. "Thyden's forces may even now be engaging those of the three fiefs. Brian and I must get back to Castle Chalmet with all due speed. I request that we be shown a tunnel up and outward to the east."

There was anger in Simon's reply, though Paul sensed he tempered it. "There is a protocol one must follow, Paul Benjarth, when one stands before the council. One does not speak to the council without permission." His tone softened. "I can understand your impatience, but our deliberations have been most difficult. We've met among ourselves for many hours before calling you here. There are many rules and regulations that govern such a small, tightly knit community as ours. But one above all others forms its backbone. It is religion to us! And that is that our world be preserved forever from the eyes of the surface dwellers. If it isn't, our way of life will be destroyed. We would become but another town under the rule of the duke of Fief Salkird. His rules would prevail over ours. His armies would ensure our compliance. We are not fighters. We've trained no armies. You will see no soldiers among us.

Do you see why our deliberations have been so difficult?"
Here his voice rose. "I know you came this way by chance. We
all do. But so what? Don't you see? We cannot grant you passage back to the surface."

"And what do you mean to do with us?" Paul screamed
back. "Keep us imprisoned in that little hanging chamber until we die of old age?"

Simon remained surprisingly calm in the face of Paul's outburst. "There are drugs to pacify your will to flee our city.
Daily injections will be prescribed until your will is altered.
With time you will be incorporated into our society. Perhaps
you will marry and have children. As for your livelihood, there
are tasks you will be trained to perform."

"Will that be your decree upon the Jarred race? To turn
your backs on your own kind and watch Thyden wipe out all
but a handful of the Jarred?"

"The survival of a handful makes more sense than the ex-
tinction of us all," countered Simon. "If we allow you to return to the surface world, then our secret is out. Should
Thyden capture either of you, then an injection of styranotide
will reveal not only our existence, but the very tunnel that can
bring his armies down upon us."

*So that was it! They were convinced Thyden's superior num-
bers would triumph!*

"Fools!" cried Paul. "Your survival lies in aiding us! Do you
not think that Thyden will find you out? Already he explores
the underside of the crohephite rock. He's built a suspension
bridge beneath the eastern land bridge joining Fief Karcan
with the Medoc Peninsula. Don't you think he's already seen
the lights of your city, as we did?"

"Your ploy will not work, Paul Benjarth," replied Simon.

"He does not lie to you," said Brian. "I crossed that bridge
myself. Do you wish me to explain its engineering to you? You
will find it no different than the bridge you've constructed
across the void in the western tunnel."

"The crohephite rock that supports the mountains of Fief
Salkird falls on all sides of us. The lights of this city are not
visible from the south."

"Can you be sure of that?" demanded Paul.

Again the council members huddled in conference.

Paul took still another step forward and strained to overhear their conversation. He dared not step any closer, for the guards posted on either side of the council looked ready to spring forward.

"Our views have not changed," announced Simon, when at last they broke off their discussion. "You will both remain here."

Paul exploded with rage. "How can you turn your backs on your own kind? The deaths of thousands of Jarred must now be borne on your consciences! Their rape, murder, and enslavement must now be borne on your shoulders! You may as well sign a pact abetting Thyden as deny us passage to the surface!"

"So, too, has the survival of the Jarred race been thrust upon our shoulders," countered Simon. "It is here, within our city, that the Jarred will survive and continue!"

"You are fools to believe that the armies of the three fiefs cannot beat Thyden!" He saw the guards tense when he leaned forward as if to take another step. He checked himself.

"You will not address this council as such again, Paul Benjarth."

"Fools, I say," cried Paul.

The guards approached him.

"Fools to abandon the Jarred forces while we possess this!" With dramatic flair he removed the medallion from around his neck and held it aloft. The guards stopped in their tracks, unsure of what to do.

"This is the medallion of the Benjarth! It was about my father's neck when Thyden surprised and captured his reconnaissance party. This is the true reason we journeyed to Castle Greyfahren. To wrest this from the grasp of Thyden!"

"For a trinket?" cried Simon, both surprised and somewhat amused by Paul's revelation. "The label 'fool' more aptly applies to you, Paul Benjarth."

"What I hold in my hand is far more than a piece of jewelry. Bring this to the council," he said to one of the guards.

The guard plucked the medallion from Paul gingerly by its chain and brought it swiftly to Simon Seagarth. The other members of the council rose from their seats and gathered around him.

"Study its construction well," said Paul. "Its seams, the fit. Now feel the substrate. Such a material cannot be found in our world." Paul went on to tell them all he knew of the medallion: its power, the bashan's guardianship, the mysterious stairway to the planet's surface, and the little he knew of his great-great-grandfather's journey there.

"A most fantastic tale indeed," said Simon, when Paul had finished. "But can any of this be verified? Don't answer. I already know. It can't. All this may be but another of your fabrications. You have an imaginative mind, Paul Benjarth. Our decision remains as before."

Paul had expected this response and he was prepared with an answer. "I ask the council to delay its decision on our fates."

"Such cannot be granted without good cause."

"I ask the council to stay its decision until the contents of the medallion are revealed."

"Do you change your story? Did you not just tell us that the medallion can only be opened by the Malhah?"

"You will find, Simon Seagarth, that if you wash the dye and dirt out of Brian's hair," and here Paul smiled in smug anticipation of watching Simon's mouth drop open, "it will be as yellow as the noonday sun."

CHAPTER 14

 Brian squinted into the eyepiece of the magnifier. He held the medallion in one hand and adjusted the angle of the ascama fiber-stub holder with the other. Finally he slid shut the cover plate on the fiber-stub and raised his eye from the lens.

"Nothing," he said.

Paul was not surprised. He'd thought it a foolish notion in the first place. How could anyone print letters to such an impossibly small scale? He took the medallion and turned it over and over in his hand. Light from ceiling-mounted ascama fibers glinted off its polished surface like a mirror-ball. The workmanship amazed him. The two halves fit together so perfectly that even with the magnifier they had not seen a gap in the seam. They had heated the medallion in fire, yet the seam had remained tight. They had smashed it with a hammer, while hot, while cold. They'd even poured acid along the seamed edge in the hope it would eat away enough of the metal to allow them to insert a blade and pry it open. It had not worked.

"There has to be a way," shouted Paul, frustrated. "My great-great-grandfather opened it!"

"So legend claims."

Paul gave Brian a dirty look. Who was *he* to question the

veracity of the Benjarth legends?

Brian wrinkled his brow in thought. "Maybe it's the hole. Maybe that's the key to it."

The hole was centered on the backside of the medallion. It was three-sixteenths of an inch in diameter and one-quarter of an inch deep. Using the magnifier, they had looked for any indentations or protrusions that would engage a mated "key" piece. To their disappointment, they'd found the sides and bottom of the hole to be perfectly smooth. They had next fashioned a rod three-sixteenths of an inch in diameter, inserted it into the hole and pushed downward, thinking the medallion's locking mechanism might be of a spring-lock type. That idea had not worked, either.

"Hold the medallion out in front of you," said Brian suddenly.

Paul did as Brian instructed, holding the medallion by its chain.

Brian flicked at the medallion with his index finger. Quickly he put his ear next to it.

"What are you doing?"

"Hold it still," snapped Brian.

Paul steadied his elbow on the table.

Brian repeated the procedure. When he drew back, he said, "It might work."

"What might work?"

"It resonates. Maybe that's how it opens. Vibration. Tonal vibrations." He picked up the three-sixteenths-inch rod and inserted it into the hole. "If we could vibrate this rod at different frequencies? Do you see what I'm getting at?"

Paul understood well enough to oversee fabrication of the entire assembly. A rod was joined across the top side of the tonal plates of a xylophone. One end of it protruded several inches beyond the end plate. Next a holder was made for the medallion. Once aligned, a base was made that joined the two assemblies together.

By noon the next day all was in readiness. Paul stood before the council and explained its operation. "As each plate is struck, the rod will function as an oscillating conductor of that tonal plate's frequency. This particular xylophone spans one octave, from middle 'C' to high 'C.' Brian and I will dictate the note sequences."

Simon nodded at one of the three musicians he had put in Paul's and Brian's service. This man, in turn, took up a position beside the xylophone-medallion assembly. He held a small, round-headed mallet in his left hand.

"He is yours to command," said Simon.

Paul approached the assembly. He felt strangely nervous and his mouth was dry. "Middle 'C'."

The note was struck.

Paul stared hard at the assembly. Light seemed to shimmer on the rod, suggesting motion. He touched the rod and felt the vibrations stop.

It was then he was aware of just how quiet the room had become. He looked up and saw several of the council members staring at the medallion, mouths agape. It was as if they had expected something to happen on that first blow; as if, with that one mallet strike, the medallion would open, a wonderful light fill the room, and unlimited power be given them. Paul almost had to laugh at how his own imagination had actually allowed him to believe that it just might happen. But as more notes were struck, he became increasingly more sober about the timetable. It might take hours. Or days.

Two hours and one thousand thirty-eight combinations later, Paul left the room. For a while he wandered the city. Simon had given him permission to do so without escort. Some privilege, he thought. After all, where could he go? The five bridges leading from the city to the rock were well guarded. Simon had seen to that!

Eventually Paul stopped beside a rail overlooking the vast emptiness of the northern sky. How much cooler it was here than on the surface, he thought. A damp, lingering chill permeated everything, and he knew this was in part because the warmth of the sun never fell upon the city. He wrapped his arms around himself and turned his face from the void. He noticed a messenger running toward him in great haste.

"Come, Paul Benjarth," the messenger cried. "The medallion has been opened!"

The two halves of the medallion lay flat on a table. They were joined by an inside hinge mechanism. A small square of paper lay within one of the halves. It had been folded over many times.

Brian met Paul halfway across the room. "F, G, C," he said, all smiles. He hummed the notes.

Paul reached for the piece of paper and slowly began to unfold it. As it grew in size, he placed it on the table. Completely unfolded, the paper measured eight inches by twelve inches. It was a map of the Eastern Mountains. Castle Chalmet was indicated on the map by a square at its left edge. A line had been drawn from Castle Chalmet through the fields east of the castle and then along one of the more popular hiking trails that encircled Mount Kiestan. Around the backside of this peak the line veered to the southeast. It twisted around the bases of several more mountains before ending at the sky-void. Paul was unsure if a trail actually followed that course; if it did, it was one seldom traveled. The line overlay the boundary line of Fief Karcan and followed its border with the sky-void to the north.

The line then jutted strangely into the sky-void. Paul could not scale it accurately, but it appeared to protrude into the void approximately a quarter of a mile. The line changed again; no longer was it drawn solid, but instead was broken and circled.

The stairway down!

The line continued in a dashed fashion, cutting back northwest beneath the mountains. Paul estimated the cutback to be in the magnitude of several miles. The line ended in a small circle beside which three exclamation points had been drawn. His great-great-grandfather had signed his name in the lower right-hand corner of the map.

Paul could scarcely contain his excitement. "It's a map revealing the location of the stairway down to the planet's surface. See here!" He indicated with his finger the circle followed by the exclamation points. "Here lies the source of that power we seek."

The council convened that afternoon. Within the same hour, Paul and Brian were summoned before it. Simon Seagarth spoke for the council.

"If a Jarred victory were assured, we might trust to the silence of you and Brian. Unfortunately, this map is little guarantee of that. From what you've told the council, Thyden is bent upon the extermination of the Jarred people. We cannot risk the lives of our people. You and Brian will remain here, and treatments with dranacyline will begin tomorrow morning."

CHAPTER 15

 Lord Thyden sat, legs crossed, floating in the air thirty feet above one end of his maze-box. His elbows rested on his knees and his chin was cupped in the palms of his hands. He was gazing with amusement at Illad Rahman, who was pawing at the space around him as if searching for the hidden wires or beams that had to be supporting him.

"Having trouble getting comfortable, Lieutenant?"

"What kind of madness is this?"

"Madness? I much prefer to use the term 'genius.'"

"But I'm . . . I'm floating in air! How is that possible?"

Lord Thyden smiled. "Have you ever dreamed of flying?"

"This isn't a dream. This is madness!"

"Please, Lieutenant, the word is genius. It took me seven years to perfect this hallucination."

"What is this place?"

"You're in your mind, and I'm in mine. Together we're somewhere in between."

"What?"

"Have you ever dreamed of flying? You never answered my question. Or have you dreamed about leaping across a wide chasm? Or have you dreamed of riding a horse faster than an arrow flies from a bow?"

"What's that got to do with any of this?"

"A hallucination is much the same as a dream. The laws of physics that imprison your body do not exist here any more than they have to in a dream."

Lord Thyden uncrossed his legs. "Take a good look at the maze-box below, Lieutenant. Try to understand how it works. Once you're inside it, you won't have the advantage of this perspective. From the square room at the center of the maze-box radiate eight corridors. Four of these end at the corners of the maze; the other four terminate at the midpoint of the boundary walls. As you can see, a corridor runs along the inside perimeter of the maze, while another four corridors trace the outline of a square halfway between the boundary walls and the center room. At the four corners of the maze are angled mirrors. These allow you to see around corners. Where the four nondiagonal corridors intersect the perimeter corridors are what I call 'half-mirrors.' These allow you to see down a central corridor from a perimeter corridor without obstructing your view of the corner mirrors." Lord Thyden paused a moment and smiled. "Note, too, that there are no exits from the maze-box."

A table materialized beside both Lord Thyden and Illad Rahman. On each was a small hand-held gadget.

"On the table is your weapon. Aim it by pointing the open end away from you. Fire it by squeezing the trigger. It fires a ray of light."

"A ray of light?" Illad Rahman forced a laugh. "Is this a joke of some kind?"

"Hardly, Lieutenant. I assure you that whichever one of us gets struck by that ray of light will die within seconds."

"But how can that be? This is . . . a hallucination! Didn't you say that?"

"That, my dear Illad Rahman, is the first intelligent observation you've made. The light ray, or more accurately the burning sensation it evokes, is only death's catalyst. Death resides in our bodies now. It is part of the molecular configuration of the drug we were injected with."

Lord Thyden realized it would take days, maybe ages, to explain the workings of the cymethadrenatyne molecule to a layman such as the lieutenant. It had, in fact, taken him weeks to digest the notes his father had made regarding his experimentation with a variety of mind-altering drugs, data that in turn would guide him in the development of the cymethadrenatyne molecule's death mechanism.

His father had prefaced his notes with a summation of existing brain theory to date. "Brain function is electrochemical. Electrical impulses carry information across nerve fibers, but between nerve fibers the transmission is chemical. The synaptic cleft, a gap perhaps only a millionth of an inch wide, exists between the dendrites of adjoining nerve fibers. Molecules of chemical released by one nerve cell seek out 'mated' receptor sites on the next. In this manner information is conveyed through the body's nervous system and the brain."

Lord Belshane had been able to isolate the protein "seratin," the principal chemical communicator between nerve cells. From its analysis he had been able to develop aseratin, a protein that would "mate" with the seratin and render it inactive. Logically enough, he had hypothesized that an injection of aseratin would halt all brain activity.

It didn't happen. Rather, to his complete surprise, quite the opposite occurred. Heart rate shot up to three hundred beats a minute, muscles tried to contract and expand simultaneously, and an electrical storm of brain activity wildly exceeded its stabilization threshold. Lord Belshane remarked that the subject exhibited many of the symptoms of an epileptic fit, only tenfold stronger. The subject had died, not because the brain had shut down, but because it had overloaded.

The pursuit of that riddle dictated the need to experiment on more subjects. Lord Belshane was discovered and banished to the unmapped lands of the west. But banishment proved a blessing in some ways. Beyond the reach of Benjarth law, Lord Belshane was free to carry on his experiments without interference.

The brain's dominant function, Lord Belshane had concluded, is inhibitory. Seratin, the chemical "messenger" of the inhibitory nerve cells, selectively shuts down those "action" nerve cells unneeded at any particular instant. When a drug such as aseratin blocks the normal functioning of the inhibitory nerve cells, there is nothing to prevent every "action" nerve cell from firing simultaneously.

"Imagine it," he had written. "All thought, all function, all memories, all motion, all muscle groups—instantaneously turned on!"

Lord Belshane would later discover another interesting fact. Aseratin was quite similar to the body's own natural "opiates," the enkephalins. These proteins were manufactured in response to physical pain, such as a burning or tearing of the flesh. Since the same amino acid chain that constituted the enkephalins was a part of aseratin, it followed that an injection of the dissimilar protein chains from the aseratin would "mate" with the enkephalin amino acid chain to form aseratin. Still of further interest Lord Belshane found that, were the enkephalins not present, these partial protein chains would gradually combine with other proteins occurring naturally in the brain's "chemical soup" and be rendered ineffective as a "mate" for seratin.

It was the logic of this chemistry that Lord Thyden incorporated into his gigantic hallucinatory cymethadrenatyne molecule. The light ray evoked the sensation of heat and that would fool the drugged body into thinking it had been burned. The doomed man's body would produce enkephalins, which in turn would combine with the partial aseratin protein chains to form the complete aseratin molecule. That chemistry took two to three seconds.

Illad Rahman picked up his weapon and turned it over and over in his hands, nervously studying it. Suddenly his arm swung out in front of him and he pulled the trigger. A green light shot out through the nozzle of the weapon, yet it traveled no more than half the distance between them.

"You insult my intelligence, Lieutenant. Did you think me stupid enough not to take precautions against such a simpleminded stunt? A clear barrier that absorbs the light separates us." Lord Thyden picked up his own weapon and turned it restlessly in his hands. "Permit me the opportunity to boast once more. One of the more difficult obstacles I had to overcome in formulating the gigantic cymethadrenatyne molecule was the creation of a light ray that was nonreflective. Else one shot would send death through half the corridors in the mazebox. And that would hardly make this contest fair or challenging, now would it?"

"True men duel with swords or knives," remarked Illad. "But this—" He eyed the strange weapon in his hand with distrust—"well, it is to be expected of you."

Lord Thyden's temper flared. "You think this an unmanly competition? You think instead we should be slashing at each other with swords or grappling with knives in hand-to-hand combat? Well, I beg to differ with you, Lieutenant. The skill in this contest lies in the mind's cleverness. The mind is something we've both had an equal chance to develop. Physically, you are, despite your bad leg, at a distinct advantage."

Lord Thyden stood up and opened his robe. Illad gaped. Lord Thyden's entire body was a fleshy skeleton.

"Muscle tissue degeneration," he explained bitterly. "The result of that accursed Benjarth sterility drug. Oh, my father was able to concoct an antidote to reverse the effects of your drug, but, unknown to him, the tronocyanimide had produced genetic damage that could not be reversed. And so I was born. A freak any mother would have killed rather than raise! But my father couldn't do that. He was old when I was born, having already fathered six children. All were freaks. All were killed. And that left just me, Lieutenant. My father needed me. He needed me because he knew he could not carry out his vengeance in his own lifetime. He needed a successor to complete the work he'd started. A cripple, yes! One without the strength of arm to wield a heavy sword. One without the heart and lung capacity within his shriveled chest to endure the rigors of a good fight. Yet, one whose mind would be keenly developed. One whose mind would be channeled toward one goal and one goal only. Revenge upon the Benjarth and the peoples of the three fiefs!" He waved his weapon above his head. "It is not heavy, Lieutenant. You can see that for yourself. And my maze-box demands but stealthy walking. So would you not agree that it is a fair fight?"

"It is not the way I would settle things," remarked Illad.

Lord Thyden grinned devilishly. "That you should have as equal a chance to kill me is more than he who betrayed Paul Benjarth deserves."

"You accuse me of betraying Paul? What kind of psychological ploy is this?"

"It's true. You talk in your sleep. A bad habit."

Lord Thyden could see by Illad's expression that he wasn't quite so ready to scoff now. "Who else but you knew when and where Paul Benjarth would cross to the Medoc Peninsula?"

A sense of urgency pressed itself upon Lord Thyden. They would be descending into the maze soon. "Of course, you did not tell me this willingly. You had to be prodded with an injection of styranotide while you slept."

"Farant?"

"The good surgeon. Of course! Who else had access to such chemicals?"

Lord Thyden felt motion.

"What's happening now?" cried Illad.

"We are descending into the maze-box. So allow me to give you a final piece of advice. The clear wall between us will disappear five seconds after our feet touch the floor. Do not be foolish enough to still be standing in the central corridor. Our little competition will be most short if you do."

The walls of the maze-box seemed to reach up toward them now, smooth, polished surfaces sparkling in a luminescence that seemed to radiate from the air itself. Seconds later, they were within the confines of the maze-box, descending between walls fifteen feet high, walls impossible to scale. Lord Thyden felt his feet touch the floor and he immediately stepped to the left. He saw in the half-mirror that Illad Rahman had heeded his advice and also stepped into the perimeter corridor.

The competition had begun.

CHAPTER 16

 That first time it had seemed little more than the sound of the wind, but the images of his dream had not vanished and he was still somewhere in the twilight between dream-state and consciousness. However, as Paul's senses became more attuned to his surroundings, the sound became distinguishable from the screaming of the wind. It was a strange sound, one akin to a wail, only deeper and more resonant.

Paul wrapped a blanket around himself and made his way across the room to the window. Above him the lights of the city shone as cold and harsh as the eyes of the council members who had pronounced sentence upon them. Below him Calferon swirled like a pot of soup slowly being stirred.

The sound rose again in his ears. This time it was menacing, nightmarish. He jumped back from the window, wary (though he knew it an irrational fear) that the sound might suck him into the void if he stood too close. The cry had come from the planet's surface, from the east.

What leaped into his mind next was an entry made in the medical log at the time of his great-great-grandfather's return from Calferon. The surgeons at Castle Chalmet had cleaned and sewn up a single deep gash inflicted inches above the duke's right hip. *The kind of wound an animal's claw might make!*

Suddenly the room pitched and Paul was thrown off balance. He grabbed for the table, missed, and fell to the floor. The table toppled over and slid into him.

A figure entered through the window. "Paul Benjarth," it called out in a whisper.

Paul righted himself. "Kellan?"

"We have very little time to talk, so listen carefully. The city is asleep now. No one knows that this room is being raised. If all goes as planned, your escape won't be discovered until morning. By then we should be far away from here."

"You're coming with us?"

"Yes."

"Why do you aid us?" Paul asked suspiciously.

"I am not of the same mind as the council. Rather, I'm in agreement with you. It will only be a matter of time before Lord Thyden learns of our city. No doubt his soldiers probe the western tunnel in pursuit of you and Brian even as we speak! Our preservation, like yours, lies in defeating him. I only hope we can get word to your soldiers in time about his hidden suspension bridge."

"Why didn't you speak your mind at the council meeting?"

"It would have done no good. Simon Seagarth hears only what he wants to hear. In fact, it might have cast suspicion on me and he may have assigned a guard to shadow me."

The motion of the room stopped.

"The elders post a single guard at each of the five bridges into the city," said Kellan. "We will cross the fifth bridge, which faces due east. The inhalation of fumes from a cloth soaked in oterzine will subdue the guard. There is a tunnel to the east that worms its way to the surface. We will flee through it."

Of Kellan's three accomplices, two remained behind to relower the room. Once the room was lowered, there would be no reason for any in the city to suspect anything was amiss until morning. That, too, was how long the guard would be knocked out by the oterzine. Kellan's third accomplice, a woman, accompanied them as they made their way along the city's perimeter walkways to the base of the fifth suspension bridge. Kellan alone crossed, disappearing into the darkness that cloaked most of the bridge.

"Who's there?" demanded the guard at the end of the bridge.

"Kellan."

"Kellan," cried the guard in surprise. "What brings you across the bridge at this hour?"

"Brolin speaks too loud," whispered the woman, whose name was Karin. "The other guards will hear."

"Do not wake the entire city, Brolin," said Kellan. "I've a personal matter to discuss with you."

A few minutes later a soft whistle alerted them the way was clear.

"Stay low," cautioned Karin.

Kellan had backtracked halfway across the bridge. He waited for Brian, Paul, and Karin to join up with him. They were not far from the end of the bridge when Kellan stopped abruptly.

"Blast, no," he said under his breath.

They could all see what concerned Kellan. The guard who had been posted at the second bridge was wandering their way.

"Brolin?" he called out. "Brolin?"

"Has he seen the body?" whispered Paul.

"Not yet," said Kellan.

"Keep moving then," said Karin. "Our only hope is to beat him there."

They arrived at the end of the bridge at the same time.

"Kellan," cried the guard. "What is the meaning of this?" He shone his lantern into Paul's and Brian's faces. "The strangers! Kellan, no!" He reached for the whistle about his neck.

Brian flashed by Paul and Kellan. To Paul, it appeared as if Brian launched himself into the air six feet before the guard. The guard managed one blast on his whistle before Brian's right foot slammed into his chest and sent him sprawling to the ground. The guard started to rise, but in an instant, Brian was above him. He slammed the side of his hand into the base of the guard's neck. The guard slumped to the ground.

"Don't kill him," cried Kellan.

"I haven't," said Brian. "Now which way?"

"Follow me," cried Karin.

They followed the wall of rock to the east.

Less than fifteen seconds later, the sleepy silence of the city was shattered by the shrill blasts of more whistles. Lights came on everywhere.

"Do either of you have an ascama fiber-stub?" Paul asked, when they arrived at the mouth of the tunnel.

"No," said Kellan. "A light would make us too easy a target for an archer."

"They'll kill us?"

"If they think we have a chance of making it to the surface, yes!"

Without another word they entered the tunnel. The grade was steep but for the most part straight. They held hands to avoid being separated. Kellan, who led, used his free hand to probe the space before him with each step.

"The tunnel curves around here," he said, halting momentarily. "From this point on there are several turns and twists. We must stay to the right. That is the route that takes us out."

A voice echoed through the tunnel. "Kellan! This is madness! Think of all you betray."

An arrow struck the wall of the tunnel somewhere behind them.

"Don't stop for anything," cried Kellan.

Again a voice cried out. "The strangers twist your reason, Kellan. Believe in your faith!"

The tunnel narrowed as they continued on. Chunks of rock jutted out from both its sides and roof. Paul found it necessary to hold one hand out in front of his face to avoid being struck while keeping the other hand on the wall to his right to maintain his sense of direction. The rock was jagged and tore at the sinewy flesh of his hands and fingers.

"They gain, Kellan, they gain," cried Karin.

Paul glanced back. The dull yellow-green light of an ascama fiber lantern shone on the wall of the turn behind them.

"How much farther?" asked Paul.

"I'm not sure," said Kellan.

An arrow skipped off the wall of the turn and bounced at their feet. Paul froze.

Karin bumped him from behind. "Go!" she cried, pushing him.

The tunnel continued straight, then veered to the right and twisted upward. There was a hole above them and through it Paul could see a patch of star-peppered sky. He stood on tiptoe and found he could just reach the ground above. Brian and Kellan grabbed his wrists and pulled him up. In turn, he helped them lift Karin from the hole.

They stood in the northwest corner of Fief Salkird. Rising up behind them were the mountains that encircled the fief. Thirty miles across the valley the eastern end of these same mountains appeared as a wall of black shadow against the pre-dawn sky. To the southwest lights shone. They marked the town of Vlar.

"There is a road that runs east-west the length of the fief," said Paul. "It joins the towns of Vlar and Ispar. The land bridge joining Fief Salkird to Fief Karcan is located south of Ispar. We can cross there into Fief Karcan."

Kellan's eyes darted from Paul to the opening by their feet. "We must plug this opening first, though."

"Kellan's right, Paul," said Karin. "Our own people will pursue us until they fear discovery. You can be sure that among them will be our best archers."

They found a suitably large rock and bent to the task of rolling it into position. They were seconds away from completing their task when two hands and a head appeared through the opening.

"Kellan," a voice cried from within the tunnel. "Think of what you do! The blood of your people will be on your hands!"

Kellan looked once toward the opening, which was now just an edge of light along one curve of the rock, and then turned his head. "Let's get away from here," he said.

They had not traveled long on the road when a caravan of one hundred and fifty men and thirty horses approached them from the east. The men were tall. Paul realized they were Jarred, most likely soldiers of Duke Orsinc. They were armed with long bows. The two groups halted when they'd drawn within fifty feet of each other.

A man stepped forward of the rest of the soldiers. "What is

your business on the road at this early hour?'' he demanded.

Paul had to wonder at the accusatory tone. Had a state of emergency been declared and were the military captains now policing the fiefs?

"We are Jarred as you are," replied Paul. "We make our way to Ispar."

"Under whose orders?"

Paul gambled with his reply. "By orders of Duke Orsinc."

"I am Duke Orsinc's field captain," the man snapped. "I know of no such orders."

Duke Orsinc's field captain! Better fortune could not have come their way! Paul had met the field captain six months earlier when his father had hosted a series of meetings to discuss the threat posed by Lord Thyden.

"Forgive me, Field Captain, for I forget your name," he said. "Mine you will surely recognize. I am Paul Benjarth."

The field captain approached Paul and grabbed him by the chin. It was obvious he suspected a trick of some sort.

"Great Malhah," he cried at last, immediately letting go of Paul. "How is it possible? Last I heard you were killed in a fire on the Medoc Peninsula!"

"We have escaped death more times than I care to remember. But we came away with what we went after. We have knowledge of a force, a weapon, a creation, call it what you wish, that will crush Thyden's armies once and for all. We seek passage across the land bridge. We must get to the Eastern Mountains with all due haste."

"I'm afraid passage across the land bridge near Ispar is impossible, Paul. Thyden now controls that piece of land."

"Fief Karcan has fallen?"

"Fief Cerus, too. And I'm afraid it's only a matter of time before Thyden directs his forces against us. This contingent I lead is to reinforce our troops stationed along the land bridge near Vlar. Thyden has amassed troops across the way."

Had Kalin and Dimistre been too late?

"Tell me, Field Captain, how did the battle go? How did Thyden gain the advantage?"

"Our combined forces were at first able to contain his advance along Fief Karcan's western border. For a full day and night the battle raged with neither side gaining the advantage. Then from the east a force of several thousand men approached. At first, we thought them Jarred reinforcements, though we could not fathom where such numbers came from. But the soldiers were those of Thyden! Our armies hadn't a chance against such numbers. Some managed to flee across the land bridge or into the mountains of Fief Cerus. Most died in battle or were taken prisoner. For the life of me, Paul, I do not know how Thyden managed to bring so many troops in from the east. I can only surmise they overran the land bridges adjoining the Medoc Peninsula."

"They did not overrun the land bridges," said Paul. "Lords Marthan and Thyden built a suspension bridge beneath the land bridge joining Fief Karcan and the Medoc Peninsula. They crossed by way of it."

For a moment, Paul tried to imagine eleven thousand of Thyden's troops descending upon Castle Chalmet. *The bastards! If they've harmed my sister or mother!*

"Have you any news of the fates of those at Castle Chalmet?"

"Thyden brags of his schemes and conquests. He posts a crier on your side of the land bridge. My archers tell me they can shoot him down, but nothing would be gained from it, for Thyden would only send another forward. Illad is dead—a contest of some sort with Thyden. Your sister is alive, but her chosen fate is, perhaps, worse than a death sentence. She is to marry Thyden."

The news weighed heavily on Paul's heart. "Have you horses to spare, Field Captain? I must consult with Duke Orsinc this morning."

The order was given and four horses were led forward. Paul started to mount, then said, "I need two horsemen, Field Captain. None of my friends can ride . . . well enough."

Well enough. He had added those words to avoid having to fabricate an explanation why none of his friends could ride. All within the three fiefs had some experience on horseback. Yet not all rode well.

"Again, Paul," advised the field captain, "the land bridge is impassable. But there is a tunnel linking the easternmost peaks of our mountains with the Eastern Mountains. Duke Orsinc will guide you through it."

"Brian! Ride with me," instructed Paul. "Karin and Kellan, ride with the horsemen. Let us make haste to Ispar!"

The flat terrain of the valley floor enabled Paul and the others to see Ispar from afar. Actually, what they saw first was not the town proper but the twin towers flanking the gate to Castle Weslan. The castle was the town's stronghold. It had been built by the Jarred in the early years of their exile from Fief Karcan. For many years after its completion the Jarred chose to live behind its massive walls. Eventually, though, as their population outgrew the castle, a town sprang up outside it.

They slowed their horses to a half-gallop as they entered the town's boundary. A wide thoroughfare led to the castle. The field captain's two horsemen dismounted and spoke with the sentry beside the castle gate. That lad, in turn, vanished through a small door.

They did not wait long before they heard the strain of gears and the slap of chains that opened the gate, which was massive, both in height and width, and it swung outward. The horses were led back to allow for its sweep.

"Well, as I live and breathe," cried Duke Orsinc, his voice booming above the rumblings of the mechanism. "Paul Benjarth! I did not believe my ears when told you were here."

The duke strode through the gate with a long, springy step that belied his fifty-seven years of age. He shook Paul's hand vigorously. In turn, he nodded a welcome to Karin, Kellan, and Brian, then he motioned them all into the castle.

The size of Castle Weslan had impressed Paul even as he'd approached it from a distance. Its battlemented gray-black walls were sixty feet high. The bottom nine feet of stone was battered, allowing for missiles dropped from above to deflect outward against an enemy. Crenelated towers were at the castle's four corners, as well as at the midpoints of its walls. The tallest of these were the two towers flanking the gate. Atop each was the gold-and-silver banner of the Orsinc royal line.

Only after Paul had entered the castle was he able to appreciate its impregnability. Massive buttresses helped support and reinforce the castle wall, which was twenty feet thick. Besides the battlements on top, there were three tiers of balconies fronting loopholes. This staging ran along the wall's entire inside perimeter. Next followed a no-man's-land of ninety feet, then another wall only a few feet shorter than the other one. It, too, was battlemented and outfitted with loopholes. Missing were the round towers that punctuated the straight lines of the outer wall. Its timber gate was smaller and lifted vertically.

Once through the second gate, Paul found himself at one end of a narrow courtyard measuring forty feet by three hundred feet. Walls twenty feet high ran its full length. Carvings in bas-relief punctuated the expanse of stone. Doors opened onto corridors every twenty-five feet.

"Those Jarred ancestors of ours who built Castle Weslan," explained the duke, "always feared the return of the Sinese and Phlogin armies that had driven them from Artan. As you know, it never happened." The duke's face clouded over. "But perhaps the efforts of our forefathers have not been in vain."

Then, almost in a whisper, he said, "We must talk in my study, Paul. Is this okay?"

Paul knew what Duke Orsinc meant. He wanted to separate him from his friends so he could speak to him in private. Paul nodded.

"Have you had breakfast?" Duke Orsinc asked the others. His enthusiasm made one think the remark had been more a sudden inspiration than a general question.

"None of us have," replied Brian.

"Then you must eat!" He called out to one of his guard captains and the man came at a run. "See to it that these three have breakfast. All they can eat."

The guard captain nodded and bid the others follow him.

"I will have breakfast brought to my study for you," Duke Orsinc said to Paul.

A messenger approached and handed Duke Orsinc a piece of paper. The duke read the memo, then dismissed the messenger.

"You must know, of course, that both Fief Karcan and Fief Cerus have fallen."

"I learned of it only this morning."

"Only this morning!" Duke Orsinc was incredulous. "How can that be? Were you not involved in the battle?" The duke did not let Paul answer. "No, wait. You went on a mission to the Medoc Peninsula. Cartag, wasn't it? I mean to ask you about that journey. But how did you arrive here? Thyden sealed off the land bridges yesterday."

They began to walk. Duke Orsinc opened a door and they entered a vaulted corridor.

"Those who managed to slip across the land bridge nearest this castle were but a few ranchers and your surgeon, Farant."

"Farant? Surgeon Farant is here?"

"In Vlar, yes."

They entered an inner courtyard through a side entrance. There was a small, shallow, square-sided pool of water in the center of the courtyard. Irregularly shaped stones of brown, sand, tan, and white made a jigsaw pattern on the sides and bottom of the pool, as well as the courtyard floor itself. Four small shade trees grew by the pool's corners.

Paul paused a moment by the pool and thought again of the wound inflicted upon his great-great-grandfather. It would be wise to have a surgeon with them, especially one of Farant's skill. Why, it could mean the difference between returning from Calferon alive or not at all!

"Can you spare Surgeon Farant?" he asked Duke Orsinc.

"He is a subject of yours, Paul. As such, he is yours to command."

"But if he is still needed to tend to the wounded at Vlar?"

"Those the surgeons could save have already been operated on."

"Would you send a messenger for him immediately? One of your swiftest riders?"

"Of course."

Duke Orsinc's chambers were off the courtyard. Paul was ushered into the den, where he settled down into the deep folds of a cozy armchair. The duke sat across from him on the edge of his desk.

"I am, naturally, curious as to the reason behind your quest."

"Do you remember," began Paul, "in the time of your own great-grandfather, an expedition put together to search for a stairway to Calferon? That search party comprised three men from each of the three fiefs. Those from Fief Karcan included my great-great-grandfather."

"I know of that history. However, I attach no special significance to it. All were killed, were they not?"

"All except my great-great-grandfather."

"That's right. I remember that. There was some sort of accident."

"A slide." Paul paused momentarily. "Or so it was reported."

Duke Orsinc cupped his thumbs under his chin and ran his fingers up across his mouth to the base of his nose. "You seem to doubt your great-great-grandfather's report. Why is that?"

"It is too convenient an explanation. My Benerit-woman always thought so, too. There are things I've been privy to with respect to that history."

"Such as?"

"The medical files for Duke Whitin. He'd lost a great deal of blood by the time he made it back to Castle Chalmet. Our surgeons thought it a miracle he was still alive. He'd suffered a deep puncture wound to the right side of his abdomen."

"The kind a knife would inflict?"

"That . . . or an arrow . . . or the claw of a beast."

Duke Orsinc stood. "The claw of a beast?"

Paul went on to remind Duke Orsinc of the facts concerning Duke Whitin's behavior upon his return from Calferon: his self-imposed isolation, his abdication of the throne, and the return of his body years later by loggers he'd befriended.

"So the truth of what happened on Calferon went to the grave with him."

"Not quite." Paul told Duke Orsinc of the medallion Duke Whitin had brought back. "Inadvertently, the medallion fell into Thyden's hands. I made the journey to Castle Greyfahren myself and retrieved it."

"Castle Greyfahren? You must tell me of that journey!"

Paul related all that had happened. However, he was careful to modify the end of his story so as to honor his confidence with Kellan and Karin that he would not betray the existence of their city. Instead he claimed they'd worked their way back to the Angena Mountains, found a route through, and made their way along the northern edge of the plain to the mountains of Fief Salkird.

When Paul had finished, Duke Orsinc remarked, "I am

most curious to see this medallion."

Paul had only a second to think up a fabrication before his pause would arouse the suspicions of someone as perceptive as his host. The medallion was in his pocket. Simon Seagarth had returned it to him, seeing no harm in his keeping it, but Paul was wary of showing it to Duke Orsinc because he would ask about the key, and it would become increasingly more difficult not to tell him of Kellan's people and the assembly they had built there to open it. "It has been . . . cast into the sky-void."

"What?"

"But not," Paul was quick to add, "until after it had been opened by us. We felt it safer if we were not carrying it on our persons. It contained a map, Duke Orsinc, a map showing the location of the stairway to the planet's surface. From the bottom of the stairway a dashed line ran northwest. The trail's end my great-great-grandfather indicated with a circle and exclamation points. There, I believe, lies the power that can aid us in our battle against Thyden. The map I've committed to memory. What I ask, Duke Orsinc, is passage to the Eastern Mountains."

"The land bridge is controlled by Thyden's men."

"There's a tunnel through the mountains to the east, isn't there? Will you show us its source?"

Duke Orsinc's answer was slow in coming. "How do you know of that tunnel?"

Paul related when and where the field captain had told him of its existence. Then, almost in the same breath, he added, "I will need supplies. Rope, food, tools."

"They will be provided."

Duke Orsinc paused as if in thought before pursuing a comment Paul had made earlier. "You mentioned that Duke Whitin's wound may have been made by the claw of a beast. A most curious remark. What did you mean by it?"

Paul realized he would again have to be careful of what he said. "I heard the sound when crossing the sky-void encircling Castle Greyfahren." He described the sound as best he could. "It came from the east and from the planet's surface. Who knows what type of creature made it? But I daresay we will find out."

The nonchalance with which he spoke those final words hardly mirrored the terror he felt about undertaking a journey to Calferon. Certainly a man knew fear when he engaged an opponent on the battlefield, but it was nothing like the fear he experienced when he went up against the unknown.

CHAPTER 17

———

The journey to the eastern tip of Fief Karcan took two days. It was now noon of the third day.

"See anything?" Paul asked Kellan.

Since sunup Paul and Kellan had sat on the eastern slope of a hill overlooking the fief's perimeter and stared at a wall of swirling sand. Powerful updrafts from the planet's surface lifted sand and other particulate matter and swirled it in a counterclockwise direction. The net effect was that a curtain of sand nearly a mile across obscured their view of the sky-void. Occasionally the wind slackened. At those infrequent moments a window of visibility ten to twenty feet opened in the curtain. But like an opening in a void, everything was quickly sucked into it until nothing but a wall of windblown sand faced them again.

"Nothing," replied Kellan.

Paul knew the stairway was near. That was what was so frustrating! The southern base of the hill they sat atop bordered the path Duke Whitin had indicated on the map. The line had then curled to the north and twisted outward.

Kellan stood up and stretched. "I think we'd have better luck toward evening," he said. "The wind might die down then."

Paul disagreed. "But we watched last night from the mouth

of the cave! Why should it be any different tonight?"

Kellan's eyes flashed. Paul had no right to raise his voice to him. "That was nightfall," he said. "I'm talking about *late afternoon*. Just as the sun starts to set."

Paul dismissed Kellan's suggestion as nonsense with a wave of his hand.

"Well, then what?" cried Kellan, no less impatient than Paul to see some evidence of the stairway's existence. "What do you suggest we do?"

Kellan's words exploded in Paul's head. "The only thing we can do," he shouted back.

In a flash he was running down the hill.

Unfortunately the nearer Paul got to the base of the hill the deeper the sand was piled. When he was no longer able to run, he tried leaping on his toes like an animal, springing from one spot to the next. It was awkward and he fell, sliding forward, elbows out in front of him until they plowed up enough sand to stop him. Damn it! Damn it! Damn it! The bastard stuff was everywhere! It was in their clothes, their food, their hair, their mouths. Didn't the wind ever stop blowing?

Paul rolled on his back and raised his head. He could see Kellan standing atop the rise, watching him. How odd he looked, he thought. The awkward contours of his body were accentuated because of the angle from which he viewed him. He was a tall, gawky fellow with a narrow, angular face that was always thrust slightly forward of his torso by his long neck. Yet he was remarkably coordinated and strong, possessing a fluidity of motion that seemed impossible for one with his physique.

There was tension between them that they did their best to subdue. Paul knew its source. They were both under a lot of pressure. Kellan shouldered a lot of guilt in fleeing his people. He feared capture and the betrayal of his people through an injection of styranotide. Thus, he was possessed with a sense of urgency to get to Calferon, because there he would be beyond Lord Thyden's reach. Whatever dangers he faced then at least did not carry the risk of betraying his people. Kellan's constant input into their plans Paul sometimes thought ludicrous, because Kellan had never set foot on above ground. *So what was his claim to expertise in guiding them to the stairway!*

Paul got to his feet and plodded down the slope. He was met at the base of the hill by Thoren, one of three men Duke Orsinc had handpicked for the mission.

"Have you seen the stairway?" Thoren asked.

Paul looked up into Thoren's hard, gray-green eyes. The man was so huge, so solid! He'd be as immovable as a spear of rock in that swirling maelstrom.

"No, nothing," he said in answer. He turned to the sand wall. "I will need a volunteer to go with me."

There was no hesitation in Thoren's voice. "You've got one."

Careful thought had gone into the selection of clothing for their journey to Calferon. It was believed the planet was a wind-swept wasteland, so one-piece outfits had been chosen. Paul had been amused by Brian's word for such clothing. "Jumpsuits" he'd called them. Boots had been selected that rode halfway up the calf, for they would prevent sand from spilling over in all but the deepest drifts. Tight-fitting caps were provided with straps that snapped around the chin. One hundred bands of porous cloth, each one wide enough to cover a man's nose and mouth, had been packed away. So, too, had two dozen pairs of goggles.

Paul and Thoren helped each other adjust their goggles and knot the cloth strips behind their heads. Meanwhile, the others looped all but one hundred feet of a coil of rope around a stump of flattened rock that rose from the floor of a cave at the base of the hill Paul and Kellan had climbed. The end of the rope would be secured to Paul; fifteen feet back it would be secured to Thoren. The rope would be let out one loop at a time as Thoren signaled for it. This he would do by tugging on the rope three times. Brian would stand at the edge of the sand wall awaiting Thoren's signal. When he felt Thoren's tug, he would alert Farant (who would be standing by the cave's mouth) with a wave of his hand. In turn, Farant would signal Rogger and John, who, like Thoren, had been hand-picked by Duke Orsinc for this mission, to uncoil a single loop of rope. Karin's job was to watch Kellan, who stood lookout atop the hill, and alert the others if he were to signal that soldiers were coming. If that signal were to be given, Brian would follow the rope into the sand wall and alert Thoren and Paul.

They did a trial sequence. Paul and Thoren walked twenty feet into the sand wall. For the most part the sand swallowed them up, though at times their shapes were visible to the others. All went smoothly and Paul and Thoren emerged from the swirling sand to signal that this time it was for real.

Suddenly Karin cupped her hands to her mouth and shouted something. The wind roared up at that moment, and Paul couldn't hear what she had said. He looked up at Kellan but saw he was making no signal. The wind swirled and for a moment Karin became but a shadow as the sand enveloped him and Thoren. Paul felt its suction and leaned away from it. This had been the reason for such caution in entering the sand wall. The wind was strong enough to sweep them both into the sky-void if they were not secured to the rope. The wind died momentarily.

"Be careful!" he heard Karin yell.

Smiling, Paul signaled with his hand that he'd heard her, then he and Thoren turned into the sand wall.

They moved forward with careful, deliberate steps. For the most part Paul stared down at the ground, making sure there was solid footing before taking a step forward. Looking ahead gained him nothing because the visibility was so limited. Only when he heard the wind ebb would he glance ahead with the hope that there would be a temporary window through the swirling sand. And always he was aware of the wind's pull.

It was his fear of being swept into the sky-void that prevented Paul from losing his concentration. Both the constant roar of the wind and the abrasive whipping sound of the sand across their clothing tended to dull the senses by overstimulation. The goggles, too, allowed for imperfect vision. The process from which they were formed—baking out of a woven disk of the stem fibers of the makraw-leaf plant—was an imperfect science. Over a controlled fire, the clear, fibrous disk bubbled up to form a lens. But the bubbled curvature of the lens was never perfect. Tiny ripples in the lens caused areas of slight viewing distortion. These all combined to give Paul an eerie feeling of detachment. It was as if he were encapsulated in some sort of shell and viewing everything from within.

The rock began to form ledges and drop, stairlike, away at his feet. He sensed he was near the edge of the fief. The wind died down momentarily and Paul suddenly had fifteen feet of forward visibility. The sky-void lay six feet ahead. He edged closer. He had to be able to distinguish where the ledge met the sky-void even when the sand was being whipped in front of his eyes. It was important. It would be the only way he'd know when he came across a protrusion of land extending out into the void. Otherwise he might continue north right past it.

He moved still closer to the edge of the fief. The suction was strong here and he leaned into the slope. They would move laterally now to the north. Paul put one foot forward of the other and slowly made his way along the ledge in this manner.

Suddenly the wind gusted fiercely. Paul's feet slid out from under him and he felt the rope go taut about his waist. The ledge sloped downward into the sky-void at this point and while Thoren anchored himself, Paul used the tension of the rope to move laterally across this slippery spot.

Gradually Paul lost his sense of time. He was not sure how long he and Thoren had been within the sand wall and could only venture a guess. Two hours? Certainly not several hours. The sand wall had not darkened, which would certainly occur when the sun swung around to the west and dipped below the towering peaks of the Eastern Mountains.

All of a sudden the wind whipped up with a roar that was deafening. Paul felt his hands being pulled from the rock he'd grabbed and he realized in helpless terror that he was being sucked toward the void. The wind whipped his body over and he rolled twice on the rock before the rope tethered to Thoren pulled taut and held him. He was two feet from the void and staring straight into it.

The wind ebbed momentarily and a window opened in the sand. He had sixty, maybe seventy, feet of forward visibility. Out of the corner of his eye, to the north, he saw the bridge. He lifted his head from the rock and stared at it. He noted its features and was amazed by how thin a piece of land it was. It looked to be no more than four feet thick. It was without railing or sides and appeared to move outward into the sky-void on a level plane.

Paul crawled to where Thoren stood. "I've seen it," he shouted above the wind. "It's to the north! We've no more than sixty feet to go!"

The wind roared as it had moments before when Paul had lost his footing by the fief's edge. Both men crouched low and waited out its fury. Although the wind always blew, there seemed an ebb and flow to its strength. As it began to ebb, Paul scampered back across the rocks to the fief's edge.

He knew immediately when he'd taken his first step upon the bridge. The rock was different. It was perfectly flat. So flat and smooth, in fact, that he half entertained the capricious notion that he could slide the length of the bridge on his belly if Thoren were to give him a strong enough push. Unfortunately he knew the crossing would not be that easy. The wind blew with gale force from north to south. He couldn't stand, kneel, or crawl. There simply were not any fingerholds. He lay belly down on the stone, allowing his left arm and left leg to overhang the bridge and grip its north edge. Were he to lose his grip or his left leg come free, the force of the wind would whip him around ninety degrees. He brought his left leg forward, then pushed off against the side of the bridge and slid forward three feet.

The snail-like pace of their crossing did not discourage Paul. Quite to the contrary, he was more encouraged than ever with each push forward. The reason for his enthusiasm was that the wind seemed to blow with less force the farther onto the bridge he moved. Soon it became little more than a brisk breeze. At that point, Paul knelt and removed his goggles.

He thought: *I kneel in the eye of a storm!*

He remembered that phrase from his talks with Brian. They had discussed weather patterns on his world, hurricanes, to be exact. The eye of this storm looked to be three hundred yards across. The beginning to the stairway, marked by two ten-foot pillars of stone, was centered in the core of the swirling sand cylinder. The sand wall rose two thousand feet above them before it spilled back over. Most of the sand particles were immediately swept back up again, swirled counterclockwise and lifted. But a bit of sand spilled too far out to be swept up again and these particles rained down within the cylinder. Above the core was blue sky. Sunlight, which slanted in from the southwest, colored the sand grains above and to the east in bright shades of gold and yellow. Below where the sun's rays struck directly the colors darkened—first amber, then ecru, then brown, then finally a shadowy gray. Somewhere far below, in the bottomless pit that was the core of the cylinder, the western arc of the sand wall lightened again. It was at this point that the sun was below the horizon line of their aerial world.

Thoren knelt beside Paul. He had removed the cloth band about his nose and mouth as well as his goggles. "What do you make of all this, Paul?"

Paul removed the cloth band from about his own nose and mouth. "It's beyond words! It truly is!"

Thoren was less awed than curious. "I would have imagined it a flat wall of sand. I mean, being formed by updrafts from the planet's surface I would not have thought it a cylinder." Thoren had been staring ahead at the swirling sand and the end of the stairway as he'd spoken. Now he turned his gaze on Paul. "Do you think it natural or manmade?"

Oddly, that question awoke a parallel but very different train of thought in Paul. *The sand cylinder was the throat of the beast! Was the beast natural or manmade?*

"Do you think it natural or manmade?" repeated Thoren.

"I don't know," Paul stammered, still distracted by the strangeness of his own thoughts.

Thoren tugged on the rope three times. "Those pillars look like a good place to tie the rope."

The stairway had existed in Paul's mind in many forms. Since Arnun had first spoken of it, his imagination had tried to construct this view from its very first step. He realized now that he might as well have been trying to imagine a slab of unworked stone when reality was a magnificently carved statue.

"It's amazing, isn't it?" he said aloud to Thoren, his eyes never once glancing up.

Thoren could only nod his head in agreement. Then, with a grin, he said, "You wouldn't want to lose your footing on these stairs."

Paul's smile was a purge of all the stresses, fears, and doubts of the past several days. That smile was an acknowledgment of their victory. They had conquered the sand wall and found the staircase. Another man might have screamed out his joy at the top of his lungs. Paul only turned to Thoren and replied, "No, you wouldn't, would you?" But it felt the same.

They studied the stairway further and realized that it had been carved from a single shaft of crohephite rock fifteen feet in diameter. The stairs had been cut around the outside of the shaft in a spiral pattern. Each step was wide and deep and shielded by a three-foot-high wall running along the outer edge of the stairway. It was narrow enough to serve as a hand-rail, though erosion had left its top edge jagged and sharp.

"How do you suppose it was built?" Thoren asked.

Paul had pondered that mystery himself. Crohephite rock formed about core-vines, so at the center of this shaft there had to be one or two core-vines. "What amazes me, Thoren, is the growth of the core-vines. Core-vines do not normally grow downward, not without curling back up or branching out. Any good bit of wind will bend them around."

After a short, thoughtful pause, Thoren replied, "Perhaps they didn't grow downward."

CHAPTER 18

The next morning Paul gave final instructions outside the cave. "The rope angles to the northeast, then cuts straight across the bridge. Thoren and I used two shorter lengths of rope in order to turn the rope just before the bridge. They are tied to the rock and go off to the right. If we all stay to the left, we'll avoid getting tangled in those ropes. Use the rope to pull yourself forward. Only when you get to the end of the bridge, to the pillars marking the beginning of the stairway, is it safe to remove cloth and goggles. Any questions?"

"What's to be done with the rope after we cross?" asked Kellan. "If Lord Thyden were to discover it . . ."

Paul had given that concern a lot of thought. "It is doubtful Thyden will send patrols this far east," he said. "Not without cause. Duke Orsinc is the only one who knows of our journey; only if Thyden learns of it from him are we in danger. We've all seen Castle Weslan—its defenses, its battlements. Duke Orsinc's people will be able to hold out far longer than our provisions will allow us to stay on Calferon." He returned his gaze to Kellan. "The rope remains. We'd wander endlessly in the sand wall without it to guide us back out."

The mouth of the cave and the ground before it were in deep shadow. When Paul and Thoren had entered the sand wall yesterday, it had been early afternoon. The sun had been at their backs, penetrating the sand wall just enough to give some definition to the ground and the sky-void. Now the sand wall was like a veil and to pass through it was to enter a gray twilight. They could not even see the ground at their feet. The best they could do was poke at the stone with their toes until sure of the footing ahead.

Paul feared the others might panic. Not that they were at serious bodily risk if suddenly overcome by such a state of mind. Each of them had a safety line looped around the crossing rope. What Paul worried more would happen was that one of them might become so disoriented he or she would freeze. The subsequent delay in their crossing would be serious. They had to descend to the planet's surface while there was still daylight, because it would be too dangerous to attempt any portion of the descent after nightfall.

Paul reached the first of the turning ropes. Squatting as low to the ground as possible to avoid being whipped forward by the wind, he untied his safety line and secured it on the other side of the turning rope. Soon he reached the intersection of the second turning rope, and finally the bridge. Here he slipped beneath the rope, crouched, and waited. He was to help guide each of the others onto the narrow rock of the bridge. One by one they filed past him. Thoren brought up the rear, and when he had passed Paul stepped onto the bridge himself.

Paul found the view atop the stairway no less incredible the second time around. He turned to Karin, who could only nod in speechless appreciation.

Just then the swirling wall of sand darkened. Paul realized a cloud had passed in front of the sun. His thoughts became more sober as he recalled his great-great-grandfather's journey to Calferon. Why hadn't Duke Whitin told anyone what he had found? Was it a horror so ghastly that it couldn't be formed into words? Or had he been afraid of the panic such knowledge would cause among those living here?

Karin seemed attuned to his thoughts, for she asked him, "What do you think lives on the planet's surface? I have heard it scream many times from the rail along the north perimeter of my city. Did you hear it the night you were there?"

"Yes."

"Do you fear it?"

Paul nodded. "It killed many years ago."

The sun was a hazy glow against the east wall of the sand cylinder when they began their descent. They rested six times, once to take nourishment. As they neared the planet's surface they were plunged into deep shadow as the sun, now midway across the southwestern sky, dipped behind the lands now far above them.

It was at this point that Paul thought he saw motion at the bottom of the staircase. Something was spinning. *Or was it?* It was difficult to tell with the sand cylinder itself swirling around them. He paused in his descent.

"What's happening down there?" cried Thoren, who brought up the rear.

They had all stopped.

"A moment, please," Paul shouted back.

"Paul? What's wrong?" asked Karin.

"Look at the base of the stairs. Do you see motion? I mean other than that of the sand wall?"

She stepped down beside Paul. "Something spins down there. The stairs descend into the center of it."

When they were five hundred feet above Calferon, Paul realized what he was looking at. It was a massive wheel whose diameter had to be in the neighborhood of three hundred feet. The top of the wheel was covered by a plate opened only along its edge and center. Sand sat atop this plate, continually being swirled and redeposited in little wind twisters caused by the mix of air currents there. Curtains of sand blasted upward from the circumferential edge of the wheel, rushing past the party with such velocity that it sucked the air inside the core upward. Their descent from this point was like walking into gale-force winds. The wheel's hub was only a few feet in diameter and protruded above the plate. The stairs descended into it.

"Do you see what it does?" cried Kellan, who had stepped past Karin and now stood beside Paul. "The wheel creates the sand wall! It spins the air up!"

Paul descended alone into the hub. He found himself in a cylindrical chamber thirty feet high and fifteen feet in diameter. Its wall was spinning so fast that its motion was a blur. Light entered only through that one small hole in the hub's center. For that reason the bottorward, lodging em of the hub was darker than the top. The stairs, which up to this point had spiraled around a central core of crohephite rock, now dropped straight, ladderlike, and ended at the bottom of the floorless hub. Paul climbed to the lowermost rung of the ladder and peered into the hole beneath the hub. The roar of the wheel's motion was deafening. He could see nothing because of the swirling sand being sucked up into the hub. He climbed back up the ladder, removing his goggles and the cloth band about his nose and mouth when he emerged.

"We will enter the hub one at a time," he instructed the others. "Be careful not to fix your gaze on the spinning wall. It may make some of you dizzy and cause you to lose your footing. Some sand is being sucked into the hub from beneath, so put your goggles on just before you enter. The same with the cloth band. It's too difficult to do it while holding onto the ladder."

Paul reentered the hub and descended to the bottom of the ladder. There he lowered himself until he was hanging from the final rung. His lower body was rocked back and forth by the turbulence. He tried to still the motion of his legs, to arch his feet, to touch the sand beneath the wheel, but the wind was too strong and he couldn't hold his legs straight. He let go of the rung.

The drop was eighteen inches.

The wind rolled him over. Twice he tried to stand but was knocked down. Once on his feet, he ran bowlegged, his steps falling wide and to the outside to better his balance against the swirling winds. He tried to run in a straight path. To follow a radius vector would be the shortest route out, but the wind gusted with such force that he found himself running in whichever direction he could. When the wind was at his back, he was swept forward; when it was against him, he was driven back or to the side. At length, he saw a rim of lighter sand to his right. Determined not to be blown back to the wheel's center, he lowered his head and, leaning into the wind, rward, lodging erward, lodging each foot well into the sand to prevent himself from being pushed back.

The wind kicked out from beneath the wheel, forming huge, rolling, mushrooming clouds of sand. Paul had to move away a good one hundred yards to get clear of them. It was from that distance that he could truly appreciate the grandeur of what he saw.

"It's a fan wheel," exclaimed Brian above the roar of the swirling winds. He had emerged from beneath the wheel near Paul and now stood beside him. He pointed as he explained the fan's workings to Paul. "See how the wind is blocked off there? It can only be funneled in through here, and then it simply passes straight through and out. The vanes must be cut on an angle to throw the air upward and through a slot that must ring the perimeter of the fan housing. That was its hub we passed through, where the walls were tight about us. The fan itself must float upon some central bearing that allows it to turn with minimal friction. But look at the size of this thing! It's enormous! The momentum the mass of the fan must generate would probably allow it to continue to spin for days even if the wind were to stop."

Paul didn't follow all that Brian had said, but Brian's familiarity with the subject of fans and airflow made him wonder. Had he been wrong? Could this—and not Palastrides—be Brian's world? "Are these structures akin to your world?" he asked Brian.

"We have the technology to build such," said Brian. "But"—Brian's voice trailed off and Paul had to strain to hear him—"I've never seen pictures or read of any." He turned his back to Paul.

Paul went to put his hand on Brian's shoulder but stopped short. He didn't really know what to say to Brian to comfort him. All along Brian had been convinced that this was *his* world. All along he had doubted Paul's story about being catapulted through space within the Saulcar Mass. Paul knew he was confused now. "We should find the others," he said.

Paul's spir they started out across the windblown terrain. It was dusk of the fourth day since they had set out from Castle Weslan. He thought their progress good. There had been no mishaps and they had all emerged unscathed from beneath the fan wheel. He was encouraged, too, as hopeful as he'd ever been, that they would find a power to crush Thyden.

The fan wheel and the stairway were creations of a civilization more advanced than his own. Even Brian had been
amazed by them. And his was a civilization that could manu-
facture a bomb capable of destroying Fief Karcan in a single
detonation!

Suddenly Karin grabbed Paul's arm. The procession halted.
"What is it?" asked Thoren.

The sound had always been there. Paul would realize this in
a moment of hindsight. The noise of the fan wheel sucking in
and discharging air, as well as the swirling winds of the sand
cylinder, had simply been louder and drowned the other out.
The sound came again. This time it seemed a little louder.
Paul knew it to be the same sound he and Brian had heard
from the hanging room of Kellan's city.

"It comes from the direction we travel," said Rogger, his
bulging eyes attesting to his fright.

They all looked toward Paul, unsure whether to continue.

"We must go on," said Paul. There was not a great deal of
conviction in his voice and he certainly didn't feel fearless issuing that command. The thought of Duke Whitin Benjarth returning wounded and alone was foremost in his mind. "Be
ready on your crossbows," he advised them.

Again the sound rose in their ears. Paul leaned into the
wind and forced himself to take a step forward. Soon they
were all trudging across the sand, drawing ever nearer to the
source of power indicated on Duke Whitin's ancient map.
They made camp that night at the foot of a narrow ridge.
Sand was piled in a semicircle radiating outward from its east
side, and the hollow between rock and sand was seven feet
deep in places.

They slept fretfully that night, perhaps Paul most of all. He
was plagued by a recurring nightmare. Duke Whitin was running across the sand toward him. He was wounded and blood
gushed from an opening in his belly. Paul stood atop the drift
by the ridge, too frozen with fear to run and help him. His
great-great-grandfather stopped frequently and tried to shout
something to him, but each time he cupped his hands to his
mouth the sound rose up from behind him and drowned out
his voice. The sound itself caused the duke to fall prostrate to
the sand. He would get up again after it passed, run forward a

little more, try to shout again. Paul knew Duke Whitin was trying to warn him of something, of a danger, of what the sound meant. But when the duke finally made it to the foot of the drift and stood but a few feet in front of him, the wind whipped up and the sand engulfed him. When the winds subsided, he was gone.

They prepared breakfast in the hollow by the ridge. The meal of unspiced capoi bread and dried vegetable bits was cold and tasteless. They finished quickly and soon were on their way. They used the sun's position to plot a course northwest, the direction indicated on Duke Whitin's map. And they were mindful of its orbit across the sky, adjusting their relative position to it accordingly. They passed one ridge and made the shelter of another by noon. All the while, the sound grew steadily louder. Not one of them doubted they would know its source before nightfall.

They had been journeying several hours when the sound roared with such volume that Rogger and Farant dove to the sand as if something had been fired just above their heads. They were all convinced it came from the next ridge, which was now a shadow rising up from the desert floor half a mile away.

Paul selected Brian and Thoren to accompany him. All had volunteered to go, but Paul knew it foolish to select more than two to accompany him on the final leg of their journey. Thoren was by far the strongest, a bull of a man who looked capable of carrying their entire two weeks' provisions on his broad shoulders. Brian was an able fighter. Still vivid in Paul's mind was the image of Brian leaping through the air and striking down the guard at the end of the suspension bridge.

They plodded toward the ridge, sand gripping their feet. The wind blew stiffly and they had to lean into it to make headway.

Thoren was the first to reach the ridge and explore its backside. "It's from beyond this ridge," he told them.

Paul climbed the east face of the rock until he was some fifty feet above the ground. There was a split in the rock that afforded him a view to the west. The sun was low in the southwestern sky and it tinted the windblown sand ahead yellowish orange. His forward visibility, despite his elevated position, was no more than half a mile.

Just then the sound blasted with such force that Paul clutched the rock as if the sheer volume of the sound alone could toss him from his precarious perch. A window opened in the sand and Paul could see another ridge some distance ahead. Then, as if that ridge were suddenly consumed by a swirling wall of fire, the blowing sand engulfed it and it disappeared from view.

Paul trembled as he climbed down. The sound had come from behind the ridge. He was sure of it, if only because that ridge was markedly different from the other ridges they'd stopped at. It was narrower, so narrow, in fact, that it seemed to be more an upthrust of a single angular stone than a broken series of them. It was taller, too, twice as tall. They reshouldered their gear and began their trek across that final stretch of sand.

Paul's fears churned the sea of his imagination. The beast that had clawed his great-great-grandfather waited for them behind the ridge. Even now it watched them, the side of its massive body pressing against the rock as one unblinking eye peered around the edge. Paul realized how foolish a weapon was his crossbow. It would be difficult if not impossible to string it in these windy conditions. Nor could he shoot it accurately into such a strong head wind. He sensed the beast knew this. It knew the Benjarth would be forced to fight up close with their puny knives. It was a fight the howling monster welcomed.

Paul was the first to step upon the rock that formed a flooring in front of the ridge. He threw down his pack and ran to the ridge wall. He drew his knife from its sheath and raised it to eye level.

The sound came again. This time it shook the rock they stood upon.

Paul had never known fear this intense. His body acted as if it were fused to the rock he leaned against. It was only with great effort that he was able to peel himself away from it and sidestep to the edge of the stone. He fought down a deep breath. Even his lungs seemed frozen, not wanting to accept the air that would provide him the energy to step around the corner. His knife seemed flimsy in his hand, useless. He moved his left foot first, curling it around the narrow edge of the stone. He gulped down another breath of air, then he brought his other foot around.

He was face-to-face with the beast.

CHAPTER 19

Lord Thyden rose from Duke Jaiman's enormous bed. The lifeless body of a Benjarth lieutenant lay slumped against the ropes that had bound him to a chair. For a moment, Lord Thyden stared scornfully at the lieutenant. He'd been no challenge at all, a waste of his precious cymethadrenatyne.

He opened the door. "Dispose of the lieutenant's body," he commanded the two guards he'd posted there.

Across the hall, the gaze of a serving woman dropped. She turned and started to enter the bedroom there.

"Stay," commanded Lord Thyden.

Lady Benjarth's serving woman, Enit, halted in the archway of her lady's bedroom.

"Turn around, old woman. I'm not in the habit of talking to my subjects' backs."

Enit turned slowly, her eyes glued to the floor.

"Does the floor speak to you?"

Enit raised her gaze and met his.

"You needn't tremble so. I'll not harm you or your lady. Her life was a promise I made to a friend."

"She is dying."

"So must we all. Do what you can to prolong her life."

"Her will to live is gone. To see her husband again would

return the desire."

"Lady Benjarth was a fool to be swept off her feet by such an insipid man as the duke! She'd have been better off had she married her first lover . . . Surgeon Farant."

"Surgeon Farant?"

The puzzled look on Enit's face surprised Lord Thyden. "She's not shared that confidence with you?" He smiled. "Perhaps she knows the character of your tongue better than I."

"I've never betrayed a confidence of my lady," Enit said indignantly.

Lord Thyden grinned. He felt a perverse delight in sparring with the serving woman. "Perhaps that is because she gave you few confidences to betray."

Enit said nothing.

"Cat got your tongue, my dear? Hmmm? Well, I trust you," he kidded. "So I will share a little confidence with you. Before your lady married Duke Jaiman, she and Farant were lovers. Although Farant was studying medicine, he and your lady shared a love of the arts. Both were painters. I daresay they would, to this day, be married and raising a family in Fief Cerus, a quaint and dull existence to be sure. However, one Farant would have preferred to the tortured life he's lived without her. The duke swept her out of his life! She was more in love with the duke's title and riches at first, but who knows, perhaps something grew from their union. I note the separate bedrooms with amusement."

"It was a temporary arrangement."

Lord Thyden grinned. "I'm sure it was."

Nothing more was said between them. Enit turned and re-entered her lady's bedroom. Lord Thyden started to call after her, but then thought better of it. An injection of styranotide would confirm or deny his suspicions. There was no reason to spook her. Perhaps it was nothing, but her face seemed familiar.

Lord Thyden made his way down a staircase and across an inner courtyard. He entered Gierfahren's Hall through a side door, crossed the hall, and stopped before an open pair of doors. There he surveyed with satisfaction the great hall adjoining Gierfahren's Hall. He couldn't remember the Ben-

jarth name for it, but that hardly concerned him. He would
rename both halls to his liking. What impressed him was its
size and grandeur. He felt it perfect for his and Christina's
wedding.

A chill rippled through his body even though no drafts blew
through the halls. "So, my bastard father, you come to haunt
me again! Well, have you seen her? The Benjarth child? Oh, I
daresay you have, floating around in whatever vacuum Fate
assigns us with death. Oh, you can see it all, more than I can,
I'm sure. Yet how does it feel, Father, to be able to look but
not touch? Have you seen the soft curves of her flesh as you
pass like a gentle wind through her garments? It is I who will
know the feel of that flesh! I, Father, I! Are you envious? I
daresay you are. Hah! Now leave me. I've things to think
over."

The sense of his father's presence vanished as he concentrated on imagining the wedding ceremony that would be per-
formed within the hall. It was certainly large enough for a
great many guests. Carpets would have to be laid down,
though, flowers picked and set in vases, and the windows
would have to be decorated. Perhaps something frilly? He
wasn't sure. Women were good at that sort of thing. Let the
seamstresses come up with something special for the occasion.

For a moment, an image of Christina lingered in his mind
and he savored it. Indeed she was as beautiful as Farant had
boasted. Her hair was as black as night's shadow and her eyes
were of the deepest brown. Those eyes! Such passion raged
beneath them. And that passion could be molded with the
proper doses of malinophorm and voalaline.

"Think of it," he had once told Farant. They had met only
once, secretly, by the edge of the forest at Fief Karcan's western
border. "These drugs alter not only behavioral patterns, but
emotional ones as well. You can induce in Lady Benjarth that
state of mind she possessed when you were both lovers at Castle Hopkitch. You can make her a school girl again with a
school girl's passion."

Lord Thyden had stared into Farant's eyes then and had
seen the hardened desperation of a man willing to do anything, even betray his friends, for the chance to be loved by
Lady Benjarth again. He'd known Farant would be easy to ma-

nipulate with the right coaxing. "She will be yours again," he
had told him. "Yours to enjoy . . . forever."

What Surgeon Farant could do with malinophorm and
voalaline to mold Lady Benjarth's passion, he could use to
mold Christina's. Those taut muscles of her youthful body
squeezed around him in the pleasure of lovemaking—Lord
Thyden could think of no sweeter pleasure.

Christina was tall, too, a physical trait Lord Thyden found
particularly appealing. Such willowy elegance was not to be
found among the squat figures of the Sinese and Phlogin
women. His train of thought almost caused him to break out
in laughter. What cattle they were, compared to this beauty!
He sucked in a deep breath, as if her exquisite beauty wafted
about the room like the finest of perfumes.

But then the face of the Benjarth daughter faded and that
of the serving woman, Enit, took its place. He remembered
now where he had seen her face. She was the maid who was
supposed to bring his infant son to the guard captain to be
thrown into the sky-void ring.

Feelings buried deep within Lord Thyden's bosom stirred
anew. There could be only one reason she had fled to Fief Karcan. Just one! She had never brought his infant son to the
guard captain. Instead she had fled with the child.

CHAPTER 20

 The *beast* was supported on eight square posts anchored into the sand. Sheet metal formed is elevated sides and its overall shape was rectangular. It protruded sixty feet from the west side of the rock. The structure was widest at its far end and narrowest where it mated to the rock. Its bottom side was sixteen feet above the ground. The posts were cross braced to add rigidity.

Paul moved around to the front of the structure. This end was open and the wind entered here. Baffles ran horizontally across the eight-foot by ten-foot opening and appeared to pitch inward and downward. He stepped beneath it. From there he could see that the structure had been built in straight segments between which, at approximately ten-foot spacings, tapered fittings had been inserted to gradually reduce the structure's width and height.

Paul found curious the fact that the posts supporting the structure were not identical. The one he stood beside consisted of two different sizes of metal somehow joined together. The top piece, which ran approximately six feet, was narrower than the bottom piece. However, the post next to it was a continuous run of the same size metal. The sides of the elevated structure were silver-gray, yet one fitting was shinier than the others, while another was darker. Paul surmised that this structure and its support legs had been built piecemeal, its architects using whatever materials were available.

He stepped from beneath the structure to where Brian stood. "Have you any idea what it is?" he asked him.

"It's a crude amplifier! Look how the structure narrows as it nears the rock. That increases the velocity of the wind. It makes the note louder."

Paul marked the word Brian had chosen to use. *Note!* "You're saying it's a musical instrument of sorts?"

"Well . . . yes! Most likely the rock is hollow." He eyed its height. "It's like a giant pipe organ. A single pipe—a single note."

The wind roared, and as it did so did the volume of the sound. Brian and Paul brought their hands to their ears. The ground about their feet seemed to shake. Moments later the sound subsided to a hum.

CHAPTER 21

——

The next morning Paul divided the party into groups of two. He paired Thoren with Farant, Karin with Kellan, Rogger with John, and Brian with himself. Each group was to move away from the rock in a separate direction. However, under no circumstances were they to go so far as to lose sight of it. If something of significance was found, one member of that party would return to the rock and signal the others by waving his arms back and forth above his head.

"I believe the rock is a directional signal," Paul explained to Brian as they searched the ground southwest of the rock. "I can't think of a better way to guide someone in this wasteland, where there's such limited visibility."

Paul believed that Duke Whitin had also been drawn this way by the sound. The dashed line on the map had scaled off roughly the same distance they had traveled up to now. Whatever Duke Whitin had meant to indicate with a circle and exclamation points was in this area. That's why he decided to split them up, so they could search the surrounding terrain more effectively.

"Paul!" Brian shouted, pointing back toward the rock.

Rogger stood beside the rock waving his hands above his head.

When they had all returned to the ridge, Rogger led them across the sand to where John waited. What the two men had discovered was a dome-shaped piece of silver-gray metal roughly forty feet in diameter protruding from the sand. Paul walked slowly around it. One full quadrant of the dome's surface was dented and the rest was laced with structural cracks. There was a hole below where the dome had been dented.

They dug away at the sand around the hole, then Paul exposed an ascama fiber-stub and thrust his arm and head through the opening. A mound of sand sloped away into the darkness below him. He pulled the rest of his body through. Suddenly the sand gave way beneath him. He tumbled down the incline and the ascama fiber-stub fell from his hand.

"Paul!" cried Kellan, who was halfway through the opening and holding a fiber-stub. "Paul? Answer me! Are you all right?"

"I'm okay," he called back. He brushed what sand he could from his clothing. "We'll need lanterns, Kellan. The light from the fiber-stubs isn't enough."

By the light of the lanterns Paul and Kellan surveyed their surroundings. The mound of sand beside them was funnel-shaped and about sixteen feet high. It had a base twenty-four feet in diameter. A rectangular opening had been cut into the floor beside the mound and stairs descended from it into the darkness below. The wall behind them was a mishmash of smashed pipes and twisted metal.

"This entire wall seems to have been crushed in," remarked Kellan, scanning its length as far as the light from his lantern allowed him to see.

Grains of sand cascaded down the mound with a faint rustle. Paul and Kellan looked up. Thoren squatted atop the sand hill.

"Are the two of you all right?" he called down.

"We're fine," Paul replied.

"Gad! Look at the size of this place," said Thoren. "Do you think this is the place indicated on Duke Whitin's map?"

"I'm sure of it."

"Will you need more lanterns, Paul? I've got two in my pack."

"Bring down all the lanterns and gear."

Rogger was next to slide down the mound. "What is this place?" he asked, looking around. "Hello," he yelled. "Is anybody here?"

Had a voice cried out in answer, Paul's skin would have crawled off his bones. The sheer desolation of Calferon was reason enough to believe in its uninhabitability. How could anything survive in a world without food and water? Yet Paul knew that rational thought did not always guide one infallibly when probing the unknown. Someone or something had taken the lives of those who'd been a part of his great-great-grandfather's expedition. Someone or something had lived in this forsaken world once . . . or still lived.

"Good lord," cried Brian, the next to slide down the sand hill. "It's a spaceship!" He held his lantern aloft. "Will you look at the size of it?"

Paul was incredulous. "A flying machine? Like yours?"

"Like mine? Hardly! The technology here is decades ahead of my civilization's. Perhaps even centuries! Good lord! It's so big!"

The floor was tiered. The lowest level was semicircular and fronted one wall of the ship. There was a tear in the wall where a second mound of sand had formed. Chairs that looked secured to the floor were half buried in it.

Brian stepped down to the lower level. "This was probably the bridge," he explained. "The control of the ship would be from this point. More than likely there was a window or viewing area where this sand has spilled in."

He climbed back up that first flight of stairs, then ascended another short flight. The three stairs that composed this second staircase appeared to run the full width of the ship.

Paul stepped up beside Brian and the two of them surveyed the ship's interior. The level they now stood upon looked to contain most of its square footage. There was furniture scattered about, mostly tables and chairs. However, there were a great many objects that Paul could not identify. Some of these hung down from the ceiling; most sat upon the floor. All threw shadows that dissolved together into the far depths of the ship, for even the light from the ascama fiber lanterns wasn't enough to fully illuminate the vastness around them.

Brian suggested they explore the ship and Paul agreed. He

instructed Rogger and John to remain behind with the gear. They then set out as two parties of three. He, Karin, and Brian composed one group; Kellan, Farant, and Thoren, the other. Paul's group was to explore all chambers and passageways to the right side of the ship, while Kellan's group was to explore the left side.

"What is it we look for?" asked Kellan.

"I wish I could tell you," replied Paul. "I only suspect we'll know it when we see it. Keep in mind the lore surrounding the medallion. 'Within it lies the power that created our world and can in turn destroy it.' "

A row of machines divided the room in half. They split into their groups and moved on either side of them.

"These look to be the ship's computers," said Brian.

"Computers?"

"Complex thinking machines. I spoke of them when we crossed the plains in the timber wagon. Do you remember? Life-support, guidance, cooling, heating—all may well have been controlled from here."

A corridor opened to their right and they turned into it. There were doors on both sides. A large, red, square button was beside each.

Brian pushed one. Nothing happened. He pushed it repeatedly, then pulled on the side of the door. It wouldn't budge. Nor would any of the other doors in the hallway.

The end of the corridor was bisected by another. Offset into a niche so it did not interfere with traffic on the corridor was a spiraling staircase of shiny metal, running both up and down. A glance down the hallway in either direction revealed more red buttons and more closed doors.

"Up?" asked Brian.

"Why not?" replied Paul.

They saw immediately that the upper level was not a carbon copy of the level below. The corridor they had stepped into curved inward toward the rear and front of the spacecraft. They stood now at its widest point. Also there was not a short hallway running toward the center of the ship. Instead there was a door. A glance in both directions revealed more closed doors, though these were on the outside wall of the corridor only. All had square, red buttons beside them.

The explorers focused their attention on the door in front of them. The button beside it was blue. They sensed its unique color coding was purposeful, not arbitrary, and that the contents of the room beyond might well hold the answer to the riddle of the medallion. Their excitement, however, quickly turned to frustration and disappointment. Nothing they tried, including the insertion of a knife into the seam between wall and door, would open it. Reluctantly they gave up trying to open it for the time being.

The forward end of that level of the ship was a vast room with neatly arranged rows of tables and chairs. The outward-facing wall was ruptured and sand entered through the opening.

"It looks like a cafeteria," said Brian. He picked up a chair. "Interesting. None of the furniture is bolted down."

Brian said nothing more. He didn't have to. Paul's mind leaped ahead to the same incredible conclusion Brian's surely had. *Not the way one would expect it to look after a crash!*

They passed more closed doors before they came upon one slightly ajar. They eagerly fell to the task of forcing it open and found within a single room furnished with a bed, chair, desk and bookcase. The walls were olive green, the ceiling silver-white. The floor covering, thin but surprisingly spongy, was emerald green.

Paul removed a book from the bookcase. The pages were of the same texture and bore the same faint greenish tint as their own manufactured paper. But the printed characters were foreign to him.

"There's writing paper in the desk," said Brian.

Paul located a small notebook in one of the drawers. The characters, as foreign as those in the books, did appear hand-printed, for they were not made with the same evenness as those in the books. Each page had some individual markings in the upper left-hand corner.

"Perhaps it is a diary," said Brian, glancing over Paul's shoulder at the notebook he held.

"What's this?" asked Karin. She held up a thin, rigid, square-shaped card no more than two inches on a side. Along one edge were many minute, irregular indentations. She had found it in another of the desk's drawers.

"May I see that?" asked Brian.

There was a red button on the inside of the door. Below the button was a slot. Brian inserted the square, which fit perfectly.

"Most likely it is a key," he said. "Probably it locked the door from within."

They explored the room further. There was some porous, gray, square material held by white painted frames at each end of the room. The frames were eighteen inches on a side. One had been mounted flush into the ceiling. Paul reached up and touched the material. It felt spongy. The other had been mounted into the wall.

"A ventilating system of some sort," Brian guessed.

There was a panel of six buttons, again square but smaller than the button by the door, on the wall beside the bed.

"Lights," suggested Brian.

Karin pushed the buttons. Nothing happened.

They found another room, two doors down and on the same side of the aisle, open, but it looked identical to the room they'd just explored and so they decided against entering it.

Paul was more excited by what they found farther down the corridor. The door to a room with a square, blue button was ajar enough to allow them to slip through sideways. This room was different from the other two. For one, it was larger, much larger. The color scheme was different, too. The walls were blue and the ceilings white. There were racks of books on both sides of them. The aisle running between the book racks emptied into an open area containing four tables and as many as two dozen chairs.

Brian held his lantern aloft. "It's a library!"

Karin took in a short gasp of breath. "Look! On that table!"

A knife had been stuck into one of the tables.

Paul's finger tensed around the trigger of his crossbow. He half expected legions of warriors to leap out from behind the bookcases, the tables, the chairs. He walked over to the table and saw that a note was pinned to it by the knife. The handle of the knife was silver and gold and its thin stone blade was nine inches long. Paul read the note without removing the knife. It said: "What's my birth date?" It was initialed "WB."

"They're my great-great-grandfather's initials," exclaimed Paul.

"When was he born?" asked Karin. "And what does it mean?"

Paul glanced first at Karin and then at Brian. Of course, he realized. It's a code! A code only a Benjarth could decipher because no one else would know such a birth date.

He was born on the fifth month, twenty-second day. The year was 212." Paul thought a moment. "It must be the numbers! It's the numbers that are important!"

"The books!" cried Karin. "Could something be hidden in one of the books?"

"Of course! Fifth corridor, twenty-second . . ." Paul's enthusiasm sank. "But which is the fifth corridor?"

The library was circular, the center room its hub. From it twelve equidistantly spaced corridors ran to the perimeter walls.

Paul grabbed Brian's lantern and inspected the small over-hung card-signs that marked the beginnings of each library corridor. He grew increasingly frustrated as he moved around the room. "These markings! They're like the writing in the books. How am I supposed to read them?"

"You can't," said Brian. "So more than likely your great-great-grandfather couldn't either."

Paul paused in his inspection of the card-signs. "What are you saying?"

"I'm saying that your great-great-grandfather probably used a reference system based on symbols familiar to him. Twelves. What else comes in twelves? The first thought that comes to mind is a clock face. Or, more familiar to you, a sundial. Wouldn't it make sense that the fifth corridor would be that one located in the five o'clock position?"

"But where would you start?" asked Karin. "Which corridor is twelve o'clock?"

"A good guess? That one that faces due north."

The early-morning sun had been directly at their backs when they'd entered the ship. Now it was simply a matter of mentally retracing their steps. There was a certain symmetry to the ship and that helped them. The stairway up to this level faced in the same direction as the first blue-buttoned door they had found. They figured they had traced an arc of one hundred eighty degrees upon coming around to the other

door, because there were only two doors entering the library
and they were at opposite ends of the room.

"Okay," said Paul, anxious to get on with the search. "Let's
consider next the day of his birth." They stood midway down
the corridor that ran south-southeast. "There aren't twenty-
two book racks along this corridor."

This time it was Karin who would contribute some insight.
"Split it. Two and two. Second bookcase. Second row."

Paul understood what Karin meant. Four circular aisles intersected the twelve radial corridors at equidistant points
along their lengths. Therefore, each corridor was five book
racks deep. "But on which side of the corridor?" he asked.

"Could be either, I guess," said Karin. "So what, though?
It means we've got to check two books instead of one."

Four books instead of two," Brian corrected her. "You could
count from either end of the book rack."

They next considered the number two hundred twelve.

"Second book, twelfth page?" Paul asked. "Or twenty-first
book, second page?"

Brian had already begun counting the books. "There are
only twenty books in this row and nineteen in the other. Let's
go with second book, twelfth page."

They found another of Duke Whitin's cryptic notes in the
margin on page twelve of one of the books. It said, "When
did I die?"

The thought was automatic. The year, month, and day of
his great-great-grandfather's death flashed in Paul's mind.
But almost as quickly as those facts had come he realized the
absurdity of the question itself. How in the world would the
duke know to the day when he was going to die?

They sat around a table puzzling over the duke's riddle.

"I don't think it has anything to do with the date of his
death," said Brian at last. "Those particular numbers are
meaningless."

"Why's that?" asked Paul.

"Well, just think it through a moment. An adversary such
as Lord Thyden, had he been the first to discover this note,
could look up Duke Whitin's birth date in, say . . . the birth
records at the castle. Just as easily, he could learn the date of
his death. This second clue is your great-great-grandfather's

assurance against that. 'When will I die?' Could it refer to something unwritten? A superstition? A ritual?"

A song!

It was a short, festive ditty known by all Benjarth men of drinking age:

"Don't want to die when I'm twenty-five,
Got women to chase and a mug in my hand.
Don't want to die when I'm fifty-five,
Got children to marry and a mug in my hand.
Don't want to die when I'm seventy-five,
Got a wife to bury and a mug in my hand.
So Mr. Fate, keep your hand off the trigger,
It just ain't time for you to deliver.
Don't think I got time to die,
Got a mug in my hand,
Got a mug in my hand."

They jotted down the numbers in the margin of a page of another book. "25-55-75."

"Second corridor, fifth book rack, fifth row, fifth book, seventy-fifth page!" Karin exclaimed.

Two papers spilled to the floor when they opened that book. Each had been folded over several times. Paul unfolded one atop one of the tables.

"It's a blueprint," exclaimed Brian, who had placed his lantern on the table and now leaned over the print with Paul. "These are blowups," he added, his finger tracing one of the lines from the main drawing to a circle that contained a select enlargement of the area indicated.

"I recognize this structure," said Paul, pointing at it with his finger. "It's Castle Chalmet." He looked up into the faces of Karin and Brian for confirmation. It was then he realized neither of them had ever seen Castle Chalmet.

A representation of the sun had been drawn in the upper right-hand corner of the blueprint. A single ray was extended to a point just above the top of a mountain. From there the line continued at a less acute angle to Tower Satchkind.

A blowup of that mountain peak revealed the existence of a concave structure with a hole in its center. Opposing it was a smaller disk. The sun's light was indicated by several rays that struck the larger disk, converged to a single point on the smaller disk, then passed through a hole in the larger disk as a single ray. The system was shown in several positions, indicating it could be moved both out of and back into the mountain.

"They're reflectors," said Brian. "Reflectors are used to collect and focus sound or light waves. Here—" His finger traced the path of the sun's light—"the sun's rays are gathered, focused onto this disk, then shot through the center of this larger disk in a single concentrated beam of light."

There was a second enlargement. This one was of Tower Satchkind. Paul saw that the beam of light entered the tower through a hole in the upper tower room that faced to the southeast. It went on to strike an object mounted to a post running vertically in the room. From there several lines had been drawn, suggesting that the light beam could exit Tower Satchkind at different vectors.

Brian put his finger on the tower. "Here it seems the beam is deflected toward the ground by, most likely, a mirror of some sort."

"Why?"

"I don't know. Such a concentrated beam of sunlight would produce, well, heat! Like a laser beam."

Paul had forgotten what Brian had told him about a laser beam. A concentrated beam of sunlight would produce substantial heat. Enough heat to rupture the jooarie sacs! "This focusing system," he asked, "could, say, diffuse, I mean, reduce the heat of the beam, right?"

"More than likely."

Less heat and the jooarie sacs would not rupture. Only the growth of the core-vines would be accelerated. Consequently the crohephite rock would form more quickly.

He unfolded the second print and spread it atop the other. His finger went immediately to an object detailed in the center of the drawing. "It's a flying machine of some sort."

"Probably similar to this one," said Brian.

Wavy lines extended from the bottom of the ship. Below them was a detailed cross-section of core-vines and jooarie sacs.

"These wavy lines probably indicated the heat produced

from the engines' exhaust," Brian pointed out.

Paul wasn't sure he fully understood all that was indicated on the blueprint, especially the second one. What he did know now was the solution to the riddle of the medallion. The *sun* was the force that could both create and destroy their world!

They made their way back to their starting point. Kellan's group had already returned.

"Have you ever seen anything like it?" Farant asked Paul. He held a bone between his thumb and forefinger. "Here! Put it in your hand and tell me what you notice about it."

Paul took the bone. It seemed disproportionately light.

"It's hollow," exclaimed Farant. "Oddest little piece of bone, isn't it? We found it on the floor of a huge cage. A cage as big as a room!"

"Let me see that," said Brian. He needed only a moment to study it. "It's a bird bone."

"A what?" asked Kellan.

"A bird bone."

Thoren did not share either Farant's fascination for or Kellan's curiosity of the bones. "I've seen enough bones for a lifetime," he said. "The sooner we leave this creepy place, the better."

Kellan explained. "This ship is a tomb! We were able to force some of its doors. Behind each was a single room—living quarters of some sort. Atop the beds we found bones. Human bones!"

"It's a ship of death," muttered Thoren.

Rogger, too, was frightened. "What do you think happened here?" He looked at Paul, his eyes as wide as saucers. "The same thing that happened to your great-great-grandfather's expedition?"

"I don't think so," said Paul.

Calferon was a dead planet. Paul realized it now. No animals roamed its barren terrain. No "beasts" lurked behind its windswept ridges except in his imagination. It was a waterless world, and as such could not support life. There was only one solution to the riddle of what happened to Duke Whitin's expedition. Only one solution that made sense.

"The rivalry between the fiefs was particularly strong one

hundred and fifty years ago," Paul explained. "The expedition was made up of three men each from Fief Salkird, Fief Cerus, and Fief Karcan. In all likelihood, the mission was organized as a symbolic gesture of the unity that could be. After all, they were all Jarred. Unfortunately they did not realize what it was they would eventually find when they first probed the sand wall. The peak from which the collector rises is in the Eastern Mountains, a part of Fief Karcan. The six men from Fief Salkird and Fief Cerus must have feared what the Benjarth would do if they were able to put in operation those mechanisms shown on these blueprints. The duke of Fief Karcan would possess the power of life and death over the citizens of the other two fiefs! He could rupture the jooarie sacs supporting their land and send it crashing to the planet's surface. Certainly these six men believed they could not allow the Benjarth to return to Fief Karcan with this knowledge. In all likelihood a fight broke out. Duke Whitin alone survived, perhaps by luck, perhaps by skill. He was wounded and I believe the gash was made by a knife."

Paul suddenly had a flash of insight. *Perhaps by the very same knife Duke Whitin had used to pin the note to the table! Its blade was nine inches long. That was the depth of Duke Whitin's wound as recorded in Castle Chalmet's medical journals.* As well, the knife had belonged to one of the three men from Fief Salkird. The colors of its handle were the royal colors of the Orsinc family line.

"In either case," he continued, "Duke Whitin had had the wisdom to realize that the Jarred were all better off if the weapon was possessed by no one."

Paul spread the blueprints on the floor for all to see. With Brian's help he explained the workings of the machinery and answered their questions.

"Circumstances are different now," he said. "We all have a common enemy in Thyden. We can use this weapon to defeat him. We can use it to defeat him if we can regain control of Castle Chalmet, for with it we can crumble the very ground on which his armies stand."

"Yet taking Castle Chalmet back will not be an easy task," Farant reminded Paul soberly. "We are only nine."

Like a candle that had flickered brightly only to be blown

out, so Paul's enthusiasm died. For some time he sat quietly with his thoughts.

The others busied themselves preparing dinner. Food was cooked over burning tins of animal fat and served on woven fiber plates. The hot food picked up the party's spirits, Paul's included. When dinner was completed, they decided to explore the room beneath the sand funnel.

"It's probably the engine room," said Brian.

They all rose to their feet. All of them, that is, except Surgeon Farant.

"You've no interest, Farant?" inquired Paul.

"Not in things mechanical, no," he replied. "What I do have an interest in is some hot sucri."

Paul was pleasantly surprised. "You have sucri?"

Sucri was an herb that imparted a bittersweet flavor to boiling water. The stem of the sucren plant, cut into lengths half an inch long, dissolved slowly in hot water. Depending upon individual taste, one normally used one or two stubs. Sucri was a luxury food item and hardly necessary for their survival on a mission such as this.

Farant smiled. "We've got more water than we need, Paul. And I do have enough sucri."

The water was boiling atop a cooking tripod when they returned from the engine room. Sucri stubs were laid out on a cloth on the floor. Farant removed the boiling water and poured. A toast was proposed: success in their war against Lord Thyden. They all drank.

Soon thereafter they retired for the night.

CHAPTER 22

———

 Lying atop his own makeshift bed with one eye half open, Farant watched them all, one by one, fall asleep. When the last of them had fallen asleep, he knew it would be a dream from which they would never wake. Hordazine was a clear, tasteless poison. Gradually it relaxed both the voluntary and involuntary muscles to where the lungs and heart would cease functioning. He'd poured it into the boiling water when they had been below. Not one of them had noticed that he had not poured the hot water into his own mug, which he'd filled earlier.

For a moment, Farant savored the memory of a much earlier and happier time in his life. He was twenty and Helana was eighteen. He remembered vividly that first night they had made love. It had been in the dorm room assigned him in the west wing of Castle Hopkitch. It was a small room, hardly big enough to contain his bed, a chair, writing desk, and a bookcase for his medical texts. Besides its small size, the room was drafty. But that night they had lain unclothed atop the blankets. It was raining and they listened to the steady patter on the stones of the inner courtyard as their heartbeats returned to something akin to normal.

"You should have enrolled with me and studied painting and drawing," she had teased. "The rooms are more spacious and there are no drafts."

The talented painter Roagarth had a residence two miles to the south. It was a private dwelling and the master took on four pupils at a time and put them up in his home. Farant had considered getting permission to sit in on some of the courses. He had some natural artistic talent.

"I'm afraid I might show up that hoary old Roagarth," he had said in jest.

"Hoary old Roagarth," she repeated. She lay facing him and she swirled the tip of her finger around the areola of his nipple. "I daresay he'd be flattered by your description of him."

"I daresay he would! Hoary, old, pompous, conceited, self-serving, perverse, bloated, fat men *should* take pride in such insults. What else are they going to hear?"

"Oh? And now it's pompous, self-serving, perverse, bloated and fat, too?"

"And conceited."

"Well, I like him anyway."

They had laughed and made love again, and many times more in the nights after that.

Farant had been devastated the night prince Jaiman Benjarth had swept Helana out of his life. The prince had met her at a party thrown by Roagarth. Helana had been his first love and Farant found it difficult to let go. Gradually time should have healed his emotional wounds and allowed him to move on to other relationships, but it hadn't. His love for Helana, now Lady Benjarth, had festered in his bosom and grown cancerous.

Helana had known none of this. She'd expected time had healed all wounds. So when the resident surgeon at Castle Chalmet passed away twelve years later she had thought of Farant as the perfect replacement for him. Farant had been powerless to turn down the appointment, because he was still in love with her. So day after day, year after year, he labored as chief surgeon at Castle Chalmet, all the while becoming more emotionally crippled in his love for Helana. Because of her nearness, his cancerous emotion grew stronger and stronger.

It was Lord Thyden who had promised his tormented soul salvation. He had told him of the drugs malinophorm and voalaline and what they could do to alter Lady Benjarth's emotional patterns. All he had to do was spy on the Benjarth. But the bargain had seemed one-sided. Lord Thyden had ordered him to Fief Salkird to spy for him there as well. Then fate had taken an even crueler turn. Paul had selected him as part of this expedition to Calferon. Now, finally, he was free to return to Fief Karcan. He had quashed the one hope the Benjarth had of defeating Lord Thyden by poisoning the members of this expedition. Now a new life, one with Helana by his side, could begin.

He rose and gathered his gear, removed the blueprints from Paul's pack, and put them in his own. Then he made his way up the sand mound and out through the hole in the ship.

The wind swirled; it did not gust and howl as it had during the day. Low in the eastern sky lay the waning half moon. The light from it, diffused by the airborne sand particles, seemed speckled, as if it were coming to him from a thousand separate pinpoints.

Farant hoped to make the base of the stairs by daybreak. That would allow him to make his climb during the day. If his stamina held out, he expected to make the cave by nightfall. The next evening he would be at the gates to Castle Chalmet.

CHAPTER 23

Such a fascinating drug was styranotide! All the higher centers of the brain—abstract thinking, judgment, logical thought—could be anesthetized by it. If the neurotransmitters of those brain centers were no longer able to send the electrical impulses of thought across the brain's network of synapses, it left only the lower brain centers operational. Lord Thyden chuckled. Fabricating a lie was an activity of the higher brain centers. Stripped of their function, one was defenseless to guard what he or she said.

One did have to be careful of the dosage, however. If too much of the drug were injected into the bloodstream, the lower brain centers would also be anesthetized. That would result in an unconscious subject. Still more, and the person's involuntary centers would be anesthetized. One would die, then.

The serving woman, Enit, had fought with the strength of a man. She'd managed to grab a knife from one of the guards and slash that fellow good. No doubt the other guard would have taken his knife to her throat had Lord Thyden not given the order that he wanted the serving woman brought to him unharmed. It had taken two more guards to restrain her and administer the injection.

"You are not Jarred, my dear, are you?" asked Lord Thyden. "Your height and bone structure betray the blood of the Sinese and Phlogin. Where were you born?"

"Lorstown," Enit replied.

"You were the maid to whom I gave my infant son. Your task was to deliver him to the guard captain, to be cast into the sky-void. This is true, is it not?"

"It is."

"Did you disobey my order?"

"Yes."

Lord Thyden's heart raced. "Why?"

"I could not be a party to any child's death, even one born of your loins."

Lord Thyden held in check an impulse to strike the woman. "Where did you bring my son?"

"Lorstown."

"But how did you smuggle the child past the guard stations on both sides of Ansona Pass?"

"I did not travel Ansona Pass."

"The tunnels? You took the tunnels?"

"I took the tunnel to the southwest."

"But there are guards there!" Lord Thyden was incredulous. "They let you pass? With my son?"

"I was hardly foolish enough to tell them it was your child."

Lord Thyden's temper flared again. "Where did you take my son? Wait! Lorstown, you said. And there? What did you do with him there?"

"I was in no position to raise the child—unmarried, a fugitive. There was a couple in Lorstown, friends of my family. For years they had been unable to conceive. The woman was sterile, or he was, I don't know. I don't even remember the lie I told them, or series of lies, about whose baby it was and how it came to be in my care. They raised the child."

"Their name, serving woman?" demanded Lord Thyden. "What was their name?"

"Harkins."

Lord Thyden recognized the name immediately. *Keith Harkins!* He was the young lad who helped him about the castle. He had been tall, too, almost like a Jarred. Then he recalled that the mistress who had given birth to the child had had some Jarred features. That was what had made her attractive to him.

Lord Thyden hovered above the serving woman as if he meant to strike her down. He was angry at her because of her deception. He was even angrier with himself because he had never thought to ask the guard captain if the baby had been brought to him. He'd always assumed his orders had been followed! Yet his emotions were confused, for in the same instant he felt overwhelming joy at the news. His son's death sentence had been the one act of passion he'd always regretted.

Not at first, however. For many years he had lived in relative peace with his decision. It had not been until the imprisonment of the Jarred and the procreation of their own kin within his castle walls that he had seen how wrong his decision had been. The Jarred children liked him and he them. Often he played with them in the nursery. Always, though, he wore his robe because its thickness gave him bulk and covered his deformities. One day he had dismissed those who cared for the children, in spite of the fact that the servants were all blind! That day he'd removed his robe and sat naked from the waist up among the children. They had played with him all the same. It was then he had realized the mistake he had made ordering his newborn son killed.

The joy that possessed Lord Thyden now made his heart feel light. He wanted to run to a window and shout, simply to hear the joy in his voice. *My son lives!*

CHAPTER 24

Paul lay motionless on the floor. His eyes stared up at the metallic hull of the ship. His breathing was shallow and difficult and he had to concentrate on it. His body seemed asleep, not that it was characterized by the tingling numbness that occurred when one's hand or foot fell asleep. It was quite the opposite. There was no feeling.

He rolled his head to the side. Karin was staring at him, her eyes wide but her face strangely relaxed. Her lips moved as if in speech, but no sound came out. Paul opened his mouth to speak and faintly heard the sound of her name, seemingly dragged out and unclear, leave his lips.

Suddenly there was motion above him. Someone grabbed his wrist and held it for several seconds. Then hands grabbed his head and turned it.

"Can you hear me, Paul?"

Paul saw Brian's agitated face staring into his own. He felt his fingers pull back on his eyelids.

"Can you hear me?"

Paul moved his lips, formed the word "yes," and tried to expel the air from between his lips.

Brian crouched beside him, his ear to his mouth. "I can hear you, Paul," he said, pulling back from his chest. "Don't try to say anything more."

Paul watched out of the corner of his eyes as Brian felt for Karin's pulse. Suddenly he knelt astride her and tore open her shirt. Paul twisted his head to the side. Brian had tilted Karin's head back and was blowing into her mouth. Then he jerked his head back and pumped her heart muscle with his two hands.

It isn't necessary! There are drugs in Farant's pack that will stimulate her heart!

He tried to cry out to Brian, to tell him of these things, but sound left his lips so faintly that he knew Brian did not hear him. Blast! Where was Farant? He could save her! An injection of corzine was all that was needed.

It seemed an eternity that Paul lay there watching Brian work to revive Karin. Helpless, he could only hope that Brian's primitive methods would work. Gradually he became aware that his own muscles were beginning to respond to his commands. He could clench and unclench his fingers. He could wiggle them. He could move his arm along the floor, though he could not yet lift it.

"Brian!" he called out.

Brian's head turned for a moment in Paul's direction.

For another minute Brian worked to revive Karin. Tears came to Paul's eyes when he saw Karin's chest rise and fall of its own accord. Primitive or otherwise, Brian's methods had worked.

"What of the others?" he asked Brian.

"They're dead."

Mirrored in Brian's eyes was a reflection of his own horror and confusion.

"You and Karin are the only ones alive," continued Brian. "And that Farant fellow. He's gone!"

The scene of death before them was one they would not soon forget. Paul felt as if a knife had been dragged through his soul and the wound left to bleed. Karin wept openly. Brian stood with his head bowed.

"It is a loss we will all grieve in the days ahead," Paul managed to say at last.

He found his words lacking and suspected the others did, too. Had he time and an orator's mastery of words, he would properly eulogize his comrades. Now, however, a sense of urgency directed his thoughts. They had to go after Farant. The blueprints he carried were far too valuable to fall into Lord Thyden's hands.

Paul had to wonder why Surgeon Farant had committed such a heinous crime. What state of mind had driven him to kill? He had always seemed a simple, quiet man mindful of his duties. He'd been especially attentive to his mother after his father's capture. It was true that no one had really been close to him. No one at the castle called him best friend. But so what? That didn't make him a killer. Illad had had his quiet moments, too.

He remembered once how Farant had taught him to use the candagge. Farant had stood behind him and placed his hands over Paul's. Paul had already placed the thimble-shaped candagge over the tip of his third finger. Cristo had had a small cut, a scratch really, and had volunteered to be Paul's first patient. The leaf of the lazan plant had already been cut to size. He'd placed it over Cristo's cut and, under the guidance of Farant's gentle, skilled hands, he had smoothed out the air bubbles from beneath the lazan. The threadlike fibers of the lazan plant grew into the skin in much the same manner one fabric is sewn into another. The candagge had to be worn to prevent the lazan from attaching to the surgeon's finger as well. As the skin healed beneath it, the plant would die and fall off.

Paul believed that Lord Thyden had somehow brainwashed Surgeon Farant. He remembered Duke Orsinc telling him that Farant had made it into Fief Salkird ahead of the invasion. Paul had been happy that Farant had made it to safety. He had not considered the fact that Farant must have had advance warning of Thyden's invasion. His soldiers might have killed him in error in the frenzy of battle.

"We cannot linger here a minute longer," he said.

Brian began to gather his gear. "How much of a head start do you figure he has?"

Paul glanced up at the opening in the ship and saw that it was still night. "There is no way of knowing. An hour? Several hours? A minute is too much of a head start with the prints he's carrying!"

The moon was high in the southern sky and its light afforded them a view of the ridge to the southeast. The wind was
from the west and would be at their backs the entire journey.
Brian led the way.

"How do you figure it, Paul?" asked Karin. "We were poisoned, weren't we? And yet . . . Brian? And us?"

Paul, too, had thought about that puzzle. "Brian's physiol-
ogy has to be different from ours, Karin. The poison had no
effect on him."

"Different from ours? What do you mean?"

"We will talk of Brian later, when the time is right. But the
two of us! I can only venture a guess, not knowing the specific
poison Farant used. You and I were served first, that I remember. Perhaps the specific density of the poison was heavier than
that of the water. Perhaps the poison settled toward the bottom of the pan."

It was many hours later when the sky along the eastern horizon washed gray. Dawn followed slowly, the gray dissolving
into an almost transparent blue, then pink, orange, yellow-
orange. Then the sun itself, hazy and distorted in the windblown sand, pushed above the horizon.

Although the sunrise took well over an hour, to Paul and
the others it seemed compressed into a time frame of minutes.
They had been in a race against the sun ever since they had left
the ship. Not until morning would there be enough light for
one to be sure of his footing on the stairs. For that reason Paul
felt Farant would not attempt to climb the stairway until then.

They pressed on until they made the final ridge before the
fan wheel. Paul climbed its west face. At the very edge of his
window of visibility, about half a mile away, he saw a man's
shape plod across the sand toward the fan wheel. He climbed
down.

"Grab a crossbow," he told Brian. "The wind's at our
back." He turned to Karin. "Have you food and water in your
bag?"

"Yes."

"Bring them and any other gear you can carry. Follow us as
best you can."

"I've never shot one of these things," protested Brian, indicating the crossbow.

"Take my knife then," said Paul, handing it to him. "We'll need the cloth bands and goggles, too."

They had not made up much of the distance between themselves and Farant when, by chance, Farant happened to glance back. Immediately he started to run toward the fan wheel. Pausing at its edge, he put on his goggles and tied a cloth band about his nose and mouth before disappearing into the swirling sand.

Several minutes later, Paul and Brian halted by the edge of the fan wheel. Brian started to put on his goggles.

"Wait a minute," said Paul.

Brian pushed his goggles up on his forehead. "What's wrong? Aren't we going after him?"

Paul had given considerable thought to what Farant might do once he realized he'd been discovered and his pursuit was close at hand. He was an older man and his stamina was no match for theirs. He could not possibly keep ahead of them on the climb up the stairway. They would catch him before he was a quarter of the way up. Farant had to realize this, too. That meant he would have to make a stand. And the best place to make a stand would be in the hub of the fan wheel. There the bare rungs of the ladder would offer them no shelter should Farant position himself on the top rung with his crossbow aimed downward. Paul realized now, too, that he could not get off a shot from beneath the fan wheel up into the hub. There was simply no way he could string his crossbow in the swirling cyclone beneath the fan wheel.

"No, not yet," said Paul. "Wait here."

He raced back across the sand.

"What is it? What's wrong?" asked Karin as Paul approached.

"Have you a blanket in your gear?" He looked past her shoulder at the ridge fifty yards beyond.

"Yes," she replied.

It was a cream-colored blanket. Paul thought it perfect because it would blend with the sand.

"Wait for us at the perimeter of the fan wheel," he told her.

Brian thought Paul's plan clever but risky. "Still," he said, "it's better than going up into that hub blind."

They rolled up some sand in the blanket and lay that bundle at their feet. Brian gave Paul his knife and Paul secured it to his belt. Each helped the other adjust cloth and goggles, then they picked up the blanket of sand and entered the swirling maelstrom beneath the fan wheel.

Although there was little to no visibility beneath the fan wheel, light and shadow could be discerned. As they moved inward from the edge, things grew darker. Glancing back, Paul could see a trace of lighter-colored sand where the fan wheel ended. Minutes later, they saw a small circle of light sand hovering off to their right. They adjusted their course accordingly and stopped to one side.

Paul was counting on two things. When they had first descended through the hub, he had noted the presence of a strong updraft of air. The suction into that opening would sweep the blanket up at Farant. Paul hoped that Farant would instinctively fire a bolt at the blanket. It would take time to nock another bolt and, in those few seconds, Paul could pull himself up the ladder, note Farant's position, and throw the knife. Hopefully the sand the blanket contained would get in Farant's eyes—he wouldn't be wearing his goggles to shoot his crossbow, because they distorted one's vision slightly—and momentarily blind him.

Paul squeezed Brian on the arm. It was their agreed upon signal that he was ready to go. Paul took up a position beside the edge of the hole. Brian grabbed both ends of the blanket and squatted by the edge of the opening, then his legs powered him upward as he hefted the blanket full of sand into the opening. Paul counted to himself. "One thousand and one." That would be Farant's bolt. He leaped up and grabbed the first rung of the ladder. He heard a scream. He hesitated.

Something fell past him. It did not drop straight, but rather came at him from the side, as if it had first been sucked against the spinning wall of the hub and then swept downward.

Had that been the blanket, Paul wondered? Had the sand blinded Farant?

He realized he had waited too long. He dropped from the ladder and jumped back from the opening. He stepped upon something soft and it compressed slightly under the weight of his foot. *Farant's arm!* For a second or two, Paul was unsure what to do. He tapped the body with his foot. There was no response. He knelt, felt for Farant's head, and slapped it again and again. Again there was no response. Brian was beside him and together they dragged Farant's body from beneath the fan wheel. When they were clear of the mushrooming sand clouds they rolled him over and felt for a pulse. There wasn't one.

"The blanket must have hit him still intact with some of the sand," said Brian. "It would be like having a weight thrown at you the way the wind sucked it up through that opening. It probably knocked him from his perch."

"It looked to me as if the blanket opened up," said Paul. "He may have lost his footing with the sand in his eyes."

Paul stared at Farant's body and wondered what his price had been. What vanity had Lord Thyden exploited? A promise of wealth and power? He shook his head in disbelief. Surgeon Farant had never seemed the type to pursue, let alone kill for, such vanities. He'd never asked for more spacious quarters or more expensive furnishings. These the Benjarth would have given him readily! Paul rolled Surgeon Farant's body over and removed the blueprints from his backpack.

The three survivors made the top of the stairway by nightfall. Guided by the rope, they crossed through the sand wall to the shelter of the cave. There they ate in silence, for each was too exhausted to talk.

Paul, the first to finish his meal, gathered his bedding and moved to the back of the cave. He remembered the ground was softer there. Unfortunately he'd not thought to expose an ascama fiber-stub to the sunlight as they'd neared the top of the stairs—he'd been too preoccupied with the climb—and he cursed this oversight as he stumbled around in the dark.

Something moved to his left. Paul reached for the knife sheathed at his side. A hand grabbed his from behind and another came around and held a knife to his throat.

"Make a move and I'll slit your throat," the voice whispered.

"Alexce?" Paul said, thinking he recognized the voice. Alexce was his sister's serving girl.

The knife was turned so the sharpened edge of the blade ran parallel to his neck. The hand atop his own loosened its grip.

"Master Paul? Is that you?"

"Put down the knife, Alexce."

The shape of another person suddenly took form in front of him. "Paul," a voice cried out.

His sister ran forward and they embraced.

CHAPTER 25

———

 The ridge they lay atop overlooked the Valley of Boulders. A trail ran north-south the length of the valley. Several of Lord Thyden's soldiers sunned themselves beside the trail at the valley's north end. The valley's west border was defined by a tree-lined ridge. Just beyond the trees lay the main road linking Castle Chalmet with the eastern land bridge. Paul and party had entered the valley from the east through a narrow gap between the two mountains that towered behind them. The eastern slopes of those mountains bordered the sky-void.

"This ridge here is the very one I parachuted onto," Brian was telling Paul.

"Where is the entrance to the suspension bridge?"

"Over there." Brian indicated the southern end of the valley. "By those large rocks."

They had talked much last night in spite of their weariness. Christina and her serving girl, Alexce, told of their escape from Castle Chalmet. There had been much revelry the night before Lord Thyden was to wed Christina. All of Lord Thyden's men had drunk heavily, even those on guard duty. It had been just past midnight when Alexce and Christina made their way unseen down the steps to Hall Creary. A concealed trapdoor led to a secret tunnel, which passed beneath the fields east of the castle and surfaced in the foothills of the Eastern Mountains. Once out of the tunnel, Christina and Alexce had tried to put as much distance as possible between themselves and Castle Chalmet. They had food and water enough for two weeks and had come upon the cave by chance.

"Our plan was to reach the sky-void and follow its border south," Christina had explained. "We were hoping to find the suspension bridge Lord Thyden's men boast of now that its presence and purpose have been revealed, or to find any other way to cross to the Medoc Peninsula. There is talk at the castle of a resistance movement there, a group of loggers. We hoped to locate and aid them."

Paul, Karin, and Brian had decided to join Christina in her search for the loggers. Nothing would be gained in returning to Fief Salkird. Christina had revealed that Lord Thyden's invasion of Fief Salkird was imminent, and Paul realized that the success of that campaign would hinge on whether Thyden could overrun the passes that cut through the mountains at the east and west end of the fief. He suspected Duke Orsinc could not hold those two passes against Thyden's troops indefinitely. Fief Salkird would fall. Thus he saw no reason to return, for their small band would contribute nothing to the outcome of that struggle.

Although there was no tree cover, there were plenty of boulders and rocks to conceal them as they made their way down to the valley floor. Brian led the way south to the secret entrance he had stumbled upon the morning after his plane had crashed. Fortunately they encountered no guards as they made their way through the tunnels to the foot of the suspension bridge.

What awaited Paul in the yawning void beneath Fief Karcan was not the damp, shadowy, colorless underbelly of rock he had expected to see. There was sunlight. A river of it. It flowed from the west, a warm, golden stream washing and splashing against the rock beside them, sparkling its somber, gray hues with flecks of silver, gold, white, and yellow. Paul cupped his hand over his eyes and squinted as he looked to the west. The sun was at such a position in the sky that it was below the line of crohephite rock supporting the flat heartland of Fief Karcan, but not below the deeper projections of rock supporting the mountains of Fief Salkird. As the sun moved inexorably west it would pass behind those inverted peaks and all would be plunged into shadow again. Only when the sun had dipped low enough in the sky to be beneath the deepest projections of rock would its light return. By then it would be near Calferon's horizon and its light, bent by the planet's atmosphere, would deepen in hue.

The appearance of the sunshine was no less a surprise than the bridge's physical condition. Crooked, tilted, and twisted, it was not at all the engineering marvel Paul had expected from someone as capable as Lord Thyden.

It was Karin who provided insight into the reasons for its haphazard construction. "The downward growth of the core-vines supporting my city are no different than those support-ing this bridge. The crohephite rock above our heads is porous, as is the rock above my city. A hole is made in the rock, or an existing hole used if its location is suitable, and a core-vine seedling nested there. The core-vine will grow downward, forming the support for a bridge, the wall of a home, what-ever. But the core-vine will also grow within the rock, anchor-ing itself simply by entangling itself within the minute passages that already exist there. Notice how each bridge sup-port has to be curled back on itself a distance down from the rock. The rope is secured to these 'hooks' and the boards sup-ported between."

"But the bridges of your city look nothing like this!"

"Do you think the city's first engineers did not make mis-takes?" Karin had been whispering, concerned that her voice might carry. She looked momentarily in Christina and Alexce's direction. "We've had more than a hundred years to perfect our craft. Besides, one must *garden* the rock constantly."

Karin's choice of words puzzled Paul. "Garden the rock?"

"The rock of my city is living, so we must always scrape and file away at it. The hairlike spinolla fibers, which exist at the surface of the rock, continually attract minute deposits of screula. If we didn't constantly garden it, such simple things as closing a door or opening a window would be impossible."

Their crossing was slow and deliberate. Where the boards were cracked or looked unsteady, they prodded them one at a time before putting their full weight on them. The bridge also bowed between its supports, and Paul thought this might be because the rope had stretched from the passage of so many of Thyden's troops.

Time marked its passage on the stone around them. First the rock warmed yellow-gold as the sun dipped toward the planet's horizon. Then, gradually, the rock turned orange, then reddish-orange. As they stepped from the bridge's last plank, the rock around them glowed red. The path before them rose steeply, then twisted to the right.

"The tunnel flattens out for a few feet at the top," said Brian. "The guards cannot see us unless they step inside."

Paul pondered their next move. Brian had told him of a clearing beyond the mouth of the tunnel, where he had been taken prisoner.

"But you must remember," Brian had told Paul, "that I did not try to make a break for the wood. I did not know where I was, or who my friends or enemies were."

"And if you had made a break for the wood?"

"I can't say for sure. I did see archers secured in the rock bordering the land bridge."

Just then they heard shouts from beyond the tunnel.

"Someone challenges Thyden's men," said Paul.

"It must be the loggers," said Christina. "We must help them!"

They climbed the path and paused a moment by the tunnel's mouth. Men were engaged in hand-to-hand combat in the clearing beyond. They could all tell at a glance those who fought for Thyden because of the gray tunics they wore. The numbers looked even.

"Death to the soldiers of Thyden," Paul cried as he ran into the clearing.

The sound of his voice, a piercing cry above the shouts and groans of the others, turned the heads of Thyden's men, who suddenly realized their vulnerability from another side. A few of the loggers were able to take advantage of their adversaries' break in concentration and, thrusting their knives, drew blood.

"Who are you?" a voice demanded, when the fighting was over.

"I am Paul Benjarth, son of Duke Jaiman Benjarth. We

come to aid those who fight against Thyden."

For a moment, not one of the dozen-or-so men around them spoke.

"Decide quickly, Jfow," a voice said. "The soldiers will return."

"Come with us, Benjarth."

They ran single file along a path through the wood. The path looped back and forth up the slope of a steep ridge, then followed the gentle curve of the rise south. The ridge top was one rock formation after another. Some were strangely human-shaped, stone warriors waiting for a wizard's hand to bring them to life. Others tapered to points like the formations in the foothills of the Angena Mountains. In a few places where the rock was broken the gnarled trunk of a stunted tree had managed to root. The branches of these trees dangled limply like broken fingers until brought to a strange, jerky life by a gust of wind. The group of warriors halted atop the great cliffs that fronted the sky-void to the south. Here the wind gusted fiercely. It was a cold, damp wind. Rain was on its way. Already the leading edge of a storm front blanketed much of the western sky.

The dominant landmark to the west was Chimney Ridge. It was a massive semicircle of upthrust rock whose flat side faced the sky-void and was, in effect, an upward continuation of the cliffs there. Two miles distant, it towered five hundred feet above the surrounding ridges and was the Medoc Peninsula's highest point.

"Our camp is just this side of it," Jfow told Paul.

The trail cut across the face of the cliffs. For much of the way there was nothing between the men and the sky-void. Fortunately the path was wide, but in some instances, where it narrowed, only fingerholds existed in the rock to assist them. The trail soon turned inward and tunneled through the crohephite rock. Lanterns were lit. These burned animal fat and their smoky odor lingered in the tunnels. The group exited the tunnels onto a great expanse of flat rock, where no path was defined. On the other side of the rock flats they picked up the trail again, which cut back toward the cliffs. This time it stayed atop them.

The loggers' base was an oval hollow six feet deep. The rock had been scooped back from its sides starting at a height of thirty inches. Blankets lay atop these crude benches, which ran nearly the full length of both sides of the oval. A ledge overhung the hollow at the far end from where the band entered, and beneath it was the opening to a cave.

A figure stepped from the cave. "So tell me, Paul Benjarth. How did you come to be at the mouth of the tunnel to the suspension bridge? The last news we had of you was your escape from the hangman in Cartag."

Arnun!

The two men embraced.

"A lot has happened since," Paul replied. He lowered his voice. "Perhaps too much to reveal here and now."

"We will talk later," Arnun said. "Ahh, but you must know, of course, that Lord Marthan has been murdered."

"By Thyden?"

"Yes. Lord Thyden had no further use for him once he'd sent his soldiers into Fief Karcan."

That fact did not surprise Paul. "Lord Marthan was a puppet. I would think the lot of a logger would change little if Thyden ruled the peninsula instead of Lord Marthan."

Arnun did not agree. "Under Lord Marthan's rule we were governed fairly. That is not the case now. The mushrooms, vegetables, herbs, and timber that grow on our land Lord Thyden now harvests out of trade. He gives what he wants to his own soldiers without giving us anything in return. Thus, we have less to barter with at the vending stalls. We end up working harder for less. Most of the loggers have accepted the change because they do not have the courage to defy Lord Thyden."

"How many are in your group?" asked Paul.

"Twenty-nine."

"And how many groups are there like yours?"

"As far as we know we are alone in our fight."

Food was passed among them. Paul was grateful, for the portions were generous and he knew the loggers' food supply was limited. After the meal he wandered away from the hollow until he stood alone atop the cliffs. The wind whipped across his face and he was careful not to step too close to the edge.

So there were only twenty-nine of them. He was glad it had been dark, for Arnun would have seen his face fall when he'd heard their numbers. They were too few to take back Castle Chalmet. Why, they would need to amass an army of at least a thousand men! That meant they would have to extend feelers into the other logging camps. For if the loggers were, as Arnun had indicated, discontented under Thyden's rule, then maybe all they needed was a little prodding. They would have to act quickly, though, while Thyden was still preoccupied with his conquest of Fief Salkird. Castle Chalmet would be minimally guarded only as long as most of his troops were needed along the border of Fief Salkird.

Paul caught a glimpse of motion out of the corner of his eye. Something had spilled from Chimney Ridge. He thought it at first rocks that perhaps an animal or the wind had loosened. But then something strange happened, so strange that for a moment Paul doubted his own eyes. Whatever had fallen from the cliffs, or at least some of it, became airborne. The wind picked it up and swirled it to within twenty feet of where he stood before sweeping it away from the cliffs. Paul stared into the vastness of the sky-void long after the objects had vanished into the darkness. The objects had behaved as something leafy or made of paper, but no vegetation grew on the sheer sides of Chimney Ridge.

The rain came sometime after midnight. It rained hard for several hours and then tapered off. By dawn it had stopped.

Paul stepped from the mouth of the cave. The morning sun, slanting in from the east, took the chill right out of him. He watched the loggers take down the ursulas set up last night at each end of the hollow. He overheard them remark that the rainfall had been plentiful and all available flasks would be filled.

Arnun joined him for breakfast.

"Do you plan another attack for today?" Paul asked him.

"My men will stay put for today. However, I will increase the watch to the east by two. I feel Lord Thyden's men may try to pick up the trail Jfow used last night. But I've little fear they will find us. Rock leaves no footprints."

"I'd like to take a closer look at Chimney Ridge," said Paul, "specifically its south face."

"There is a deep crevice that splits the land between us and Chimney Ridge. There is no trail leading to the bottom of it, but if you pick your way down carefully through the rocks, you can make it. What is your interest in Chimney Ridge?"

Paul told Arnun what he'd seen last night from atop the cliffs bordering the sky-void.

Arnun did not know what to make of it. "Are you sure you saw something? The wind and the night can play tricks on your eyes."

"I'm sure."

Arnun shrugged. "Take a look, then. There are no logging camps nearby and our watch has yet to spot any of Lord Thyden's troops wandering this high on the ridges. I'll have one of my men show you the way."

Paul nodded his thanks.

Arnun turned his attention to the efforts of two of his men to pack up one of the ursulas. He shouted instructions to them.

Paul placed his mug on the rock beside him. The brew was strong and bitter, and not to his liking.

"It's an acquired taste," said Arnun, noticing that Paul's mug was still full. He signaled one of his men to bring Paul some water.

Paul gulped the water thirstily. Over the rim of his cup he could see Arnun watching him, smiling, as if he'd known all along that he would find their morning brew distasteful and had been having a little sport at his expense. Paul put down the empty cup.

"How far is the nearest logging camp?" he asked.

Arnun's gaze turned cold and suspicious. "Why do you want to know that?"

Paul explained the need to amass an army. "The time is now, Arnun, while Thyden is engaged on other fronts. Now is the time to take back Castle Chalmet."

Arnun argued vigorously against the idea. "I know full well the trust I can place in my own men. They are true to our cause and would never willingly betray our group, but I cannot say that about the loggers in the other camps. Lord Thyden may have been able to buy the allegiance of some of them. What happens if one of my men talks to such a logger about your plan? Lord Thyden is tipped off and my man is captured. Then he's given an injection of styranotide and tells Lord Thyden where our base is. The risk is too great, Paul."

Paul would not deny the risk, yet he argued that it made more sense to attack than to wait for Thyden to pick their day of execution. "Do you really believe you stand a chance the day Thyden decides to throw his full muscle at you?"

But Arnun would not see it that way, and the more they debated it, the more it became apparent to Paul that Arnun was perfectly content with the small successes he'd enjoyed so far against Thyden's troops. To attempt something on a grander and more meaningful scale was to risk failure. Reluctantly, Paul dropped the subject.

"Would your man show us the way to Chimney Ridge now?" he asked.

The crevice was narrow and about seventy feet deep. The slope on their side dropped at a forty-five-degree angle. Across the way the drop was vertical, the wall being a part of Chimney Ridge's east face. Paul and Brian began a slow and careful descent into the crevice as one of Arnun's men stood watch. The crevice's floor was a trough three feet wide, and they walked single file to its southern end. There they had an excellent view of Chimney Ridge's south face, for the land on their side jutted beyond the cliff face by several feet.

"There it is!" exclaimed Paul.

Chimney Ridge's south face was almost completely flat. There was an occasional ledge, but the amount of indentation or overhang at these points was more in the nature of inches than feet. But at one point, at about eye level with where they stood and to this side of the approximate center of the cliff, there was a sizeable outthrust of rock. This protrusion left the face of the cliff at a downward angle and overhung it by about five feet. To both men there appeared to be an opening into the cliff beneath it.

Brian, who was an experienced rock climber, pointed to a crack running across the rock to the overhang. "If I had the proper equipment," he shouted above the wind, "I could move laterally across the cliff face to that opening."

"What would you need?" Paul asked eagerly.

"A good hammer, some rope, two dozen pitons."

They stepped around the corner so they would no longer have to shout above the sound of the wind.

"What are pitons?" Paul asked.

"Metal spikes with an eyelet to pass a rope through. I would hammer them into that crack I pointed out and use them to pull myself across."

"Perhaps we can fabricate something," suggested Paul.

"Fabricate something! Do you understand the difficulty of this traverse? The wind alone makes the climb extremely dangerous, let alone the fact that we don't have the proper equipment!"

"We can secure you with ropes from atop the crevice and from here. We crossed the sky-void ring that surrounded Castle Greyfahren without mishap, didn't we?"

"Yeah, well . . . so we did. But still! I need pitons! Where are we going to get them?"

"I think I know."

Not all crohephite rock formed with equal density. The concentrations of spinollas along a given length of core-vine determined how much screula adhered and thus its density (its thickness was determined by the length of the spinolla). Blocks of stone hewn from areas of denser crohephite rock formation were used to make the blades of swords, cutting utensils, axe heads, and the like. No doubt Arnun and his men had a few of these blocks, for the implements of their trade were formed from such. At the very least, they had to have them for sharpening the edges of their existing hatchets, axes, and knives.

When they had returned to camp, Arnun confirmed that they had such blocks stored in the back of the cave. "But the labor required to chisel out these . . ."

Brian filled in the blank: "Pitons."

". . . Yes, well, it will take the efforts of several of my men for perhaps as long as an entire day. It is time taken away from other projects. What is the importance of investigating a hole in Chimney Ridge?"

Paul's answer was in the form of a question. "What do you do, Arnun, when you've a load of scrap branches to dispose of?"

"Find a dumping hole for it."

"And if you're logging the outer slopes of the ridges?"

"Dump it in the sky-void."

"Exactly," said Paul. "Now you may not be familiar with castle design and construction, for your trade is that of a logger, but their wastes and scraps must be similarly discarded. There is a patch of land off the back of Castle Chalmet where the depth of the crohephite rock is thirty-six feet. When the castle was first built, a dumping chute was carved through the rock, one whose path was carefully made so as not to rupture any of the jooarie sacs. What I might have seen the other night were scraps of paper. Scraps of paper dumped from a garbage chute!"

Arnun's face was a sheet of disbelief. "Are you suggesting that people might actually live within Chimney Ridge?"

Paul nodded.

Arnun was more than a wee bit skeptical. "My people have logged these woods for centuries! There has never been a shred of evidence of anyone living within the rock."

"That is not true, Arnun. Loggers *have* spoken of hearing voices from atop the ridge. Others claim to have seen an occasional speck of light from up there."

"Such are stories only, Paul, as is the winged beast Saulcar."

Paul tried a different tack. "I'll barter with you for the labor of your men."

"A trade?" Arnun was vaguely amused. "You've my curiosity, Paul Benjarth. What could you possibly offer us from your three bags of gear?"

"Ascama fibers."

Paul smiled as Arnun reached over and shook his hand to cement the deal. He'd known the loggers had no way of growing ascama fibers. They did not have access to the basement levels of a castle where absolute darkness could be guaranteed. They had to rely on the light of lanterns that burned animal fat, which were smoky, limiting their use to areas that were well ventilated.

Paul stood alone again by the cliff's edge that evening. He was deep in thought and for that reason did not hear his sister's approach.

"Why do you make this traverse tomorrow, Paul?"

Paul continued to stare into the sky-void. "Arnun is shortsighted. He believes he can lead his small band of loggers-turned-soldiers up and down the Medoc Peninsula for years to come. I'm not belittling their soldiering abilities. They may be the best soldiers that ever lived! But what chance do they have when Thyden has finished with Fief Salkird and dispatches thousands of his troops to mop up any remaining pockets of resistance here? We have the power to destroy Thyden's armies if we can only retake Castle Chalmet and put into operation the light-beam machinery. The possibility that a civilization might exist within Chimney Ridge must be explored. These people may be able to help us. With manpower, with weapons . . . possibly in ways I can't even imagine now." He turned to his sister. "Every opportunity must be pursued."

The next morning those loggers not assigned to guard posts stood atop the east wall of the crevice and watched Brian hammer in the first piton. From that same lookout Karin, Christina, and Alexce watched Brian attach his safety harness and begin his traverse of Chimney Ridge's south face. A rope was joined to that first piton and its other end secured around a stone atop the crevice. So, too, had a permanent safety line been attached to Brian's belt. Paul had helped Brian secure a knapsack across his back. It contained a small quantity of food and water, two lengths of rope, the pitons, and an extra hammer. He watched Brian from the floor of the crevice.

It took Brian until early afternoon to reach the overhang. When he did, he removed the shorter of the two coils of rope from the knapsack. Securing one end of it to himself and the other to the eye of the last piton he'd hammered in, he lowered himself beneath the overhang. With a wave of his arm he signaled Paul that there was indeed an opening into the rock.

Karin descended into the crevice. The plan had been that if Brian was successful in traversing the rock, and if the overhang concealed an opening into Chimney Ridge, both Karin and Paul would also make the crossing. At first, Paul had been against Karin joining them. He'd spoken of the danger and the uncertainty of what they would find. Yet he realized, even as he voiced his objections, that there was no basis for his concern. Hadn't she made the journey to Calferon and faced all the dangers they had? Had she not been closer to death than he? He knew his motives were personal and emotional. He wasn't questioning her capabilities at all. He was simply voicing his fear for her safety. He thought she realized this, for while she had reacted hotly to his suggestion, she had come to him afterward, squeezed his hand, and given him a quick kiss on the cheek.

Brian hammered two pitons into the underside of the overhang. He secured one end of the second coil of rope to both pitons. The bulk of the rope he now held coiled in his right hand, and he signaled to Paul that he was ready to make the toss. The rope struck the rock of the crevice that extended beyond the cliff face. Paul secured it to two pitons driven into the rock behind him. He and Karin helped each other secure their safety lines. Then, hand over hand, they pulled themselves forward along that length of rope.

There was a ledge up inside the opening. Brian pulled himself onto it and waited to help the others. Paul was the first to arrive and Brian grabbed his arm and pulled him up. They both helped Karin up.

The ledge was not large, roughly six feet on a side. At one end was an open door. It was wooden and rounded on top. An unlit flight of stairs rose behind it and curled around to the right. Beside the door, hung from a peg that protruded through a hole in its handle, was a broom.

Paul thought: *The ledge has been swept clean of garbage!*

No, not entirely, he realized a moment later. He saw a small scrap of paper protruding through a thin crack in the floor. It tore when he pulled it free. The paper felt slick, as if it had been used to wipe something greasy. Paul held the ripped half up to a beam of light (the space around them was lit only by sunlight seeping through small holes and slots in the rock of the cliff) and studied it. There were words written on it. Unfortunately, the ink was smeared and most of the words were illegible. Whatever the greasy substance was, it had mixed with the ink and begun to dissolve it. Paul could only make out two words: "sew jackets."

"What does it say?" asked Karin.

Paul handed her the paper.

"Sew jacket." She looked at Paul with an almost comical look of profundity. "Does it mean something?"

"Yes!" exclaimed Paul. "It means someone's jacket needs

to be sewn!''

Paul would have charged up the stairs had the darkness of the stairway not given him reason to be cautious. There was a civilization flourishing within Chimney Ridge! A civilization whose people wore jackets that wore out and had to be mended. What else could it mean? The waste needs of a few individuals would not require a huge garbage chute such as this.

The staircase was narrow and spiraled upward. There was a landing after each completed helix. Atop each landing were two doors. One opened onto the garbage chute; the other exited from its opposite side.

The higher Paul climbed, the more the symmetry of the stairs and landings impressed him. By the eighth landing he understood the logic of the chute's construction. Rubbish could be discarded into the chute at each landing. That was for the convenience of those Paul believed lived and worked on each level. The chute narrowed to make the opening in the cliff face smaller and less obvious to any logging at the higher ridges. The bottom landing allowed access in case garbage became stuck where the chute narrowed.

The stairs ended at the thirteenth landing. Paul opened the door and they entered a narrow corridor. The joints where the roof and floor met the wall were rounded, indicating the corridor had been carved from the stone rather than built from blocks. The stone was a creamy beige and Paul had to believe that it had been treated with a tinted wash. Light entered the corridor through an open archway midway along its length. The light was surprisingly soft and white, unlike the yellowish green light that would be cast by an ascama fiber. They passed through the archway and found themselves on a balcony. An elderly woman, gray-haired and with thin, bowed shoulders, dropped the tray of food she was carrying and gaped at them. Her eyes were dark brown and her face was a mesh of wrinkles. She wore a white, full-length apron over gray slacks and a pale-blue, collarless shirt. Her slipper-shoes were greenish gray. But Paul, Brian, and Karin paid the woman no mind. The view before them had captured their complete attention.

Chimney Ridge itself was an upthrusted semicircle of stone whose flat side faced the sky-void. Within, another semicircle had been hollowed out, one whose flat wall lay to the south as well. They stood upon the highest of twelve stone balconies. Each followed the gentle curve of the rock from the eastern corner of the open space a full one hundred eighty degrees around to its western corner. The radius of that smooth curve was in the neighborhood of three hundred feet. The twelve balconies across the way ran straight, for they were joined to the flat wall of the semicircle. The wooden rail of the balcony ran waist-high. Its wide top was ornately carved, as were the posts that supported it every fifteen feet or so. Paul had felt the carved surface when his hand had first touched the rail. Now he looked down and saw that its detail was of a long, leafy vine from whose stems a variety of fruits and vegetables grew.

Paul looked up and saw that the curved balconies on their side and the straight balconies across from them joined at those points where the flat of the semicircle abutted its curved side. Two diagonal stairways were cut into the stone of the south wall above the balconies. Viewed together the two stairways formed a massive "X" one hundred feet high. Where they crossed, a small, rounded balcony jutted outward. The stairways ended at notches in the rock, and appeared to provide access to the top of Chimney Ridge.

They were now all staring upward.

"What is it?" asked Karin.

The top of Chimney Ridge opened to the sky. At least it appeared to do so at first glance. Now, however, they saw that a membranous film was stretched across the opening. They were aware of its existence because, although it was transparent, it did have a slight grayish brown cast to it.

Paul looked to Brian for an answer. As he did, he noticed that the woman who had stood gaping at them earlier was gone. He suspected she'd gone to alert the guards. If she had, well, so be it. They would not be able to hide from whatever security forces existed here. Besides, he was anxious to meet those who presided over so incredible a place.

"Perhaps it retains the heat," Brian guessed, "or filters out a certain spectrum of the sun's light. I really don't know."

Paul directed his gaze downward. Vast gardens covered the floor of Chimney Ridge. He recognized such staples as corn, peas, tomatoes, squash, and cucumber. A small orchard grew in the center of the gardens, but from their vantage point above its small trees it was impossible to identify the fruits being grown. Bridges arched above the gardens, some in turn arching above each other. They were made of wood and had been stained in earthen hues. These bridges joined together the many footpaths that wound and twisted through the gardens.

Everywhere there were people. Some labored in the gardens. Others walked briskly along the many tiers of balconies across the way, most seeming to pop out of one archway only to pop back out of sight through another. Paul heard the shrill cry of children's voices and saw them running along the edge of the gardens. From somewhere below came the sound of wood being hammered.

Paul sensed motion behind him and his hand went instinctively for the knife sheathed to his belt. Yet when he turned he saw that the five men who stood before him were unarmed. Nor did they stand in a defensive posture as if to engage them in a fight if they tried to pass. Three of the men huddled together while the other two stood apart. The five were elderly. Paul guessed them to be in their seventies. All had long, white hair tied back behind their heads. Their hairlines were very pronounced along the top and sides, framing the large foreheads and broad cheekbones. Their eyebrows were bushy and ran straight across. They were not, on average, as tall as the Jarred. Their skin was pale but not totally without color. All five wore loose-fitting, silken, yellow pullover shirts. These had wide half-sleeves and were pleated under the arms. Where sleeve joined shoulder was a dark-green triangular patch. Two short bands of green had also been stitched to the fabric over their hearts. Two of the men had a third bar that was purple. Paul had to believe these bars indicated rank. Their pants were loose-fitting and dark gray, with drawstrings at the waists. They wore the same slipperlike shoes the woman had been wearing. Paul noticed that these shoes had thick soles that would cushion the step of one who walked across rock all day.

One of the men took a step closer as if to separate himself from his colleagues. He was the shortest of the five. His forearms were surprisingly brawny for one his age. Small pockets of fat protruded from beneath both gray-brown eyes. Paul couldn't help but notice they were the color of his own.

"Who are you?" the elder asked.

There was no threat to his voice, so Paul removed his hand from his knife. "I am Paul Benjarth, son of Jaiman Benjarth, Duke of Fief Karcan. This is Karin and Brian."

"How did you get past the wall of rocks?" The man spoke with the simple curiosity that a child would in asking his parents to explain something to him. "How did you learn of the doorway?"

"Wall of rock? Doorway? You must speak of another entrance," said Paul. "We traversed the rock facing the sky-void and entered through the rubbish chute."

As if all five gaping countenances had merged into one consummate face, five looks of amazement stared back at Paul.

"You scaled the southern cliffs?" asked the man in astonishment.

"There is a crack that runs across the face of the rock." Brian removed an extra piton from his pack. "I hammered these into the rock and pulled myself across."

"May I see that?" asked the elder who stood forward of the others.

Brian handed it to him.

"Interesting," he said, after studying it briefly, "so simple, too." He passed it among the others. "Do others know of your traverse and entry into the rock?"

"A band of loggers-turned-soldiers does."

"Turned·soldiers?"

"Yes," said Paul. "They battle Thyden."

The man turned and whispered to one of the elders behind him. Then, grinning broadly, he asked Paul what he thought of all he'd seen from the balcony.

"It's incredible," Paul exclaimed. He smiled, too. "Naturally, I've a thousand questions for you."

"They shall be answered in time. For now, though, please follow us. I am Olgar. You shall be our guests at dinner."

They were shown to rooms where they could clean up. Hot tubs of water were prepared and fresh clothes laid out. The pale blue pullovers did not have triangular patches or bars sewn on them. Pants and shoes were the same as the elders'.

When they were alone, Paul asked Brian what he thought of their hosts.

"They seem friendly enough. I'm suspicious, though." He shrugged. "Perhaps it's just my nature to be so."

"Suspicious? Why?"

"I told you it was just my nature, Paul. Well, no, perhaps there is more. This place reminds me of Karin's city. Her people were friendly enough and all, that is as long as we did not want to leave. It's obvious these people have gone to great lengths to conceal their society. I doubt they're about to let us walk out of here and announce its existence to the world."

Paul realized, somewhat sadly, that Brian was probably right. They were prisoners again! Prisoners, though, only if they couldn't convince these people to aid them in their battle against Thyden. He had failed to convince Karin's people. But this time there was a difference. This time he knew of the light beam. They could defeat Thyden if they could put into operation the machinery that harnessed the sun's destructive power.

Brian submerged himself in the tub. When he popped back up, some of the dye Paul had colored his hair with at Castle Weslan had washed out.

"What are you staring at?" he asked Paul.

"Your hair is two different colors."

Brian shrugged and submerged himself again.

Then Paul had a flash of insight. These people were a mix of the Jarred, Sinese, and Phlogin races. There was a chance, therefore, that they had religion. They might even believe in the Malhah. He had Brian wash all the dye out of his hair.

They dressed and waited for Karin by the door. She had changed and bathed in the adjoining room.

"You've not been waiting long, have you?" she asked, as she stepped into the corridor.

There was an aura of femininity and beauty about Karin that caught Paul off guard. Not that her beauty surprised him; no, he'd suspected it the very first moment he'd seen her. It was just that she had never had an opportunity to showcase it, at least not until now. Paul could not help staring. She wore a green cloth dress that fit so perfectly he would have sworn it had been tailored for her in the time it had taken him and

Brian to bathe and clean up. Her hair had been washed, trimmed, and shaped. It seemed to glow as if backlit by moonlight. Her cheeks had been touched with rouge, her lips shaped and colored in a soft, fleshy red, her eyes highlighted. She wore earrings and a single jewel suspended about her neck.

Karin's eyes were on Brian. More precisely, they were on his hair. "Your hair! It's yellow!"

Brian looked to Paul, unsure what to say to Karin by way of explanation.

"Does it have any significance, Karin?" asked Paul. "Does it mean anything to you?"

"No, it's just that, well, I've never seen hair that color before. I never knew *anyone* had hair that color! A significance? What do you mean?"

"Nothing," mumbled Paul, deep in thought.

So they've eliminated the concept of a savior from their religion. Of course! It made sense to carry on the lie that nothing worth seeking or understanding lay beyond the boundaries of their city! Didn't it make sense to imprison both the body and the spirit in that hanging citadel?

Paul was not optimistic now that revealing Brian's true identity to these people would gain them an advantage. The belief in an enlightened one probably had no more place in this hidden society than it did in Karin's. He realized now that Brian's yellow hair would only gain Brian the humiliating status of a curiosity or freak.

CHAPTER 26

———

 They were shown into a small dining hall. Forty people sat around a single table that stretched the length of the room. For the most part they were elderly, and their ages made Paul wonder if the elderly ranked highest in the caste system of this society. Both men and women wore the same buttonless yellow shirts with the dark-green triangle patches between shoulder and sleeve. But the number of bars stitched to the shirts' left front varied from zero to three. Always the colors were the same. The first and second bars were green, the third purple.

A feast was laid before them. Apples at the peak of ripeness were carried into the room in coarsely woven half-baskets. Ginsel, a small, hazel-colored fruit that grew on a vine, had been mixed in a fruit salad with square chunks of pear and apple. Steam wafted up from wooden bowls heaped with more than six varieties of vegetables. Some, such as peas, corn, and squash, were familiar to Paul. Others, such as besapt, a long, stringy vegetable that lay like wet strands of ribbon on his plate, were new to him. A number of casseroles were offered that baked combinations of these vegetables together with spiced capoi bread crumbs. Freshly baked loaves of bread were brought in on thick serving trays, and the room soon filled with their warm scent. A fermented drink called calsanor was poured from ornately painted pitchers and carafes into earthenware mugs.

Nothing of a serious nature was spoken of during the meal. Entreaties were made to Paul and the others to put a little of this on their plates or to try a little of that. When one of them proved unfamiliar with a particular food, their hosts were only too glad to tell them not only what it was, but how it was grown, how the seed sprouted, its germination time. When the meal was over, the table was cleared. More fruits were brought in as dessert.

At this point, Paul became aware of the growing silence within the dining hall. Looking around, he noticed that the kitchen staff had left the room.

Olgar spoke to Paul, Brian, and Karin in a voice loud enough for all present to hear. "Those seated around you are members of the governing council of our society. We are sure that you have questions of us, of our society, about our existence. Perhaps we can answer some of them. But we've questions to ask of you first and we expect you will answer them truthfully."

"I assure you it is not our intention to deceive this council," said Paul. "Please, ask your questions."

"How is it that you came to suspect an opening in the rock? It was designed to be hidden from the view of one standing on the surrounding cliff tops."

Paul described what he had seen two nights ago from the cliffs facing the sky-void.

Olgar pursed his lips in thought. "Yet why did you risk such a difficult climb? I cannot believe your motivation was simply that of curiosity." He paused. "What is it you wish of us?"

How quickly he came to the point, thought Paul, admiring the intelligence and accuracy of Olgar's instincts.

He took a deep breath. "We need your help to defeat Lord Thyden."

"Who is Lord Thyden?"

Paul told the council all he knew of Belshane, Thyden's father, and Lord Thyden. He concluded by summarizing Thyden's recent conquests and the horrors he had inflicted. "Now he invades Fief Salkird. Like Fief Cerus and Fief Karcan, it, too, will eventually fall. When it does, he will turn his attention to the few pockets of resistance here on the peninsula. If we fall, there will be none left to oppose him. His reign of terror and darkness will go unchecked."

There followed the murmur of many voices, but Olgar's voice rose above the others. As it did, the others fell silent.

"We are not soldiers, Paul. Our society has persevered because of its isolation, not its armies. We harbor those secrets that have prevented your societies, be they good or bad, from obliterating each other. From obliterating us all! We possess knowledge that could aid you. But there is a danger in revealing it to you. It is something this council will have to consider, though I already suspect what our answer will be. Our first loyalty is the preservation of our own society."

"We know of the light beam's existence," said Paul. "We know of the collector in the Eastern Mountains and the focusing mirror in Tower Satchkind."

Those of the council exchanged surprised looks.

"How do you know of these things?" asked Olgar.

"We descended the stairway to Calferon and explored the ship there. We found drawings detailing the mechanics of the light beam in the ship's library."

"Tell them no more," cried out a council member. "It is a trick of some sort! They could not have found the ship. Those who built the stairway could not find that ship!"

"Calferon is wind-swept," said Olgar, addressing his fellow council members. "The sands will shift over time. It took ten years to build the stairway. The ship may have been buried over when that first expedition of our ancestors crossed those sands."

"That was nearly the case when we came upon it," revealed Paul. "Only a bit of the . . . the . . ." He looked to Brian for the proper word.

"Hull," said Brian.

"Only a bit of the hull was visible. It was torn open and we were able to gain access through it."

That brief exchange between Paul and Brian had not gone unnoticed by Olgar. "Tell us of yourself," he said to Brian. "You seem knowledgeable in the terminology of space vessels. Your hair color also intrigues me. It is not genetically possible for any of the Ornan, Sinese, Phlogin, or Jarred races to reproduce with yellow hair."

Brian was unsure of Paul's strategy and how much he wished him to reveal to these people. But Paul signaled him with a head nod that he was to tell the council what they wished to know, and so he began his story.

"I am a pilot." Brian felt the need to explain that term. "One who flies airplanes . . . ah, flying machines. I learned to fly in the Air Force. It's a branch of the services back where I'm from. A buddy of mine and I opened a sky-diving school when we were discharged." He hesitated. "This can't be making a lot of sense to you."

Olgar smiled. "We understand far more than you might think."

"Well, I was putting one of our two planes through its paces because we had a jump scheduled for the next day. I like to fly at night. So there I was, west of Cincinnati, cruising at an altitude of fifteen thousand feet."

Paul noted curiously the brief smiles that crossed the lips of several of the council members at this point. He was unsure whether Brian had noticed it or even what had triggered it.

"Suddenly the sky went pitch black and what looked like a rolling cloud bank engulfed the plane. An electrical storm the likes of which I've never seen flashed around me. The engine sputtered, and the dashboard lights blinked! Suddenly I was out of the cloud bank and there were mountains around me. About that time the power quit completely. I bailed out." He remembered Paul and the others' confusion with regard to that term. "Bailed out? You know? Jumped with a parachute?"

Olgar nodded his head to indicate he understood.

"The prophecies spoke of his coming," interjected Paul. "Look at his hair and the fairness of his skin! He is the Jarreds' Malhah."

"The Jarreds' Malhah?" The speaker was that elder who'd earlier challenged Paul's claim that he'd found the ship. His voice dripped with arrogance. "Your Malhah is nothing but a silly fabrication meant to give depth to otherwise shallow lives."

"Sanur, please!" entreated another. "We've not considered this in council."

Sanur looked ready to shout back a reply, but Brian's voice cut him short. "But is Calferon my world? Paul insists I was catapulted through space from a neighboring planet. Truthfully, I do not believe that explanation. But you, Olgar, you must know. You hint at knowledge of my world and its things. Can you tell me?"

Olgar hedged his answer. "Well, I suppose . . ."

"I see no harm in revealing that truth," said the elder seated beside Olgar.

Others enthusiastically voiced their agreement.

"So be it," said Olgar. "You were catapulted, not through space, but through time. Whether it was forward or back only you can answer for sure, Brian. Yet I do have my suspicions." Again he smiled. "The Saulcar Mass is a time door. It is a gateway in and out of the dimension of time. It is colorless except when it passes through our atmosphere and draws screula to it. Then it gathers shape and form and its path can be seen. It, like Calferon and the other planets of this solar system, is trapped in orbit about the sun."

Olgar's tale seemed equally as fantastic as Paul's. "A scientist named Albert Einstein theorized the existence of a fourth dimension," began Brian, "but it was all an exercise on paper. His field was theoretical mathematics. You'll not convince me time travel is actually possible!"

Olgar smiled as one bursting with a secret to tell. "If the council votes on it, I've something to show you that may very well change your mind."

Brian pressed Olgar for details.

"Give us time, my inquisitive friend," said Olgar. "As I said, any decision will require the full council's permission." Olgar paused a moment before continuing. "You realize, the more that is revealed to you, the more limited our options are in dealing with you."

Olgar's remark disturbed Paul. "Just what do you mean by that?"

"Please don't view what I've just said as malicious. Try to see it as . . . well, necessary. We did not request the presence of outsiders, yet you are here. We are unsure whether we can allow you to leave. As I said before, our first priority is our own people's security."

"And that is precisely why you can't afford not to let us leave!" cried Paul. "Others watched us traverse the rock and saw us enter."

"They'll believe you had an accident if you do not return," Olgar answered. "That is not so unlikely a possibility, is it? If another party attempts to traverse the rock, well, we'll escort them up here, too."

Paul noted how Olgar avoided the more direct phrasing, "We'll take them prisoner, too!"

"You don't understand," Paul told the council members. "You've got more to lose by holding us here. The three of us are not the only ones who know of the collector and the focusing lens. Those loggers who follow Arnun know of its existence. What if one of them should be taken prisoner by Thyden's patrols and be given an injection of styranotide?"

That part of his argument was bluff. He'd only revealed the knowledge of the collector and focusing lens to his sister, but by claiming others had that knowledge, he put more force behind his argument.

"The power to destroy this rock," he continued, "or the entire peninsula for that matter, will lie in Thyden's hands. And sooner or later he will learn of your society. For remember: the three of us disappeared inside this rock and two dozen loggers know this. Thyden knows I am not a fool, so he can't help but be curious. And when he does learn of your existence, you will be offered two choices: submit to his autocratic rule, or see all you've built here reduced to rubble by the light beam."

"Arrogant child!" cried Sanur. "How dare you thrust such an ultimatum upon us! Reduced to rubble." He ground the words between his teeth. "You had no business coming here."

"Sanur, please," said Olgar.

"Don't attempt to chastise me, Olgar. Our people do not deserve such misfortune cast upon them."

"Not one of us would disagree with you on that point, Sanur. But haven't we all had to consider, even if it's been but a thought in the back of our minds, that one day we would face this crisis? Perhaps each of us has hoped that such a crisis would not occur during his or her tenure on the council. Unfortunately it has now, and we gain nothing by wishing it hadn't."

Sanur offered no rebuttal, so Olgar addressed his thoughts to Paul. "Let us assume that we must now act either in conjunction with Arnun's men or separately. What is it that you would have us do?"

"We need men. Not soldiers! You've already told me that you have no army. But surely some of your menfolk are skilled with bow and arrow? Swords? You must have organized contests of some sort here."

"We do."

"Good. Those men are needed. We need men also who are able fighters. Wrestlers?"

Olgar nodded, indicating that wrestling was a sport practiced in their society.

"Unskilled volunteers would be trained by Arnun and me. If we can get together enough men, we can beat Thyden. And the time to strike is now! His defenses about Castle Chalmet are minimal because the bulk of his forces are engaged in combat to the north." Paul glanced at Sanur, then back at Olgar. "Our futures are now entwined, not by your choice, as Sanur has pointed out, nor by ours, but our lot has been cast together and now we must act as one."

Paul, Brian, and Karin were dismissed and escorted to sleeping quarters, Paul and Brian sharing the same room.

"What do you think their decision will be?" Paul asked Brian. "Olgar said they would debate as long as necessary to reach a consensus."

Brian rolled his head to the side and looked at Paul from the other bed. "Olgar seems open-minded, but Sanur seems dead set against helping us. And did you notice the bars he had on his shirt? Two greens and a purple. The same number as Olgar."

The next morning, breakfast was brought to their quarters. Afterward they were summoned to the dining hall. The entire council had reassembled.

Olgar spoke. "Our futures are now entwined! Those were your parting words last night, Paul. This council is in agreement with you. Either we will break our isolation and band with you in your fight against Thyden, or you and your two friends will *remain* here with us."

The inflection Olgar used on the word "remain" had a ring

of permanence to it that frightened Paul. He knew Olgar had purposely emphasized the word to indicate that escape would be impossible.

Olgar continued. "You have convinced us of the seriousness of the dilemma our society faces. To do nothing is perhaps only to postpone our eventual discovery by Thyden. But to act upon a poorly conceived plan of attack would be most foolish! Our final decision may well rest in the soundness of your plan and in its chance for success. We therefore feel that you should have at your disposal the knowledge we ourselves possess. If any part of it can be used to aid you in the formation of your plan, then it will have been worth revealing.

"Sanur made a comment that the Malhah was a fabrication, a fable not unlike that of the winged beast Saulcar. That fact is true. Yet, of itself, that fact isn't as important as what it hints at. Yours was a programmed society, Paul, one set up as a desperate hope for the genetic continuity of the four races. Certainly the guidelines used did not establish a perfect society. If one such as Thyden could come to power and dominate, then it is quite an imperfect society. However, those who founded your society faced a more frightening monster than Thyden.

"The planet Eost is the homeland of our ancestors. Eost orbits the star Irita. I could point out Irita to you come nightfall if you wish. Records kept by the crew indicate that it was a twelve-year journey. How they knew Calferon had an atmosphere similar to theirs is unclear. Perhaps they didn't. Perhaps it was by chance they discovered this planet. Perhaps what was more important was not that they arrived here but that they left Eost.

"The monster they faced was the same one you've uncovered—the light beam. In the old tongue it is known as 'Eron-tornatu.' If the beam is correctly focused, the heat energy from it will accelerate the growth of the core-vines. Those who first colonized the skies did not have the years to wait for the grazing lands and the crop fields to develop. Their needs were immediate. There were four to five hundred of them to feed, as well as their animals.

"Now if the beam of the Eron-tornatu is focused too narrowly, the heat produced will rupture the jooarie sacs and the ground will crumble. Surprisingly enough, both of these can be constructive forces. In the hands of a skilled operator the beam could be focused to rupture the jooarie sacs when the crohephite rock turned upward. Thus, only a flat plain would develop. Let the core-vines develop of their own accord and, well, I'm sure you've seen the mountains that can result."

"But what of the Eastern Mountains?" interrupted Paul. "Core-vine dating shows that they preceded the development of the plains and rolling hills in and around Castle Chalmet."

"And well they should! For they were wherever the four ships hovered as they seeded the skies below them. The heat from the exhaust of their engines greatly accelerated the growth of the core-vine seedlings and formed the crohephite rock upon which the ships could land."

"Yet the heat from the exhaust of the engines must have been intense," remarked Brian. "Surely that would have ruptured the jooarie sacs?"

Olgar smiled. "An astute observation. However, the degree of heat energy is relative to the distance away from the engines. Do you understand?" He continued. "Naturally, they had no control over the formation of those first core-vines. Thus the Eastern Mountains."

"Yet we found one of the ships in the sands of Calferon," pointed out Karin.

"Perhaps that ship's engines failed while in the hover mode. Perhaps that ship was never able to engage the hover mode and simply couldn't brake itself in its descent. It's unclear exactly what went wrong. So many records were destroyed."

"What do you mean?" asked Paul.

"Those who came here desired to bury their past in order to preserve their future. That principle underlay the other guidelines set up to govern the programming of your society. Perhaps a brief examination of their history can serve as explanation. Try to imagine, if you can, Paul, the skies above Calferon filled with crohephite rock formations. Link some by vast bridges. Position others at different elevations from their neighbors. Then imagine them all destroyed in one final war. Imagine four ships fleeing this destruction, four ships commanded by people who foresaw this doom, four ships laden with all the people they could carry to start a new civilization on a new planet."

"What was this war about?" asked Paul.

"Does it matter?" replied Olgar. "Why does Thyden attack your fiefs? Does the reason make any more sense? Is it any more justifiable?" He paused to give Paul a moment to think about the questions he had raised. "What is crucial here is that Thyden does not yet know of the Eron-tornatu. Thyden may subjugate you—he may kill many of you—but he cannot wipe out everything. Without knowledge of the ultimate weapon, genetic continuity will be possible. That was why those who settled here desired to destroy all records of the planet Eost and their twelve-year journey. Consider what that left them. It granted them the power to selectively reintroduce into a new society those elements they believed good and beneficial, while discarding those they saw as bad or dangerous. With this in mind, they scrutinized their technology carefully. They kept what they believed beneficial—advances in medicine, knowledge of drugs, of plants, their craftsmanship in stone. They eliminated sophisticated weapons and reintroduced the more primitive bow and arrow. Books on physics, astronomy, and their star charts were destroyed, for they stood as evidence of a more advanced civilization. Most importantly, they denied the existence of their most awesome creation—the Eron-tornatu. They did this because they believed that technology, while it moved a civilization farther into the future, also pushed it ever closer to its inglorious day of self-annihilation. It was the hope of these people to retard that progress.

"The key to the success of their plan lay in the upbringing of their children and their grandchildren. Strict birth control practices were adhered to during their years of space travel. Those who were children when they boarded the ships were, upon reaching this world, old enough to be brought into the confidence of their elders. And that confidence was this: that Eost, their homeland, as well as those portions of their technology they wished not to reintroduce into their new society, were forbidden topics. Nothing was to be written or spoken concerning them. In time, all who knew of the past world would age and die."

"But what of the ship on Calferon?" asked Karin.

"And what of your own knowledge of all this?" inquired Paul. "What went wrong?"

"Let me answer Karin's question first," replied Olgar. "The stairway down was built at the same time the Eron-tornatu was assembled and the focusing tower built. It took ten years to build those stairs, and I'm sure the scizans involved must have had an idea it would take that long. Perhaps they hoped there was some sort of substance on the planet's surface on which those aboard the ill-fated ship could survive. But in the back of their minds they had to consider that they would find the crew of that ship—"

"Who were mostly Ornan," interjected Paul, the realization just come to him.

Olgar smiled. "Four ships—four races. It was perhaps in hindsight not a perfect solution. Perhaps there were politics involved that resulted in the concentration of numbers as they did. In any case, someone had the presence of mind to at least splinter off a handful from the other races and place them within each ship. That way one race could not be wiped out entirely."

Olgar continued with his previous train of thought. "First and foremost it was regarded as a rescue mission. But in the back of their minds they must have realized that they would find no one alive, that their mission would be to destroy what remained of the ship."

"Destroy the ship? How?" asked Brian.

"None of us know the technology involved. We have to assume that each ship could somehow self-destruct, dissolve itself, whatever. There are no traces of the first three ships and they certainly weren't small structures."

"Yet they never found the ship, did they? It was buried in the sand."

"That's right, Karin, but they did find something else." Olgar looked at Brian. "Something you'd be most interested in seeing."

"Show me," cried Brian. "I'm interested, damn it!"

Olgar's smile revealed that he enjoyed teasing Brian on this particular subject. "Patience, my friend. I've yet to answer Paul's question. Then we shall take a little walk."

"You asked about us. It must be obvious from what I've

told you that their plan was an imperfect one. Think about the staircase. It's still there, isn't it? Have you not stopped to wonder why that is after all I've told you? You've seen the fan wheel! Instead of destroying the staircase, they constructed a swirling wall of sand to conceal it." Olgar paused, searching for just the right words to make his point. "It's difficult to dissolve one's past completely. A part of them wanted to preserve the marvelous creations of the very same technology they were trying to deny. The stairway was truly a feat of engineering and they found they couldn't destroy it. Perhaps they rationalized that one day they might want to explore Calferon. So, too, the Eron-tornatu remains concealed in a mountaintop, for it was no less an engineering marvel than the staircase.

"Those who hollowed out Chimney Ridge started as a band of eight men and eight woman. They were grandchildren of those who came in the ships. These sixteen set out to preserve what knowledge and records they could, for it was their passion to keep alive the past. Yet they also believed that they should not be the ones to jeopardize the experimental society of their grandparents. So they set off to build their own secluded society. That was over three hundred years ago."

Olgar smiled at Brian. "Now it is time to show you a bit of your own world."

They climbed a narrow set of stairs to a small shrinelike room. Its ceiling was high and vaulted. Through a hole in it a shaft of sunlight fell squarely onto a small, bare table centered in the room. The wall to their right and left each had a semicircular niche cut into it. A writing desk and chair snugly fit these openings. A niche had been cut into the far wall as well, and within it sat a metallic capsule four feet high and two feet in diameter. Shelves had been cut into the stone on either side of and above this niche. About two dozen books sat upon these shelves, as well as a gadget of some sort and some thin, flat items.

"As you know," said Olgar, specifically addressing Brian, "that first expedition to Calferon did not locate the Ornan ship. But what they did find protruding from the sand was that capsule. Please, explore the room. I believe these are the artifacts of your time."

Brian approached the capsule. He saw a seam in the metal

three quarters of the way up. "Cincinnati—2005" was inscribed in pronounced letters in the upper piece.

"There were more volumes when the time capsule was first found," said Olgar, indicating the books on the shelves. "Those who founded Chimney Ridge had enough trouble securing these."

Brian spoke aloud the authors and titles of some of the books. "Hemingway, Shakespeare, Dr. Seuss, Webster's Dictionary, Encyclopedia Britannica, Volumes 1, 7, 21. May I?" he asked, indicating his desire to look more closely at the gadget above the time capsule.

Olgar nodded his permission.

Brian removed the device from the shelf and placed it squarely in the shaft of sunlight on the table. Immediately two small, red indicating lights came on.

"It's a solar-powered cassette player," he said in amazement.

He realized then that those flat disks on the shelves were cassettes.

"It is how those who came in the ships learned to speak your language," revealed Olgar. "That was perhaps their most ambitious undertaking—complete erasure of their native tongue. That way, even if notes and records were one day found on the Ornan ship, who would understand them?"

"Yet that, too, has not been a complete success," remarked Paul. "Some names are still of old tongue origin. Some words remain, too. My great-great-grandfather could read and translate bits of old tongue scribe. I can see how it aided him in his exploration of the Ornan ship."

Brian had gone back to studying the time capsule. Suddenly he whirled around. "What year is this?"

Paul's immediate thought was to tell him it was the year "358."

However, it was Olgar who answered. "There's no way of knowing. You've gone into the future, haven't you?"

"My god!" said Brian, visibly trembling. "Cincinnati!"

CHAPTER 27

The view from the balcony at the intersection of the two crossing stairways revealed new sights. A pool of water was visible this side of the orchard. A bench of raised stone ringed it. A couple sat upon the bench, their shoes off, feet splashing in the water. Absent was the sound of running water Paul had heard the other day, so he asked Olgar about this.

"You entered Chimney Ridge the second morning after the rain. When our storage containers are full, we allow the excess from the ursulas to fill that pool. There are pipes running through the rock behind us. The pool will be drained in a few days so the water does not become stagnant."

Paul noted something else of interest. From the floor of Chimney Ridge there flashed a bright point of light. "What is that glint of sunlight?"

Olgar smiled. "That is a signal beacon. The intense light is produced by a specially developed ascama fiber-stub. It's how we communicate between the floor of the rock and the plateau above."

Olgar explained another phenomenon they had been curious about. "It is a woven fabric," he said, indicating with a sweep of his arm the covering across the top of Chimney Ridge. "Actually the threads are derived from the leaves of two plants. One leaf gives it its strength, the other its properties of absorption. Both are transparent, as you can see."

"There seems," remarked Brian, "a slight grayish brown cast to it. What is the reason for that?"

Olgar smiled again. It was evident that he took great pride in revealing the wonders of his civilization. "It does not start out that way. It's perfectly clear when it is first pulled taut around its holding fixtures. This one will be replaced soon. The grayish brown tint is from the smoke of our fires. Some of our heating needs are accomplished by the sun, but stone does not absorb the heat well. At night, especially in the colder season, fires must be lit. Naturally, we must cook year round and that also requires flame. Yet how secluded could we remain if smoke were visible issuing from the top of Chimney Ridge?" Olgar paused, then added, "the wood for our fires we harvest atop the rock."

Atop the plateau was a forest unlike any Paul had ever seen. The trees were thirty feet high, two feet in diameter, perfectly straight and without branch or leaf.

Olgar looked at the woman and two men playfully, enjoying their amazement. "How do they grow? Ask it! I'm waiting for that question from one of you."

"All right," said Paul. "How do they grow?"

"Isn't it obvious? The bark is the leaf." He noted the looks of skepticism on all three of his visitors' faces. "I'm serious. Touch one of the trees."

The bark did not feel like bark should. It was soft and spongy.

"This outer layer," explained Olgar, "which we call crileen, is roughly an inch thick and capable of all the photosynthetic chemistry a leaf is. Where growing space is severely limited, as it is here, trees such as these enable us to grow and harvest more wood. They can be planted at three-foot centers and do not have to be transplanted or pruned."

They began to walk through the forest.

"The floor of this plateau," continued Olgar, "lies thirty-five feet below its rim. This allows the trees to grow hidden from the view of those who live and work on the Medoc Peninsula." He pointed at the ridge top and traced its shape. "A walkway encircles the rim."

Even more amazing than the strange trees was what lay within a translucent fabric dome beside an ursula at the far end of the plateau. It was an airplane. They entered the dome through doorway flaps that closed back on themselves.

"Where did this come from?" asked Brian.

"The same place you did, my friend," replied Olgar. "The Saulcar Mass."

The plane was a small, single-engine, single-wing, two-seater. The cockpit was open. A machine gun was mounted behind the propeller. The plane was numbered, and its markings were clearly American.

"How did the pilot land it here?"

"We'd just harvested a band of trees. Perhaps you've noticed that each crop runs west to east. There are no stumps left when we harvest. If there were, we'd be unable to plant a new tree in the same spot. Roots and all come up. So the pilot of this craft had a smooth path to land upon. He did tear a quadrant of an ursula apart, for he kept going beyond the trees. He would have smashed into the far wall had the fabric not slowed him."

"She's well preserved," remarked Brian, stepping onto the wing beside the cockpit. "Why, she doesn't look to have suffered any damage at all!" He looked suspiciously at Olgar. "Where is the pilot? He couldn't have been killed in the crash."

Olgar was not quick to answer Brian's question. "It is a part of our history we speak of seldomly. I do not feel we acted irrationally. Perhaps he could have been captured. At least then he could have told us the reasons for his actions."

"What the hell are you talking about?"

Brian's impatience was obvious to the others. So, too, was his reason for it. The pilot would be another person from *his* world.

"There are those who, upon occasion in the summer months, sleep atop the plateau. The plane landed and they came running to investigate, to *help!* The pilot stepped from the plane. He held a weapon of some sort and started firing it. Hard metal pellets it shot."

"Bullets, yes! He fired them from a gun. But why? What did your people do to him?"

"Nothing," replied Olgar defensively. "He simply climbed down from the plane and started firing his weapon."

"That doesn't make any sense! Why would he just start shooting? There's something you're not telling me."

Brian's accusation infuriated Olgar. His face reddened and the veins of his neck swelled noticeably. "I'm telling you what happened! He was unprovoked! There's nothing else to tell!"

Brian fell silent, bowing his head like a child who had just been scolded.

Olgar finished his account of the story. "Some of our people managed to get help. A bow and arrow was secured and the man killed. We dumped his body into the sky-void."

"How many years ago did this happen?" asked Brian, still looking away.

"Forty-five."

"The beginnings of World War II," Brian said, half to himself, half to the others. He ran his hand along the fuselage. "It's an old aircraft. Perhaps they were going to press it into service. Did any ammunition come with this?"

"Ammu-what?" asked Olgar.

"Pellets," said Brian. "We call them bullets, or rounds. This is a machine gun mounted up here. It's designed to fire rounds of ammunition through the spinning prop."

"A great many bullets came with it. Strung together, you know what I mean? And some larger cylinders."

"Good lord," said Brian. "Bombs?"

"Bombs?" repeated Olgar. "I guess."

Bombs, thought Paul. Brian had told him of bombs. He'd told him of bombs that could destroy an entire city, even one the size of Fief Karcan. He'd called them warheads.

"Can you fly this airplane?" he asked Brian.

Brian nodded.

Paul smiled with anticipation. "Good. I've an idea."

CHAPTER 28

 Paul stood, arms outstretched, grasping the handrail of the balcony. He'd let his head fall forward and his eyes were closed. Karin's hands felt good massaging his shoulders.

Earlier that evening he'd made his presentation to the council. He'd thought his plan a good one. No, he'd thought it better than that. He'd thought his plan to recapture Castle Chalmet from Thyden an excellent one. He only hoped the council would feel the same way. They were debating it now. They had guaranteed him a decision in the morning.

Paul opened his eyes ever so slowly, as if awakening lazily from a restful night's sleep. He saw in the gardens below a man and a woman sitting by a pool of water. Their forms were but shadows by the faint light of an ascama fiber lantern. They sat apart. Yet, as if on cue with his own thoughts and desires, he willed them together and they embraced. When the passion within him rose to the point where he could no longer watch them, he reached up and put his hand atop one of Karin's. Suddenly her hand felt very frail and he sensed it trembling slightly. He turned and kissed her.

CHAPTER 29

—

Morning brought the news Paul had hoped to hear.

"We are yours to command," announced Olgar.

* * * * *

Paul watched the shadows of the late afternoon sun slowly lengthen and fill the passage between the rocks. These shadows concerned him. He would have preferred to wait until the sun had fallen below the horizon. The darkness would mask their attack and give them just that much more of an advantage. Yet, already, the four archers secured in positions about the rock face were getting difficult to see, and it was paramount that those archers be knocked out first. His would be the first arrow shot. It would signal the others in the trees around him. Arnun's men waited within the shadows of the forest just beyond the clearing. His whistle would signal the storming of the eastern land bridge.

His muscles felt cramped and he did his best to stretch himself without shaking the limb he straddled. He and the other archers had been in the trees bordering the clearing close to eleven hours, having climbed them before dawn to avoid being seen.

The minutes crept by.

Paul waited for something to happen, something to ensure that his first shot would be true.

"C'mon, c'mon," he mumbled under his breath. "Do something."

One of Lord Thyden's archers stood up to stretch.

Paul's arrow was true. The archer pitched forward and fell from his perch. Arrows whistled through the limbs as bow strings twanged. Another archer fell from the rock. Paul strung another arrow and fired into a crowd of soldiers about their weapons pile. A soldier fell forward into the pile of bows, an arrow in his chest. Another soldier tried to run back across the land bridge and fell as an arrow pierced his calf.

Suddenly an arrow whizzed through the leaves around him. Paul whistled.

Arnun's men charged across the clearing. Some carried bows and let fly their arrows at Lord Thyden's men while others threw their knives. A few charged with hatchets raised above their heads. Lord Thyden's soldiers fell under the onslaught.

Paul let fly a final arrow, then tossed his bow to the ground. They'd only risk hitting Arnun's men now. When he'd climbed down, Arnun was waiting for him.

"It is done," he told Paul. "This end of the land bridge is secure."

Paul was confident that any guards Lord Thyden might have posted at the other end of the land bridge had not seen the attack here. Such was the topography of the land bridge. The rock formations that formed the walls of the bridge were high, and because the trail itself bent slightly to the northeast, it would obscure the view of those at the other end.

"Shall I send for Olgar's men?" Arnun asked Paul.

Paul shook his head. "I've got to consider the possibility, as unlikely as it may be, of an ambush. We'll cross first as a small group and secure the other end. Then we'll signal for Olgar's men to join us. Have your men change into the guards' uniforms."

"Even our small numbers may arouse the suspicion of Lord Thyden's guards at the north end. We have perhaps a dozen more men than Lord Thyden's guard contingent had at this end. They'll be suspicious if any more than a few men approach, even if they wear the garb of the soldiers."

Arnun's point was well taken. "What do you suggest?" asked Paul.

"How many men do you figure Lord Thyden has posted across the way?"

"As few as he figures he can get away with. He needs men for his assault on Fief Salkird. So maybe six?"

"Then I will lead five of my best men across the land bridge. We'll leave immediately."

Paul could do nothing now but wait. The minutes passed slowly. More than once Paul thought about sending men after Arnun. Several times he thought he saw a shadow move in the darkness engulfing the land bridge, but it was only his mind playing tricks on him, his fears projected into substance, then dissolving. Finally one of Arnun's men emerged from the darkness.

"We've secured the other end of the land bridge," he told Paul.

Paul sent a messenger for the men of Chimney Ridge, who waited atop the easternmost ridge of the Medoc Peninsula. Soon the forest crackled with the sounds of twigs breaking underfoot and branches being brushed aside. The men of Chimney Ridge were four hundred strong. Paul led them across the land bridge.

For a time they followed the main road north toward Castle Chalmet, but where the road veered to the northwest, just before the cultivated fields east of the castle, they left its broad path for a narrow trail that cut behind the foothills of the Eastern Mountains. A small contingent of Olgar's men split off from the main group at this point. It was their mission to activate the Eron-tornatu and have it raised by dawn. Olgar had told them of its location; that knowledge his people had preserved. A second contingent of Olgar's men would leave an hour after the first. This organizational detail had been included as a precaution in case something unforeseen happened to the first group. The rest of the men continued north. Soon they came to the stunted trees that marked the entrance to the secret passage beneath the crop fields to Castle Chalmet. Paul pushed aside the thick brush that grew around the entrance. He unlocked the door with the key Christina had given him earlier and stepped into the tunnel. He held an ascama fiber-stub aloft, and it lit the first fifty feet of tunnel. He found a place to secure it on the wall.

"Have the men enter the tunnel," he instructed Arnun. "I've got to signal Brian and Christina."

Paul had not been enthusiastic about his sister riding in the airplane with Brian. Too many things could go wrong. Although they had cleared a path through the trees atop the plateau, Brian had advised him that the runway was short. The condition of the plane concerned him, too. Brian had said there was no way to test it prior to flight other than pulling its levers while it was still on the ground and making sure the proper things worked. Still Christina had insisted on going. The buildings of the village of Canter, which bordered Castle Chalmet, would look similar at night, and only she would know which were of wood and which were of stone. Brian's targets were the wooden buildings. Hopefully one would catch fire when bombed. Lord Thyden's men would have to put out the fire before the jooarie sacs ruptured and that would divert a sizeable amount of manpower from the castle.

Paul climbed the nearest hill only as high as he had to in order to see Chimney Ridge. From his pocket he removed another small box. This one contained an ascama fiber-stub of the type those within Chimney Ridge used to signal each other. Paul opened the box for a second, closed it, opened it again, closed it. He counted to ten and repeated the sequence.

Several minutes later he thought he heard the drone of the airplane's engine. He could not see it, not yet, so he crept closer to the ridge top. Suddenly he was aware of someone beside him.

"Can you see it?" asked Arnun.

"No. The night sky is too dark. Wait! There!" Paul indicated a shadow that seemed to sweep north across the sky over Castle Chalmet.

"I see it, too."

The plane swept past Castle Chalmet, then circled west. Paul and Arnun soon lost sight of it.

"What's Brian doing?" asked Arnun.

"I don't know."

They did not see or hear any sign of the plane for a full minute.

"Something's wrong," mumbled Paul.

"No, wait," said Arnun. "I can hear it. Listen!"

Paul could hear it now, too. It came from somewhere to the south. It grew louder.

Seconds later, its presence seemed to momentarily fill the sky above them. The plane swung around due west toward Castle Chalmet. Moments later, they heard an explosion rip through Canter. However, no ball of fire followed. Brian's second pass netted the same result. But it was on his third pass, when more than one explosion ripped through the village, that flames shot up into the night sky.

CHAPTER 30

 Brian banked the plane to the right and watched the flames as they engulfed the building they had hit. Christina had thrown down several bombs during the last run. Within moments, Castle Chalmet blocked their view of the blazing structure.

"Have you any bombs left?" he yelled back to Christina.

"Yes!" she screamed above the noise of the engine.

"Good! We're going to make a run along the mountains of Fief Salkird. Throw the bombs into groups of soldiers."

Earlier Paul had advised him that Lord Thyden would, in all likelihood, throw his muscle against only one of Fief Salkird's two mountain passes, guaranteeing him a better chance of success than spreading his forces thin between the two. Yet they had both remembered Duke Orsinc's field captain's early morning mission to shore up their defenses on the western pass. That was where Lord Thyden had been clever. He'd kept Duke Orsinc guessing by parading troops at both land bridges.

From the air Brian had seen concentrations of men near the eastern pass. As he and Christina approached the eastern pass, he saw quite a battle raging there. Lord Thyden's men swarmed like ants on the southern face of the mountains. Brian swung the plane into position and grabbed the handles of the machine gun. He was in position to make a west-east pass across the southern slopes of the mountains.

C'mon, baby! Let's work!

The sound of the machine gun exploded in his ears as a hail of bullets rained down upon those scaling the mountains.

"Hold your bombs, Christina, until I make my next run!"

Brian banked the plane around one hundred and eighty degrees. This time the pass he made was over the rolling hills of Fief Karcan bordering the mountains. Here most of Lord Thyden's forces were still gathered. He came in low, no more than one hundred feet above the ground, and squeezed the trigger handles of the machine gun. Christina threw her bombs into groups of men. Brian checked the fuel gauge as he banked the plane around again and saw that it was low. There hadn't been that many rounds of ammunition, either, not for a gun clicking off twenty rounds a second. They exhausted the ammunition and the bombs on their next pass.

Christina took a look behind them. "They are running," she cried. "Do you hear me, Brian? They are running!"

Brian turned the plane around and made another pass. This time many of Lord Thyden's soldiers dove for the ground and covered their heads. Riders were thrown from their mounts.

"We've beaten them," shouted Christina, shaking one arm triumphantly above her head. "We've beaten 'em!"

"We've only confused them," Brian shouted back. "It's up to your brother to beat them."

He banked the plane to the right and soared up and over the mountains separating Fief Karcan from Fief Salkird. To the east was Castle Weslan. Brian swung the plane around to the east and began his descent.

"What are you doing?" asked Christina.

"Landing! Hold on tight!"

He brought the plane in as close to the mountains as he dared. He and Christina left the plane and ran toward Duke Orsinc's men.

"Shore up your defenses now," cried Brian. "Thyden's men are confused and will need to regroup. You must hold the pass for one more night. That's all the time Paul Benjarth needs!"

Duke Orsinc was located and Brian explained the situation. He told him of the Eron-tornatu and Paul's attack on Castle Chalmet. When Brian had finished, Duke Orsinc called for a horse, then rode to the top of the pass to personally see to its defenses.

CHAPTER 31

Paul opened the trapdoor beneath Hall Creary just enough to see into the room. The hall was deserted. He pushed up and back on the trapdoor and signaled the others to follow. The corridor beyond Hall Creary was likewise deserted. Side by side, Paul and Arnun led the men up a wide flight of stairs located at the end of the corridor.

There was a guard atop the landing. Arnun's knife flashed, and the guard crumpled to the stone. Paul ordered the men to spread themselves out the length of the walkway bordering the inner courtyard. The wall there was waist high and would act as a barrier behind which they could kneel and take aim with their bows.

An arrow flew from the top of Tower Satchkind and struck the wall behind them. Voices cried out in alarm.

"Where's the entrance to that tower?" shouted Arnun.

Paul pointed out the doorway.

Arnun instructed Charnen to lead a group of four men around the perimeter hallway to Tower Satchkind. Charnen nodded and was on his way.

A guard contingent burst through a doorway across the courtyard. Paul and the others shot their arrows, and the guards crumpled about the door. Another arrow flashed from

Tower Satchkind. This time one of Arnun's men fell back, the arrow in his shoulder. Two of Lord Thyden's guards appeared on the balcony overlooking the courtyard. They let their arrows fly across the way to where the men of Chimney Ridge still scampered to take up positions. Arrows seemed to fly from all around Paul. The two men atop the balcony fell to the courtyard.

Paul tried to think amidst the confusion. *Where is Thyden? Where would he set up a command post?*

Another arrow flew from the bow of the guard atop Tower Satchkind. Another of Arnun's men fell back.

Of course! Whitin Hall!

"Follow me," cried Paul, as he leaped the barrier wall and ran for the door that opened into Gierfahren's Hall, a small entrance hall adjoining Whitin Hall. An arrow glanced off the stone of the courtyard by his feet. He threw himself against the door and it flew open. The loggers and the men of Chimney Ridge followed him in.

Gierfahren's Hall was deserted. The men crossed the hall and pushed open the entrance doors to Whitin Hall. A wave of gray-green uniforms charged them. Swords raised, faces set in battle frenzy, the soldiers of Lord Thyden closed in too quickly for Paul's men to use their bows. They barely had time to draw their swords before the soldiers were upon them.

"Spread them out," cried Arnun.

Whitin Hall filled with the noise of the soldiers' battle cries. They slashed wildly with their swords, each stroke delivered with the arms fully extended to make the most use of the sword's size and weight. Each was armed with an Edor-Bandi-style sword. Its heavier, broader blade was designed for cutting and slashing rather than thrusting. The blade could cut the spinal cord or lop off an adversary's head with a single swing, but the blade was too heavy for the skillful parries required to defend against the sword thrusts of an opponent. The Edor-Bandi sword was usually given to a strong but unskilled swordsman who stayed on the offensive until he exhausted himself and was slain.

The screams and shouts of the soldiers was a tactic meant to confuse an opponent. But Illad Rahman had taught Paul to shut out the noise. He crossed his sword in front of him to

block the downward hack of a soldier's blow, grabbing his
wrist with his other hand to steady his blade. But the soldier
had put his full weight behind the blow. Paul's sword dipped
and he was forced to crouch, slipping beneath the crossed
swords to gain more leverage. Now the upward force exerted
by the triangular brace formed by his arms and body equalled
the downward force of the soldier's outstretched arms. Suddenly the soldier drew his sword back over his head to deliver
another blow. Paul moved sideways just as the soldier started
to bring his sword down. Its weight, as well as the momentum
generated by the force imparted to the stroke, made any
change in its direction impossible. The blade cut harmlessly
through the air and struck the wood floor. Now the soldier was
off balance, his sword too low. Paul drew his sword up and
across and sliced the soldier about the rib cage.

Paul readied himself for another opponent, but none engaged him. Many of Olgar's men had pushed into the hall behind Arnun's and their combined forces outnumbered Lord
Thyden's. The soldiers backpedaled as Arnun's and Olgar's
men pushed forward. Paul saw Lord Thyden shouting instructions from an elevated stage at the far end of the room. His
gaze was directed . . . *upward?* Paul saw then the trap Lord
Thyden had prepared. Concealed among the wooden bracing
of the first roof support beam were more soldiers. They
jumped before Paul could shout a warning to his men.

Paul had entered Whitin Hall first and had moved toward
the side of the room as their ranks had fanned out. The men of
Chimney Ridge were running forward and moving into positions beside their fellow warriors. Lord Thyden's soldiers had
jumped into these groups of men, their swords flashing as they
swung them forward while in free fall. Two soldiers were killed
before their feet even touched the ground, their own weight
impaling them on upturned swords, but the rest delivered
deathblows as they fell. Paul circled back toward the center of
the room and squared his stance to deal with a soldier who had
turned to challenge him. For a moment, their eyes locked.
Then the soldier's head jerked back, his eyes rolling upward as
his face caved inward with pain. Paul looked down and saw the
blade of a sword protruding from his abdomen. The sword was
twisted and then withdrawn. Blood squirted from the wound

as the soldier fell forward.

"Thought I'd save you the trouble," said a woodsman Paul knew by sight but not by name.

The soldiers' advantage was momentary. Again they were pushed back. Suddenly they started to run, opening up the distance between themselves and Paul's forces. Then they squatted. Arrows ripped through the air above their heads. Paul dove for the wall, doing so not because there was any cover there, but rather because it was instinct to move away from the openness of the room's center. He raised himself on one elbow. The front line of his own forces now lay on the floor, arrow shafts protruding from their chests. Paul could see archers perched atop the second roof support beam.

Fortunately the men of Chimney Ridge were skilled archers. They knelt and returned fire. The wood joists above the support beam offered minimal protection and, one by one, Lord Thyden's archers fell from the beam. Paul's men pushed forward again, doubling up on Lord Thyden's remaining soldiers, easily killing them or taking prisoner those who threw down their swords in surrender.

Paul looked for Lord Thyden but saw no sign of him. He knew immediately his escape route. There were no doors at that end of Whitin Hall, but there was a trapdoor located at the back of the stage. It was used in theatrical productions to allow an actor to appear unexpectedly from behind a piece of scenery. A narrow flight of stairs accessed the trapdoor from a basement room used to store costumes and theatrical props. There was only one door into and out of that room. It opened onto an inside road that passed beneath that end of Whitin Hall. Posts helped support the south end of the building, as did the two embankments bordering the road. The basement room had been built into the slope of the southern embankment.

Narrow windows ran the full height of Whitin Hall to the underside of its pitched roof. These windows were spaced every twenty feet and ran the length of both walls. The window nearest Paul was open, and he slipped outside into the cooler night air. The sounds of the battle grew faint as he moved away from the window. Soon they seemed a part of another world as his concentration was turned to other business. He was alone now, in a private battle with Lord Thyden.

The cloud cover had cleared and the moon shone brightly in the southern sky. The earthen embankment in front of him was studded with rocks, their rounded surfaces glowing white, looking like prehistoric eggs buried in the ground. Tufts of yellow-green grass grew between the rocks. The roadbed was constructed of stone as well, though these were larger and flatter than those used for the embankment. Gaps in the roadbed were sealed with mortar-paste, now chipped and riddled with cracks because of age. Paul quickly descended the slope and crouched behind the wheel of a hay wagon. He'd sheathed his sword and now he loosened the harness straps that held his bow and a quiver of arrows across his back. The forward edge of the cart's wheel protruded beyond the front of the cart. Paul peered out from between its spokes.

Tower Satchkind was fewer than two hundred feet east of Whitin Hall. The road ran straight ahead, then narrowed before ending at a lower level door to the tower. A man's form moved into the circle of light thrown by an ascama fiber lantern that had been mounted above the tower door. Paul strung an arrow, his fingers working automatically as he considered the shot before him. It would be a challenge for even a skilled marksman at this distance. Therefore, the possibility that he would miss was good, and an errant shot would only serve to alert Lord Thyden that he had been pursued. Lord Thyden glanced his way and Paul flattened himself against the side of the wagon. Lord Thyden turned and entered Tower Satchkind. Paul slipped from behind the cart and ran into the shadows of the southern embankment after restrapping his bow across his back. He drew his sword as he neared the tower door. Slowly he opened it and entered.

A dark sweep of stair followed the curve of the tower's wall. Paul walked with his sword held upright, its hilt at chest level. He could feel the uneven ripple of the stone against his back as he moved along the inside wall of the stairway. He could feel moisture through his shirt and wondered if it was the cool sweat of the stone or his own perspiration.

Paul heard something move above his head. He ducked instinctively, spinning completely around as he dropped down several steps. He squared his body to the line of the stairs as he spread his feet for balance. He crossed his sword in front of him, ready to rip it up and across, left to right. Yet only the darkness of the stairs lay before him. *What had he heard?* He thought it had been Lord Thyden's sword cutting through the air. He took a cautious step forward, listening for the retreat of Lord Thyden's footsteps up the stairs. Something had happened. Or had it? Was his mind playing tricks on him? He heard the sound again. This time he held his ground. *The wind!* He remembered there was an opening, more a slot than a window, high in the wall ahead. It was used to ventilate the stairway.

There was no mistaking the next sound he heard. It was a man's scream. A *dying* man's scream. It had come from the main tower room, which was at ground level. Paul proceeded cautiously, still keeping his back against the inner wall and his sword raised in front of him. When he reached the top step, he paused by the open doorway to the tower's main room. Slowly he stuck his head out and peered around the stone's edge.

A man lay facedown on the floor, his arms pinned beneath his body. He was spotlighted in a circle of light thrown by the ascama fiber lantern hanging above the south door. He wore a brown cloak and hood. Paul recognized the garment as one worn by some of Arnun's men. He remembered that Arnun had sent Charnen and three other loggers to Tower Satchkind early in the fight. Had Thyden surprised this man, cut him down, and fled the tower? The man was moaning, and Paul knew he would have to see to his wounds. He laid his sword on the floor and knelt beside the man, then reached for his shoulder, meaning to roll him over.

The man slashed out with his right arm as he rolled up onto his elbow. Paul saw the knife and threw himself backward, falling on the stone. Lord Thyden was on his feet in an instant. He unsheathed his sword and laid its point against Paul's chin. Paul, propped up on his elbows, tried to inch away from the blade, but his elbows were well forward of his shoulders and he couldn't apply any leverage to push himself. All he could do was twist his head back. Lord Thyden pricked Paul's chin with the tip of his sword. A thin flow of blood rolled down his neck.

"How pathetically like your father you look, Benjarth pup," Lord Thyden said.

Thyden's hair, cut short in the front but longish elsewhere, fell forward, framing his sunken cheekbones and convergent brow line in a three-sided rectangle of gray and white. His eyes were more oblong than round—a Sinese trait—yet their coloring was the true gray-brown of the Jarred. His white eyelashes were unnaturally long, almost spiked. His nose was extremely thin with little tip.

Paul realized Lord Thyden had killed a logger and disposed of his body. He had then donned the logger's hooded cloak and feigned injury. He had known all along he was being pursued and had set up this trap.

"You've seen your father, haven't you? Face to face? He's not a pretty sight, is he?" Lord Thyden laughed. "Perhaps his blindness will prove a blessing for him. He won't be able to see his son's corpse."

Lord Thyden parted his thin lips just enough to show teeth. It was a gloating smile, a momentary acknowledgment of his victory. Then his face hardened as he raised his sword above his head.

Then, oddly, Lord Thyden's sword seemed to continue up in an arc of its own, and it slid from his grip. Even more incredibly, Lord Thyden himself rose in the air.

Charnen tossed Lord Thyden like a limp rag to the floor, then he helped Paul to his feet. Paul saw that the south door was open and that Charnen had slipped inside behind Lord Thyden.

CHAPTER 32

Brian stayed atop the ridge all night with Duke Orsinc's troops. Maybe he napped once or twice; he wasn't sure. Now and then he could make out a faint shadow of motion downhill. He knew Lord Thyden's archers were attempting to establish positions high on the mountain to provide cover for a morning assault. Occasionally he could hear the twang of a bowstring as one of Duke Orsinc's archers drew a bead on a soldier. Sometimes he heard the arrow strike the rock and knew the archer had missed. Other times there would be no sound. The arrow might have missed then as well, sailing high of its mark and striking the softer ground of the plain below. Or maybe a soldier had been killed, his flesh soundlessly absorbing the arrow's impact. There was no way of knowing; not once did Lord Thyden's archers return fire.

Brian was very aware of the subtle changes in light that preceded the dawn. The stars that blanketed the sky—a good sign, since it indicated little or no cloud cover—began to fade the way an ascama fiber-stub would burn out, its glow becoming softer and softer until its light was finally extinguished. This was followed by a very gradual lightening of the sky, gray dawn replacing the darker colors of the night. The sky above the Eastern Mountains turned pale blue, lit by a morning sun still hidden behind Calferon's horizon. The blue expanded across the sky, then the peaks of the Eastern Mountains appeared backlit by a soft, yellow-orange glow.

Suddenly a flurry of arrows ripped through the air above their heads. Lord Thyden's soldiers charged up the south side of the pass while others climbed the steeper slopes of the mountains on either side. Duke Orsinc's archers returned fire and cut down the first line of advancing soldiers. Their places were immediately taken by other soldiers as a wall of men continued to push up the pass.

A soldier leaped out from behind a rock only a few feet downhill from the ridge top. He had managed to climb to that point unobserved. His knife was drawn and he killed one of Duke Orsinc's archers immediately. He would have killed others except that, by the time the soldier had picked out another opponent, an archer had cut him down. Brian had watched the attack and was reminded of Duke Orsinc's sobering words to his commanders last night. He had said that Lord Thyden's numbers were so great that three soldiers could die for every one of their men and still the soldiers would overrun the ridge. That confrontation had been a one-for-one trade!

The battle raged for an hour, the main body of Lord Thyden's troops pushing ever closer to the ridge top.

An archer holding a spyglass came running toward Duke Orsinc. Brian moved toward them to hear their conversation.

"Something's happening in the Eastern Mountains," the archer cried. "See for yourself!"

He handed Duke Orsinc the spyglass. Duke Orsinc took a look, then gave it to Brian. "Is that the Eron-tornatu?" he asked.

A thin, needlelike structure had split the ball of the morning sun in two. The upper half of the needle then divided in three. Next the two outside pieces moved downward and stopped when the structure resembled a cross. Each of the three arms and the stem of the Eron-tornatu opened radially. The pieces joined together to form a bowl-shaped disk that eclipsed all but the outer edge of the sun.

Something flashed before their eyes, forcing all who had been staring in the direction of the Eastern Mountains to shut their eyes momentarily until the brilliant afterimages of the light had passed. The air crackled. When Brian opened his eyes again, he saw a beam of light in the sky above their heads. Slowly the light came down toward them. Brian was aware that all fighting had stopped. Lord Thyden's soldiers, as well as Duke Orsinc's, were all gazing up into the sky. The beam of the Eron-tornatu struck the ridge east of the pass, the light glowing brightly against the darker stone of the mountain. The beam was thirty feet in diameter. It continued downward until it reached the base of the slope.

Minutes later, Brian heard a popping sound as if something were trying to boil up from beneath the ground. There quickly followed another pop, then another. Brian knew what was happening. The selevium gas was expanding because of the heat and the jooarie sacs were rupturing. A sudden rush of selevium gas spurted loose stone into the air. Moments later, the ground ripped open.

* * * * *

Paul sat on a stool atop the flat roof of Tower Satchkind. He gripped the two turn wheels that controlled the pitch of the Eron-tornatu's deflection mirror, which was located in the room below. Arnun stood nearer the wall encircling the roof, a spyglass raised to his eye. Paul had a view of the mountain slopes of Fief Salkird through a crenelation, but he could not see the grassy plain that bordered them. At some point in the past, after the Eron-tornatu had formed the open plains to the north and west of Castle Chalmet, the tower wall apparently had been raised for defense. Paul assumed this because it seemed illogical for the operator of the Eron-tornatu not to be able to see the ground he was molding. Arnun had agreed to help Paul direct the light beam.

"The ground has opened up!" Arnun cried excitedly.

Paul got up, took the spyglass from Arnun, and focused it on the hole. He could see the nubs of green where the core-vines had sheared, as well as the porous crohephite rock and the chartreuse skins of the jooarie sacs bordering the hole. The opening looked to be fifty feet across and two hundred feet long.

"Move the beam southwest," said Arnun, again looking

through the spyglass.

Paul turned the wheels. The mirror could pivot horizontally, as well as tilt forward or backward. The two worm gear
screws joined to the turn wheels were finely threaded, allowing
for precise adjustments in the mirror's position.

"More west," Arnun said.

Paul turned the right wheel one degree clockwise.

"A little more. . . . That's it!"

Paul let go of the turn wheels. He was aware of the windy
sound of the turbulent air currents swirling around the light
beam, and then, for a moment, his thoughts drifted. Earlier
he had watched the Eron-tornatu's collector, focusing mirrors,
and lenses slowly unfold above the peaks of the Eastern Mountains to receive the energy of the morning sun. Then there was
light, a thick rope of yellow-white light that was so concentrated it appeared solid. The superheated air crackled as if it
were fabric being torn apart stitch by stitch. The beam had
struck the mirror, then angled northward, diffusing to a point
in the sky well above the mountains of Fief Salkird. Paul had
slowly tilted the mirror forward, bringing the light beam
down against the dark stone of the mountains.

Paul's strategy was to burn a "moat" around the soldiers,
isolating them from the rest of Fief Karcan. Once the moat
encircled them, he would chip away at the land, shearing off
huge chunks of crohephite rock, some perhaps as thick as
ninety feet near the mountains. Soldiers and horses would fall
to the planet's surface. Duke Orsinc's archers would kill those
soldiers who remained on the mountains or who had retreated
to the lower slopes.

Minutes later Arnun told Paul the ground had ripped open
again.

"Look at that!" Paul cried. A large fragment of crohephite
rock had risen into the air and was blown to the east by the
wind.

"A strange phenomenon," remarked Arnun. "For some
reason a jooarie sac did not rupture." The weight of the rock
still encrusted to it was less than the weight the selevium gas
could displace. The jooarie sac eventually would adjust its production of selevium gas, but it could not do so instantly.

Paul watched the rock begin to descend as the jooarie sac

adjusted to the change in altitude and released gas. Then, with Arnun's help, he centered the beam of the Eron-tornatu on a section of plain west of the opened ground. This time the sudden outrush of selevium gas spurted loose stones into the air moments before the ground collapsed.

"The jooarie sacs rupture quickly now," said Paul.

Arnun nodded. "That first break took almost twice as long as the others. No doubt the rock, bordering where the ground is being directly heated, is being preheated as well."

Paul nodded. He was pleased with how well things had gone so far. Last night Olgar's men had found the Eron-tornatu. A single door located on the mountain's east side accessed its hollow top. Inside, eight shiny metal girders angled upward from points equidistant along the circumference of the floor. These were bolted to a metal ring thirty feet in diameter near the room's ceiling. The machinery of the Eron-tornatu, except for its computers, was located in the center of the room atop a circular platform. The collector was folded, allowing it to pass through the ring. A single worm gear ran straight up beside the platform to a point just inside the metal ring. The grooves in the worm gear were widely spaced and allowed the Eron-tornatu to be raised quickly.

The top of the mountain had been fitted with a cone-shaped piece of metal. This artificial top had slid back on rails when the Eron-tornatu had been raised. A bank of solar cells energized the tracking computers, which had kept the disk aligned with the sun.

Paul had used the blueprints retrieved from the Ornan ship to measure the size of the opening that had once existed in Tower Satchkind but had since been walled over. It was through this opening that the concentrated beam of the Eron-tornatu had been directed. The mirror and the rods on which it pivoted were joined to the ceiling by a bolted pin-and-clevis joint. His ancestors had concealed the mirror by strapping it in place against the ceiling, then constructing a false ceiling below it. Masons had labored by lantern light to lower the mirror into position, four of them supporting it and its pivot rods while the other two unfastened its straps.

An opening had to be made in the ceiling of the upper tower room to allow both worm gear shafts and their atached turn wheels to pass through. The control of the mirror was meant to be from the roof of Tower Satchkind, most likely because the heat generated by the light beam made it impossible for an operator to remain in the same room as the mirror.

"Lord Thyden's soldiers have discovered our strategy," Arnun advised Paul. "They are climbing down the mountains' slopes."

"What about his cavalry?"

"They've already mounted. No doubt they plan to flee west near the Void of Carcin. There's open ground there."

"Direct me to where the riders gather," said Paul, realizing another of the Eron-tornatu's powers as a weapon. Crohephite rock is not the only thing the Eron-tornatu can burn holes in."

Arnun smiled as it dawned on him what Paul intended to do. "Bring the beam north," he said, "toward the mountains, and a little to the west."

Paul moved the turn wheels as Arnun had instructed him.

"Yes! That's it," shouted Arnun. "The horses buck and unseat their riders. The heat must be intense." He turned to Paul. "Move the beam east to west and back again. They're spread out."

Arnun raised the spyglass to his eye. "Keep doing it! Back and forth!" He shook his fist triumphantly in the direction of the soldiers. "Retreat, you bastards! Fall back toward the mountains!" He gestured to Paul. "Quickly now. Bring the beam forward. They're confused and we can crumble more land."

Paul followed Arnun's instructions until the light beam was in position to burn away the next section of grassland. Then he jumped from the stool and took the spyglass from Arnun. Paul focused it first on the plain, where he could see dozens of horses and soldiers lying on the ground, but he saw that the dead accounted for only a small fraction of Lord Thyden's total forces. He raised the spyglass and scanned the mountains. Duke Orsinc's archers had crossed the crest of the ridge and were now establishing positions behind mounds of rock on the upper slopes.

Just then the beam of the Eron-tornatu vanished. Paul jerked his head skyward. A small cloud moved in front of the sun. To the northwest he saw a cloud bank moving in their direction. Already the wind had picked up.

The beam of the Eron-tornatu reappeared as the cloud moved from in front of the sun. Minutes later the ground split open where the beam had been focused. Paul sat back down on the stool. He knew which way to move the light beam without Arnun's instructions this time. West by northwest. He moved the left wheel two degrees counterclockwise and the right one a degree clockwise. He was beginning to close the circle.

The ground crumbled minutes later. This time a jagged opening ran for several hundred yards in the direction of the Void of Carcin.

"The ground is thin near the void," said Arnun. "It crumbles quickly."

Paul glanced over his shoulder at the approaching clouds. Not quickly enough, he thought. "What do Thyden's horsemen do?" he asked.

"They wait for the clouds." Arnun looked up at the cloud bank. "We won't make it, Paul. We have only a few minutes of sunlight left." He glanced skyward again. "If even that." He looked at Paul, desperate, then, with a shrug of his shoulders, said, "What can we do? We're better off just to run the beam through their midst and kill as many of them as we can."

No, thought Paul. Thousands of solders would still escape. Lord Thyden's commanders might reorganize them in the days ahead, and they would prove a formidable army to defeat.

It was then Paul had a flash of insight. The jooarie sacs produced or released selevium gas in response to a change in surface weight, but they could not do so *instantly*. The time factor was the key. It was the only chance they had to prevent Lord Thyden's armies from escaping justice.

"How much land remains to the Void of Carcin?" he asked Arnun.

"Maybe eighty yards, but we only have a minute or two of sunlight left. It's not enough time."

"Forget about the time," Paul shouted back. "I just need you to help me direct the beam to that final strip of land."

"There's not enough time, Paul! Just sweep the beam through them."

"Damn it all, Arnun! Do as I say!"

Arnun gave Paul an uncertain look, but helped him guide the beam. Paul moved the light beam up and down the length of the strip of land. Maybe he could rupture a few of the jooarie sacs—he was sure he could—and a few were all he needed. The land itself did not have to collapse; it only had to weaken. A change in surface weight would be created by the thousands of horses and riders crossing the strand. The jooarie sacs would not be able to produce selevium gas fast enough to compensate for the sudden, massive increase in weight.

Paul continued to move the light beam back and forth. Not once did he look over his shoulder at the approaching clouds. He had to concentrate on his hands and the motion of the turn wheels. Two degrees counterclockwise with the right turn wheel and two degrees clockwise with the left, then, slowly, the reverse of that. The light beam had to stay focused on that narrow piece of land.

The beam vanished as the cloud bank moved in front of the sun. Paul jumped from the stool and ran to the tower wall. "What's happening?" he asked Arnun, who was viewing events through the spyglass.

"They ride across," said Arnun. "Wait! It's happening! The land has dropped."

Paul grabbed the spyglass from Arnun. The southern edge of the land between the sky-void moat and the Void of Carcin had dropped six feet. This newly formed wall of crohephite rock was too high for the horses to jump over. The riders that followed continued to spur their mounts forward, only to realize too late the predicament of the other horsemen. The southern edge dropped again, forming a deeper wedge into which horses and soldiers helplessly fell. A crack formed along the northern edge of the land, then the crohephite rock gave way, completing the moat. Soldiers and horses alike hurtled downward toward Calferon's surface.

CHAPTER 33

—

 Lord Thyden watched the Benjarth guard walk back and forth in front of his cell. He was flattered. *So the Benjarth fear my cleverness enough to post a guard!* Unfortunately there was no way he could escape. The cell had been built solidly. The guard was unnecessary.

"Stop your pacing, fellow," he called out irritably.

The guard, who had been absently staring at the ground as he had been walking, stopped and looked at Lord Thyden. "How I wished Paul had ordered you brought atop tower Satchkind. From there you would have seen the ground crumble beneath your ill-fated cavalries and foot soldiers."

Lord Thyden pressed his face against the bars of his cell and spat at the guard. The guard rolled back his head and laughed as the spittle fell short of its mark.

Lord Thyden had learned of the Eron-tornatu from the boastful Benjarth guards who rotated shifts to watch him. Such an incredible weapon! He had heard the roar of its destruction all morning. Only two hours ago the sound had stopped. Lord Thyden suspected this was because the sun had moved into the western quadrant of the sky and its weakening light could no longer be amplified sufficiently to produce the beam.

Lord Thyden knew his armies stood no chance against such a

weapon. He suspected many of his men had been killed and the rest—*cowards!*—had probably surrendered. The Benjarth had won the war. Now only thoughts of revenge mollified his feelings of defeat. The thin band of jewelry he wore on his left wrist concealed a tiny dart outfitted with a self-activating plunger. The dart was filled with cymethadrenatyne. He would slip the dart into his mouth and spit it in Paul's face when he was brought before him for sentencing. A hollow cap on his tooth was filled with the little bit of cymethadrenatyne he had left. Biting down sharply on that tooth would spill the drug, and the two of them would have twenty minutes together in the maze-box. That would give him enough time to kill the Benjarth pup and take his own life with his light-gun, depriving the Benjarth of that final satisfaction.

Yet the arrogant confidence of these guards gave him reason to consider a second option, if only to knock them down a few notches. Wouldn't his victory be more satisfying if the rest of Paul's lot were to know that he, and not their boy-warrior, was the better fighter? He could laugh in their faces as they stared open-mouthed at their dead leader. Certainly they would be curious to know what had happened to him. So he would tell them. Tell them every detail of the boy's defeat in the maze-box! What was the worst that could happen to him then? It was a known fact that the Benjarth were *civilized* and did not torture. Death by hanging? How painful could that possibly be? A trapdoor sprung, a rush of motion, and then the mind tumbling into the dark, peaceful recesses of death. That instant in time when the neck snapped had to happen too quickly for the brain to interpret the nerve endings' messages of pain.

Lord Thyden heard a swish of air. The guard suddenly doubled over and clutched at something about his midsection. He fell dead to the stone before he could pull out the knife.

A figure stepped in front of his cell.

"Keith?"

"It is I, my lord." He inserted the guard's key and sprung the lock.

"But how?"

"Paul's army is a mix of woodsmen and a people from within Chimney Ridge. Not all are known to the other by sight. My dominant features are Jarred, so I walk among them freely. To any who ask I am a stable hand in the employ of the Benjarth."

Lord Thyden slowly nodded in agreement with his son's remarks. The boy did possess the Jarred's thinness and the telltale gray-brown eyes. His grandfather, Lord Belshane, had been of pure blood.

"Do you have a plan?" he asked.

"I've tied two horses to a eucloid tree near the stable compound. We will ride west to the forest. Even if the Benjarth pursue us, they will not enter the forest at night because of the snow-tigers. That is why I had to wait until late afternoon to make my move. It is a three-hour ride to the forest."

"How do we cross?"

"I've concealed a vessel of mythorian in each saddlebag. Its vapors will ward off the snow-tigers. It will eventually kill the horses—an unfortunate side-effect—but I suspect we will be another day's journey beyond the western border of the forest before that happens. The drug was something my lord was working on and told me about. Certainly you remember?"

Lord Thyden smiled. He did remember, but that wasn't the reason he smiled. The boy was smart, skilled, and crafty. He was the kind of son a father could be proud of, not like that careless Paul Benjarth! That fool had laid his sword on the ground before identifying whether a fallen man was friend or foe. He'd have been killed if that gargantuan mutant hadn't saved him. Thyden's son's plan was a good one. Those who might pursue them would have to wait until dawn to enter the forest. He and the boy would ride southwest to Lorstown. There were many there who believed in their supposed cause—the Sinese's and Phlogin's right to take back the Jarred lands—and they would conceal them from any Benjarth search parties.

Keith held a bow. A quiver of arrows was strapped across his back. He rolled the dead guard over, extracted his knife, and sheathed the bloody blade in a holder bound to his belt.

"Which way now?" asked Lord Thyden.

"This corridor, my lord."

My lord. Those words made Lord Thyden realize how much he yearned to tell Keith Harkins that he was his father. *This corridor, father.* Unfortunately, the timing was bad. It would be an emotional moment and one followed by questions. Already he had delayed their escape with his own questions. Now every second was precious. Another guard might appear in the dungeon corridor at any time. The revelation would have to wait until they were safely on their way.

They began to run down the corridor. Keith led and Lord Thyden followed. Suddenly two guards appeared from a side doorway. Keith let fly an arrow and the lead guard fell back against the stone, the arrow's shaft protruding from his chest. He cut down the other guard with a second arrow before that guard had even drawn his knife to throw. But the second guard had managed to cry out for assistance just before he fell. As Keith and Lord Thyden reached the doorway, they heard the sounds of more Benjarth guards coming their way.

"We can't go this way, my lord."

"Keith!" cried Lord Thyden. "Ahead of us! More guards!"

There was an archway in the wall to their right, and they made a dash for it. An arrow flew from the bow of one of the guards, and it glanced off the corridor's low ceiling. Keith knelt beside the archway and struck down one of the guards with an arrow. Then he, too, ducked into the archway.

"The are stairs here," said Lord Thyden, as his foot dropped down.

"I've a fiber-stub in my pocket." Keith held the fiber-stub aloft. The light from a nearby lantern hanging in the corridor initiated the chemical change and soon the fiber-stub glowed brightly.

The stairs were narrow and twisting and ended at a wooden door.

"Is it unlocked?" asked Lord Thyden. "We'll never make a stand here."

"It is," said Keith, yanking it open. He entered the room, holding the fiber-stub high.

"No!" cried Lord Thyden. "Cover the light!"

It was too late. The light-catalyzed change was instantaneous. A wave of illumination swept the length of the ascama fiber growing room.

Lord Thyden heard the footsteps of the Benjarth guards atop the staircase. "Run for the door at the other end of the room," he told Keith.

Already the ascama plants glowed brightly. The two fugitives managed only a few strides before the molten glare forced them to shield their eyes with the backsides of their arms. But even that did not afford their eyes enough protection and they had to close them, making it difficult to keep their sense of direction. The corridor was narrow and the plants thick on either side. Something struck Lord Thyden about the knees and he fell forward, his right arm splashing into a trough of solution.

Get up! Must get up!

Lord Thyden opened his eyes for an instant as he got back up on his feet. The light was blinding and he felt his eyes sink back into his skull as he squeezed them shut. For a few seconds, thought was impossible, then it returned with astonishing clarity. He remembered from the glimpse of the room he'd had when they opened the door that the troughs ran in straight rows from one end to the other. They could use the waist-high edge of the troughs as a series of handrails to help keep their sense of direction. He knew archers couldn't set themselves at the open door and cut them down. They couldn't look into the room for even a moment because of the intensity of the light. But they had to know or suspect that the other side of the room had a door as well. It would be a foot-race now.

"Keith!" Lord Thyden cried. "Use your hands! Grip the edge of the troughs!"

He heard a splash behind him. This was followed by the heavy thump of a body hitting the floorboards.

"Keith!" he screamed. "Answer me!" He couldn't open his eyes, not even for an instant, to see if his son was conscious or unconscious. He took a step back, felt a sliver tear into his palm, and pulled his hand from the wood. "Get up, Keith!"

His voice echoed without answer. Lord Thyden hesitated, unsure whether to go back and help his son. What could he do for him? He wasn't a strong man. He couldn't carry him from the room if he were unconscious. He couldn't even open his eyes to see where the boy lay. He would have to feel the floor until he located the boy's body. Maybe he could revive him by splashing solution from the troughs in his face, but all this would take time, and he didn't have time. Certainly one or more of the guards had already backtracked up the stairs. Thyden wanted to help his son, but he had to keep moving. He had to go for the far door. "Keith!" he screamed one last time.

There was no answer.

Lord Thyden moved forward again, feeling his way along. He bumped into the door, felt for the latch, found it, opened the door, and closed it behind him.

Even before he opened his eyes, Lord Thyden could sense the soothing darkness of the stairwell. As he made the first turn in the stairs, his eyes adjusted to the dim light, allowing him to see the steps. Relieved, he hurried up.

He paused at the top of the stairs to catch his breath. He could hear the footsteps of the Benjarth guards running down the main corridor to his left, but he knew exactly where he was in the castle. The corridor to the stable compound ran off to the right, perpendicular to the main corridor. He knew he would make it to the stable compound now. Whatever guards arrived here in the next few seconds would immediately descend the stairs, thinking they had trapped him in the ascama fiber growing room. He took a deep breath and ran off down the corridor. He was careful to quietly open and close the door at the end of the corridor, lest the guards hear him, then he was out into the light. The eucloid tree was to his right, and concealed in its shadows he could just make out the two horses. He opened the saddlebag of the first horse, took out the flask of mythorian, and smashed it against the wall of the castle. He untied the horse and shooed it, whacking it hard about its hind flanks, then he mounted the other horse.

The noise attracted the attention of a soldier who had been in the stables. He saw the horse run past him without a rider, so he drew his knife and peered into the shadows of the eucloid tree.

Lord Thyden knew the soldier couldn't see him. He waited as the man drew closer and closer, then he dug his knees sharply into the horse's sides. The mare charged forward, springing from the shadows of the eucloid tree. The soldier never had time to get out of the way and Lord Thyden ran the horse over him. A moment later, he was out past the stables. The main gate of Castle Chalmet was to his left as he cleared the north wall of the castle. He looked back once to make sure he wasn't being pursued, then he lowered his upper body into the neck of the horse. He could sense the mare's strength by the way it ran. It was a good horse. His son had picked well.

Thyden then felt a moistness forming about both eyes. He had been raised on hate, and these new emotions were strange to him. He couldn't think past them or put them out of his mind. This feeling of loss was different from the mix of emotions he'd felt knowing his forces had been defeated at the hands of the Benjarth. This was more personal, more painful. Thoughts of revenge did not soften its sting. A single tear spilled from the deep hollow of one eye and split into tiny rivulets as the wind blew it back across the flat of his cheek.

CHAPTER 34

The battle had gone well that day for the Benjarth. Paul stood atop Tower Satchkind, the spyglass raised to his eye, and observed the surrender of Lord Thyden's remaining forces. Columns of prisoners were being marched up the mountain pass, bound for the dungeons of Castle Weslan. The soldiers' horses were being rounded up and would be driven over the pass before nightfall. When the cloud bank had passed, Paul had crumbled huge segments of the plain, pushing Lord Thyden's forces back toward the mountains and within range of Duke Orsinc's archers. Now, as Paul folded together the telescoping segments of the spyglass, he did so in the same satisfied manner that a victorious warrior would sheath his sword when the battle was over. He placed the spyglass on the stone, then bent his head forward and swept his hands outward across his temples, pushing his hair back. He was alone atop the tower roof, Arnun having left earlier. Paul closed his eyes and took advantage of a few quiet moments to rest.

When he opened his eyes, he gazed to the west. The sun would soon set. A few distant clouds, hovering on the horizon, would burn magenta as the sun dipped behind the curve of Calferon. It would be a sunset of unparalleled beauty, because it marked the end of Lord Thyden's dreams of conquest.

The dawn would herald a new era of Benjarth rule, free from the threat of tyranny.

Paul saw the rider as soon as he came out from beneath the castle wall and into Paul's line of sight. The man, who wore a brown, hooded cloak, seemed in great haste and was riding due west. Paul focused the spyglass on the rider, who was leaning forward, hugging the horse's mane. Then the man looked back over his shoulder and his face filled Paul's spyglass.

Lord Thyden!

Paul's first thought was to organize a team of riders to chase after Thyden, but he dismissed the idea after only a moment's reflection. Olgar's and Arnun's men had fought beside him and neither group had experience on horseback. Paul doubted any of them could even ride! He then knew that he alone would have to pursue Lord Thyden.

He threw the spyglass on the chair and ran down the stairs of Tower Satchkind. The shortest route to the stables was through a narrow corridor off the main courtyard. It passed near the cells and Paul had to wonder if Lord Thyden had used this same corridor to get to the stable compound. The corridor was lit only to its intersection with the main dungeon corridor. Paul unhooked an ascama fiber lantern from its wall hanger and used its light to illuminate the final length of corridor.

A man sat on the ground outside the stable compound. He was bent over and holding his right leg and looked up when he heard Paul approach.

"Are you hurt badly?" Paul asked him.

"That bastard ran his horse right over me! Go after him, Paul! I'll be all right."

"Is there a fast horse in the stables?"

"Over there." The man pointed to where a saddled mare stood by the edge of the grazing fields. "It's his other horse. He must have had an accomplice."

Paul ran toward the horse and grabbed its reins. He mounted and urged the horse to a gallop.

The ground immediately west of Castle Chalmet was gently sloped, enough so that it created two horizons—a near one that was the top of the rise and a more distant one consisting of the converging mountain ranges of Fiefs Cerus and Salkird. It was beyond this small rise that the land flattened out into

the great plain that stretched all the way to Fief Karcan's western border. It wasn't until Paul reached the top of the slope
that he could see the distant figure of Lord Thyden. He
spurred his horse onward. The shadows of night would soon
sweep across the plain, and if Lord Thyden were to get too far
ahead, Paul would lose sight of him. He rode past unattended
herds of cattle and flocks of sheep. He rode past fields of
wheat, barley, and oats, unworked by field hands since Lord
Thyden's invasion.

Paul reached the westernmost fortifications of the Benjarth
after nightfall. Blocks of stone, dragged from quarry sites
along the Void of Carcin, had been piled in rows across the
plain. These fortifications had been built a half mile back
from the forest. They were to give a line of archers protection
against Lord Thyden's charging cavalries. Unfortunately, Lord
Thyden had surprised them by attacking from the east after
crossing into Fief Karcan via the suspension bridge. Paul could
see the bodies of the Jarred dead, and to a lesser extent the
dead of the Sinese and Phlogin. Lord Thyden's commanders
had not even had the decency to dump the bodies into the
Void of Carcin.

The last quarter mile of ground before the forest pitched
gently downward. Paul stayed his horse atop this slope. Lord
Thyden had halted before the wood. Paul's strategy would be
to move laterally now, preventing him from slipping away to
the north or south. He wouldn't attempt to close the distance
between them. Not at night. Many of the corpses and fallen
horses beside the fortifications appeared to have been mauled
and eaten by the snow-tigers. He felt himself safe at this distance. The snow-tigers were fast, but only in short bursts. He
would have his horse turned around and at a full gallop before
one of the snow-tigers could reach this rise.

Then Lord Thyden trotted his horse in a circle several times
and, to Paul's complete amazement, rode into the forest.

Paul wanted to believe Lord Thyden was mad enough to
have made a gross mistake in judgment. Certainly the snow-
tigers would come this way, as they had every night, drawn by
the scent of horse and human flesh. Yet to believe Thyden insane was too convenient an explanation. It was the type of explanation a crafty adversary such as Lord Thyden would *want*

an opponent to believe. Paul was confused now. There had been something deliberate in the way Thyden had ridden his horse before entering the forest. Such deliberateness spoke of a strategy. Yet what was his plan, Paul wondered? Was it to lure him near enough the forest to leap out at him, sword in hand? Was Thyden just crazy enough to play a waiting game and risk being killed by the snow-tigers first?

Paul unsheathed his sword and coaxed his horse down the slope. How well Lord Thyden understood his resolve. He *had* to investigate his disappearance into the forest. He'd rode all this way to avenge the Jarred dead by killing him. He couldn't be absolutely sure the snow-tigers would do the job for him. Maybe the scent of the dead here on the plain was stronger than that of the living.

Paul held a lantern aloft as he rode slowly along the edge of the forest. The lantern was the same one he had used to illuminate the corridor leading to the stable compound. Certainly its light would alert Lord Thyden where he was. But Lord Thyden would see him anyway if he had indeed concealed himself by the edge of the forest. This way, at least, Paul had a chance of seeing him as well. He stopped before the spot where Lord Thyden had entered the wood. He smelled . . . *chemical!* It was then Paul understood Lord Thyden's strategy. He was using a chemical substance, a gas, to keep the snow-tigers away. That was why he had circled his horse. He'd wanted the scent to envelop them both.

There was another matter to consider now: his father's safety. Paul realized it would give Lord Thyden immense pleasure to sour the Benjarth's victory by killing his father and the other blind captives in the chemical gardens. He had to pursue Lord Thyden *now*. Lord Thyden would reach Castle Greyfahren by dawn if he rode all night.

The lantern gave Paul an idea. He remembered Etan telling him that the eyes of the snow-tigers were extremely sensitive to light. That's why they hunted at night. The standard fiberstubs might not be brilliant enough to blind the snow-tigers, but Olgar had given him a spare fiber-stub for the signal lantern. These stubs had been developed by the people of Chimney Ridge and their light was five times as bright. Paul had used one of them to signal Brian and Christina atop Chimney

Ridge. He carried the spare in a flat pouch he wore beneath his shirt and about his waist.

Paul removed the fiber-stub from the pouch and cupped it tightly in his hand. He balanced the lantern in his lap as he carefully removed the other fiber-stub. The smooth surface of the stub was warm, but only slightly so. He held the glowing fiber-stub between his thumb and forefinger. Slowly he opened his other hand. Instantly the second stub started to glow. Paul threw the first stub to the ground and quickly placed the new stub in the lantern. Two elastic fabric squeeze clamps held the rigid fiber-stub in position. Within seconds the fiber-stub glowed brilliantly. Paul held the lantern high above his head.

The shadows of the forest were like voids that had suddenly been filled. The underbrush was now a single mass of lime green broken only by the overlapping lines of its own shape and form. Trees stood like forest sentinels, the forward sides of the nearest crisply defined by the light, making visible each snaking ridge of bark and protruding knot. The more distant trees rose up like pale gray pillars into the fingerlike canopies of branches too high to be defined by the light. Paul felt the light was indeed bright enough to keep the snow-tigers at bay, but what he didn't know was how long the fiber-stub would glow. A normal stub glowed for fourteen hours, but Olgar's people had developed these to signal with, not light a hallway. Paul swallowed. It was a dry swallow, one that resulted from his fear. Beads of perspiration dotted his forehead, and his heart hammered in his chest. He was scared, every bit as much as when he'd been glued to the rock on Calferon, the noise of the "beast" screaming above the desert wind on the other side. Yet he *had* moved around that corner of rock, and he knew he would have to enter the forest now. His father's life depended on it. Gently he urged the horse forward.

Branches hung low across the trail and Paul had to duck to pass beneath them. A small rodentlike animal scurried across the path. It paused to look at them, eyes red, confused by the light. A large snake slithered out of its bed of leaves and away from the lantern's glow. Soon the trail bent around to the southwest. Here the forest was more open. Vines twisted around the trunks of some of the trees. Others were stained with spots of yellow and brown, indicating some sort of fungi.

Just then Paul heard the dry, rustling sounds of an animal walking through a bed of leaves. The sounds had come from his left, just beyond the circle of light. A twig snapped, then another. Paul gripped the lantern's handle tightly. The horse acted nervous and started to trot. Paul pulled lightly on the reins with his free hand. "Easy now," he said. "I'm as scared as you are, girl."

The forest grew still again and Paul almost dared to think that the danger of the snow-tigers had passed, then he heard the rustle of leaves again. This time the sound had come from behind him and nearer the trail. He gently stroked the mare's neck, trying to keep it calm.

A snow-tiger growled somewhere ahead of and to the left of Paul. The sound was guttural and raspy, as if the cat were rolling its own salivary fluids in the back of its throat. A second snow-tiger answered the first, its throaty snarl coming from behind. The horse bolted, and Paul leaned forward against the left side of the mare's neck, the lantern held beside his shoulder. The branches were low overhead and he had to keep his head down. His right arm was around the mare's neck, and he pulled on the reins after he'd grabbed them closer to the bit. He shouted at the horse as well, but the animal was driven by fear, and that instinct was stronger than any command he could give. Suddenly the horse stopped and reared. Paul was thrown to the ground. Luckily he managed to stick a leg out, and this absorbed some of the impact of his fall. He spun halfway around and fell on his buttocks. Throughout he'd managed to hold onto the lantern. He jumped back up on his feet and saw the huge form of a snow-tiger slink away from the light and disappear into the darkness of the forest. Paul grabbed the mare's reins and quickly tied them to a tree before the horse could run again. The mare pulled against them only once, then was still.

For Paul the night passed with agonizing slowness. His thoughts were on his father and the possibility that he had failed in his mission to rescue him. Lord Thyden was increasing his lead with each passing minute, and Paul was helpless to pursue him. Twice he had untied the mare and attempted to ride it. The first time it had whinnied skittishly and had been difficult to control. The second time it had reared up again, kicking at the air near his head. He had been fortunate to get the horse tied to a tree again. Sometimes Paul could hear the movement of a snow-tiger through a thicket of branches or across a bed of dry leaves. Once he thought he saw a pair of glowing red eyes floating in the darkness. He had been sitting down then (the lantern hanging from a low branch of a tree) and had bolted upright, fearing that one of the snow-tigers was going to attack in spite of the light. But nothing happened. There was food in the saddlebag, but Paul was afraid to unwrap it, fearing the smell of the meat might enrage the snow-tigers. There was a flask of orca as well. Paul recognized the drink by its odor when he unscrewed the cap. It was a stimulant and he drank it to keep himself awake.

When the change in the light first came, the forest colors fading into the softer hues of dawn, Paul was aware that the sound of the snow-tigers had been gone for some time. He immediately mounted the mare and rode west through the forest. Three hours later he caught his first glimpse of the forest's end and the sunlit field beyond. He felt a rush of exhilaration at the sight and he urged the mare to gallop faster. Twenty miles to the northwest lay the Angena Mountains, jagged black stone peaks framed by a cloudless sweep of cobalt blue sky. Paul could feel the strength of the mare beneath him as it galloped across the field. He knew it would run hard for him.

It was early afternoon when he came upon a horse lying in the field. Paul circled the animal once and realized it was dead. The horse's saddlebag, still strapped to its side, was identical to his own. He was sure this had been Lord Thyden's horse. For a moment, he puzzled over the reason the animal had died. He saw no dried blood that would indicate the mare had been wounded by a snow-tiger and had managed to run this far before collapsing. He couldn't see any cuts to the neck or chest, indicating the animal might have broken its leg and Lord Thyden had mercifully killed it with his sword. Paul remembered the scent of chemical and wondered if that had anything to do with the animal's death. Had Thyden's cleverness backfired? He looked in the direction of the Angena Mountains. They were four miles distant now. Lord Thyden had had to walk from this point on.

Maybe I haven't failed you yet, father!

As Paul reached the base of Ansona Pass, his eye was immediately drawn to a figure on foot. Paul recognized Lord Thyden by the hooded brown cloak he still wore. He was leaning forward, laboring with the effort of the climb, three quarters of the way up the slope. Two hundred feet above and to Lord Thyden's right was a timber wagon. Its left front wheel lay on the ground beside it, so the wagon pitched on its axle to that side. The wagon was at a sixty degree angle to the slope, its right backside pushed up against the rock. It was loaded with six cuts of timber.

Paul realized he couldn't gallop the mare up the steep slope. The trail of hard-packed earth rose for half a mile at a thirty-five degree pitch. Its backside, as Paul remembered, was only slightly less steep, but Paul knew a horse could still make better time up the slope than a man on foot. He spurred the horse up the incline.

Paul was nearly halfway up the slope when Lord Thyden looked once over his shoulder, then started sprinting, as if somehow he had just found an untapped reserve of strength. When he drew level with the wagon, he turned and ducked behind it. Moments later Paul heard the sound of wood striking wood. The left back wheel of the wagon fell off its axle. The wagon pitched onto its side and spilled its load of logs. Five of the logs rolled across the width of the pass at the same angle the wagon had pitched forward, and they piled into the far wall. The logs then moved as a single mass, sliding down the left side of the pass as if in a chute at a sawmill. But one log had turned when it had spilled from the wagon, and it pounded down the slope toward Paul. He whacked the mare's back, and the horse bolted across the pass. He had only one chance to survive this trap. He had to get to the right side of the pass. The log just might miss him if he could squeeze against the stone there. The log kicked up off a rock and struck the mare's hindquarters. It spun the horse around, and Paul was thrown from the saddle. His shoulder cushioned the initial impact of his fall, but his head still struck the hard ground.

Paul struggled to remain conscious. In his mind he found himself spinning around the edge of an ursula filled with black water, which was draining and caused a whirlpool to form in the ursula's center. The swirling water tried to pull him down into the blackness of unconsciousness. He thrashed his arms wildly, slapping at the water as he felt himself being dragged under.

No! No! No!

The whirlpool dissolved in a sea of blue. For a few seconds more Paul remained disoriented, not understanding this abrupt change in images. Then it dawned on him that his eyes had opened and he was looking up at the sky. Slowly he got to his feet. The horse lay on its side, its back legs broken. Paul would have to destroy the animal, but that mercy killing would have to wait. His mind was focused wholly on his mission to kill Lord Thyden. He could see his foe again walking up the slope, his back to Paul.

Paul realized that Lord Thyden had arrived at Ansona Pass earlier than he had first thought. He had removed the pin that held the wheel of the wagon in place, then moved the wheel forward until it just teetered on the end of the axle. He had then walked back down the trail only to give the impression that he had just climbed to that point. He had thrown some object, perhaps a block of wood, at the wheel from behind to knock it off the axle.

Paul ran up the slope after Lord Thyden. He felt surprisingly strong, and knew it was both from the adrenaline his body was producing and the effects of the orca he had drunk earlier. His shoulder and the side of his head hurt, but he could concentrate past that pain. Ten minutes later he stood only twenty feet downhill from Lord Thyden. It was then he unsheathed his sword.

Lord Thyden whirled around at the sound of Paul's sword sliding from its scabbard. His hood fell back as he unsheathed his own sword. "You've not the big man to help you this time, Benjarth pup!"

Lord Thyden leaped forward, almost as an animal might spring up on its toes. As he landed, he swung his sword down and across. Paul easily jumped back out of his way. Lord Thyden took a step forward and slashed his sword back the other way. Again Paul stepped back, and the blow swung harmlessly in front of him. But in one continuous motion, Lord Thyden used the momentum of that missed pass to bring his sword above his head. He leaped again, this time slashing from left to right. The suddenness of the move caught Paul off guard and he had no chance to defend against it with his sword. He ducked and Lord Thyden's blade sliced through the air only an inch above his head.

Lord Thyden had put his full weight behind the force of that blow. Before he could lift his sword and slash back the other way, Paul, knees bent, leaned into the slope and whipped his sword left to right. Lord Thyden shrieked as the blade severed his right hand at the wrist. He grabbed at the stump of his forearm as he crumpled to the ground.

Paul realized it was over. He stepped forward, both hands gripping the hilt of his sword. The Benjarth *would* be avenged now. Yet he had never dealt out justice in this manner. He had never run a sword through a beaten man to finish him off. He hesitated a moment, trying to gauge the exact position of Lord Thyden's body, desiring to make the kill instant. But then he was distracted, his gaze drawn to Lord Thyden's face and the curious expression there. Lord Thyden's eyes were beginning to roll back into his skull. Something was happening to him, something beyond just the pain from his wound. He opened his mouth and Paul saw that his tongue was stained purple.

He saw Lord Thyden's left wrist snap toward him too late. He recognized the motion—Lord Thyden had thrown something at him—and he instinctively brought his sword tight to his body, hoping the blade would by chance deflect whatever had been thrown. He felt something sting his face and it caused him to take a step back. It stuck there and Paul brushed it away with the back of his hand.

Paul believed he had been poisoned, but he felt no sorrow for himself at that moment. His thoughts were again focused like those of a true warrior. If he was going to die, then he would be sure to kill Lord Thyden first. He held his sword in both hands and raised it high above his head, then the landscape seemed to cave inward, then swell outward. Lord Thyden's body appeared to shift to the right. Paul took a step in that direction and felt his knee buckle. Again the landscape caved inward, as if everything that existed on the periphery of his vision had been sucked inward to one narrow focal point.

Paul fell to one knee as the ground seemed to flow away from him. His sword fell from his hand as he dropped to his other knee. He teetered like a rag doll waiting to be pushed over, then he fell forward, managing to get his arm out in front of his face just as he hit the ground.

Paul was no longer cognizant of his surroundings. A squishy, gelatinous substance that he thought of as his "self" fell away from his skin, painlessly ripped from the sensory organs that gave it contact with an outside world. He had a momentary thought that this must be what a baby sensed floating in its mother's womb, only there was light, a strange yellowish orange light. Its source was his body, only it wasn't his body anymore, because there was no pigment or color to define it as such. Instead a thin, translucent shell filled with a glowing yellowish orange liquid surrounded him. For a moment, Paul felt wonderfully relaxed and carefree.

The change was abrupt. The substance of his "self" began to swell like a sponge soaking up water. He was pressed against the rigid shell of his body. He hurt everywhere. Yet, strangely, he was aware that the pain wasn't physical, for his nerve cells had fossilized like his skin. The pain was mental. He felt like he was slowly and helplessly being crushed. He screamed again and again, then his body shell exploded into thousands of luminous yellow-orange fragments. They flew in all directions, scorching the darkness of the infinite void where there was no sense of up or down. In an instant they were but pinpoints, strangely colored stars in a horizonless sky. Then, like an eggshell tapped with a knife, a jagged seam of light opened in the void. The void rolled back and Paul found himself floating thirty feet in the air above a phosphorescent red maze. He had his body back.

"Welcome, my young friend," said Lord Thyden jovially. He sat at the opposite end of the maze from Paul.

"What is this place?" Paul screamed back at him.

Lord Thyden smiled with delight. "Are you impressed with my creation? You needn't say it. I can see that you are. I call it my 'maze-box.'"

"But where are we? Spatially?"

"If you would cease with your foolish outbursts," he said, "perhaps I could explain all this to you. Spatially? We're still atop Ansona Pass. Only we are in a dream state now and share the same hallucination. Certainly we would be a curious sight to any who might come upon us. We would appear as two warriors who had fallen asleep in the middle of their battle." His expression turned sober. "I find it curious how relentlessly you've pursued me. The battle won, and yet you aren't satisfied with that. Did you fear that I'd rise again? Attack with another army and another plan of battle? Or do you fear for your father's safety? You are right to be afraid for him. For after I've killed you, I will kill him! How pathetically defenseless a blind man is! So many ways to kill him. His death will not be pretty."

Paul seethed with anger, but he knew Lord Thyden was baiting him, trying to drive reason from his mind and fill it instead with hate and emotion. Illad Rahman had told him once that a fighter could use emotion to finish off an opponent, but he must never use it to plot the strategy of his fight.

"You control your emotion well, Benjarth pup, but it will not help you defeat me. My advantage is my familiarity with the maze-box. As for my future? There are many Sinese and Phlogin families who will harbor me from the Benjarth's search parties. I will live out my days in peace. Perhaps, before I die, I will hear of another man assuming control, and of another army rising to challenge the Benjarth."

"The Benjarth will be ready for them," Paul said defiantly.

"But are you ready for this?" cried Lord Thyden, gesturing to the maze-box below.

Paul listened in amazement as Lord Thyden told him of the cymethadrenatyne molecule. He told him of the miniature dart with the self-activating plunger that he'd concealed in his wrist band and then thrown at Paul. He explained the placement of the mirrors and advised him to study the maze-box while he floated above it. When their light-guns materialized, Lord Thyden explained their operation. Paul fired his once at Lord Thyden. The shot was absorbed by a clear barrier wall between them.

Lord Thyden glanced down at his hands a moment. He had been absently folding and unfolding his fingers. "Do you wonder about my hand? Why I have it back? Your lucky blow was quite painful. It caused me to bite down hard and rupture the hollow cap on the tooth holding my own supply of cyme-thadrenatyne. But my mind had yet to adapt to the fact that I had lost a hand. My own denial and surprise at your lucky sword stroke prevented it from becoming incorporated into the parameters of this hallucination."

Paul felt motion and realized they were descending into the maze-box. When his feet touched the floor, he stepped quickly out of the center corridor as Lord Thyden had advised him to do. Five seconds later the clear barrier between them dissolved.

Paul watched Lord Thyden's movements in the corner mirrors. The double reflection created the illusion that he and Lord Thyden were slowly approaching each other from a great distance. Paul's strategy was to imitate his foe's movements. If he were to move just as his opponent did, theoretically, Lord Thyden could not gain the advantage.

Or could he?

Suddenly Lord Thyden raised his weapon and fired it.

Paul threw himself to the floor, rolled once, aimed, and squeezed the trigger of his light-gun. A bolt of green light struck the mirror at the end of the corridor and splintered.

Mirrors! We've only shot at each other's reflections!

Lord Thyden was running now, his backside visible in the corner mirror. Paul leaped to his feet and whirled around. In the half-mirror in front of him he saw Lord Thyden charging toward him.

He's in the center corridor!

Paul took a step forward.

Suddenly the intersection with the center corridor flashed with bolts of green light. Seeing that the location of Lord Thyden's shots were high, Paul sprang forward and thrust his light-gun around the corner only inches above the ground. He fired repeatedly, spraying his shots back and forth across the width of the corridor. When he peered around the corner, Lord Thyden was nowhere to be seen.

Paul ran to the right corner of the maze. In the far corner mirror he saw Lord Thyden's reflection. He whirled around and saw his reflection again, this time in the half-mirror located where the center corridor bisected the perimeter corridor. For an instant, he seemed suspended in air, both feet off the ground. Then his reflection was gone.

Damn it! I don't understand these mirrors!

Paul jog-walked up the right perimeter corridor. He suspected he'd be a harder target to locate if he kept moving. As he stepped across the entrance to the right center corridor, a bolt of green light flashed. It struck the light-gun he carried in his left hand and splintered, producing an instantaneous radial wall of light. The weapon fell from his hand, struck his knee, and tumbled forward into the corridor, sliding six to eight feet on the smooth surface.

In an instant Lord Thyden was in the corridor. Bolts of light flashed from his light-gun as he charged.

Paul saw his weapon was impossible to retrieve. Now all he could think to do was put as much distance between Lord Thyden and himself as possible. He ran for the far corner of the maze-box. Lord Thyden appeared in the mirror in front of him. His image was small. A reflection of a reflection of a reflection. Paul lunged for the corner of the maze, sliding headfirst along the floor. Surprisingly, the points of friction between his body and the floor produced a cold sensation not unlike that of sliding on ice covered with a slight dusting of snow. Two bolts of green light hammered the wall above his head as he slid into the corner mirror. Paul rolled his body to the left and scrambled to his feet.

What had Thyden said? The corridors of the inner square were hidden from the view of the mirrors. Yes! And so were the diagonals!

Paul ran down the diagonal corridor in front of him. Where that corridor intersected the inner square, he stepped to the right and threw himself against the inner wall of that corridor.

"Hear me, Benjarth," Lord Thyden's voice rang out. "I gloat now. I gloat because my victory is near at hand."

Where is his voice coming from?

"Unfortunate child," continued Lord Thyden. "You've dropped your weapon. How do you expect to win now?"

Paul inched closer to the diagonal corridor to his left. It had sounded like Lord Thyden's voice had come from the center of the maze-box. He remembered the aerial view of the maze. From that center room all corridors were visible except those of the inner square.

He knows I'm in the inner square!

He inched still closer. If Lord Thyden were to come from the left, he could duck around to the right, or up or down the diagonal corridor. If he were to come from his right, he could run back to his left.

But if he comes down the diagonal corridor, I'm doomed! Does he know where in the inner square I am?

Paul heard footsteps.

Which way is he moving?

Paul thought himself too vulnerable from the right. He swung his upper body around and into the intersection point. He was half in one corridor, half in the other. He heard Lord Thyden's footsteps draw nearer.

Is he coming from the right or the left?

Lord Thyden appeared to his left. Paul leaped into the diagonal corridor just as a bolt of light blasted the wall where he'd been standing. He started to run toward the perimeter of the maze and then thought better of it.

That's exactly what he expects me to do!

He doubled back and peered into the inner corridor. He heard footsteps and realized Lord Thyden had turned up the right center corridor and run back to the center room. Paul stepped to the left. Once again he was within the inner square. The sound of Lord Thyden's footsteps stopped. For a while there was no sound in the maze at all.

"You've shown a bit of cleverness, Benjarth," Lord Thyden shouted, "but your luck won't last."

Paul suspected Lord Thyden might be right. He knew he couldn't dodge the energy blasts from Thyden's light-gun much longer.

It was then he had a clever thought. He unlaced his shoes and undid his belt. His belt was a double wraparound and there was plenty of length to it. He secured a shoe to each end of the belt, then he moved quickly to where the right center corridor bisected the inner square.

"Your time runs short, Benjarth," Lord Thyden cried. "Prepare to meet your end!"

Paul thought: *I'm too vulnerable if he approaches me from either of the diagonal corridors. He must know exactly where I am!*

"Hear me, Thyden," he shouted. "*Your* time runs short! It is I who hold the upper hand!"

Lord Thyden charged down the center corridor, a light-gun in either hand.

Paul grabbed his belt in its middle and, allowing enough length for his hand to grip it, raised it above his head and swung it. He listened to the sound of Lord Thyden's footsteps approach. Just as they seemed upon him, he reached around and flung the belt and shoes at Lord Thyden's knees. The belt wrapped about Lord Thyden's legs and tripped him up. He twisted as he fell, landing on his back. Paul dove forward and slid into him. He grabbed Lord Thyden's wrists as his foe tilted the light-guns back. Bolts of green light flashed just above Paul's head. However, he'd grabbed Lord Thyden's wrists cleanly and his strength was far greater. He pushed his hands back the other way.

Lord Thyden let go of the light-guns. The momentum of his hands falling forward was enough to fling the weapons down the corridor half the distance to the center room.

Paul scrambled to his feet. He had to get to the light-guns first! He leaped over Lord Thyden's supine form. But Lord Thyden managed to raise a leg and trip him up. As Paul stumbled forward, Lord Thyden got to his feet. He stepped free of the wrap of the belt and ran toward the light-guns.

Paul pushed himself across the corridor on his belly by kicking off from the wall. He swung his forearm across his adversary's shins and knocked his feet out from under him. But Lord Thyden's momentum carried him forward and he slid toward one of the light-guns.

Paul saw in an instant that Lord Thyden had beaten him to the light-guns. He scrambled to his feet and ducked back into the right-hand corridor of the inner square. He ran to its intersection with the diagonal corridor and looked once toward the center room. When he saw that Lord Thyden was not there, he sprinted down the diagonal corridor to the corner of the maze. From there he could see Lord Thyden in the half-mirror to his left. He still sat on the floor, but his light-guns were up; he was ready to shoot if Paul should return. He got to his feet slowly, steadying himself on one knee before standing up. He acted fatigued and Paul wondered if his stamina was affected by his *real* physical condition. He had lost his right hand and had to be losing blood. But Paul remembered how Lord Thyden had fooled him earlier. He had walked with a plodding shuffle up Ansona Pass only to run to the wagon and spring his trap. The fact that he appeared tired might only be a pretense. Maybe Lord Thyden wanted him to believe he was exhausted only to catch him off guard moments later.

Paul flattened his back against the wall and looked up at the top of the maze-box. If only there was some way out. But the walls were icy smooth, as slick as the blade of a sword. They could not be scaled. Paul looked again in the mirror. Lord Thyden was walking with a slight limp.

It's a trick! I know it is!

Lord Thyden disappeared into the inner square. Paul decided to move now that Lord Thyden couldn't see him. He ran the complete length of the perimeter corridor to his right. Fortunately he'd had a good jump on Lord Thyden and made it to the far corner of the maze before his foe reached the perimeter corridor. Lord Thyden didn't even attempt to fire a shot as Paul ducked around the edge of the wall. Instead he retreated back up the diagonal corridor toward the inner square.

Paul continued to stare into the corner mirror even after he could no longer see Lord Thyden. The seed of an idea had begun to germinate. He stepped forward and touched the mirror's surface. It felt different from the walls. It was harder, yet at the same time it felt brittle. Paul removed the medallion from around his neck. The medallion was constructed of *metal*. There was no substrate as hard anywhere in their floating world. Paul wondered if the same held true for Lord Thyden's maze-box. Perhaps this metal was harder than the surface of the mirror. He cupped the medallion in both hands with one curved edge exposed. He brought his hands up over his head, then slammed the medallion into the mirror. A thin crack appeared. Paul struck the mirror again and again. The crack lengthened and eventually ran to the top of the mirror, which was the same height as the wall. Paul threw his weight against the left half of the mirror. It moved inward eight inches. Its exposed edge was two inches thick.

The crack that had formed was not straight. Instead the seam had rippled in a rounded way. This produced small fin-

ger and toeholds along the cracked edge of the mirror. Paul
wedged his toe into one such notch, then he pushed upward,
grabbing onto the edge of the mirror for balance. He found
another inwardly curved edge above him, grabbed it, and
pulled himself up.

Paul wondered what he would find atop the maze-box.
Would there be a clear barrier, an unseen continuation of the
existing walls, that would prevent him from climbing over the
edge? Would his motion somehow be restricted if he tried to
leave the maze-box, as it had when he had sat floating above
it? Both were possibilities, but Paul doubted Lord Thyden had
designed such safeguards into the maze-box. Not in all his genius could Lord Thyden have foreseen someone finding a way
to scale its walls. That conclusion made Paul even more curious
about what he would find. What lay beyond the boundaries of
a madman's hallucination?

Paul grabbed onto another chunk of the mirror's edge and
pulled himself higher. He was almost to the halfway point in
his climb. If he could climb a few feet higher, then establish a
firm toehold, he might be able to extend himself and reach
the top.

He then caught sight of Lord Thyden in the mirror. He was
running down the straight corridor that terminated in the
middle of the perimeter corridor to his right. One fact impressed itself upon Paul at that moment. If he could see Lord
Thyden, then Lord Thyden could see him. He grabbed at a
protruding edge of mirror above him and felt his hand slip.
Fortunately he was able to grab hold of the mirror with his
other hand. He grabbed again for the edge, this time making
sure his grip was more secure. He pulled himself up, lifting his
legs as high as he could, then located a toehold. He pushed off
with his leg and found he was able to reach the top of the wall.
He pulled himself up and straddled its narrow edge. The outside of the maze-box was the same phosphorescent red as its
inner walls, but everything else was a void of darkness.

Lord Thyden appeared in the perimeter corridor, his light-
gun already held out at arm's length. The first blast of green
light streaked through the darkness above Paul's head, so he
leaned to his left and fell from the top of the maze-box.

Paul caught a glimpse of the maze as he tumbled through

space. Already it was just a glowing red square far above him.
Each time he rolled and looked in that direction it was farther
away. Finally it was no more than a single red star in an otherwise blank sky. Paul threw his arms and legs out, a position
Brian had told him parachuters used for stability when they
jumped, but he was disoriented. The red star had vanished.
He had no bearing on which direction was up or down, right
or left. His shoulder dropped and he began to tumble again,
then he wasn't falling anymore. He didn't remember anything breaking his fall; he had just stopped falling. There was
something hard beneath him, and he scraped at it with his
fingers. A crack appeared in the void and an edge of blue
traced its seam. The void rolled back, but only to open up
around a figure. The figure took a step forward and filled
Paul's vision.

Thyden!

Paul rolled to the left. Lord Thyden's sword missed him,
smashing instead into the hard-packed ground of Ansona
Pass. Paul was aware of the slope of the ground and rolled with
it. He heard Lord Thyden's sword hit again, but the sound was
more distant than it had been the first time. He got to his feet.
He was standing about forty feet below the crest of the pass.
Lord Thyden was standing fifteen feet above him, his sword in
his left hand. Paul looked for his own sword but didn't see it.
He realized Lord Thyden had come out of the hallucination
earlier than he had, probably only seconds earlier, but the
time difference had allowed Lord Thyden to grab his own
sword and throw Paul's on the other side of the pass. His sword
had to be there! The walls of stone bordering Ansona Pass
were too high to throw a sword as heavy as his over them.

"Your cleverness be damned, Benjarth!" Lord Thyden
snarled. He took a step forward, stumbled, and caught himself.

Paul watched Lord Thyden's face twist in pain. He knew the
madman's wound was bothering him. Paul had to get his own
sword. Lord Thyden would be no match for him with only one
hand. He moved to the left. Lord Thyden moved laterally to
block his path, then stepped forward, holding his sword out in
front of him, challenging Paul to come closer, *foolishly close*.

"It's still my victory, Benjarth," Lord Thyden taunted him.

Paul walked slowly back the other way. Lord Thyden kept pace with him, then took a step forward, closing the distance between them. Paul matched this move by taking a single step back, all the time continually moving to his right. He watched Lord Thyden's eyes carefully. He saw them glance to the left. It was the second time he'd glanced that way. Was his sword lying on that side of the pass? Or was Lord Thyden deceiving him? Everything he'd learned of Lord Thyden so far told him that he was an extremely clever adversary. Therefore Paul suspected his sword lay to the right, just on the other side of the pass. He changed direction, walking back toward the left. He took a step forward, ever mindful of Lord Thyden's sword. Lord Thyden moved laterally with him.

Just then Paul saw Lord Thyden grimace, his eyes closing as another wave of pain swept over him. It was the opening Paul had been waiting for. He jumped forward and to the left as if he meant to run that way. Lord Thyden's response was delayed because of the pain from his wound. When he finally moved left, Paul was already changing direction. Lord Thyden couldn't recover in time. Paul ran past him to the crest of the pass. There, twenty feet downhill, lay his sword.

Paul sensed rather than saw Lord Thyden's presence beside him as he stooped to pick up his sword. He swung his sword up and across just as Lord Thyden's sword came down. Paul's hand shook from the force of the blow. Lord Thyden leaned forward, bringing his full weight to bear over his sword. Paul realized his strategy. He was trying to push Paul's sword down and forward. If he should be successful, he had only then to flick his sword to the right and Paul would suffer a fatal blow to the head. Paul realized he had to keep his sword above his head until he could stand.

Suddenly there was no more pressure. Lord Thyden had brought his sword above his head, preparing to strike another blow, but, for an instant, he seemed distracted. He was looking past Paul, focusing on something in the distance. Lord Thyden's hesitation was only for a fraction of a second, but Paul took that moment to push up with his legs and rip his sword up and across. The blade slashed into Lord Thyden's neck, slicing it open. He was dead before he hit the ground.

Paul glanced down the slope and his eyes widened in

amazement at the sight before him. Around the edge of the mountain, on the trail leading to the base of Ansona Pass, men and women walked hand in hand, linked together like a vast human chain. The man who led them held a wooden club in his right hand, no doubt meant to be used as a weapon if necessary. The man poked the ground in front of him with it, feeling the difference between the hard ground of the trail and the softer ground of the grassy field bordering it. He held a woman's hand with his left. Paul recognized both the woman and the man. The woman was Elsa, she who had led Paul and Brian up the back stairway into Castle Greyfahren's kitchen. She had been their first link to the medallion.

The man was Paul's father.

EPILOGUE

The sunrise was magnificent. Tongues of pink and gold licked the peaks of the Eastern Mountains. Paul chose to ignore its beauty. Instead he gazed into the grayness of the west. There he thought he saw the trees of the forest bordering Fief Karcan, but he realized it was probably an illusion, his memory recreating an image that his eye could not see, for the distance was too great.

It had been across that stretch of forest that both Dimistre and Kalin had tried to cross into Fief Karcan. Dimistre had done so successfully, though he'd been too late to warn Illad of the suspension bridge. He and his men had been forced to flee into the mountains of Fief Cerus. Neither Kalin nor any from his group had resurfaced. Paul had to assume they had been killed by Lord Thyden's soldiers. He had built a marker at Fief Karcan's western border in their memory.

The Angena Mountains lay farther to the west. Jessie, Janon, Ewechuk, and Etan had fled toward Kietro across the foothills of those very same mountains the same day he and Brian had ridden in the direction of Kiev. They had discovered the tunnels Lord Belshane had hollowed out beneath the Angena Mountains and had escaped to the south. The tunnels had been guarded and Etan had been killed as they had fought their way out.

"He must have killed five men before a knife dropped him," Jessie had told Paul upon their return. "I owe my life to him."

Paul's mother was doing better now that his father had returned. Lord Thyden had deserted Castle Greyfahren, expecting to make Castle Chalmet his new residence. The blind captives had figured out how to lower the drawbridge and had crossed to Kietro. That town was nearly deserted, as its menfolk were serving in Lord Thyden's army. The women and children of the town had only stared at the escapees as they had made their way along the worn trail east of the town.

Paul turned to the sunrise. He remembered as if it were only yesterday the night he and his sister had stood in Tower Satchkind and seen the reflection of the lightning off Brian's airplane. He missed Brian. He hadn't contemplated that his friend would try to return to his own time. Why, he hadn't even realized it was possible! He'd envisioned another future for Brian, one spent at Castle Chalmet with him, Karin . . . and Christina. He had hoped Brian and Christina would get involved. He'd thought he'd seen the beginnings of a relationship developing between them, but he realized now that his own wishful thinking had blinded him to what Brian had really been thinking and feeling.

It had been nine months since Paul and Karin had been married, and a few nights before the passage of the Saulcar Mass, when Brian had brought up the subject.

"Olgar tells me it is possible. The Saulcar Mass is simply an opening. There are no tunnels, or mazes, or doorways that need to be navigated. On one side is my time and the world I left. On this side is your time and world."

"But how does Olgar know this? Have any from Chimney Ridge gone through and returned?"

"No."

"Then how does Olgar know these things for certain? How can *you* be sure that you'll be going back to what you left?"

"I can't, Paul. Olgar can only theorize. But I have to believe I can."

Paul realized now that it wouldn't have mattered to Brian if Olgar had told him there was only a five percent chance of returning to his own time. He would have made the attempt.

He had to. His sense of being, of belonging, was in his own time. Paul had watched the airplane's flight with Christina and Karin from the watchtowers at Castle Weslan. The plane had been but a speck in the night sky, visible only because of the two ascama fibers attached beneath its wings, when the Saulcar Mass had engulfed it. Paul had followed the course of the storm until it had passed over the Angena Mountains. Only then had he turned his head away.

An edge of sun appeared in the vee of a crevice between two mountains. Soon the castle would awake to the tasks and chores of another day. Paul looked down into the courtyard below. Karin walked leisurely across the flattened stones. Their son, Brian Whitin Benjarth, rested on her shoulder.

"Hey! Up here!"

Karin looked up and smiled. He could see her mouth the words as she pointed. "See da-da."

Paul waved both arms above his head. He stopped, then he waved his arms again, this time lightly bouncing up and down on his feet. In those simple motions geared to elicit a smile from his son, a wondrous feeling of joy swept over him. He raced down the stairs of the tower.

GLOSSARY

———

Ascama fiber: a stem portion of the ascama plant, which glows after exposure to light.

Asharan tree: large, high-branched tree found on the Medoc Peninsula and in the Sornk Mountains.

Bashan: an observer.

Benjarth: a member of the ruling family of Fief Karcan. Can refer to all who live within Fief Karcan.

Benerit-woman: a teacher.

Besapt: a noodlelike vegetable.

Calsanor: a fermented beverage.

Candagge: a thimble-shaped medicinal device used to smooth the lazan plant into the skin.

Capoi: the large, edible, almond-shaped seed of the capoi plant.

Capoi paste: an oatmeallike cereal, usually eaten dry.

Clandi-cabbage: a wild species of cabbage that grows on the wooded slopes of the Medoc Peninsula.

Core-vine: the foundation plant or root. From it develop the spinollas and jooarie sacs.

Crileen: tree bark capable of photosynthesis.

Crohephite rock: solidified cloud mass.

Cymethadrenatyne: a hallucinogen that allows two combatants to enter the maze box.

Eucloid tree: a thick, flowering, bushlike tree.

Fiber-stub: the cut-to-size (usually to fit a lantern) stem portion of the ascama plant.

Ginsel: a small, hazel-colored fruit.

Jarred: one of the four races and the dominant people of the three fiefs.

Jooarie sac: a bulbous protrusion of the core-vine wherein selevium gas is stored.

Kejote: a thick, flowering bush.

Lazan plant: a plant used medicinally as a "living" bandage, whose fibers attach to the skin.

Makraw-leaf: a transparent plant of extraordinary strength.

Malhah: the enlightened one; savior.

Mankekin: a water-repellent material that forms an ursula.

Morcain gas: a clear gas found in the stems of the ascama plants that glows upon exposure to light.

Nicomene: a sleeping gas.

Orca: a coffeelike drink.

Ornan: one of the four races.

Orquil: a fire ditch.

Phlogin: one of the four races.

Reiswaner: an alcoholic drink.

Relzan: a priest or minister.

Saulcar Mass: an atmospheric disturbance trapped in orbit around the sun. It intersects the orbit of Calferon four times a year and has religious significance to the Jarred.

Scherling: a deerlike animal.

Scizan: a scientist. Used as a suffix, as in geoscizan (geologist).

Screula: an unsolidified cloud mass.

Selevium gas: a lighter-than-air gas produced by the core-vines and stored in the jooarie-sacs.

Sinese: one of the four races.

Spinolla: the hair-thin fiber of the core-vine plant. These fibers draw cloud mass to them, then compact and solidify it into crohephite rock.

Star-gate: a Jarred word for the Saulcar Mass.

Styranotide: a truth serum.

Tronocyanimide: a sterility drug.

Ursula: a large funnel-shaped water-collecting structure.

Wood people: a general term used to label those living on the Medoc Peninsula.

Token of Dragonsblood **Damaris Cole**
To Noressa, raised by simple rural folk, a curious prophecy means nothing. She has vowed a lifejourney to answer the summoning that compels her eastward. But from the beginning, the fates are against her. Hunted by demons and possessing a talisman that awakens strange powers within her, Noressa learns that the prophecy means everything. August 1991.

Lightning's Daughter **Mary H. Herbert**
In this sequel to *Dark Horse*, young Gabria comes to terms with her magical ability and her role as a strong woman leader in a male-dominated world. The magic-blessed outcasts from the horse clans make Gabria their mentor, but before she can become their teacher, she must lead them against a magical creature bent on destroying the Dark Horse Plains. December 1991.

DARK·SUN™
WORLD

Prism Pentad
BOOK ONE

The Verdant Passage

Troy Denning

KALAK: AN IMMORTAL SORCERER-KING WHOSE EVIL MAGIC
HAS REDUCED THE MAJESTIC CITY OF TYR TO A DESOLATE
PLACE OF BLOOD AND FEAR. HIS THOUSAND-YEAR REIGN OF
DEATH IS ABOUT TO END.

BANDING TOGETHER TO SPARK A REVOLUTION ARE A MAV-
ERICK STATESMAN, A WINSOME HALF-ELF SLAVE GIRL, AND A
MAN-DWARF GLADIATOR BRED FOR THE ARENAS. BUT IF THE
PEOPLE ARE TO BE FREE, THE MISMATCHED TRIO OF STEADFAST
REBELS MUST LOOK INTO THE FACE OF TERROR, AND CHOOSE
BETWEEN LOVE AND LIFE.

SPELLJAMMER™ novels

◇ The Cloakmaster Cycle ◇

Follow one unlucky farmer as he enters fantasy space for the first time and gets caught up in a race for his life, from the DRAGONLANCE® Saga setting to the FORGOTTEN REALMS® world and beyond.

Book One
Beyond the Moons
David Cook

Little did Teldin Moore know there was life beyond Krynn's moons until a spelljamming ship crashed into his home and changed his life. Teldin suddenly discovers himself the target of killers and cutthroats. Armed with a dying alien's magical cloak and cryptic words, he races off to Astinus of Palanthas and the gnomes of Mt. Nevermind to try to discover why . . . before the monstrous neogi can find him. On sale in July, 1991.

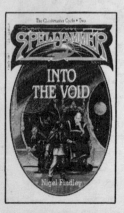

Book Two
Into the Void
Nigel Findley

Plunged into a sea of alien faces, Teldin Moore isn't sure whom to trust. His gnomish sidewheeler ship is attacked by space pirates, and Teldin is saved by a hideous mind flayer who offers to help the human use his magical cloak—but for whose gain? Teldin learns the basics of spelljamming on his way to Toril, where he seeks an ancient arcane, one who might tell him more. But even information has a high price. On sale in October, 1991.